I0606675

the *ANAERRIS CODE*

a Gemma Sinclaris Series

Part 1

the

Gemma

By LK Kelley

DragonEye Publishing

The Anaerris Code– Part 1 The Gemma
a Gemma Sinclaris Series
Copyright © 2017, by LK Kelley

Published by
Space-Time, an Imprint of DragonEye Publishing

Mass Market Paperback: First Edition
First Printing: July 3, 2017

ISBN 13: 978-1-61500-137-8 (Trade Paperback)
ISBN 13: 978-1-61500-198-9 (Mass Market PaperBack)
ISBN 13: 978-1-61500-158-3 (PDF)
ISBN 13: 978-1-61500-141-5 (EPub Ebook)

Library of Congress Control Number: 2016963820

Printed in USA

Publisher info. Contact
DragonEye Publishing
753A Linden PL.
Elmira, New York, 14901

Website: DragonEyePublishers.com
Email Orders@DragonEyePublishers.com

The Anaerris Code - Part 1 The Gemma

Above me, two, ancient moons shine – one of brilliant lavender, purple, and white, and one of blood red, yellow, and black. Both obscure one-fourth of the night sky, casting an eerie light on the world of my birth, which is charred and blackened by hell-fire and blood. I stand upon an enormous bluff, and stare down into the great, blackened valley, while the final war rages. A massive river of red races toward the brilliant lavender moon...the blood of my people and his. Tears of blood stain my cheeks and clothing while I watch the end of two races of beings. My race will be gone – including me, if I refuse to agree to be turned. A sound behind me. I know it is he. I can feel him as I have always done, since we met. Our kind should never be together, but it is as inevitable as time itself. I turn to see my attacker's body, which no longer has its head attached. Blood gushes forth from it. I meet his frightened eyes, and follow his horrified gaze down to the fatal wound in my chest where blood runs freely. I will bleed out in seconds.

"NO!" he yells, as I begin to collapse.

He catches me long before I hit the blackened earth below me. I stare at the man I love, knowing I should not love him. We are enemies. He has no tears to shed, but he gently cradles me in his arms, his tortured red eyes begging me with the same question he has asked many times. I can barely move my head, but I nod once, knowing the precious cargo I carry for my race and his. I want to be with him forever. And, if I'm still alive, my own race will also continue. I must change, no matter what, into whatever form. His mouth lowers to my neck kissing the pulse that is rapidly quieting as my heart silences. I feel a momentary sting as his fangs bite into my neck. To be with him forever is all I ever want, and I must complete the task that I was given by the ancients. Warmth trickles down the back of my neck as I feel the liquid of life slipping from me, echoing the death of my planet. I hope we have not waited too long. He lifts his head, his mouth dripping with my blood. I see in his sad eyes that he is hoping the same. I slide gratefully into the unknowing.

Time and space stand still. For how long, I know not. I awake, naked, on a soft bed covered in crimson silk. He sits with his back to the headboard, still cradling my lifeless body in his arms, patiently awaiting my awakening, and then, I will always be with him. I lift my eyes to stare at the man I will be with forever. I am ready as his lips lower to mine while my new, strong arms pull his nude body over mine. He is not gentle with his kiss, and I would never want him to be. I kiss him back frantically, feeling wetness between my legs as he spreads mine with his. He plunges into my heat, sheathing himself as deep as possible, and thrusts hard and fast into my body. My hips meet him with the same desperation and desire. I need him like I do not need air to breathe. As our orgasms reach their climax, I feel his hot seed jet into me. I can feel it enter my womb! He has so much! He stills, and I open my eyes that I know are still ripe with inhuman desire. I stare at the couple that is reflected in the mirror above our bed. My bright red eyes look back at me. I am whole again, and in the arms of my great lover for all time to come.

It is time. He shows me the crystal that I had entrusted to him, and I breathe a sigh of relief. It is safe, and ready for the one who must receive it. One who knows not of his part in the great scheme of the Creator. I must make sure that the Codex is written, and both it and the crystal must be kept apart. Both are dangerous alone, but together would cause unimaginable chaos. Our race has always been banned from writing about our history. I have been charged with finding a way to write what I was given in an indestructible method. But, I will use not only my own powers, but those given to me by my mate. I will make sure that we do not lose our heritage. If we must sacrifice our own lives, then so be it. At all costs, the one safeguard I carry must be kept safe until a time when the "gem" is needed.

Time ceases to exist in the realm we chose for its magic, where an ancient friend of mine offered to help. An ally who believes, as do we, that nothing can be left to chance. It is time to travel to the one place the Council would never expect us to hide the book. As for the crystal? My love has given it to one we know we can trust to protect it, sending him to a primitive planet known as Earth. And, we will hide the flesh-blackened codex – sealed with the most terrifying of magic that cannot be opened by any living soul, or they will die. My magical friend sees the future, and tells us that a time will come when both crystal and book will join together. Because of this, she sends an envoy with the "gem". And, now, we are leaving behind the only one who has the power to open and to read... the codex. And, then, it passes into legend and myth.

And, this book will forever be known as...

the

ANAERRIS CODE

The Beginning

"DADDY!" screamed eleven year-old Gemma Elwood, as she ran toward the house, and down the driveway with a tiny little dog at her feet. "DADDY! DADDY! HELP! HELP! MOMMY!"

William Tyler Elwood flung open the door the moment that he heard his daughter scream over the thunder and lightening that scraped the sky. Gem flung herself into his arms. Gemma and his love had just left the house minutes before he heard Gem's voice.

"DADDY! MOMMY! HELP MOMMY!" she screamed, finally getting her words right.

Tyler felt his stomach draw up in knots as he heard the terror in her voice. Without a word, he threw Gem into the new, red truck that he had just purchased, and drove like a maniac to where Gem pointed. Tears ran down her cheeks as she sobbed. Tyler stepped out of the truck.

"Gem. Stay here," he told her, then turned to see smoke and flames coming from below him on the mountain.

Terror gripped him as he flung himself over the edge, and started slipping and sliding his way down the embankment to get to the black Honda SUV that lay at the bottom of the mountain side. As he got closer, he saw his wife, Corina, laying on the ground in an unnatural position. He slid his way down, using his hands to keep him upright, rocks and grit scraping them to almost bloody pulps until he reached her. She had been flung almost thirty feet from the vehicle, and she hung from a low branch, where she had been impaled. He gulped as sobs racked his body. He had no option but to pull her down. She was dead. There was no life left in her beautiful green eyes. Crying uncontrollably, he slid her off the eight inch limb, and gently laid her down on the ground pushing her blonde hair back from her face. Looking into the face that had held his love for so long, he found himself in an almost catatonic state as he held the love of his life.

"Oh, Corina! My beautiful love! How did this happen?" he asked as reality set into his mind.

His clothing was blood soaked with her precious life, and he buried his face into her neck. The storm crackled around them, and rain poured from the sky mixing with his own tears and her blood from the massive hole in the middle of her body. And, then, he heard crying above him. Who was crying? Then, he remembered. Gem. Gem was crying. He turned his head upward, and saw her peering over the cliff. Corina would want him to watch after her, now. All he wanted was to join her in death! But, he couldn't. Not with his precious little girl needing him. He took one last look at his wife, laid her body down, then began the long climb back to the top. Once he was there, he fell on his knees, and pulled his crying daughter into his arms.

"It's OK, Gem. It'll be OK."

"No! It will never be OK again, Daddy!" she cried.

"I know, Gem. I know."

~1 ~

"Alone is never where I wanted to be, but then, I do have Lola!"

Lola, the pug, dodged a pillow that her pet just threw. Lola had been very worried about her over the last few weeks. She hadn't been able to write one, damn word on her laptop. She must have writer's block. The next words confirmed it.

"I'm so sorry, Lola!" Gem apologized, whipping her up into her arms, and giving her a kiss on her tiny head. "I didn't mean it! Really, sweetie, I didn't. Oh, Lola! What am I going to do? I don't have an idea for my next novel series!"

Lola loved her little pet, so she did the only thing that was really in her power. She turned her head, and licked her pet in the mouth. She and her pet had much in common, since both of them were adopted. Gemma Marie Elwood adopted Lola from a Pug Rescue organization in Denver, Colorado, and she had been with Gem for a very unusually long time. In fact, Gem really didn't know when Lola came to live with them, and truthfully, Lola was a bit anxious that Gem might discover that very soon. Strangely enough, though, all Lola knew was that she had never been happier. She had only complaint with her pet, and that was that Gem should be feeding Lola much more food than was placed into her bowl twice a day! Gem claimed it was to keep her trim and healthy. Lola didn't believe that for one minute! Nevertheless, no matter how many times Lola pulled the "I'm really starving" face, Gem never bought it, and would never give her any more, or less. However, sometimes, Gem would give in and cook her an egg, or maybe put some peanut butter in a Kong Ball, which kept

Lola busy for hours trying to eat it all, with a bone treat, sometimes. In consequence, Lola grudgingly admitted to herself that she was healthy, trim, and had tons of energy! She could run rings around other pugs her age, since most were kind of fat! In addition, her Vet was very pleased with her health, and it always made Lola a smug pug! Pugs had a problem with weight, causing them to become sedentary with little energy. Another condition specific to pugs was with impaired breathing due to their flat little noses. And, being overweight just made it worse. At least Lola just didn't have that problem, so she forgave Gem for not feeding her as much as Lola really wanted. OK. So.   If she could, she'd eat all the time! Lola loved everything – well, except for lettuce. She hated it! Ick!

Gem carried Lola over to the sofa flopping down, and leaned her head on the back of it.

"Lola, I'm stumped! I don't have an idea in my head!" Gem told her. "My publisher is about to have a cow! I have to come up with something really soon!"

Since she was little, Gemma Marie Elwood kept spiral notebooks that she called her "Dreams Diary". Spiral notebooks weren't the most elegant diary, but then, they never had much money. In them was written every dream she ever had that she remembered. It was those dreams, which gave her great ideas for her books. After her Mom had died, she became plagued by new and horrible dreams that were terribly disturbing. She would awake, screaming, and every time, her Dad would come to her rescue, holding her until her shaking and terror calmed.

Questions followed those dreams about her Mom's death – and, one particular question she repeatedly asked, yet was never supposed to ask, she did anyway.

"Why? Why? Why?" she would ask, but that question was never answered, of course.

The Anaerris Code - Part 1 The Gemma

There were things that never added up in her Mom's death, and her Dad had not been forthcoming with any information. Whatever the mystery surrounding her Mom's death was, her Dad took it to his grave. He had always told her that her Mom had hydroplaned during a horrendous storm, sending her SUV flying over the cliff. Gem could remember running and running back to her house after she found the wreck, but, she could remember nothing more, and her Father would never answer her questions. Most importantly, though, she always had the queasy feeling that she was in the SUV with her Mom. If so, though, she had no memory of it. But, another question plagued her. If she was, why wasn't she hurt or killed? She had not had a scratch on her!

Her therapy doctors had told her Dad that she had deliberately blocked out what she had seen that night. However, despite all her therapy sessions, the dreams continued to escalate. The night her Mom died was also the first night she dreamed of a frightening place of blood, death, and war. Pick something! During the nights, Gem would awake in a cold sweat that drenched her sheets. Of course that meant that she had to change them in the middle of the night, before she could go back to sleep. And, then, the dreams repeated. During the days, though, she tried to reason it all out, but when she thought of it too much, her head would feel as if it were about to explode. That one particular dream, though, had always remained the same. But lately, it had begun to change. Now, *she* had become *a participant* in it! Because of this, she could see from both the objective and subjective points of view. However, trying to figure out which was which, was becoming increasingly harder, especially since she kept hopping back and forth between someone else's eyes and her own. Confusing was not the word for it! She needed to do something about them!

Putting that aside for the time being, she walked to her desk where she kept a drawer under lock and key. Gem inserted her key, unlocked, and opened it, pulling out one of her older diaries. Because she actually believed that sometimes it was beneficial to hand-write, Gem grabbed a pencil, and curled up on her sofa, while Lola plopped her tiny body on the arm of it, falling asleep almost instantly. Gem began to write out her dream, trying to remember the omniscient point of view, and the first person point of view. And, in this case, it was really hard since the scenes kept switching constantly.

"Let's see," she said aloud, and while biting the top of her pencil, she began to write. Gem's mind escalated, and her hand began to write as if possessed!

"OK. I'm standing on a bluff. Everything around me is blackened as if burned to a crisp. Nothing is alive here. There are no trees, no grass, no water, no signs of habitation any longer. And, it is certainly not Earth, but another planet somewhere. Two moons – or were they planets – take up half of the sky above me – one in lavender and white, and the other black and red! Below me is an unbelievably deep valley – so deep, that those fighting below resembled ants scurrying to and fro. And, even though everything seems so dark, I can still see everything."

"How weird is that?" she asked herself, still nibbling on the eraser. Then, Gem continued to write and mutter to herself. She smirked, and said, "And, that is the fate of an author!"

The Anaerris Code - Part 1 The Gemma

"Massive armies fighting beside a red river spanning the ground below her, as if it were a vein within a giant being in the cosmos."

"Suddenly, I feel a gut-wrenching pain in the middle of my stomach and look down. A large spear is piercing my body. *Scene switch.* I see what happened from my own point of view, now. A bastard of a coward stabbed me – uh her – from behind, and a look of glee flits across his face. *Scene switch, again.* Where before, I saw the man who had stabbed me, now, I am the woman, and I see a man leaning toward me with red eyes that have no hatred, but are filled love and concern. I am weak, but I don't know why. Pain! The cause of my pain is sticking out from my chest. And, I'm sticky with blood! A lot of blood! My eyes jerk back to his in shock, and they seemed to ask me a question. Without my own volition, I nod my head slightly, and turn my neck. I see him lean down with fangs, and feel a sharp prick on my neck – no, wait. *Scene switch.* Not my neck...*hers! Scene switch..*
"I'm getting damned tired of this!" she growled to herself.

She continued. "I can feel the pricks in his bite, followed by incredible desire despite the weakness due to loss of blood. *Switch back.* I see her body through her eyes lying on a massive bed covered in red silk. I am completely naked, and my legs are on top of the man's shoulders who bit me – uh – her...and he is fucking me hard! I can feel every single stroke of his cock as he pounds deep into her body! And, I could not stop it! I didn't want it to stop! A mirror hangs from the ceiling over us, allowing me to see the back of his body that was toned with the tightest ass I've ever seen! I am beginning to lose track of where I start, and the woman begins! My hands, no the woman's hands, were digging into his ass, trying to push him – uh, her – deeper into my body. His hair is coal black, but I can see nothing else, since his mouth is suckling my neck as he was biting me. And, more? I stare into the mirror that is above the bed. My eyes were bright red just like his! Although what I could see was so erotic, it was embarrassing – epecially since it wasn't even me!"

"Ah, hell!" she almost screamed aloud. "*I always wake up at this point in the dream, feeling wet, horny, eager, and ready for my new life to begin.*" But, aloud, she said, "And, that is the...End of dream, Lola," Gem finished with a flourish of her pencil! Her face was flushed, and very red.

Gem put her pencil down, and remembered that the dream *always* ended with her screaming when she awoke. Worse, and even more embarrassing and frustrating, was the fact that she was so horny, she had to touch herself to get some kind of release! Thank goodness her Dad wasn't alive to see the change in her features that had manifested over the last five years. Her arousal after the dream caused her eyes to glow red just like the woman's in her dream. And, it happened every single time she was aroused. It was so scary, she had refused to write it in her diary in the past. Gem had made the decision to put her diary away, and never write in it again – until now. All her other dreams were more dreamlike. But, some of them were so erotic, she had to bring herself to an orgasm, and the last couple of weeks, it was almost every single night!

Gem had no idea why this was happening to her, but she sure *wanted* to know. No. It wasn't a want, but a *need* to know!

Lola watched her little pet, while cocking her head to the right. Lola meant the word "little" as it pertained to her pet, because Gem was barely five-feet tall, and sported long, bright red hair, and cool, emerald green eyes. She had milky white skin that was pale, but had a luminosity that caused her skin to have a faint, but soft glow. Her nose was smaller, while her lips were full and naturally pink, so lipstick wasn't necessary. And, let's face it! She never went anywhere, and never had dates, so why should she wear makeup? But, when her eyes twinkled, it gave her a mischievous glow, bringing a smile to whoever was the recipient of it. She wore only a minimum amount of other makeup. Her figure was all woman! Her breasts had always been larger than most girls, her waist was not skinny, but perfect, and her hips gave her that hourglass figure most girls would die to have!

All these features, when seen as one, simply gave Gem an almost ethereal look. But, still, Gem was the epitome of what some might call a "pixie", and it fit the description of her personality perfectly. Always smiling, she bounced around with plenty of energy, and she cheered up everyone she met – even when she was miserable.

Barely five years before, when Lola had seen her red eyes for the first time, she knew the time had arrived for Gem's destiny...and, Lola was so not looking forward to it! However, she was Gem's guide, so she sucked it up, and waited for the event that she had waited for over the eons that would change everything.

Watching Gem put her notebook away, Lola could tell she was very despondent. No ideas meant no writing. And, writing was absolutely her entire life. And, where was the best place to get new ideas? Why, Gem needed to go to that odd building she called the " library". It had lots of books, and might provide Gem with the ideas she might need. Hmmm. Periodically, Gem would take Lola with her, dropping her off with her other pet human, Taylor Tamson, who was Gem's best friend. The two were the exact opposite in personality. And, they really got along great!

Gem and Lola lived at the base of the Rocky Mountain Foothills, about forty minutes from downtown Denver, Colorado – in the middle of nowhere. There were also no internet connections, so Gem couldn't do research for her books online with her computer, iPad, or even her iPhone. She barely got cell service, and it was "iffy". So, she nudged Gem until she lifted her head, and frowned at Lola.

"What's the deal, Lola? You can't be hungry! I just fed you breakfast!"

Gem got up, stretched, and paced as she fought for some kind of an idea. She stopped, and turned back to Lola.

"Well, I could do the usual, you know. Werewolves, Demons, Vampires, or Fae are the popular things these days," she said to Lola, who yawned.

And, that was really what the LaMonte Publishing House wanted her to write about. The few times her cell did connect, which was last night, she received a call from Norman LaMonte, her publisher.

"Come on, Gem! The public is clamoring for those types of books, and you are my best writer."

"You can't be serious, Norman! Do you know how many of those types of books are out on the market? How could I compete?"

"Look. It would sell, because you are one of my finest writers!" Norman had told her. "Besides, it's what the public wants! We are in the business of selling entertainment for the eyes. So, get over it, and start writing! I need that book in a couple of months!" Then, he had disconnected the call, leaving her angry, and even more frustrated than ever!

Gem had fought against writing those kinds of novels with every single breath. All of them were pretty much alike. And, they were not what Gem wanted to read. She wanted something unique like her last Trilogy. Despite the fact that she was one of the more popular writers, and her books were making a small amount of money on Kindle, it was just not enough. She wanted to be able to live as a writer. Since Gem couldn't do that, yet, she was forced to supplement it by working as a cashier at the only grocery store in town owned by Macklin Simmons of Simmons Grocery. In addition, she also held a part-time job at the library. Since she was majoring in writing, it was the best possible world for her! After all, not only did she have to live and eat, she also was paying off her Father's hospital bills that had incurred after he spent two months there just before he died. She figured she would be paying those off even after she was dead at this rate!

Pacing more, she muttered, "I just need a new angle on the supernatural, Lola. But what?"

Lola flew under her feet, and nudged Gem, again. She only did that when…wait. Gem's eyes grew wide. She just realized that Lola only did that when Gem went to her hole-in-the-wall town's library. Her eyes narrowed with suspicion looking into Lola's eyes with shock. Was Lola communicating with her? How the hell could that be? She was a dog. No. That would be the most ridiculous thing she had ever heard!

"Are you talking to me, Lola?" Gem just had to ask, anyway. Lola cocked her head to the other side, and nudged her nose against Gem again. Frowning, she squinted her eyes at her. "No, you can't be, right? I mean, animals can't talk," she said, and laughed as she deliberately slapped her forehead with her hand, causing a loud cracking sound. "Gem, you're losing it! You really are! You've been living alone for far too long, and writing way too many fantasy novels! Now, you're starting to believe what you write?"

Looking at Lola, she said, "Well, I guess going to the library will get me out of the house!"

To which Lola just nodded, receiving another surprised look from her pet. Well, she did love to look at the ancient books that were in the climate-controlled room. She was so good with books that she had been put in charge of the ancient books and documents. She stood up, and slapped her legs.

"You're right, Lola! I do need to go to the library. I'll be back before dinner. You want to go out, or stay in today?" she asked her not expecting an answer.

Nevertheless, Lola cocked her head at her well-trained pet. It sure did take her long enough to get through to Gem. While Lola usually loved inside, today she just wanted to run and play. After her brief potty break earlier, she had seen that it was already a perfectly beautiful fall day. And, she figured the shit was going to hit the fan soon enough, so she had better take her breaks, now, before she couldn't any longer. Lola darted to the back door, and looked back at Gem wagging her tiny, little curled tail. With the fenced yard, Gem didn't have to worry about Lola getting in too much trouble, and she had a huge place to run. She had meant to put a doggy door in, but kept forgetting to do it. On the patio, Lola had a little doghouse just in case Gem didn't get back in time if it rained, or was later than usual. In the winter, Lola would always stay inside! She hated the cold, especially when it snowed outside, and her butt was always so cold! But, it was still nice even though Thanksgiving was just a few weeks way. Right now, all Gem needed to do was to leave a few snacks, and Lola would be all set for the day.

"You know, Lola? If I didn't know any better, I would swear you could understand every word I say!" she muttered.

Lola heard her, stopped, and barked, bringing another shocked look from Gem!

"Nope! Not going there, Lola! I already have enough of an active imagination!" she laughed.

Gem set a large bowl of water for Lola on the deck, a small snack, then closed and locked the door. As if she had anything valuable in the house. She grabbed her purse, phone, and laptop, then jumped into her rattletrap of an old, rusted-out Ford truck. People laughed at it, but she loved it. It was all she had left of her Father, except for the house. While she drove, she reflected, yet again, on how her Mother had been killed in a car accident eleven years ago. Gem had been running on the road, but she still had no memory of why! Her Mom had been driving to Simmon's Grocery, simply because she was out of sugar, eggs, and milk. No matter how hard she tried, she had never been able to remember. Since her Dad had died, his truck was more important to her than ever.

Anyway, she had to drive, and she certainly couldn't afford to buy one, used or new. She was barely making ends meet as it was. Jobs were scarce since the 2008 mortgage debacle, and the only real job she could find was at Simmon's Grocery Store. At least, both the house and truck were paid for, and just recently, her book trilogy had begun to sell in spurts all over the world. Even so, it would be quite some time before she saw any money from it. She had several rejections at large publishing houses, so she had found an Independent Publisher who accepted it immediately. She really didn't know why the sudden sales were happening, and neither did her publisher, but hell! She wasn't complaining. Maybe, just maybe, she could finally become a best-selling author. But, still, it was hard work to get her name and books into the outside world. If only she had the money to go to book signings, and other appearances. But, where she lived, there was only the Sinclair Library owned by the tiny college, where she worked from four to ten every other day, and a couple of very tiny bookstores which never had booksignings. Even sadder? They wouldn't even carry her books! So, her only alternative was to rely on social media – especially Twitter. At least this way, Gem could get her name out faster all over the world!

When Curt and Jerry Elwood adopted her as a baby, they legally changed her middle and last name to Gemma Allen Elwood, her middle name taken from her Mom's maiden name, and her Dad's last name, of course. Her publisher wanted to change her name, and she balked at it. Together, they decided that she should write under the alias of her real name, G.A. Elwood. At least they never changed her first name, because, as her Dad always said, she was the brightest "gem" in their lives. Her Dad had toyed with the idea of calling her "Rusty", because Gem's hair was the exact color of rust. Gem was one of the few girls whose red hair did not run riotously around her face. She kept it a long length down to the middle of her back, and it was loaded with soft waves that only emphasized her pale skin, and of course, the freckles on her face. OK. The freckles she didn't like, but that just wasn't something that could be changed, and she had accepted that fact long ago.

Sighing, Gem had to finish her research, before she would head to work as a cashier at Simmons from 9 to 11 pm. It was really lucky, because the grocery store was right next door to the library. She wanted, and needed, a full-time job, but the economy was very bad in their neck of the woods, and at least her part-time job gave her money for food.

The Sinclair Library had assigned Gem her very own parking place, because she was the well-known celebrity in town thanks to her books. And, that meant that she didn't have to waste gas! So, Gem turned into the library's parking lot, putting the truck into park – just as a huge bolt of lightning flared, making her jump.

"That's just great!" she whined to no one as she stepped out of her truck, and into the random hard drops that always comes with a bad storm. What the hell?

She totally ignored the black lettering above the door that declared the name "Sinclair Library of Fate" in her desperation to get inside. The name had too much of a conotation to it, so it had been shortened by the public to just the Sinclair Library, and finally, just the library. Hoping she could get into the building before the next lightning strike shot from the sky, Gem quickly ran up the three short steps into said building. The second she stepped inside, high winds began to whip about in almost hurricane force. The trees bent halfway, and then, a deluge broke loose. Gem paused in the foyer to look out the door's windows. Watching the wind blow, she was truly thankful to the fates that she was allowed to get her toe inside, before she was caught in it!

"Whoa!" she whispered, drawing back in surprise when she saw a metal something fly by the door. Not good to stand here with that happening!

Turning she ran up the ten stairs leading into the main room of the library. As usual, no one was present at two o'clock in the afternoon. Ordinarily, the only other person inside it was Taylor Tamson, who was Gem's best friend. Taylor was about nine years older than Gem, but their friendship was immediate the day that they had met six years prior. She was about five-foot seven inches tall, and had an absolutely gorgeous figure! She was extremely well-proportioned, despite giving birth to her two children – Shirley who was six and seven year-old Marcus. Taylor had two very unusual features. First, her snow white hair flowed down her back to her waist, which she deliberately kept in either a tight bun or a long ponytail. Her second feature were eyes of lavender, so pale, they were almost white. And, her eyes drew men to her like flies, even though she had been married to Richard, or Rick, Tamson for the last ten years. None of them even had a prayer of getting anywhere with her, and she generally ignored them. Not that it deterred them in anyway, but her skin was fair, her lips pink and plump, and it looked as if her legs never ended they were so long. And, that kept the men – and boys – trying to gain her favor!

Both little Shirley and Marcus loved Lola to distraction, and Lola returned that love when Gem let them pug-sit for her. There was no doubt whatsoever that Lola would protect them with her life if need be. Recently, Taylor and Rick had been thinking about adopting a pug from Colorado's Pug Rescue just as Gem's family had done. And, Gem was encouraging them to do so. She wasn't thinking of herself, but if they did, then, Lola would have a friend to play with when she would stay with the children.

Gem headed for the librarian's desk that was situated within the middle of the library to put her things into the file cabinet, and then looked up into Taylor's face.

"Hey, tall and lanky!" Gem laughed. Between the two of them, Gem was short, and maybe had a few extra pounds, which didn't show even though she thought they did, while Taylor was just tall and skinny.

"Hey, yourself, Ms. vertically challenged!" Taylor laughed back at her. "So, back for more torture? And, why are you here so early today, anyway?"

Gem plopped herself on the stool that sat behind the desk, ignoring Taylor's question for the moment.

"Man! Did you notice the storm outside? I mean, I've never heard or seen the wind blow this hard!" As if on cue, a huge gust of wind hit the side of the building, and shook the narrow windows above that circled the building. Both girls jumped.

"Wow!" Taylor gasped. The girls had dropped to the floor when they heard all the rattling.

"Yeah! What you said," Gem agreed. "Oh. To answer your question? I needed to do some research to find something new and different for my next book."

Both stood back up, and Taylor signed onto the computer.

"OH! Well, I get that. Besides, I really don't think we're going to have that many customers today!"

While Gem agreed by nodding her head, Taylor grabbed two dusters, and tossed one at Gem. Following Taylor, the two women started dusting the shelves. For the next two hours, they circled the room talking as they dusted. No one entered during the entire time, but then, the storm had not abated at all.

"Anyway, to answer your question of earlier, before I was so *rudely interrupted by that big blowhard,"* she grinned, "when am I not here for torture! I so miss not having an internet connection, Tay! But, I'm stumped. Writer's block," she poked herself in the temple. "I need a demon idea, before my publisher is put into the hospital with a coronary!"

"So, that publisher of yours is giving you a hard time?" Taylor asked as she ran the feather duster across the shelves and the top of the books as if there was dust when they both knew there was none.

"Yeah. He wants me to write...wait for it.... A Demon series!"

Taylor stopped dusting, and turned around with wide eyes.

"Seriously? Why would he want that? Most all of them are alike! Why would he want you to write one of those?"

Gem stopped dusting. She tilted her head as something came to her.

"Taylor, will you explain to me why we are always dusting dust-free shelves and books?" Watching Taylor shake her head, Gem continued. "Oh...he thinks it's going to be good for his publishing company, and wants to get in on the bandwagon, I guess. At least that's what he told me. I think it's really silly. I wrote my fantasy books without the normal paranormals on purpose! I didn't want to be like everyone else," Gem giggled. "Seriously, though? I almost wanted to tell him to vamp-off!"

Taylor, who was standing on the third rung of the ladder, dropped her duster, fell off the ladder, and onto the floor erupting in boisterous laughter.

"V-vamp-off?" she roared. "Did you really just say that? That's just s-so h-hilarious!" she gulped between breaths. "W-whoa, girlie! You are sure full of *something*! Gem, you should be writing comedy!" Taylor laughed even harder.

"Hey! You mean bullshit? Taurus, remember?" Gem pointed to herself. "And, let's face it! I have always had that talent!" Gem joined Taylor on the floor laughing so hard, they had their arms holding their stomachs.

Their laughter almost drowned out the hurricane force winds and rain outside. It was really lucky that no one was in the library at the moment, because the girls were laughing just far too loud. After about ten minutes, their giggle boxes landed right side up, but stopped immediately, when a man came through the door with a disappoving frown. They picked themselves up off the floor, and strolled back to the desk with huge smiles on their faces. Both women knew he came every other day at exactly four thirty pm every Monday, Wednesday, and Friday...and he was never late. The last two hours had flown by, Gem grinned at the pun, and she had gotten nothing at all done with her research!

The two women quickly went about doing their job. While Gem perched herself onto the stool that was behind the desk, Taylor opened the locked, desk drawer, automatically pulling out the key to the climate controlled room. Turning, she frowned in dismay as she walked toward him, noticing that he had already removed his coat, and was shaking it out, drops of water being flung everywhere!

"What a jackass hypocrite!" Taylor told herself. *"I bet you'd never do that in your own really fancy home!"*

Professor Hawkins sat in an overstuffed chair with a table and reading lamp that sat to the right of the chair. Gem had deemed this chair "Professor Hawkin's chair", and they kept it vacant at all times. Gem had told Taylor over and over that she thought he was a dick, andTaylor agreed with her every time.

Taylor asked which books he wanted to see today, and after he "ordered" them, she turned to go back to her desk when to her surprise, he actually addressed her! That was a new one!

"My dear Mrs. Tamson," he began, condescendingly, "Must I remind you both, that it is highly inappropriate to find our Librarian and her assistant, laughing loudly – and on the floor – inside the Sinclair Library?" he admonished her, then glared at Gem who pretended she hadn't seen it.

Professor Jaxxon Philip Hawkins was his name...and...he was the bane of her existence! Always complaining about something, he was a true enigma. He always sat in the same chair, always had the same, black leather, duster on with a hoodie underneath, and the hood flung over his head! No one could see his face that well, since it hid most of it, but, when one did get a glimpse of his eyes, they were indescribably gorgeous, deep brown eyes with flecks of blue glitter. And, from what she could see of it, his face was tan, as if he spent a lot of time in the sun. He would come and go from the Sinclair Library like clockwork, always asking for ancient manuscripts and books, but never the same ones, which was a bit peculiar to her. But, he also did one other thing that made Gem grit her teeth over and over to keep from smarting off in a retort. He always butted into other people's conversations without remorse, interjecting complaints into those conversations. He thought he was right and smarter than everyone else! And, even though he rarely addressed either Gem or Taylor directly, when he did, it was to criticize them for some stupid infraction. She narrowed her eyes at him when her "inner imp" invaded her body, which gave her the courage to do what she did on the spur of the moment, to finally say something to him. Of course, that led her to slap her hand over her mouth after the words spewed forth! Without thinking, Gem stood and walked over to him. Taylor saw her, and recognized that look! She quickly started shaking her head at Gem, who paid no attention to her.

"Oh, shit!" Taylor murmured under her breath, seeing Gem's eyes turning bright green as she approached Professor Hawkins. There would be no stopping her, now. As for Hawkins? Anyone on the receiving end of Gem's sharp tongue when she got started, well, Taylor cringed when Gem spoke.

"Oh?   And, just why the hell do you object to laughter, Professor?" she demanded with hands on her hips.

His piercing, brown eyes glared with disapproval at her, raising his eyebrows in surprise that anyone would actually talk back to him! He smirked at her audacity.

"I do not object to laughter, young woman. Only where it happens and when. And, it is most obvious that a library is not that place!" he answered with sarcasm in his voice.

Gem started toward him, when a hand touched her shoulder. It was the only thing that made it through her angry haze. She turned to look at Taylor.

"Don't, Gem. It's OK. He was correct to point our inappropriate behavior out to us. I apologize, Professor Hawkins," she told him.

He darted the same piercing eyes at Taylor, and sharply nodded once in approval. Gem glared at the Professor, then turned to glare at Taylor. She took a deep breath. Professor Hawkins was clearly waiting for her apology.

"Tough shit! He'll be waiting for an apology until hell freezes over!" she thought, looking into his eyes. He was clearly not going to back down. *"Nope. Never gonna happen!"*

Aloud, Gem told Taylor, "I'm going to the CCR, now."

Gem turned on her heels, and stalked off in a huff toward the CCR room. Taylor turned, and walked back to the desk, when several things happened simultaneously. A huge bolt of lightning crashed, causing a fireball to appear inside the library, and just missing Gem. She was stunned into silence as she watched the ball of fire travel leisurely across the library, before it dissipated, knocking out all electricity to the building. Anyone who has ever seen one knows that it is a scary sight to behold. Then, immediately, a massive gust of straight-line winds blew out the windows on one side of building, hitting books and bookshelves as waves of various sized glass flew toward Gem.

Watching as if in slow motion, Gem knew she would never make it, even if she ran! She knew, without a doubt, that she was going to be struck by millions of shards of glass, and would be cut to pieces! There was no way that she would be able to move out of the way in time. Dropping to her knees, she tried to cover as much of her body and head as possible, and slumped forward waiting for the shards to slice her. That's when she heard Taylor scream, as if from a distance, followed by another scream, "NO"! Then, suddenly, Gem was slammed by something that felt like a tank, knocking her out of the way of the oncoming glass.

"Umpf!" was the sound Gem made as she felt her body fly sideways, and out of the path of the glass. One of the tables stopped her from going any further, as she smashed into it. Her head hit the corner of the table, and she uttered an oath.

"*Fuck*!" she said yelled.

More lightning and thunder followed, and rain began to blow into the library onto the shelves showering down water onto the precious books.

"Taylor! Do you have something to cover these books?" Professor Hawkins yelled, as he knelt next to Gem to make sure she was alright.

"Yes!" Taylor told him loudly, then turned and ran to the storage closet grabbing a couple of tarps that were only there, because of the manager's convertible, antique T-Bird.

"Are you alright?" Professor Hawkins asked her in a tender voice.

"Y-yes, I-I guess," Gem answered, rubbing the bump that she had on her head. Her hand came down, and she saw that it was bloody. She stared at the blood dripping from her hand, but tried to stand, anyway. That was a futile move, since she fell back down on her ass, as a wave of dizziness hit her.

Hawkins obviously tried to help her, but she waved him away.

"I'm fine! Go! Help Taylor get those books covered!"

"But, you're bleeding," he stated the obvious.

"Yeah, yeah! I know! Don't care! Please, Professor! Help her cover those books! It's just a little bump on my noggin'!" she whined, closing her eyes.

Nodding, the Professor darted to help Taylor. Gem opened her eyes. Wait! Noggin'? Who the hell says that type of word? One word came to her...concussed! Yep. That's what was wrong, because the minutes that followed had her questioning her sanity.

"Jaxx!" yelled Taylor. "Take your time, but hurry the hell up!"

Hawkins left her, while Gem shook her head, trying to clear her vision, and decided to lean against one of the table legs closing her eyes. That's when her blurry vision saw Professor Hawkins and Taylor fly up to the top of the shelves to cover the books. She frowned. Flying? Gem closed her eyes, and when she opened them seconds later, she saw Taylor on the ladder with Professor Hawkins, helping her cover the lower books with one of the tarps. Gem groaned, and rubbed her head, again. Where the hell was the tank that had pushed her out of the way? It had saved her body from being scarred for life, if not saved her very life. But, what was it that hit her in the first place? Gem tried to stand to her feet, but they collapsed from under her, and she fell back onto her ass.

"Damn! That's twice!" she murmured in anger.

She tried, again. This time, she managed to pull herself up by holding onto the table edge. Her legs were really wobbly – probably from a bit of shock. Her body was bruised, but at least the bruises would be temporary. No such luck if she'd been hit by the flying glass! She'd just be in a lot of pain until the bruises healed. That was alright for her! Bruises were good!

Professor Hawkins dashed to her side when he saw Gem trying to walk unsteadily toward them.

"Are you alright?" he asked her, grabbing her arm as she stumbled, almost falling, again.

Nodding, "Yeah. I think so. I'm sore as hell from that tanke that hit me, and knocked me against the table," she said, "But, at least I'm still alive."

"Good. Stay here," he ordered, earning a "no one tells me what to do" look, which he ignored, of course.

After he finished helping to cover the windows, Taylor asked him a question.

"Professor Hawkins?" Taylor said. "I wish we had some wine, or other booze in here, but we'll just have to make do without it. Could you get some coffee for Gem while I finish hanging the tarps?"

Without question, Professor Hawkins, first, helped Gem to the chair where he usually sat, pushing her gently down into it. His heart, if he had one, would have still been pounding in fear! He could have lost her! Instead, he turned to Gem.

"Ms. Elwood? How do you take your coffee?"

"Oh…uh…two sugars, please?" I think.

He put the sugar into the cup, and brought it to Gem as well as one for himself, and Taylor.

"Damn! It knocked out everything even the phones!" Taylor complained, taking a sip of her coffee. She tried her cell, and threw it down on the desk. "Even the cell towers must be down!"

"More coffee?" Professor Hawkins asked Gem as he poured a cup of coffee for himself.

"Sure. I suppose. Thank you, Professor Hawkins," Gem told him.

"My pleasure, Ms. Elwood," he answered in such a soft voice, Gem's head shot up in surprise. But, he had already gone back to the drink station provided by the library.

Finally, Taylor finished, and rushed over to Gem's side.

"You OK?" she asked, kneeling next to the chair. "I am so very, very sorry I couldn't get to you, sweetie!"

"Hey, no worries! But, yeah. I guess I'm OK. My head hurts, though," she complained. "By the way...did someone get the license plate of the tank that hit me? Anyone know what it was? What knocked me out of the way, anyhow?" she asked.

Taylor looked at Professor Hawkins as if for an answer. With a sarcastic grin, she asked him.

"Well, Professor Hawkins? Did you get the "tank's" license number?" she asked sweetly, earning a glare from him.

"There," he pointed to one of the library tables that was lying on its side – right where Gem had been before she was knocked out of the way.

Gem looked at the table in surprise, then turned to look where the Professor was pointing. How had she missed it? She didn't remember seeing it there earlier. But, then, again, her head was still woozy. She shuddered when she thought that if the table hadn't hit her, she might have been cut to pieces! But, how on Earth did it get thrown there? She looked back at him, and he shrugged.

"Must've blown sideways, and caught you in its path."

Really? Gem wasn't sure she bought that, but then, with her head hurting so badly, she decided to let it go – for now, that was.

"You want me to call Simmons and tell him that you won't be in tonight?" Taylor asked.

"No. That's OK. I'm all right. I'm only going to be there for a couple of hours, anyway."

"You're sure? Head injuries are not to be taken lightly, you know."

"Yeah."

"OK." Taylor looked at the clock. "It's only six thirty, so I want you to stay right where you are until you need to go next door, OK?"

Gem nodded without an argument.

"Wow! No argument? Who are you, and what did you with my best friend?" Taylor smirked.

"Very funny. Ha ha," Gem answered, leaning her head back on the chair, and closing her eyes.

Taylor walked toward Professor Hawkins who was standing at the inside glass doors looking out on the still-raging storm. Gem raised her head, and looked on in puzzlement when she noticed that their heads twere ogether, and whispering – almost as if they were great friends who like to argue, that is! Gem leaned her head back. She decided the worst thing she could do was to think, and began to doze.

A shake on the shoulder woke her, and her eyes opened to lights once again.

"It's five till seven, Gem. Are you sure I don't need to call Simmons?"

"Oh, goodness! No, no, Tay. Really, I'm fine. I see the lights are back on," Gem remarked. Standing up, she tested her legs, and equilibrium. Actually, she felt quite a bit better! "Seems, everything is in place! I'm OK. I'll get my purse, and walk next door. Has it let up at all, yet?"

"Seems so," Professor Hawkins told her picking up his belongings and walking to the door. "Well, I'd better leave while it has let up. Besides, my night has officially gone the way of the dinosaurs, so I guess I'll come back in a couple days."

"Strange man," Gem murmured in consternation, when he left.

"You have no idea," Taylor agreed under her breath, and watched as Gem left the library.

"Hey, Simmons," Gem called as she walked to her register, and logged on.

"That was some storm," Simmons said casually.

"Yeah, it was."

"Anything interesting happen when the lights went out?" he asked her with narrowed eyes.

Gem cocked her head. He couldn't know what had almost happened to her. So, ignoring his narrowed eyes, which was weird in itself, her intuition told her not say a word about her almost being sliced to pieces.

"Well, as a matter of fact, yes!" she rambled while putting on the purple vest that all employees had to wear. He waited. "The lights, the phones, and even the cells were knocked out, too! I mean, I thought that Taylor was going to have a coronary! You know how she is about her iPhone! It's like an extension of her arm and her fingers! And, a couple of windows blew out, and we had to cover the shelves underneath the windows – you know how high they are – and the books from getting ruined by the rain."

Simmons just looked at her.

"That's all?"

"Well, yeah. That's about it."

"Where did you get the bruise on your forehead?" he asked.

"Oh, that?" Thinking fast, she made up a lie on the fly! "Lola. She was rambunctious to a fault this morning! She leaped out of the bed while I was on the floor, looking under the bed for one of my socks, and jumped onto my back, using me like a step stool, and landed on my head, which pushed my head into the bed's steel leg!"

Narrowing his eyes again, she could swear that he didn't believe her, and even more than that, he seemed as if he was irritated at her. But, she shrugged, and her first customer appeared who had braved the storm's aftermath to shop.

Ignoring him, "Hi, Mrs. Wayne! Storm didn't keep you away, did it?"

Two hours later, when her shift was over, she grabbed her purse, and hung up her vest.

"Night, Simmons! See you in a couple of days!"

All he did was nod. He was just acting so damned strange tonight. And, she hadn't been the only one who noticed it, either. The rest of the employees were gossiping about it as they left.

"What was wrong with the boss, tonight? Anyone have a clue?" asked Timothy.

"Dunno, but one thing is for damn sure…he looks as if he's a man who was angry at something not going his way!" Jane remarked.

"Well, maybe. Night everyone!" Gem said.

Gem walked next door to her rusted bucket of bolts. Just as she opened the door to the truck, she got a really, really strange feeling. Nothing ever happened in this little out of the way town of about six hundred people. Well, not counting the excitement of the library. Starting the truck, Gem pulled out of the parking lot. Musing as she drove, about seven years ago, some really old woman on the opposite side of the world, had left all her books, oddly, her entire collection of first editions of books as well as money to establish a building with enough to keep the library self-sufficient for a hundred, or more, years – if it lasted that long! The money also included the funds to build a climate controlled room inside the building to keep them safe. The collection was so old, many were written in the forms of Tomes, scrolls, and even the oldest known type of books, codices. No one in the town knew who she was, and as far as anyone could determine, no one was related to her either. Even now, people were puzzled about it, and very curious as to who the woman was who left it to them. But, it was such a curiosity, people from all over the area came to it. And, it also drew the academic world as well such as Professor Hawkins.

The collection was amazing, and extremely expensive. Only a few people were allowed into the CCR, because of their value. If anyone, including the academics, needed anything, only the manager, Marshall Adams, Taylor, and Gem were actually allowed into the room. It would be very difficult for someone to escape with any book. It was rigidly controlled as were the few who were chosen to sit down with them to study. Clean, white, and disposable cotton gloves were always provided for those who touched the books, and they had to have experience with ancient documents to be allowed to handle them.

That was just about the only thing exciting to have ever happened around here. But, Gem's gut instincts were rarely, if ever, wrong, and it was coming through so strong, now, it caused her to be nervous. She'd never felt this way. But, there was definitely something wrong! Shadows were everywhere there was no light. In fact, she could almost swear one of them was moving! Lately, she had a fanciful, and over-active imagination.

Just as she reached home, and got out of the truck, it clicked, and she totally forgot about her terror and pain! She had it! Her story-line and plot for her Demon series! Gem threw up her hands, and wiggled around like Rocky while humming the tune.

"YES!!!!" she cried joyfully.

Unseen by her, a moving shadow disappeared into the night.

~ 2 ~
"What is it with the Storms?" ~ Gem

Gem stretched in her bed like the Cheshire Cat from Alice in Wonderland. The sun was a dancing glow on the horizon, quickly heading below it as dusk hit. Brilliant, orange and pink fluffy clouds caused patterns in her room as she lay there for a while just looking out the window. Last night seemed a long time ago! She turned to look at the clock on the table beside her bed, and that's when she felt the bruising all over her body. She had slept the day almost completely away! And, still, her body ached!

"Ouch!" she whined, and a tiny little body jumped on top of her stomach, causing more pain!

Licking her face, Lola had decided her pet had stayed in bed long enough! She really had to go outside, like, now! Using her teeth, Lola pulled the covers away trying to force Gem out of bed.

"Why, what's the matter, Lola?" she grinned.

Lola looked at her.

"Want to eat?" she laughed.

Lola jumped off the bed, heading to the kitchen door.

"Ah! Potty time?" Gem laughed harder when Lola just stopped, sat down, and glared at her pet. Seriously? Her pet was laughing about it?

Finally, Lola couldn't hold it any more, and barked loud. Gem laughed, got up, and padded to the kitchen to open the back door. Lola practically flew off the deck with Gem's laughter following her. Gem just stood at the door waiting, and…opened the door again to allow the much relieved pug back into the house. Now, Lola had more energy as she ran in circles between her pet's legs. Food! She was soooo hungry!

Gem scooped one-third of a cup of Lola's weight controlled food, and waited for her opportunity to put the food into her tiny metal food dish. Seeing no opening, she bent down, and before she could empty it all into the bowl, Lola jumped, and knocked a lot of food from the cup. Gem wasn't bothered, though. She knew that Lola would wolf down what did make it into the bowl, then she'd make sure she had every piece that fell on the floor.

While Lola swallowed her food, which took about a half a second, since she was more like a vacuum cleaner, Gem made a cup of coffee with the Keurig Taylor and Rick had given to her last Christmas. It was her favorite gift – ever! While her coffee was making, she placed her Fruit Loops in a bowl, then realized she had no milk! Damn! Oh, well. She reached for a snack for Lola, and tossed both of them out the back door so Lola could finish her regimen.

Gem traipsed to her computer, and began writing. She'd send her publisher an e-mail when she went into town later. She had a great idea, and that should pacify him for a few days. She hoped.

A noise at the door brought her out of her "in the zone" area. Realizing it was Lola, she opened the door, and let her into the house. Lola started bouncing around like she did for her food. It wasn't time to be fed! Or…was it? She turned and looked at the clock, feeling her mouth drop. It was already nine o'clock? It sure didn't seem like it could possibly be that time, but it was! It *was* way past time to feed Lola – an herself as well!

Gem realized her own stomach was growling, as she placed Lola's food into her dish making sure she still had plenty of water.

"Well, there's a shocker, Lola! Why do you think I'd be hungry? I had a couple of cups of dry Fruit Loops and coffee. I only missed lunch...and, snacking...and, dinner!" she muttered while raiding her refrigerator only to slam the door. "Fuck! There's nothing in this place to eat!"

That meant a drive to town to get some groceries. She hated to shop at the place she worked, but she didn't have any choice in a small town. Or, she could just run down to the convenience store to pick up something, and buy her groceries tomorrow either before or after work. Yes. That would do.

"Hey, Lola? Wanna go with Mommy to the store?"

She sure didn't have to ask Lola twice, because she started leap-frogging all over the place as Gem tried to put her harness around her! Lola always enjoyed it when she got to ride in the truck. Her pet was just so slow!

Gem looked down at her clothes. Oh, well. She had on her lounge pants and a black tank top, so she pulled on her flip flops and grabbed her purse picking Lola up in her arms.

"OK. Let's run down to the Sip 'N' Stop, and I'll pick up a treat for you, too. Shouldn't take more than ten minutes," Gem said to Lola.

It only took her about five minutes to drive to the Sip 'N' Stop, and she pulled into a parking space in front of it. Getting out of the truck, she heard a rumbling in the sky, and looked up into the sky. A small bolt of lightning crossed its way across. She looked into the truck at Lola.

"Lola. Looks like we have a storm brewing, so you wait here. Mommy won't be long at all."

Lola didn't mind. She just loved to get away from the house sometimes. She put her paws upon the door pulling herself up to look out the window. A flash of lightning startled her for a moment, and she narrowed her eyes. That was never good. She was charged with taking care of her pet, and she couldn't get to her. Now what?

Something was odd about the lightning. She'd seen it before, but she sure hoped she was wrong!

Gem charged into the store quickly.

"Hey, Gem."

Newton was the store manager, but was all by himself in the store.

"Hey, Newton. By yourself this evening?" she answered.

"Yeah. Tina couldn't make it. So…whatcha doing?" he asked.

"Out of food. Well, except for Lola's, that is. I'm out of *human* food. Just grabbing a couple of things."

"How's the pug?" he said.

"She's in the truck. She really wanted to come with me."

"Well, better hurry. Looks like it's blowing up a storm."

"Yeah. Just like last night," she murmured with her head stuck inside the refrigerator, dragging out some soft drinks and milk.

"Last night?" Newton asked with a frown.

"Yep." She shut the door, and went down the canned aisle first, then the snack aisle.

"What storm, Gem? Last night? There wasn't a storm last night!" he told her.

Gem slapped her purchase down on the desk, and proceeded to swipe her debit card in the reader. It beeped at her reminding her that she had to use the chip in the card. It was a recent change by the government.

"What do you mean there wasn't a storm? It was awful! Blew out the windows in the library, and I almost got sliced into beef tips by the glass!"

"No. There was no storm, Gem. We are not that far from the library. We would have heard it if there had been one."

"Well, Taylor was there, and so was Profess...."

Wind whipped across the glass windows accompanied by massive rain. Lightning flashed without stopping, and thunder was so hard the entire building vibrated. Things flew off the shelves on the store, and a loud screech was heard outside. In horror, Gem watched as her old rust bucket of a truck was picked up, and thrown sideways. It disappeared somewhere outside, and they both heard it hit – hard. Gem was already to the door. Newton tackled her to keep her from going outside just before she reached for the handle on the door.

"LOLA!!!!!!!!!!!!!!!" Gem cried in the middle of her screaming. "LET ME GO! I HAVE TO GET TO HER. FUCK YOU! LET ME GO, Damnit!"

"You can't go out there, Gem! It would be suicide!" Newton yelled, trying to hold her back.

Another huge wind gust hit the windows, and broke one side of the glass throwing tiny glass pieces into the store. Both Gem and Newton hit the floor. Then, suddenly, it was just as quiet.

"Fuck!" Newton cried, while standing. "Is that what you meant by a storm last night?"

Gem shook Newton off of her when he tried to help her up, and sprinted toward the door. Tears were cascading down her cheeks as she thought about Lola in the truck. Why had she brought her? Why? Now, she could be hurt, or worse, dead. As she jerked open the door, she ran flat into Professor Hawkins, and fell on her ass. She didn't stay, but jumped up to run past him. He caught her arm.

"Ms. Elwood. You can't go out there. It's a mess."

That just made her angrier than she had been.

"Get the fuck out of my way, Professor! Lola is out there!" she screamed, and tried to push by him.

Suddenly, she heard something breathing hard. Something that sounded like Lola. Gem turned, and saw Professor Hawkins was holding Lola in his arms, and she looked just fine! Gem darted toward him, scooping Lola out of his arms, and hugging her tightly burying her face into her soft fur. After a few minutes, she looked up into the Professor's dark brown eyes, and stared into gorgeous...red eyes? She blinked. No. Must have been her imagination. They were as brown with those blue flecks of glitter as ever.

"How? Where?" Gem stuttered.

"She was crawling out of a rusted truck, and ran toward me. It's obvious she was trying to get to the store and to you," he explained.

"The truck?" she asked while kissing Lola and holding her tightly in her arms.

"Well, what was left of a truck, anyway."

Tears flowed down her face. Both men found her extremely attractive in her PJ bottoms and tank top. Holding Lola to her as if she would never let her go, Jaxx's eyes narrowed at her. This could be a problem.

"Look, Ms. Elwood, let me take you home. "You and… what's her name?"

L-Lola she cried silently.

"Right. Lola. Let me take you both home. I'm assuming that rust bucket of bolts was yours?"

She nodded. Her truck was gone, and of course, it wasn't insured, because it was not worth insuring. She turned her head up to him.

"I don't want you to go out of your way, Professor. I can walk it. It's only a mile up the mountain."

Gem had never been one to be so emotional, but this was far too real. Lola could have been killed, and it was all her fault!

"Thank you so much for saving her, Professor! I will never forget it," she told him, and moved to leave when Hawkins grabbed her arm. Electricity, or something that sure as hell felt like it, shot into her in mere seconds, and covered her body right down to her toes! Her eyes jerked upward seeing his eyes staring at her with…what was it? She shook her head. No she hadn't seen anything on second thought. That would be way too weird! He was an older man!

"I don't think so, Ms. Elwood. You've had a trauma, and you don't need to walk in the dark alone. That would be extremely foolish."

Even though his tone was usually rough, it wasn't, now. The electric pulse that flowed from his body into her was completely unexpected. That was unusual, and he'd never felt it before. Not in his entire, long life! The pulse not only flowed from him into her, but he felt a pulse from her flood into him! What the hell was wrong with him? He felt…what? Sorry for her? Anger? No. Not anger. Irritation? No, that's not it, either. He focused his eyes on her terrified ones. She had believed she had lost Lola, and the tears marking her beauty only made him want to hold her forever. To take her pain away. So, what is that called? He never stopped to consider humans before. At least not until now. She knew him only by his designation as Professor, and that's the way it was. Shaking his head, Jaxx was here for one purpose, and one purpose only. Whatever this feeling was, he had to get rid of it. If he didn't find what he was looking for, his entire mission would be a failure. Everything would be gone. And, so, frankly, would the human world. What he couldn't figure out was why Lola was here. Listening to her soft words as Gem cuddled Lola was anathema to him. And, he wondered what Lola thought of it.

Jaxx's eyes held hers for what seemed like hours on end, when in truth, it had to be a few seconds if that long. But, it felt like an eternity. Then, he dropped his hand from her arm as if he had been shocked. Still they stood staring at each other.

Finally, Gem shook her head slightly as if to free cobwebs from her brain. For some reason, she didn't want to be in a confined space with the Professor. This situation was way too weird.

"T-thank you, sir, but it's OK. Really. I've walked from town, before when the weather was nice," she said by way of an explanation.

He narrowed his eyes at her, then he said, "No. You will not. You will allow me to escort you to your destination. I will brook no argument on this."

Surprise gripped her. She had never heard him say more than a short sentence here and there over the last six years. And, usually, he did not address her, but when he did, his statements were always blunt, and really mean! In fact, she had been certain that he didn't talk much at all! Well, this incident sure blew that out of the water! And, did he really say he would "brook no argument"? What the hell kind of talk was that? Who actually said stuff like that any more. Well, he was an older man, so she'd give that to him. He had to be at least sixty-five. She really couldn't tell. Give or take an inch, he had to be six-feet two inches. He always had that infernal hoodie on, just like now, and never took it off even in the library, so she couldn't see the color of his hair. His eyes, though, were always mesmerizing. The reason she hadn't been able to look away. But, those eyes pierced her as if he was trying to see through to her soul. She couldn't move her eyes from his, and it appeared that he was having the very same problem. Oh! That's just sooooo gross. Never gonna happen! Somehow, she found the strength to rip her eyes from his.

"Thank you, Professor, but…" she started to decline his offer again.

"Do not argue," he ordered, and she found herself obeying him.

Jaxx turned to Newton.

"Insurance?" he asked.

"Yeah, man. I have it."

"Good. If you need anything else, let me know," and with a nod, he grabbed her elbow to lead her to his car, which amazingly, was still intact.

Opening the door, she remembered why she came in the first place.

"Oh! My food!"

Jaxx cocked his head, nodded once, and went back inside to retrieve her purchase.

It was a very short trip to her house, but as they rounded the corner, they saw a brilliant orange glow. Gem's heart almost stopped. It was fire! As they drove closer, Gem gasped in horror as she realized her house was almost burned to the ground. It had obviously been struck by lightning. Despite the rain was falling hard, she stepped out of the car leaving Lola inside of it. All she could do was stand and stare as the rain erased the tears that were streaming down her face.

"Why?" she whispered almost to herself.

Jaxx turned to watch her. He had never felt the need to be attached to a person, place, pet, or thing, so he was having a difficult time processing why she was crying. She dropped to the mud on her knees. Her tank top was thin, and he could easily see through it. She wore no bra, but then, she'd probably been going to bed before she realized she was out of food. Her pants were muddied, and sagged enough to creep lower than her butt crack, so he got a good look at it! He felt a sudden rush of desire enter into him. Sex was fun, yes. He never felt desire, no. But, her nipples were easily seen through her top, and the sight of her crack made his cock swell with blood anticipating thrusting into her body. He had never felt physical desire for any woman – his kind or not. He also had a sudden burst of jealousy, knowing that Newton had seen her breasts as well! Shit! What the fuck was wrong with him? This woman was vulnerable. His entire existence was to protect the innocent. But, how would he protect her from him when he felt this way? Well, he couldn't leave her kneeling in the mud, and there was no way she was going to move, so he picked her up in his arms, and putting her in the front seat of his car, got behind the wheel.

Again, the soft whisper, "Why?" came from her. Her soft, sexy voice just increased the size of his cock. He had to take her somewhere, but where would she be safe?

"Gem?" he asked softly. No reaction. He asked louder, "Gem?" Still nothing. Finally, he raised his voice even louder.

"Gem!' he yelled, and her head jerked toward him.

"I'm sorry, but you're in shock. Is there someone I can leave you with?" he asked her, but his body was demanding that he take her home, and bury his body inside of hers. Fighting it was almost too hard.

"I-I guess you can take me to Taylor's house, Professor," she said quietly. Then, "What am I going to do?"

Everything was in that house. Everything she had in the world – including her job! She had no idea why everything had been taken from her. What had she done? And, she almost lost her best friend! She turned to see

Lola was alive, and sound asleep in the backseat. At least she still had her.

"What did I do to deserve this?" she muttered so quietly that a normal person would never have heard it.

But, Jaxx did.

"Nothing, Gem. You did nothing wrong. There is always a reason behind everything. The fates will allow it to be seen when it is time," he told her.

"Really?" she cried louder. "I don't believe that! The 'fates' my ass! They can all go to hell!"

Cursing the fates? Did she just actually curse the fates? What was wrong with her?

"Cursing the fates is never a good idea, Gem," he told her.

Without turning her head, she sneered.

"I don't care! First of all, they aren't real. Second of all, I don't care, and I'll curse them all I like, MR. Hawkins!"

Damn the man! Acting as if the Fates were real! Idiot!

"I'm a college graduate, and believe me…no one I know would ever treat them as 'real'…because they are not real! Surely, you, a Professor, know that?"

"Here," he said ignoring her, and giving her his cell. "Call Taylor. I have her number stored."

"Thanks," she muttered, wondering why he would have Taylor's number in his phone.

Desperately punching the buttons on his iPhone, she kept missing, and had to dial at least three times. Taylor answered on the first ring.

"Yes, sir. Your orders?" Taylor's voice said.

Orders? Sir? Why would Taylor be saying something like that?

"Hey, Taylor?"

"J – uh – Gem? Is that you? Why are you using Professor Hawkin's phone?" Gem could hear the surprise in her voice.

"Another massive storm hit, Taylor. I was out of food, and ran down to the convenience store. It hit, and Lola was in the truck, which was picked up and thrown sideways."

"Oh, no! Is Lola…?"

"No. She's fine. Professor Hawkins showed up, and brought her to me."

"I was wondering why you were talking on the Professor's phone? He's there?" she sounded surprised.

"Uh, yeah. He tried to take me home, only…" Gem gulped.

"What, Gem? What happened?"

"Lightning strike. My house is gone," Gem gulped tears back, again.

"Oh, sweetie! I'm so sorry! Tell me that you're coming here with Lola. You are, right?" Taylor asked.

"H-he's bringing us, yes," Gem's voice broke, and she couldn't speak any more.

Jaxx grabbed his phone out of her hand.

"Taylor, she's about to have a nervous breakdown…not that I blame her at all, of course. She's been cursing the fates." He heard a gasp of horror from Taylor. "Yes. No. Yes. We're on our way."

He shut the phone down, and put it in his pocket. He hated using the damned things! They were just too ridiculous for words considering he was able to contact anyone he wanted at any time without them. But, to function in this world, he had to appear to be like humans. Taylor could easily have blown their cover. He sighed, and turned to look at Gem. He never had a heart. He wasn't built that way. But, her sadness was piercing him where a heart would be, and that was so not good. No.

Not good at all. He'd never have feelings for a woman. Ever. Oh, he used them for sex and fun, but that's it. This girl, though. She could turn out to be a real problem for him, and he couldn't let that happen.

Jaxx turned down Taylor's street, and stopped in front of her house. He still couldn't believe she had not only married a human, but had children with him! How could she be happy? But, she sure seemed to be. Nope. Jaxx just couldn't understand it at all.

Beside him, Gem sniffed as she exited the SUV, and opened the back door to pick up her tiny little dog who was sound asleep. Lola didn't even move, but snored adorably as they walked to the front door with Professor Hawkins, who seemed to think that she needed him to hold onto her arm to keep her from falling, or whatever. When he had reached for her elbow, a bolt of electricity shot through her entire body, again! It had startled her so much, she had flinched. Her eyes shot up to the Professor who looked at her with the same dumbfounded look that said, "What the fuck?"

The tense moment was interrupted when Taylor threw open the door, and ran out to grab Gem in a huge bear hug! Richard and their two children followed after her. Over Gem's head, Taylor glared at Jaxx. What the hell was he up to this time?

Letting her go, Lola, who had just woken up, almost suffocating when Taylor hugged them, started to wiggle to be let down. Gem sniffed, and handed her over to the two kids who hugged her tightly, much to Lola's happiness. She had awakened when Taylor had almost suffocated her in the bear hug she had given Gem. Lola admitted it. She was truly worried about her pet, but it was also nice to be loved by so many after that harrowing close call when the wind blew the truck sideways, and into the tree with her little love pug inside it! Lola excelled at being loved! Her very size and face made everyone love her instantly. While she wagged her tiny, curly tail, Gem was caught in a wooly mammoth hug by Richard, who was, quite literally, a giant of a man at 6 feet nine inches.

"I'm so sorry, Gem. I truly am. I know how much the house and especially the truck meant to you," he told her quietly.

Richard always had the ability to calm her down just by his voice, and Gem felt calmer than she had over the last couple of hours. He pulled away from her.

"We'll help you, Gem. You know that, right?" he asked her.

Gem couldn't trust her voice at the moment, so she just nodded. Then, her legs buckled. Jaxx was behind her, and caught her while Richard grabbed her from the front. Jaxx couldn't believe the surge of jealousy he felt when he saw Richard touching Gem, and he growled at Richard, whose eyebrows rose at the sound in surprise! Richard carefully released his hold on Gem, giving Jaxx a knowing grin. Jaxx's surprise at the grin made him wonder why he felt that way? He'd never felt jealousy – ever. In fact, his emotions were non-existent. At least, that was what he had always been told. It was his lack of emotion for anything, or anyone, that made him so dangerous.

Gem turned around.

"Thank you, Professor, for bringing me here. I'm so sorry, because I just know you wanted to have a hysterical woman on your hands," she managed a tight grin at him. "And, thank you for saving Lola for me! I'm just so glad that she was o-okay."

Gem broke down into tears once again, and Richard guided her into the house with Shirley and Marcus following him, holding tightly to Lola who wanted her pet, and tried to wiggle down to get to her.

"I'll be right in, honey!" she called after Richard, then whirled on Jaxx.

"What in the fuck is wrong with you?" she demanded.

"Nothing! If she wasn't your best friend, I would have left her alone!"

"Gem Elwood is *not* your responsibility. You know it!"

"Oh. So, what? Had you rather me stand aside, and leave her to her own devices after her entire world hit the fucking fan?"

Taylor narrowed her eyes at him. Something wasn't right.

"Since when do you care about humans?" she asked warily.

"I don't, so don't get any ideas, Taylor. I have my orders just as you have yours. Gem is not your responsibility, either!" His voice was low, but held a note of authority.

"So, why didn't you just leave her?" she asked.

"Taylor, hon?" Richard called.

"This isn't over, Jaxx. I'm considering telling the council about this!"

Jaxx snorted.

"Go ahead. You know I don't give a fuck what that group of blowhards says or does. I have never bowed to anyone. I will *never* bow to them, and you know it."

"Fine. Go away!" Taylor hissed, and turned to walk into the house. She stopped when she heard Jaxx's voice.

"I will leave for the moment, Taryln, but I will not stay away," he growled at her.

Taylor turned on her heel, and shot him an angry glare.

"You *will* stay away from Gem!" Taylor answered with her own growl, then slammed the door behind her with finality.

Finding himself standing, staring at a shut door, surprised the hell out of him! No one had ever shut a door in his face! He was livid, and stomped back to his SUV. Just before he stepped into it, he looked into the distance where the rumble of thunder, and the lightning was slowly dissipating. He got behind the wheel, then put his arms on it staring. Something was not right about this. The thunder and lightning last night, the heavy deluge, and the shards of glass heading straight for Gem – as if they were guided. And, then, tonight. He'd been on his way out of town, and drove upon the devastation that wrecked Gem's life with her dog and her truck. Also, caused by a storm. But, what he didn't tell anyone was that hers was the only vehicle that had been thrown into the tree. If she had been inside it, she would be dead. If he didn't know any better, he could have sworn that the two storms were after her – or someone was causing the storm to target her! No! That was just plain crazy! In his entire life, never had he seen a force of nature target one particular human. Besides, who would do this in the first place? He slid his arms off the wheel, and turned the key. Fuck these stupid vehicles! He didn't need one at all, but he had to continue to play this charade until he found what he had been sent to find. He drove off, and straight to his house.

"Gem, I'm so very sorry!" Taylor kept telling her.

"It's okay, Tay. I-I'll have to figure out what I'm going to do, now, though. I have no car, or house. Hell! My computer was burned to a crisp, my clothing, and everything I owned! The house wasn't worth a dime, and neither was my truck, but they were free, and I didn't have to pay rent. My books are just beginning to give me a little bit of money every third month, but now, I have to find a place to live, pay rent, figure out how to get from point A to point B, and to do my writing." Gem's voice sounded defeated, and Taylor had tears in her eyes.

"Don't worry, Gem," Richard said. "You can stay with us as long as you need until you can figure out what to do. Besides, we have three cars. You can have one of them."

Taylor smiled at her husband. Who said that humans weren't awesome! To hell with the council who thought they were nothing but animals beneath them! They believed that they were made to serve them, but through a glitch in the system, had been given total freedom! The idiots on the council were fucking bastards! And, if she didn't know better, she would bet a month's salary that Jaxx hated them, and a second bet that the Council was terrified of him! Why, she had no idea, but she would swear it was true!

"I can't take your car, Richard," Gem gasped.

"Yes, you can, sweetie," Taylor backed her husband up. "Look. We can't drive three cars at a time, and one just sits in the garage, anyway. We drive it, what, Richard?"

"Maybe, if it's lucky, a couple of times every three months?" he surmised.

"Close enough!"

"And, cars are not made to just sit," Richard added. "You'll be doing us a favor."

Gem looked from one sweet face to the other while she considered their offer. It would help her out for the time being. And, if they would let her stay until she could find something really, really cheap, then that would help.

"Okay. I will. But, just until I get back on my feet. I'll pay you back."

"The hell you will!" Taylor growled. "We are as close to family as any blood bonded family. Come on, you can take the basement room."

"I thought you had been using that as your workout room, Taylor."

"Uh, well, yeah, but we had it renovated into an apartment for Richard's, uh…," Taylor stumbled over the words as she tried to think up something.

"My great aunt. She came to stay with us a while back for a couple of days," Richard finished.

"Right," Taylor agreed. "She wasn't here that long, though, and we just didn't want to change the room back, so we just kept it like it is."

"Yep. And, I moved all our exercise equipment to the building out back, and fixed it up into a full gym," Richard finished.

Great aunt? Gem was a bit confused.

"You never mentioned it, Tay," she stated.

"Oh, right. Well, you see, the woman is a menace. She's a bit of a jackass, and I just don't like to talk about her."

Gem frowned, then yawned, and Taylor laughed throwing her arm around Gem.

"Look. When Jaxx told me he was bringing you here…I mean Professor Hawkins…I rooted around in my closet for some clothes that should fit you. Tomorrow, you and I will go shopping for some new clothes, OK?"

Gem just nodded.

"Well, let's all eat. What does everyone want tonight?" Richard called to the kids.

"Pizza!" was the unanimous answer, and even Lola was wagging her little tail at the word.

Gem laughed a little at that one.

"Well, I could have made book on that answer!" she joked.

"Then, pizza it is!" And, Taylor pulled out her cell.

53

~ 3 ~

"Well, when the shit hits the fan for your friend, you gotta drag out the big guns!" ~ Taylor

The children decided upon cheese pizza, and the four pizzas that they had ordered were delivered to the house in record time, and they all sat down to eat. Taylor ate quickly, and then gave a nod to Richard who understood what she meant.

"The room is dusty, I'm sure. I'll just toddle on down there, and make sure it's clean, Gem."

"Oh, please, Tay! Don't go to that kind of trouble. A little dust isn't a big deal."

"Hell, Gem! If you had someone to stay with you, would you let them go into a dusty room?"

Gem looked at her, and grinned.

"Touché!" she laughed at Taylor.

"OK. Give me an hour. Kiddoes, play with Lola, and be nice! Be back up in a little bit," and Taylor took off down the stairs, and entered the exercise room. She had an hour. That was it. So, she pushed her sleeves up, and started to work.

Richard and Taylor were rich. There was never a question about it. Their house sported five-thousand square feet of living area, and even though Gem knew that she could live with them in the house – maybe never seeing any of them for days at a time, it just wasn't in her nature to sponge off anyone. She'd been pretty much alone most of her life from the age of sixteen, and so she had learned to take care of herself. Granted, if she couldn't find a place to live she could still live here, but it had to be a worse case scenario. Right now, though, she just needed a bit of time to recoup. That's it. Just a few days. She sure hoped Tay wasn't going to a lot of trouble with the room. Pushing that thought away, she settled down to play with Lola, Rick, and the kids.

Downstairs, Taylor was just about finished. Brushing her hands together, she had moved all the equipment to the building into the guest house that was at the back of the property, then designed the room, beating her own record! It was lovely, and she knew that Gem would love it. It was a room straight out of Taylor's favorite series, Gem's "King Triton". She slapped her hands together to get rid of the dust to clean up the room, before she put the furniture into it. In seconds, another clap of her hands, and the room was transformed! Critical of her design, Taylor cocked her head as she walked through the new apartment. Having a five-thousand square foot house had its advantages, and since this room had its own entrance, Gem could easily stay here for months without even seeing them! For years, she had tried to get Gem to stop being a nut about being alone, but she had finally stopped bugging her about it. Gem wouldn't change even though Taylor's family considered her family.

Nodding her head in satisfaction, she headed back up to get Gem.

"Gem?" Taylor said, looking through the railing while she stood on the stairs. "It's ready. I hope you like it."

Gem only laughed at that, because it was pretty hard not to please her! She stood up, kissed the kids on the head, told Lola to behave, and descended the stairs while Taylor went before her.

Taylor opened the door, and let Gem enter first. Gem took one look at the room of blues, greens, and creams, and gasped! She recognized it! It was straight out of her last book series! She almost couldn't breathe! It was so beautiful it took away her breath! She moved reverently through the huge room that her own house would have fit into three times over!

It was split into three different areas, and all the walls were painted a seafoam blue as if one was under the ocean. To her right, and at the back of the room, a small kitchenette complete with full size fridge, stove, sink, and even a dishwasher that was shining and new! Large, sixteen inch, sand colored tile, covered the floor. Distressed cabinets of cream and a dark gray granite cabinet top completed the small kitchen. A small, cream wooden table, also distressed, was accompanied by wooden chairs – two green and two blue.

Two dividers separated the three areas. The one separating the kitchen from the living space was painted a coral pink, and resembled a bookcase with various sized square and rectangle cubbyholes. Adding some books, shells, and marine knick-knacks, and interspersing them within the cubbyholes, enough were still empty for Gem to fill. And, she had an idea about what she could put into them.

Next, came the main room. A full-size sofa sat side-by-side at a ninety degree angle with a matching love seat, and the upholstery was dark sand in color. The floors were light wood, but covered with a large rug of seafoam blue-green resembling the color of the ocean depths. On two end tables of mahogany sat solid brass anchor lights with cream shades, and a small, rectangular mahogany coffee table sat in the center in front of the larger sofa. Underneath it sat two blue-green storage/seats. A rocker recliner in the same blue green sat opposite the love-seat.

The second divider was textured in a sand colored tone. In the center was a very large opening that held a 50" flat screen TV. Taylor darted to it to show her the cool feature the TV had!

"We bought this a while back, and it was still in its box, because it wasn't large enough for the family room. It has a tiny feature in it that we absolutely love. Watch!" she giggled, as she swiveled the TV completely around so that it faced the sleeping area behind it.

"That's so cool, Taylor!"

"Yes. It keeps one from needing to buy another TV!"

More cubbyholes were in this divider, and most were empty for Gem to fill.

"Come on! Look at the sleeping area!" Taylor gushed.

As Gem walked around the divider, her mouth dropped open! The bed was placed opposite the TV, and behind it, a mural had been painted. The entire wall had a sandy beach leading up to the palm trees that appeared to actually sway as a person moved toward them. On the opposite wall, sat a tan wicker chair with a stand next to it with yet another solid brass lamp on top, and positioned at the side of the mural which looked out upon the ocean! To the right of the bed, sat a multi-drawer large cream wicker dresser.

"Oh, Taylor! This is just beautiful! And, so relaxing!"

"I've worked on it for weeks, Gem! I loved the description so much in your books, I just had to match it here. I never dreamed, though, that you would be staying in it! After she left, I had planned to show it to you."

"It's absolutely beautiful, Taylor, and spot on the money from my description!"

"The door on the left of the bed is a closet, and just wait till you see what I did for the bathroom!"

OK. That was enough for Gem. She headed straight for the bathroom, opened the door, and came to a dead halt!   You know those OMG moments? This just happened to be one of them!

The bathroom was completely tiled in the same seafoam green. The ceiling was painted in a deep midnight blue, almost black, dotted with stars of every color that actually twinkled as if one was literally looking at the night sky. A long cabinet on the left side was painted in a distressed cream, again, and the doors and drawers underneath were shuttered. The top of the sink was clear glass while one of the glass basins was blue and the other was of green. The handles were gold seashells, and the faucets were ribbed. Gem turned to what she was really interested in seeing. The bath and shower.

In front of her was a humongous, sunken tub with plenty of jets for a whirlpool. Two sets of steps led down into it. But, one set also let up into the shower next to it. There were two steps in both, and the backs of each step curved.   Both were completely open, except around a corner of the shower where rocks had been stacked to the ceiling with a spout at the top resembling what Gem could only describe as "spouting hole" that she had seen at Hanging Lake, Colorado! It took Gem a moment, but she realized....

"Taylor? If I use the shower...I mean does water...I mean does it flow into the tub over the steps like a waterfall?"

"Yep! Isn't that great?   There is one, larger than normal drain in the tub, and that is where both the tub and shower drain!"

"This is a real dream, Taylor! I can't believe you did this!"

"I thought it would be a great idea to take a photo or two of all of this, so that you might use it in the advertising of your book."

Tears appeared in Gem's eyes. Her best friend had done all of this…for her! She threw her arms around Taylor, who held her tightly while Gem finally let her tears flow. She needed to cry! She'd truly lost everything she had, yet had gained so much more!

After a while, she wiped her eyes, and sniffed.

"Thank you so damn much, Tay! You guys are the bestest friends in the entire world!" She pulled back, and then said, "I think I'm going to go to what's left of my house, tomorrow, and see what I can salvage."

"Want me to go with you, sweetie?" Taylor asked with compassion.

"No. But, thanks. I need some time alone. No offense," Gem hastened to add.

"None taken. I understand. We can let you drive one of our cars."

"No. I think tomorrow morning, I'll just run *to* the house, instead of from it. Whatever I find, I can leave to pick up later."

"Sure, Gem. Just take your cell phone, and check in with us a couple of times."

"Oh, Tay?" Gem asked.

"Yep?"

"Could you, or the kids, let Lola into the room when you go to bed? But, if she wants to sleep in the kids' room, that's just fine. I know how much she loves them. But, I'm betting that she will want to be with me tonight, especially after what happened."

"No need!" Taylor pointing to the door as she turned to leave. "I made sure a tiny door was put into the door so she could go in and out whenever she wanted!"

Gem just smiled even bigger! Lola wouldn't have to be trapped!

"Oh. Almost forgot!" Taylor opened the outside door onto a multilevel deck, and a small fenced yard. "We also put in a deck, a small, fenced yard, and doggie door, so she can run in and out to do her business, too! Now, I put some extra clothes in the dresser. A couple of lounge outfits, some T-shirts – short and long sleeved – but, I just don't have jeans to fit you, so I left you a couple of my jogging pants, and panties for the short term."

Gem's eyes filled with tears at how they had gone to so much trouble for her – even if they had designed it for that great aunt they had never mentioned!

"Thanks, Taylor," she sniffed. "For everything, and for taking Lola into account, too! She will love it!" Gem blew her nose into a tissue, that she had taken from a box on the nightstand. She took a deep breath, then continued. "After I finish at the house, I'm going to the store to get some things."

"Want some company?" Taylor waggled her eyebrows, and laughing.

"Sure, I do! I mean…who's going to tell me if my butt looks big when I try on some jeans?"

Throwing her hands up, and her head back hooting with laughter, Taylor closed the door behind her, and traipsed up the staircase.

Instantly, Gem ran to the bathroom! She was going to soak in the tub for a while. Turning on the faucet, she let the tub fill, stripped, and stepped down into it sitting on one of the two built in seats in the whirlpool. Once the water reached the right depth, she pushed the button, turned on the jets, then settled back, and let the tears run down her face.

Slurp! Slurp! A warm, wet tongue slapped itself across Gem's face. She moaned, and turned over in the bed. Then, a tiny little body started to bounce up and down on her legs causing Gem to open one eye, which glared at Lola. Knowing Lola needed to go outside, she dragged her body out of the bed, and sleepily found Lola's leash. She stumbled to the door, and opened it onto the multi-level deck that was outside the room. Lola led her outside, and spent her sweet time just finding the "perfect spot" so that she could relieve herself. Gem yawned, and almost dislocated her jaw. She had no idea that she was this tired! Lola danced around her feet when she was finished, and the two of them walked back inside. That's when Gem stopped, turned to look at Lola who actually had a snarky look on her face. She looked back at the door, then burst out laughing at the doggie door Taylor had put into it. She looked back at Lola.

"Oh, you little stinker! You knew about the doggie door, and deliberately didn't remind me, didn't you?" she laughed.

Lola's expression of "I have no idea what you're talking about" was so ridiculous, Gem just laughed all the more. Still laughing, Gem took off Lola's leash, and the two of them shuffled to the kitchen. Opening the cabinet door in the kitchen, Gem found a 5 lb bag of Lola's favorite dog food, a brand new doggie bowl for her food with a matching water dish, along with a mat to go under them. She filled the water dish, and put it down, then filled the bowl with 1/3 cup of the dry dog food, setting it down next to the water dish. Before she could get it down, Lola leaped up, and knocked some of the food out of the bowl into the floor. She did it every time Gem fed her. Knowing Lola would have her food downed in about ten seconds or less, Gem stumbled into the bathroom. She washed her face, brushed her teeth, and combed her hair. She'd gone to bed with it wet, and naturally, it was curling and frizzing.

Giving up on it, she pulled it back into a ponytail, then went to the dresser to pull out what clothing was in it.

Everything except a bra was there. Taylor was a 38-C while Gem was a 36-B. No way could she wear any of Taylor's. But, she had washed her sports bra out in the sink the night before, and even though it wasn't totally dry, she pulled it on over her head anyway. She pulled on panties, the yoga pants, and then, grabbed the long sleeved matching yoga jacket. Turning to Lola, who was still busy snuffling around for more food, Gem scooped her up, receiving an enthusiastic kiss.

"So, Lola? Wanna go with me, or stay with the kids?" she asked.

Lola looked at her pet, then cocked her head. Was her pet serious? Go on a hike all morning, or stay and play games with her second favorite two humans? No contest. She wiggled, which told her pet to put her down, then she dashed to the door, pushed open her little doggie door, and sped into the small hall that led to the first floor above.

Gem shook her head, she muttered, "Traitor."

Well, just as well. Lola did love to get off track when they went for a walk. Oh, well! Gem would never get things done with her stopping at every little thing, to inspect it! Not noticing, Lola grinned at her words. Gem grabbed a water bottle, filled it with Gatorade, then grabbed her keys, her phone, darted out the door got her thirty minute jog to what was left of her house.

It was a good thing she was in great shape! Passing the Sip 'N' Stop, she decided to tell Newton that she would have the truck towed. Before she went into the building, she...stopped. She looked at the tree, but her truck was gone? She jogged over to it, and saw where the truck had been thrown into it, but no truck! Far too curious, she dashed into the building.

"Hey, Newton? Where's my truck?"

"Your truck? Huh? Well, I didn't even notice! Are you telling me that it's not there?" Newton asked in surprised.

"No!" she exclaimed with surprise.

Newton followed Gem outside, and looked at the tree. She was right. The truck was gone.

"I have no idea where it is, Gem," he told her. He shrugged.

"Well, I need to find out where it is, and if you didn't have it towed, then who did?"

"I have no idea," he answered.

"Look, I'm going up to what's left of my house, and when I come back down, maybe you can help me."

"OK. Sure. No problem! I'll see what I can find out while you're at the house."

"Thanks, Newton!"

She waved at him as she jogged out of the store, and headed to her house.

Angry, narrowed eyes watched Gem leave the Sip'N'Shop. What the hell was wrong with him? He'd spent last night watching over her across the street. The dark shape he had shadowed had suddenly disappeared about 2 am. So, why didn't he leave? He had no answer. Well, an idea was forming, but he refused to believe it, so he pushed it aside. There was no way he was going down that road! Mainly because it was a total impossibility!

Professor Hawkins discreetly followed Gem to make sure she didn't get into any more trouble. The storms were bothering him – a lot. There was something not right about them, but for the life of him, he couldn't put his finger on what it was. If he didn't know any better, he would swear that the storms were going after Gem! But, that wasn't possible. Was it? If so, he'd never seen anything like it in his long, long life! He needed to talk to Gem about it. Maybe she had the key to why, although how she could know was out of his zone of understanding. After all...she was only human.

Gem finally stopped in front of the burned out house. She just hoped that something was left! She looked behind her expecting the cops or the fire department to come along and stop her. But, they weren't, and they didn't, so she walked into the ashes. Not much was left, but she was going to look anyway.

After going through the living room, and finding her burned up computer on the floor, she proceeded to the kitchen. The kitchen looked as if it hadn't been so badly burned. She opened a cabinet door, and it fell off the hinges, making her jump as it hit the floor. Inside, her Mother's stoneware looked pristine! Not a speck of ash on them! Tears beginning to form, she pulled out one of the plates, and blew on it. A bit of dust, but that was all! She almost broke down into tears at this one, small thing still left of her life! Holding the plate, she turned around. Where would she put it till she could take all of it back with her? Her eyes fell on the patio table that hadn't been hurt. She put the plate down on the cabinet, and made her way carefully back through the house, until she walked out onto the lawn.

Pulling the table across the grass was tough, but she managed to do it, leaving it just outside the kitchen area. Then, she walked back into the kitchen, and began to pull the stoneware out of the cabinets, and set them on the table. Next, she looked into each cabinet, and discovered she had some pots and pans along with the utensils still relatively intact. She left the things that looked burned, crooked, or bent, and took the good condition utensils and pans to the table stacking them, then, she went back into the ashes.

Diligently, Gem silently, and methodically, worked through all the destruction. She found her parent's photo still fairly intact in a frame that had been in her Dad's room. A few other things such as a watch, two rings, an engagement ring, and a pair of slippers. She rattled around inside his closet, and pushed and pulled her way through the clothing that had smoke damage, and burns.

Just as she turned around in the closet to leave, her foot hit something sticking out, and she heard a squeaking noise, then a twang. Gem looked behind the clothing pushing them aside. A small door at the baseboard had swung open, and inside it was a royal blue velvet box. She looked at it, and frowned. Why had she never seen it before? She stooped down for a better look, and then, reached out, and pulled it out of its little cubbyhole. It was about 3 inches wide x 4 inches long, and at least 1 inch high. The size of one of those costume jewelry boxes one bought at Christmas containing a bracelet, necklace, and earrings. Gem ran her hands over the soft velvet, then turned it upside down, and sideways. It looked as if it had no opening at all! No hinges, no lock. Nope. She couldn't find any way to open it. Scratching her head, she had to wonder why would her Dad have something like this? What was it? Where did it come from, and did Dad even know about it? OK. That was a dumb question! Of course her Dad knew about it! He would have had to hide it, for goodness sakes!

While she puzzled about how to open it, Gem heard someone stepping through the broken boards and ashes. For whatever reason, Gem grabbed one of her Dad's coats off the hanger, and quickly wrapped the box inside it just as Professor Hawkins came into the room. Why she felt she needed to hide it from anyone, she didn't know, but at the moment, it just seemed imperative that she keep that box from everyone. At least until she had time to figure out how to open it.

Hawkins had yet to see her, since she was still in the closet, and it gave her an opportunity to really look at him without his noticing. He had been coming to the library as long as she had been working there, and she had noticed him, but had never really *looked* at him. He always sported that hoodie, and duster. But, now, he had a flight jacket on that was zipped almost up to his neck, and a cap with his favorite baseball team on it. He wore ragged blue jeans, which she had never seen him in, since he always wore khakis. It was fall and after the solstice, so the mornings and evenings were colder, now. He had his glasses on with a strap holding them in place, so he could run without worrying he would break them. He was rather non-descript, and it was just darned hard to get a read on him.

"What are you doing here?" Gem rudely demanded, as she stepped out of the closet with the coat tightly held in her hands. She realized it, and offered an apology immediately. "I-I'm sorry, Professor. Just everything has gotten to me."

"No worries. I understand. I thought I'd come look to find if you had anything left. I was going to filter through it, and sort out anything that was still salvageable."

Gem wasn't altogether sure that he was telling her the truth, so she frowned, but thought it better not to tell him that she didn't believe him.

"Uh-huh. OK. Thanks, but I wanted to see if there was anything left, before the fire department got here with their investigation."

"You do know you are not supposed to move anything, right?" the Professor asked.

Hmm! Why was it that she still didn't believe the reason he gave for being here? She'd never had cause to distrust him before, so why now? She narrowed her eyes at him trying to discern the truth. She twitched the right side of her lips upward as she considered it.

"Yeah. I know, but who knows what would happen if they got in here, and stepped on something that was OK till their boots stomped on it. I truly appreciate your offer of help, Professor Hawkins, but I think I have everything that I could find. I laid it all on the patio table in the backyard over there," she pointed. "I'm going to borrow Taylor's car, and I'll pick them up later today."

"Well, if you're sure?" Professor Hawkins asked.

"I'm sure," Gem answered cautiously.

The two stared at each other forever. At least, it seemed that way to Gem.

"Care to join me in a jog back to town?" Professor Hawkins asked.

Trying to get out of it, Gem replied, "Oh, I don't want to take you out of your way, Professor."

"It's not out of my way. Please," he added.

Damn! Well, she was obliged to go with him, now. She took another look around, and nodded.

"Sure. Why not?" she answered him. "Give me a sec to get my jacket."

The Professor went outside, and Gem quickly unwrapped the velvet box, stuffed it into her pocket with her cell phone, and joined Hawkins outside. The two started off at a loping jog, both silent as they concentrated on their run. They picked up speed, after they reached the bottom of the mountain, and took off toward town. When Taylor's house came into view, the Professor waved, and took off in a different direction.

Gem just stopped, watching as he put distance between them. What the hell was that all about? He's certainly not her type, of course, but then, she didn't think he was any girl's type! What an odd bird! She shook her head, then let herself into Taylor's basement. Taking her now dead cell phone out of her pocket and the blue velvet box, she opened the drawer of the bedside table, and put them inside it. Then, she headed to the shower, stripping as she went. The most fun she had was in the bathroom, where it was relaxing, Gem could swear she could live in there forever! She giggled, turned on the shower, and stepped inside of it.

After her shower, Gem took Taylor and Rick up on their offer to drive the car she had been offered. She drove back to the house to scoop up what she had left on the table. There was no way she was going to let anyone else take her stuff. It would take forever to get it back from the authorities.

After she rescued everything salvageable, she contacted her insurance company. Next, she spoke to the fire department, who apparently had appeared just after she had picked up the things she'd dug out of the ashes. But, except for the blue box, plates, and cookware, there just was nothing left. Gem knew she shouldn't have disturbed anything, but there was no way she could go without checking everything. Imagine if the door had popped open, and anyone could have stolen the box from her – even someone from the fire department, or a passing bum. The insurance, of course, insisted upon investigating it, before they would give her any money, and they told her it could take several weeks, if not months. In other words, they practically accused her of burning the house down to get the insurance money!

Sighing with resignation, Gem entered the library as usual, quoting under her breath that it was the – "same Bat Time, same Bat Channel" from the old Batman TV series. Man! What she wouldn't give for something exciting that didn't have to do with storms!

"Nothing ever changes!" she muttered, as she went to the desk and clocked in, before taking her new purse, and its contents to the file cabinet, and putting them inside. She realized just what she had said, and amended to herself – *"I mean without the storms, fire, and losing everything!"* She really didn't want to tempt the fates, even though she didn't believe in them.

Earlier, she had gone shopping at Wal-Mart that was close to Taylor's home – the really fancy one – for some new clothes. Gem was wearing all new everything. Luckily, she found some "short" jeans, and several long sleeve t-shirts. Other things she bought were underwear, of course, four bras, a couple of lounge pajamas, a belt, two pairs of tennis shoes, and a pair of boots. She also purchased a couple of fleece tops, two sweaters, and a coat. She'd have to get another, heavier one later, but this would do for now. A purse and a billfold she added into the mix, even though she didn't lose those things. Next, Gem had to stop by the bank to get a new bank card. If they hadn't known her, it would have been a long time, before she got one since she would have to prove who she was without any documentation! All of it had been destroyed in the fire. Tonight, she'd apply for a replacement social security card online at the library, and tomorrow she would have to get her driver's license replaced. She didn't use credit cards, but it surprised her how much there was to do! You never really think about those things until something happened, and they were gone. But, first things first. Right now, she was about finished cataloging the books in the CCR! She never thought she would finish! Taylor floated into the library, and nodded at Gem, so Gem grabbed the key, and entered the room with the equipment she needed to catalog the rest of the books. Like always, when she entered it, she wondered about the odd woman who had donated to the town. As far as anyone knew, she had no contacts, relatives, or connection at all with anyone in Colorado, let alone anywhere else! No one around here knew her, or who she was. It was a true mystery to everyone.

The sight before her never ceased to amaze her, as she looked around at the books. The room was small and oval in shape with bookshelves, which rose to the thirty-foot ceiling on all walls except the door. There were scrolls, documents, and books, and most were old – very old, and in some cases, extremely ancient. The entire library had been donated fifteen years ago by a woman – a Mrs. – who lived somewhere in Italy. And, that was about it. They didn't know much about her, or anything else. However, from the small information they did have, it was assumed that perhaps she had a relative in this town to whom she actually left them. And, even that was just a guess. It was rumored that she had been a very, very old, and extremely eccentric woman, as well as a total recluse. Immediately after she had donated the building to the small town, she had disappeared with her only living relative being a great-grandson. The house, or mansion and property, was sold to a wealthy land baron, whose property was adjacent to the Sinclairs. And, then, they just disappeared from existence.

"Well, I guess stranger things have happened!" Gem giggled as a thought came to her. "She's probably pushing up daisies by now!"

OK. Technically, she really shouldn't laugh about it, but hey! It just struck her giggle box as funny! So funny, tears began to run down her face.

Trying to actually work at the moment was going to be impossible as she gasped for air, and even then, she found herself giggling off and on for a while. It took her almost an hour, before she was able to control herself.

Gem looked around. After her laughter, there was no way that she would have have any time to finish cataloging the CCR. She just had too much to do, so, she locked up the room, and walked to the desk, promptly propping her butt onto the stool behind the desk, and opened the computer. Taylor was feeling sick, and Gem just waved her away, and told her to go home.

It didn't take her long to fill out a replacement application for her social security card, so she checked her e-mail. She found no less than fifteen e-mails from her publisher. He was having a fit by the time she opened the eleventh e-mail. After last night, she'd just not had time to worry about contacting him. OK. Truth. She never even thought about it! A virtual numbness had set in over the entire incident, and she still wasn't quite over it, and she doubted that she ever would.

Gem shot off an e-mail telling him, briefly, what happened, pressed send, and shut the computer back down as her first evening customer walked into the building.

At 8:30 pm, one of the young students came in to take over from her, and Gem left for her shift at the grocery store. Prompt, as he always was, Simmons closed the doors at eleven, and then, became chatty. Simmons was never talkative. He was a quiet man, and not prone to chattering. But, whatever the reason, he sure was yakkity yaking tonight! He wanted to know all about the truck, her house, and Lola. When Gem escaped after ten minutes, she knew that she had a thirty minute walk back to Taylor's house, and it was already late. Earlier, Gem had left Rick's car at the house, before she walked to work. She continued walking to the back of the store, forcing Simmons to follow her. She answered a few of his questions, then told him she had to get back to Lola, because she was traumatized. Good thing Simmons was a dog lover, so he waved her out the door, because he understood that dogs need consistency. And, Gem began the long walk to Taylor's house.

~ 4 ~

"Didn't I say I wanted a hunky, gorgeous, drool worthy man of my own? Why, yes...yes, I did!" ~ Gem

Gem had class two days later. Since all of her books had been destroyed in the fire, she had nothing to take with her. She was almost finished with school. Just two weeks left to go. She knew her Professors would understand, and probably lend her the books for anything she needed for her finals. She took what she had picked up at Simmon's Grocery the night before, such as pens, pencils, and a notebook, then headed out the door. Her novel would just have to wait until she was back on her feet, again. She had sent off, yet, another e-mail to her 'perfectly, panicky publisher" last night. She laughed aloud at her description!

Gem rounded to the front of the house, where she met Rick walking to her. He caught up with her, and threw something at her. Usually, she couldn't catch anything, nor could she hit the side of a barn if she threw something at it, but her hand automatically caught the jingling item that he had tossed. Surprised at catching it, she opened her hand to find the keys to his vintage Mustang! His fully, restored, antique 1965 Mustang?

"Drive it until we can help you find another car," he told her.

She looked way up into his dark brown eyes in shock, while the keys dangled with a cheerful jingle from her hands. He was so good-looking, it startled Gem sometimes. With that big, goofy grin on this massive man, who looked like a wrestler with dark brown, cropped hair and dark skin, he was devastatingly handsome! She shook her head, though.

"Uh-uh! No way, Rick! If something happened to it, I wouldn't be able to forgive myself!" she told him. She was hyperventilating at the mere thought of driving it!

"Come on, Gem! You can't hurt it. Don't you remember the way it looked when I bought it? It was as if it had gone to hell and back! Besides, I have the best body man in the business!"

Well, that was true. Rick had Stanley Ryker who lived in town. And, that was just another drool worthy man! Well, over six-foot three, Stan sported dirty blonde hair, an incredibly dark tan, which he never seemed to lose, and eyes the color of teal, he was just another man that made her want one of her own! Like that was going to happen anywhere but in her dreams! But, Gem did remember how the car had looked when Stan had brought the Mustang home. Rick had picked it up about eight years prior, and it had been in horrendous condition. Neither she nor Taylor had ever thought it could be salvaged. But, if you have enough money, and Rick and Taylor had plenty of it, Gem figured one could get just about anything done!

"I don't care, Rick! The answer is nope, nope, and, did I say...no frickin' way? There's no way in hell I'm going to drive it, so you'd better just shut it right now!"

Laughing at Gem, Rick whined.

"You are far too independent, Gem!"

Gem just grinned at him, and began walking to her classes. She stopped, and looked back at him when she heard the keys jingle, again.

"Rick, it's barely a ten minute walk! For goodness sakes!"

Rick just waved at her, and went back inside the house.

Gem kept walking. It was true. It wasn't all that far, but for some reason, it seemed longer that morning. Her first class was English Lit with Ms. Know-it-all Patterson, who was appropriately nicknamed by the students. She was one of those people who thought she was smarter than anyone else, and believed she never made a mistake. *Really believed it!* Unfortunately, Patterson made them all the time, but refused to acknowledge that she was fallible. To her knowledge, she had never apologized when she made a mistake. But, then, that's the way of egocentric human beings! Following her Lit class, was World History. Henry Rollins was her Professor. The man had her on tenterhooks all the time with his unending barrage of questions to his students. So studying, and learning was a necessity if you wanted to pass it.

"OK. So. His class is really interesting," she grudgingly muttered.

But, he had also enlisted her as his assistant two years ago, and it did give her some extra money. Not a lot, but combined with her job at Simmons, and sales of her books gave her enough money to live on, and what little she had left, she was able to save. Well, that was until the fire, of course. Now, she was going to have to figure out a way to pay rent somewhere! She was seriously beginning to believe she would have to rely on Rick and Taylor's generosity longer than she had wanted. Gem straightened her shoulders when she arrived at the campus, and walked into the building that housed her first class. Something would have to give, and whatever that something was, she definitely wasn't looking forward to it.

Walking into class, Gem came to a dead stand-still. Professor Hawkins was sitting at Professor Rollins desk! What in the hell was he doing here? He looked up as she came in, meeting her eyes with a smirk. She had no problem letting him see that she was angry, and practically stomped to take her seat with the other students. She flopped her backpack down with a loud thud drawing looks from some of the others, dug out her notebook, while everyone else had their computers, and was ready to hand-write her notes as he began to speak.

"Welcome, students. Professor Rollins has had a family emergency, so I have offered to take his class for the next few days. Today, our subject will be Ancient gods and goddesses, and why the people of the day were so devoted to them. The god of the day is Poseidon. Now, can anyone tell me which god he was, and what you do know about him?" No one raised their hands, and Hawking stared at Gem, who glared, daring him to call on her! So, Hawkins decided on someone himself. With a mischevious grin at her, he said, "Jacob Lawrence? Tell me about Poseidon."

Four o'clock, on the dot as always, Gem entered the library. She had grudgingly admitted that Hawkins was really great at history! Especially the Poseidon thing! She had found herself rapped up in the story of Poseidon, and his great love, Cleito, who gave him five sets of twin sons. She was so interested, she wasn't paying attention to the wind beginning to blow hard just like it had the day before the fire. Luckily, she, again, made it into the building, before the heavy downpour. She really hoped it wasn't going to be a repeat of the other day! She really felt blessed, because all her Professors and teachers were kind to her when they found out about her plight, and had loaned her the books she needed. She knew they would, but still she was wary, before finals and graduation. Even Ms. Patterson had relented, and told her that she was sorry about Gem's loss. Gem had tried, very, very hard, not to roll her eyes when Patterson had told her she knew exactly how she felt, because she had lost a toy when she was a kid .

Gem had a bit of a struggle carrying all the books that her teachers had loaned to her, but even without her backpack, she managed to do it! She reached the desk, and plopped them down on the floor. Now, all she needed was a computer! Luckily, the night of the fire, she had saved what she needed onto her flash drive, and hadn't realized that she had shoved it into her pocket when she and Lola went to the Sip 'n' Stop. So, she had all of her school papers, and her books. That was a true miracle. But, she still needed a computer to access them. She hated it, but she would have to ask Taylor if she could borrow hers. She knew Taylor wouldn't mind at all, but it was the fact that she had to borrow it that bothered her. She had always been self-sufficient, and hated to ask others for help.

As much as Gem wanted to dive into the CCR, Taylor was still under the weather, so Gem was by herself tonight. She had to close, too, and this was her closing night at Simmon's as well. The library closed at 8 pm, and she had to be on duty at Simmons at 8:30. I was rare that her hours changed, but she had asked Simmons for a little less time over the next couple of weeks, and he had kindly gave it to her. Hopefully, there wouldn't be many people in tonight because of the storm. She turned to the computer terminal, and got ready for business.

Gem closed and locked the library door behind her at exactly 8:45 pm. Hell and damnation! Where had everyone come from tonight? She hadn't stopped for two seconds, since she took over for Marie who was there from 8 to 4 pm! Even finding time to use the bathroom was almost impossible! At least the storm had passed, She juggled her books from one side to the other, and wobbled into Simmons' Grocery, at 9:01 pm. Simmons was patting his foot when he saw her.

"You're almost thirty minutes late, you know," he muttered, a twinkle in his eye.

"Yeah, yeah. I'm late. Suck it up!" she muttered back to him.

It was a game they played every single night. The customers didn't get it, but the two of them had a great time putting up a front, well, in front of them! Simmons and Gem were convinced that their acting skills were superb!

Gem put her books in the break room, and her purse in one of the six lockers. She grabbed her apron, and went to register number one, relieving Larissa, who was very happy to leave! The store was just as busy as the library had been. Gem could only conclude that after everyone visited the library, they came next door to do all their shopping. Gem didn't draw breath until Simmons locked the door.

"What the hell was all that?" she asked him.

"I have no idea, but after the recent storms, people seem to be getting paranoid."

"Why?"

"Well, some of them believe that they are out to get the town from the way the lightning has been striking us!" Simmons told her.

"Well, that's just about the silliest thing I have ever heard!" Gem told him, as she untied her apron, and put it on the hook in the break room. She retrieved her books, juggling them back and forth along with her purse.

"Gem, Gem, Gem," Simmons said shaking his head. He turned, and pulled out a small, squared Rubbermaid cart on wheels. "Here. This should help. I know you're walking."

Tears misted her eyes at the generous gesture.

"Thank you," she sniffed.

He helped load her books into it, and she said goodnight to Simmons. Gem walked toward the library parking lot, tooling the cart behind her. She knew Simmons would take her home, but she just wouldn't hear of it. His wife hadn't been feeling well, and he needed to get home to her.

Just as she rounded the corner of the library, she came to a dead stop as her eyes beheld a sleek, red truck sitting in the parking lot. Under the few bright lights that still worked, an extremely well-built man was leaning against said brightly painted red truck. It looked so much like her Dad's truck when it was new, she gulped back tears. It was beautiful, and looked newly restored.

She turned her attention to the man leaning against it. His arms were muscular as they crossed against his massive, strong chest. His waist and hips were lean, and his skin was heavily suntanned. A black, ornate tattoo began somewhere under his charcoal gray t-shirt, winding its way down his left arm, ending at his wrist where a black leather bracelet with a watch in it rested. His stance exuded power, even though his ankles were crossed in a relaxed pose. His head was tilted down, and she noticed his shoulder-length hair was the color of midnight black, slicked back, and tied in a ponytail with a leather cord. He wore a pair of what looked like designer jeans. and a dark gray t-shirt that stretched tightly over his chest, and his arms. She had a sudden urge to yank his t-shirt over his head so she could see the rest of that tattoo! He was sex on stick, and she felt every bit of that draw!

Hells bells! She wasn't exactly "scared", but walking home at night in the dark always gave her the creeps! Her instinct told her to go around him by walking behind the library. It was obvious that whoever he was waiting for had yet to show. She turned to pull her cart as silently as possible across the grass, and took two steps before....

"Is there some reason you are walking in the dark alley behind the library, Ms. Elwood?"

Gem squealed in surprise, dropped the cart's handle on the ground, and jumped! Professor Hawkins! She'd know that voice anywhere! She slowly turned to see him shrouded in the darkness of the library. There were no lights here.

"Oh, uh, hey, Professor," she stammered.

He stared at her. At least she thought he was staring at her. She couldn't see him very well.

"Oh, well, you see...I-I was...." and for the life of her, she couldn't think of an explanation. Then, "Wait a minute! Just what business is it of yours anyway?"

"I never said it was my business, Ms. Elwood," he drawled.

Damn that man! He was right!

"Well, OK. I-I guess I'll just be on my way, then," she said to him, picking up the cart turning to walk behind the library, again.

"Ms. Elwood." She turned. "What kind of man would I be if I let a young woman walk – alone – at 11 o'clock at night? Come along."

He turned and walked toward the front of the building. Without turning, Gem considered mutiny, then shrugged. What was the point? She would like a ride home with all these books, so she headed toward the front of the library. When she came around the corner, the same man was still leaning against the truck, still with his head down. But, looking around, there was no Hawkins! Gem slowly started across the parking lot, hoping the man wouldn't notice her. Just as she passed the truck without looking at him....

"Ms. Elwood? Still trying to walk home alone?"

The voice brought Gem to a complete, and total stop. She was truly afraid to turn her head. Oh, hell! It couldn't be! No! It just couldn't be! Afraid of what she might see, Gem tried to turn her entire body to face the voice, but she just couldn't get the courage.

"Ms. Elwood. Will you kindly turn around?" Hawkins demanded. His tone brooked no argument.

Gem slowly – very slowly backed up pulling her cart with her until she was within sight of the man she'd had the "hots" for since the second she saw him. Gulping, her eyes started at his black loafers and slowly – very, very slowly, she allowed her eyes to drift upward to his legs, his slim hips, and she was absolutely positive that the black t-shirt hid six-packs abs and a large, strong chest underneath. Finally, her eyes came to rest on his face, and her eyes widened in shock. A "god" of six-feet six inches stood before her! Dark brown eyes stared back into her green eyes without flinching. His mouth was turned up into a lopsided grin – as if he knew what she was thinking.

Did you ever have one of those incredible moments in your life, where you just knew your life was going to change? Or, you were so stunned and shocked that you couldn't move your eyes from someone's face? Well, this was Gem's moment as she she met the eyes of the most devastatingly gorgeous face she had ever seen in her life! How in the fuck had she not known that the Professor was so handsome, that the only word she could use to describe him was – Angel? Maybe, but even that title seemed completely off the mark! A god? No. The ancient gods would pale against this man! She had no words to describe him! There were no words in the English language, and she doubted if there were any in any other as well!

She shut her eyes tightly, shaking her head in disbelief! What the hell was wrong with her? This was Professor Hawkins? *Professor Hawkins*? This had to be a nightmare! No, not a nightmare, but if she had ever felt horny in all of her life, she had only imagined that it would be for a man as gorgeous as the man standing before her right now! Not even her own made up male characters looked this sexy! Oh, shit! Did she have to say the word? She was damp between her legs already!

"I-I d-don't understand? Professor? I-I don't... I-I mean.. I-I...." Gem stammered still in shock.

Something was tossed at her, and she automatically raised her hand to catch it. Again, Gem actually caught something that someone else threw at her. It might have happened once, but twice? She still couldn't look away from his eyes, but she dragged them away to look at what was in her hands. Keys? Wait a minute! She jerked her head up to look at him again, and then the truck.

"T-these are my t-truck keys?" she stuttered.

"Indeed," he answered her.

"B-but...."

Gem tried very hard to put one foot in front of the other as she attempted to maneuver toward the cab. She glanced at Hawkins once more, before she peeked into the truck grabbing the handle at the same time. Opening the door, and looking inside, she saw everything that was familiar to her except that it was sparkling new and clean! Even a large, old brown stain on the passenger side dashboard that had been there for over thirty years was gone! She breathed out, and looked at Hawkins.

"I-is t-this...." her words trailed into nothing.

"Yes."

Gem jerked her head toward Hawkins in shock.

"B-but h-how is it possible? It was damaged badly! I saw it!" she said softly. "It was altogether destroyed!"

"I called Stan Ryker," he told her as if that was all the explanation that he needed.

Gem's eyes met his – again. Wasn't that who Rick said he used?

"B-but h-how?" she breathed softly.

"I had him check it out to see if it could be salvaged in some way. He towed it, and told me he could fix it."

"Why? Why would you do this?" she asked him, meeting his brown eyes.

"Why would I not?"

"But, fixing it! Painting it? That requires getting rid of the rust, and primer, then paint and gel coat! It's barely been forty-eight hours! No one can complete those kinds of repairs in such a short time! And, apart from all that, the cost would be enormous!" Her voice was tight in her throat as she tried to understand.

"Yes."

Gem was getting a bit pissed with his one-word answers, but she quelled that since he'd done this as a kind gesture.

"But how? No one could repair, and do all this on this old truck that fast!"

"Stan can," he replied with a shrug.

"But…"

"Ms. Elwood. Will you please stop asking questions that do not apply, and please just get into the truck?"

Gem was surprised when she realized he was already sitting in it! How had she missed him move? She was just looking straight at him! Staring at him, she turned to get her books to put them in the bed when she realized they weren't there! She looked around quickly, but didn't see them.

"Your books are in the back, Ms. Elwood. Now. Will you please get into the truck? I would highly suggest it in light of the storm that's coming," he told her, pointing to the sky behind them.

Lightning struck terribly close to them, startling Gem who immediately jumped into the truck, and shut the door just as another lightning bolt hit a tree near the truck. She hadn't even noticed a storm had been brewing! And, why? All because she didn't want to take her eyes off of this magnificent specimen of a man! Really Gem? Get you head in the game!

"Put it into gear, and get us the hell out of here!" Hawkins yelled.

His voice knocked Gem out of her hormone induced haze! In seconds, Gem was speeding out of the parking lot, and putting the pedal to the metal. Again, lightning struck too close for comfort. Her foot slammed onto the brake, and they came to a sudden stop at a stop light.

"Which way?" Gem yelled in panic.

"Left!"

Gem turned the truck left, and stepped on the gas. Behind the truck, the storm seemed to be following them. Gem looked into the rearview mirror in shock! She wasn't seeing things! That storm *was following them*! She pushed the truck to its top speed as she wove in and out of the mostly deserted streets of the town. Neither spoke, but while Gem kept her eyes on the mirrors, Hawkins' head was turned, looking behind them.

"Faster, Gem!" he yelled.

Gem didn't argue, and just stepped on the pedal pushing it to the floor!

"I can't go any faster! It's to the floor, now!" she complained in fear.

"Just do it!" he yelled back at her.

Gem did as he told her, until she heard a relieved sigh come from his lips. And, they were such amazing lips! Suck it up, Gem, and shift your libido back into normal!

"Yeah. I'll just get right on that!" she thought.

"The storm has subsided. We managed to get through another one without being hurt!"

Gem slowed the truck down, pulled over to the side of the highway, and stopped. She laid her arms on the steering wheel, leaning her head on them while she desperately tried to catch her breath.

"What the fuck is going on around here?" Jaxx muttered, opening the truck door.

Gem huffed as she, too, stepped out of it. She cornered Hawkins who had walked back about a block watching the thunder and lightning die in the distance. Gem stomped toward him. She was sick and tired of people not answering her questions, and acting as if they knew something that she didn't. Coming to a halt, she turned, and almost stood toe to toe with him. If she had been taller, she could have said face to face.

"What the fucking hell is going on?" she demanded.

Without looking down, he answered, "I don't know."

Really? Did she actually hear him say that to her? His eyes were still staring at the storm behind them, so she knew that was a flat out lie.

"Professor Hawkins!" she yelled, slapping his left arm.

Jaxx seemed to finally have heard her, and his eyes slid down to hers. He had avoided looking into her eyes on purpose. After what Stan and Stacey had said to him earlier in the day, he didn't want to know that they might be right. After unending time by himself, to find his mate, now, was just ludicrous! And, of all the women he had to meet, the one he would never have chosen! But, he might as well have tried to get away from the flood that destroyed Atlantis! It was inevitable.

Gem had no idea what was happening. How could she or Taylor have missed this man's charisma, charm, and out and out gorgeousness! Was that even a word? There was no way on this planet that she could look away from him! She looked deeper, and began to think she saw something so enigmatic, there wasn't a name for it. What she did know was that her heart beat heavier and harder until she almost couldn't breathe. Her breath came laboriously, while trying to figure out exactly she felt. How could she describe it? Anticipation? No. Excitement? Yes, but that wasn't all. It was then she realized that there was heavy dampness at her sex. Her jeans were soaked with it! Gasping in shock, she felt more flood from her! Breasts heavy with the need to be caressed grabbed her in the throws of excitement. Sexual desire. Gem had never felt this before. Even in school, she'd never felt what her friends talked about all the time. It was just this mystery that was out of her reach, because she had never had any feelings for the opposite sex. But, with the Professor? He was this "god" standing before her, and even though she was thoroughly mad at him, if he wanted her right now, she'd gladly strip, and let him do whatever he wanted with her! In fact, if she got the least hint, she'd demand him to thrust into her body! Oh, man! She couldn't have these thoughts! For heaven's sake! He was a Professor!

While Gem's body was trying desperately to stop her desire, Jaxx's eyes narrowed darkly. What they say about narrowly escaping eminent danger, or even death, was true. Even the thought of losing Gem gave him a hard-on that was so large, the only thing that would keep Gem from seeing it was the fact it was dark. His desire for her was running rampant, and he could feel his own fluid leaking from his slit, and dampening his briefs! If this kept up, his pants would be visibly wet very fast. But, his eyes could not tear away from hers, while her eyes were staring into his, heavy with need! He was about to lose control something he had never done in his life! Yet, here he was. A sudden breath of air invaded his nostrils with the most entising scent he had ever smelled! He breathed deeply. Oh, no! It was the scent of arousal, and pure intoxication. With that, he lost control of his rational faculties and his senses in his desperation to claim his mate. His arms reached out, and pulled her toward his body.

When Gem felt his strong arms around her, she groaned in anticipation of the kiss. In seconds, his mouth was on hers, devouring her as if he needed her lips like he needed to breathe! In truth, she needed it, too. In seconds, his tongue raked over her closed lips, and without thought, Gem opened her mouth allowing his tongue had full access. His lips sealed theirs even tighter while his tongue dove in and out tasting the sides of her mouth, her tongue, and anything else he could reach! Hesitatingly, Gem matched his tongue with hers, and he let her dive into him freely. Her tongue was like velvet against his! His scent and taste overwhelmed her senses. Apparently, it overwhelmed him as well, because his hands slipped down to her hips, and brought her tightly against something rock hard, pressing into her belly. In seconds, she realized what it was, and she gasped in shock! It was his arousal! It was hard, and grinding into her. Her sex flowed with her hot, silky juices readying her for him to plunge into her depths. She wound her hands into his black hair, pulling him even harder against her mouth and body.

A very low groan emanated from his chest – almost like a growl. She tasted wonderful! Gem's arousal was a scent unlike any other woman. He drank her into his body with each kiss. His cock was so hard, he believed he would come just by kissing her! But, that's not what he wanted. Jaxx wanted…no, needed…to plunge deeply into her body. Then, Jaxx wanted to pound it into her until he released his seed into the depth of her womb! Just the thought made him grind into her harder and harder. He could smell her juices that were covering her jeans. He couldn't wait. Jaxx stopped the kiss staring into her eyes, breathing and panting heavily, watching her do the same. Without hesitating, he swept her up into his arms, and streaked back to the truck laying her down across the seat. Climbing into it, he lowered himself down on her body that arched along with her deep moans of desire. Hell! He felt like a horny teenager on his first date!

Gem groped at his shirt's buttons, but they wouldn't cooperate with her hands, so she ripped his shirt down the front sending buttons flying everywhere. She was too far gone with desire and need. She needed him inside of her – now! Watching him as he divested himself of his shirt in a second, his naked chest hovered above her. Oh, my Creator! He did have six packs! But, the tattoo, which covered the left side of his chest to his waist, was very ornate. It was like runes combined with wings in certain areas. And, as she looked, she saw that it went downward into his pants! She wanted to see the full tattoo, but that would mean that he would have to remove his pants and briefs! She licked her lips, as her eyes swept downward, then back up to his face. He had a smirk on it, so he knew exactly what she was thinking. Her fingers started tracing his tattoo slipping ever lower on his body, until they reached the waistband of his jeans. Grinning, she looked back into his eyes.

Jaxx was beyond hope, now. With that grin, he knew that she was his...or he was hers...or...what the hell! Lowering himself down onto her, again, he felt her soft fingers and nails stroke his back. It caused him to shudder in desire. He needed to feel her bare breasts against him. He lifted himself up, and in seconds divested her t-shirt so she lay in nothing but her bra and jeans.

"So beautiful," he whispered, as his lips claimed hers once again.

Gem writhed underneath him! She could feel his bare chest on every part of her except her breasts. She needed to feel his rugged chest against them.

"Unhook my bra," she whispered in between the kisses that he was lavishing upon her.

He stopped, turned her just a bit, and deftly unhooked her bra as if he had tons of practice – something she didn't want to think about just now. He lowered her back onto the seat, removed her bra throwing it onto the floor of the truck, and let his eyes gaze on her full, voluptuous breasts teasing him with their hard tips. Gently stroking, he let his hand start at the base of one breast, and looking into her eyes, circled lazily to its peak, where his finger brushed against the hardened, rose-colored tip before lowering his mouth to suckle.

Gem arched her chest upward when his mouth closed over her nipple, and begged for more and more as she pulled his head tighter struggling against crying out his name as he licked the ripe bud.

The sound of her muffled cry just spurred him on to the other breast. He kneaded and suckled her breasts to his heart's content. Never had he tasted anything as good as this! He could spend the rest of their lives just like this, and he'd be happy. Happy? He'd never countenanced such a thing in his entire life! It was not unusual for his kind to take a mortal human for their own. Their mate. Once they had sex with a human, and bound them with the Blood Chain, they became immortal as well. And, then, it would be possible for impregnation to occur! Just look at Taylor and Rick. They had bound themselves together, and she had become pregnant immediately! The idea of Gem's belly swollen with their child startled him in a way that he never imagined. He lifted his head to look into her eyes. They stared at each other in surprise, shock, and acceptance. Stan was right. There was no doubt at all in his mind. She was his mate. That's why he went to all the trouble about the truck. Why he followed her to protect her after the walk and tonight. Jaxx would protect her against everything – but him. His hand reached down to unbutton and unzip her jeans, which he could feel were soaking wet.

When she heard the sound of him lowering the zipper on her jeans, Gem started to groan and writhe in excitement and anticipation! Then, she felt his hand slip down between her jeans and panties, sliding down to her curly patch that hid her sex.

"Spread your legs for me, Gem," he whispered breathlessly.

She couldn't answer, but she did as he asked. She placed one leg down onto the floor of the truck opening her sex to his touch. He groaned, allowing his fingers feel her soft folds and slick liquid that coated her entire sex. His fingers slid along the incredibly soft skin until he felt her swollen clit. Holding his breath, he felt the swollen nub, and began to gently caress it adding just enough pressure to make her desire his cock inside of her instead of his fingers with which he plunged into her heat.

When those two fingers entered her body. Gem's last vestige of control was lost, and she cried out as she felt his fingers move in and out of her wet channel. OK. That was way to bookish. No. He moved in and out of her tight, wet walls, causing more and more fluid to rain down from inside of her womb.

"Please!" Gem cried, not knowing what she really wanted, but knowing without a doubt that she did.

She wanted him. Her channel was throbbing, almost convulsing, for his thick cock inside her. His fingers were moving fast and hard, until they came together at the height of orgasm! She wanted to feel his hot seed as it shot deep into her.

Jaxx prepared himself, now that she was ready for him, and he rose to his knees between her legs, and wrapped his fingers around the waistband of her pants. Jaxx began to strip them off of her hips, while Gem raised her hips to let him uncover her to his gaze, when a sudden noise made it through their consciousness. They looked at each other, and froze.

"Keep down," he whispered as he slowly raised his head above the seat to see what they were hearing. A car approached, its lights shining into the cab. Luckily, it passed them by, and as the sound disappeared into the distance, Gem suddenly became aware of what she had been about to do. About what she was going to let him do. One glance at his face saw that his thoughts were with hers.

"Damn!" he muttered under his breath as he zipped her pants. Then, he helped her to sit while slipping her t-shirt over her head, but forgetting her bra.

Picking up his damaged shirt from the floor as well, he slipped it back on. Both faced forward without looking at each other.

"I live in the Montgomery mansion."

Gem just nodded as she slipped under the steering wheel. She knew that she couldn't answer him at all. Starting the truck, she shifted into gear, and drove on down the road even while she was shaking with unquenched desire. The Montgomery Mansion was the town's strangest house anyone had ever seen. Gem had never been inside it, but those who had said that the design was unlike anything they had ever seen.

Driving up to the gates, Jaxx gritted his teeth as he ground out, "Let me out here."

She nodded, and stopped. He stepped out of it. Without looking back, Gem turned the truck around to drive back to town leaving him to stare as the truck disappeared into the darkness. Jaxx opened the gates, and stepped onto his property. Never had he ever felt so frustrated as he did at this moment. His hands shoved into his pockets, and his dick still huge, he walked down the down the road to his house.

~ 5 ~
"How is it Possible to have an Affair in her own Father's Truck?" ~ Gem

Gem felt tears running down her face. She couldn't stop them! How had she let this get so out of hand? She had lost her mind – and her head! The two of them had totally forgotten where they were, and acted like horny teenagers! And, they would have had *sex – inside her* Father's *truck – on the side of the highway*! The car that came by had stopped them, but that didn't ease her frustration and sexual tension. She knew his wasn't, either.

Slamming her hands against the wheel, she cursed them for not having had better sense! Especially her! What the hell was wrong with them? Holy crap! How in the hell had all of that happened? Neither of them had ever had feelings for each other, so what had changed? The moment she asked the question, she knew the answer. The sight of him without the way he was normal dressed was her downfall. He had never been nice to her, nor had he shown her any kindness. Except? Her mind rewound as her memories unfolded. Until she saw him standing in the door holding Lola...until she saw him standing in the middle of her burned out house with caring eyes...and...until she saw him standing by her truck – her fully restored truck that he paid for, and delivered to her, personally. It wasn't his clothing. This not-so-simple acts of kindness, and those gorgeous, brown eyes had done it! Then, the storm that seemed to chase them fueled their terror helped even more. Their need for each other had overwhelmed them.

As she drove into the separate drive to her apartment, she slammed her hands against the wheel, a second time, before she emerged from the truck. Turning around to look at it's fully restored beauty, Gem had to wonder why he would have had her truck fixed for her? She didn't understand, or if truth be known, she really didn't want to understand. She'd been without love for years, and no guy ever seemed to want her. That's why this was so damned hard for her to believe that someone who looked like Professor Hawkins, would care for her. It was quite clear that they both would no longer have control over their sexual desires whenever they were together! That was a bridge they had just crossed, and like all bridges...once you crossed it, you couldn't go back.

Rubbing her head's rapidly expanding headache, Gem stepped into her apartment, and headed directly for the bathroom. She really needed a bath. Besides, her panties were sticking to her. Ah, hell! That just brought back how horny she was for him all over again! She dropped her belongings on the sofa, then practically ran to the bathroom. She stared into the mirror. Her face was flushed, and her eyes still shimmered with deep desire! She felt moisture return as she slipped out of her clothing, again. Stepping into the shower, she sat down letting the water flow over her, while her eyes closed as she remembered each second of his touch, and the touch of his naked chest against hers. Her core throbbed as if he were still with her. She needed release!

Reaching down, she touched her clit, and began to massage it gently, lightly. It didn't take that long, before her excitement allowed fluid to rush down, and she placed three fingers within her channel. Pulling them in and out, she increased the tempo until she finally felt her orgasm hit. Her body throbbed over and over as it released some of the tension that it carried. Even though she would have rather had Jaxx inside of her, at least it provided a temporary relief. It wasn't what she wanted, but it would have to do. Drying herself, she walked back into the room to see Lola lounging on one of the sofas. She wrapped the towels around her, and sat down. Lola crawled onto her lap. Burying her head into Lola's fur, Gem began to cry.

"Oh, Lola! What am I going to do?" she murmured.

After a while, she forced herself to get up, and she slid into bed. That's when she remembered the blue velvet box that she had put away for safe keeping. Quickly, she retrieved it, and sat looking at it, turning it every which way. She fingered it, feeling no catch, or opening. But, when she moved it, she heard something rattling around. Something was inside of it, but how to open it? Gem shut her eyes in frustration. When were things ever going to go her way? She thought of her Dad and her Mom, and a wave of love swept over her. They were gone, yet she still felt as if they were here! Suddenly, she felt a shift in the box, and her eyes flew open and her mouth dropped. A gentle glow came from the top as the box split open in two pieces, and a brilliant white light spread outward into the room, blinding her for a few moments. As the light dimmed, she saw something silvery that shown from within, and she spread the box open gently. She issued a gasp at what lay inside of it. Reaching inside, she scooped the item up, and let the amulet drop from the heavy chain that held it. It glowed with a gentle light, and its silvery look bathed her eyes in beauty. She knew that it belonged to her. She stared at it as she moved it around and around, then looked at it carefully. She felt imbued with some type of power that she could not explain. She slipped it over her head, and laid down. Sleep came quickly.

Lola snuggled closely. Whatever had happened it wasn't good. So, Lola sniffed. Hmmm. Her pet smelled different. She smelled of…arousal. Yes. That was it. Sexual arousal! Lola looked up at Gem. Sex, yes, but she had not indulged in it! But, the other smell? This one was…Professor Hawkins! No! She couldn't get involved with him! She had to speak to Taylor, now!

She jumped up, and ran through her outside doggy door, and in seconds, Lola shimmered into nothing, and disappeared! She re-emerged inside Taylor's kitchen as a shimmering young child. Taylor, startled, looked at her in surprise. Who was this?

"W-what the f-! Who are you?" Taylor demanded. "*What* are you?"

"I'm Lola, Taylor," Lola explained in a little tiny voice.

"What?" Taylor all but sputtered. "B-but…?"

"That is not important right now. Who I am, and what I am will come to light soon enough. But, because of what has happened, I chose to change into this form, so that I could speak with you. 'Houston…we have a problem'!" she quoted from one of her favorite movies, "Apollo 13".

"I don't understand," Taylor said. And, she really didn't. It was one thing to know you were a supernatural being as it was, but to find out another existed of which she had no knowledge made her very upset!

"I have been with Gem's family for…well, I'm not sure how long I have been with them. We just don't see time in the my Realm. But, I have changed forms from generation to generation. I was assigned long ago for their protection. Or more accurately, for Gem's protection."

Taylor stared at the vision before her. She was tiny. About 4' high. Her long pale, blonde hair reached almost to the floor, along with the robe that she wore, and even her skin was white with tiny facets of glitter. She was very beautiful. No wonder Lola appeared enchanting more than other pugs. But, the most startling of all were her brilliant silver eyes that seem to glitter with stars. Suddenly, Taylor knew.

"You are Fae!" Taylor began, only to have Lola wave her into silence.

"Yeah, yeah. Whatever. Doesn't matter. It is my job to make sure that Gem finds her destiny when it is time. I must ask you about Professor Jaxxon Hawkins. What do you know of him?"

Well, what was Taylor going to tell her about him? Apparently, Lola didn't seem at all concerned about Gem, but seemed to have some problem with Jaxx. Well, that wasn't new. Who *didn't* have a problem with him, given his propensity to get into trouble with the powers that be?

"Jaxx is a Professor at the local college, and…"

"No. I don't want his profession, and you know it!"

"Man! Always heard Fae were damned rude," Taylor thought to herself.

"I want to know who, and what, he is. Tonight, I smelled him all over Gem, Taylor."

Taylor jerked in shock.

"What?"

Lola nodded.

"Yes. There is no doubt the two of them were together. The smell was unmistakable."

"You mean…sex?" Taylor squeaked.

"Yes, and no. It was apparent that they were together, but it did not end in sex. Yet."

Taylor slumped against the wall. Why would Jaxx seduce Gem? That made no sense at all. Well…not unless…unless…unless...oh, shit! It couldn't be! But, what other explanation was available?

"Shit!" Taylor said aloud.

"I see. So, there is a problem," Lola stated quietly.

A problem? Yeah! There sure was! But, it depended upon what Lola might see as a problem.

"Depends. If what I suspect is true, Lola, then there is, and is not, a problem."

"What does that mean?" she asked, obviously irritated by Taylor's cryptic answer.

"Simply that if, as I believe, Jaxx has found his mate, then he will go to the ends of the Earth to protect her – and even beyond if necessary."

"His mate?" Lola's eyebrows rose. That sure wasn't what she was expecting to hear!

"Yes. Our kind is emotionless, Lola. That is until we meet our mates. When this happens, our submerged emotions shoot to the front of our very being, and from that time forward, we appear no different than humans, except that we are not human. Rick is my mate, and human. Once the Blood Chain has been achieved, then we become one, and he lives as long as I. Our children will grow until they reach maturity, and then, will live as immortals as well."

"Ah. I see. You believe that Gem is Jaxx's mate, then?"

Taylor thought back on what had happened recently. Surprised at herself for just realizing it, she did believe it.

"Yes! I do! Absolutely!" she answered. "I have no doubt whatsoever, Lola."

Lola nodded. "Then, that is good. There is no problem as I feared."

She turned to leave.

"Uh, Lola?"

"Yes?" Lola looked back at her as she began to shimmer.

"Protect Gem. Something is very wrong around here. Those storms just cannot be a coincidence!"

Lola nodded her head, and again, became a pug. Taylor let her out so she could pretend to return to Gem. As she turned, Rick came into the room.

"I overheard you, love. I have observed Jaxx over the last couple of days. His agitation only makes me sure of it. I agree with you. Gem is his mate."

"Yes, but Rick?"

"My love?"

"Jaxx is not like the rest of us. I didn't tell Lola everything. I just couldn't! The ramifications could be disastrous!"

"But, he is one of you, right?" Rick asked puzzled.

"No, he's not one of us, Rick. He is not Anaerris. However, he is a creature who is older than any of us. Even we do not know his age. And, he is one of the ancient ones who were doomed by the fates to go through their lives without a mate."

Rick's left eyebrow rose.

"Not one of you? Does that mean he is – one of those who lusts after blood? Why would he be the mate of a human?"

She nodded. "Yeah, he is. If the fates have assigned him a mate, I don't know why."

"And, it worries you?"

"Indeed it does, my love. Indeed it does!" Taylor answered.

"Or, perhaps…?" Rick was pensive, as he rubbed his scruffy, barely-there beard with his thumb and forefinger.

"What?"

"Perhaps the Fates have decided to change the rules, because the status quo has changed?"

"Huh? What status quo?" Taylor's eyes shot up to his in surprise.

"Well...it is quite possible that whatever they had decided for him prior to meeting Gem has changed in some way. Do not the Fates change outcomes?"

"No. They do not change things. Fate cannot be changed." Taylor said so puzzled, her brows were drawn into a frown.

"So, if they cannot change things, that means someone else has. And, that means that whoever did change things has caused the fates to provide her with a mate of bloodlust."

Taylor's eyes lowered, as she stared into oblivion. Was that possible? Has someone else interfered with fate, and the Fates had to change as well? Her eyes slowly drifted to Rick's as understanding dawned.

"If you're right, then who the hell could have the kind of power to change Jaxx and Gem's fate. Something isn't right here, Rick."

Rick planted a quick kiss onto her lips, then picked her up to carry her to their bed.

"I love you, Taylor. If we are right, then things should get very interesting very soon!"

"I love you, too, Rick," she said softly throwing her arms around his neck, and pulling him in for a kiss. "But, Creator help us!"

"Exactly, my love," Rick said as the dawning of lust began to show in her eyes.

Gem woke refreshed, and filled with energy. She scrambled out of bed, grabbing a Little Debbie snack cake, and shoved it in her mouth. Running to the bathroom, she stepped into the shower, washed her hair, then towel dried it. She grabbed the blow dryer, then stopped as the amulet around her neck glowed. It hadn't been a dream! She had thought it had, but obviously it wasn't. She would love to stay and see if she could figure it out, but she had to go. She slipped it over her head, then gently placed it back into the blue velvet box, which sealed immediately as if it had never opened! She petted the velvet box.

"You're little mystery will just have to wit for me to solve," she cooed to it. Still puzzled, she replaced it into the drawer, then resumed dressing. Petting Lola, after she had shot into the room, delaying Gem long enough to feed her. Gem jumped into the mustang, making it to the library in record time.

The CCR always managed to excite Gem, and she was always eager to explore it as she pulled on her white, cotton gloves, and grabbed her library sanctioned mini-iPad, before climbing one of the ladders. She had pushed what had happened the night before to the back of her mind, because if she didn't, she believed that she would seek him out to finish what they had started! And, she just couldn't risk it. She knew he would probably show up at the library today, but she'd cross that bridge when she came to it. It was a good thing that she had not had a class today! She needed to be out of his proximity soon. Today, though, she was bound and determined to finish all the cataloging of books this afternoon!

Gem was still excited when she reached the top shelf. Using her hands, she glided the ladder to the shelf that was just to the right of the door. The room had low light, but she used her tiny flashlight to see the names of the books on the dark shelves. When they had received the library, there was a stipulation that the CCR was to be thoroughly cataloged, and was contingent upon the donation of the books. The top shelf, and those below it, were labeled A-B. Next to that group, the books were labeled B, followed by the next section labeled A-D. It was pretty simple, and each book had both a virtual, and physical, card assigned.

This was her last shelf, and she quivered in excitement at the accomplishment that she had finally almost completed.   Finishing the first section, she proceeded to the B section. In C section, she saw an interesting book she wanted to check out later called "Corisone Di Alva".   She thumbed through it, and registered disappointment.

"Hmmm. Sounds like an autobiography of someone. Nope. Written in Italian, of course. Can't read it," she muttered putting it back, and grabbing another. She filed a mental note to begin studying the language. With her almost photographic memory, it shouldn't take long to learn Italian so she could read it.

Gem proceeded with each book, cataloging with her iPad, until she reached the bottom shelf. She noticed one book sticking out further than the rest. Then, another, and still, another. There were eight in all, and the group was protruding slightly outward further than the rest. Setting her iPad down, she reached for one of the books.

"You bookies are in the wrong place. Not even alphabetized? Now, you..." she said to one of the books as she extracted it from its place, "...you should be with the larger books on the opposite."

Gem placed the book on the other side of the room where she saw a few empty, and said, "Now, that's where you are supposed to be!"

Placing it into the empty opening, she proceeded to do the same with the other seven – until the last book. While it was not any larger than the others, when she reached down to pull on it, it wouldn't budge. Looking at it further, she realized that it was a bit different by just a touch. Scratching her head, she realized that those eight books had all been protruding, but just in that one area of the entire CCR. But, why? Gem sat on the floor, and leaned sideways on her elbow, so she could look into the shelf, Gem aimed the tiny flashlight, into the spot. She still couldn't see a thing, so Gem tried to pull the book out again. This time it moved easily, and she laid it gently on the floor, so she could shine the light behind it, again.

"That's odd," she mumbled to herself, noticing something unusual in the back. "What is that?"

For whatever reason, her light would not illuminate the object. Very strange, but finally, she laid on the floor, and reached into the lightless cubbyhole. Her fingers stroked something that made her hand draw back in disgust!

"Damnit!" Gem muttered, while trying to reach the book. Then, "Ewww! That's so gross!"

Gem continued to try and grab hold of it, but she wasn't very successful. She pulled her hand back, and thought maybe it was the gloves keeping her from grasping it easily, so she yanked one off, and then stuck it back into the cubbyhole. Seconds later, she her hand away.

"Ewwww!!!! Yuk! It feels like very dry skin!" she said in astonishment.

She looked at her hands, but nothing was on either of them, nor the glove she had discarded. So, she decided to try again. Fumbling with her fingers, she reached back into the darkness, and traced the outline of the object. No doubt about it! It was a book. Then, she grabbed it, and tried to gently pull it out of the shelf. It was stuck! Knowing she shouldn't do it, she tugged a bit harder. The book suddenly loosened, causing her to roll onto her back, while the book flew out of her hand hitting the opposite bookshelf.

"Shit!" Gem said, rubbing her head after hitting it on the floor.

She sat up, turned, and reached for the book. For the first time in the light of the room, she could look at it. Her mouth dropped open. It was flat black. It seemed to neither absorb nor reflect light. She flipped it back and forth in her hands. It really looked as if was made out of skin. Not unusual since there were all kinds of books with leather covers, but this one was like nothing she had ever seen before. She needed to get a better look at it.

"I wonder if Taylor might know what this is?" Her voice was definitely puzzled.

Gem stood, and with the book in hand, unlocked the door. Walking out of the room, she carried it into the light in the main room, laying it on the closest table to her, and just stared at it. She sniffed, and frowned. Was she detecting a faint odor coming from it? She leaned forward, and sniffed again drawing back in shock. It smelled as if it had been in a fire of some sort. It smelled of sulfur, and…burning flesh?? Gem gagged.

"What is this?" she whispered to herself, then paid attention to the cover, and an emblem on it. "Strange."

Gem leaned over the book to try and see what was embossed onto the cover. It was a circle with something that looked like a triangle in the center...maybe a pyramid? There were other symbols on it as well. From the top, and clockwise, she puzzled over the others. At the right base of the triangle, there seemed to be something that looked like wavy lines. Hmmm. Perhaps that is supposed to be water? The next symbol was a mountain with smoke rising from it. Volcano, maybe? She couldn't see anything else, until she lifted her head a bit, and she saw two more. The center of the triangle was not a pyramid as she had first thought, but it was actually a huge, double mountain covered by something she couldn't distinguish, and in the center of it was something swirling like a spiral. And, right in the center was a burst – kind of like ball lightning! She leaned back, and plopped down into the chair that was behind her. This was very odd to her. She had never seen a book like this one, and quite frankly, the embossed design looked a bit familiar. Gem was deep in thought, and did not hear Taylor walk up to her to peer over her shoulder.

"What did you find, bestie?" Taylor asked.

Gem jumped in surprise, stepped back, and almost stepped on Taylor's foot! She stumbled a bit, but Taylor grabbed her arm to steady her. Gem waved her hand at the book, and looked at Taylor.

"I found it in the CCR, Taylor. This has to be the strangest book I've ever seen! Have you ever seen anything remotely like it? It feels like scorched skin, and it smells very faintly of sulfur and burning flesh – as if it has been in a volcanic eruption!" Gem exclaimed.

Taylor's eyes widened as her gaze fell on the book. She swallowed hard, and began to have a fit of coughing having drawn in air through her mouth in shock.

"You OK?" Gem asked, pounding on Taylor's back.

Taylor glared at her while she coughed even more.

"Right. Dumb question. I'll get you some water?"

Taylor nodded, and watched as Gem walked to the water fountain next to the restrooms. She turned and looked at the book, again. She knew she dare not touch it!

"No! It can't be!" she exclaimed, knowing that it was real – the Codex – bound by the charred flesh of the enemy! *The Codex!* Only one book fit that description, and the faint smell of sulfur proved to her that that it was here, on the table, and in front of her! Taylor had long believed that it was something that had been made up by story tellers throughout the eons! Yet, here it was! In front of her! It was real! And...did that meant that the *legend was really true?*

"Holy crap!" Taylor mumbled under her breath.

She was beyond shock, and knew she had to get a hold of herself, before Gem returned carrying a mug of water. Taylor grabbed the mug from Gem, and started chugging it. Her throat was already dry, and while the water didn't quench her thirst, at least it stopped her from coughing. She had to tell Rick and, now. They couldn't risk the book out of their sight, even for a second! She'd have to get one of the tarps, so she could handle it. Then, she reconsidered using a tarp. The ancient lore was that nothing, and no one, could touch the book at all. At the moment, it never occurred to ask how Gem had brought it to the table.

Gem watched as Taylor's cough subsided. As long as she had known Taylor, she had never seen her cough, get sick, or even look as shocked as she appeared to be. While Taylor was battling her cough, Gem reached toward the book, and though Taylor tried to scream at her to not touch it, she was unable to speak! That's when she completely froze. Taylor suddenly realized that Gem had already touched it! Her eyes widened. There would be no way Gem could have taken the book from the CCR, and put it on the table! She should be dead! Yet, here it was – in front of her, and Gem was alive? How?

Gem turned from her friend to run her bare hand gently over the cover. Taylor continued to be stunned! According to their legends, the Codex was ancient, bound with the charred flesh from a burned enemy warrior in the Great Battle of The Warriors. But, it was not just any warrior.

Taylor searched what little information she had held within her mind. The battle had been so long ago, most of them had little knowledge of it. Her own parents had lived through it having been lucky enough to have survived. Few did, but since that time, the few Anaerris left had flourished, and their race continued, much to the ancients' furor. The Council of Ancients had ordered their enemies to destroy her race completely. Why, no one really ever knew, but luckily, some on both sides refused to do so, and they bound together as allies, which continued even today. Her parents had told her some of their past, but believing that if they withheld the information, Taylor would be safe, apparently was not happening with the discovery of the book. Whatever their reasoning, one thing was for sure. Jaxxon was the oldest of their enemies. He had lived through the destruction of the war, and survived. But, he wasn't exactly an enemy, now. He was more like an ally. Oh, they had their disagreements, but if she ever needed help, Taylor had no doubt he would have her back. Taylor had long believed that Jaxxon had his own agenda, but never could figure out what it was. Furthermore, it was also said that only one hundred warriors survived – fifty from each faction – with her Father being one of them, and Jaxx being another. It was also said that five, each, of both factions had decided to form a new Council of Ancients, and after they divested the original Council – the translation being killed – this group "ruled the roost", so to speak. To defy them was to court one's own death!

Her Father and a few others had struck a cease-fire, and had led the small remnant of both to Earth thousands of years ago. It was here that her Father had found his human mate, Sylvia, where she became a part of the supernatural world, and after the Blood Chain, her Father had given her an almost immortal life as long as he lived, and their daughter, Taryln, surprisinly inherited her Father's immortality. That was something that none of them could ever have forseen! And, Taryln, in turn, passed that immortality to her mate, Richard.

Her mind traveled back over the long years to remember something she had heard. She had been little, and had deliberately been eavesdropping on her Mom and Dad. What eight year old Taryln had overheard, she didn't really understand. It was in the evening, after their dinner, that she had heard low voices. Inching closer to her

Father's study door that was almost shut, she saw a small crack just large enough for her to hear them speak. She remembered it well, and why it had been engraved on her mind, she just didn't understand. Whatever evil tracked their race was within it, but it also came with a blunt warning. She remembered the description of it listening to them.

"It was written by an Anaerris," her Father had told her Mother.

"Who?" she had asked.

"The survivor who changed, Millicent."

"What the hell does that mean, Jacol?" His name had been misinterpreted to Jacob, and except for their home, everyone else called him by that name including the Federal Government.

"Neither I, nor anyone else, knows who it was. We only know that she was 'changed', and if I really let myself believe she changed into what, it could be disastrous for the Anaerris."

"So, not even me will you trust with this secret?" she asked wistfully.

He had taken her into his arms, and kissed her head.

"No, my love. Not even you. If I dare mention it, it is possible that the Council of Ancients may hear, and a death would be on my hands."

"Whose death?" When Jacol had not answered, she huffed, and said, "Well, what *can* you tell me? What does this book look like?" she asked.

"It is said to be made of the charred skin of two warriors – one from each race."

Its cover was the charred skin of both Anaerris and Onaerris! Now, she remembered! And, that accounted for the sulfur smell that Gem had told her that she had scented.

"Within the book, it is said that the pages are a thin, solid silver, which was carved with our history, its destruction, and what will come."

"Will come?"

"Yes. I only know that the one who wrote it would have been called 'witch' by humans, only she was much more. She was also a 'seer' - one who could see the future. She and her mate fled at the end of the battle long ago, and neither of us know where they are. We do not wish to know. Knowing would put us all in danger. Only Jaxx and I managed to make it to Earth bringing a few survivors with us. We never knew what happened to the other two."

"I thought that there were only four of you?" Millicent asked in surprise.

"That is the official story. We brought, as I have told you, a few with us."

"Anaerris, though?"

"It is what I thought, but now, I am unsure," he told her.

"Taryln?" she whispered in terror as it dawned on her that if they could find them, they would learn about their children!

"They must not know about any of our children. Taylor was an incredible gift. We were always told that we are not compatible with humans, because of our physiologies. And, quite frankly, we were never designed to procreate. Or, so we thought. We know that it is not true, now."

Millicent looked into his eyes.

"Then your belief was flawed. We are physically compatible for children, obviously," she told him with a sneer, brushing his brown, shoulder-length hair away from his face.

"Well, that truth cannot be denied," he answered, laughing.

He stopped to look at his mate. Why the hell had he not seen this before?

"I mean, if it changed for your people, then why could it not change for the others?" she reasoned.

"Hell! It never occurred to me to think of why it changed. I was so excited when you gave birth to Taryln, I never thought about the rest!" How dumb could he have been! "If the few who had children with human women, then, our race would survive – diluted, yes, but it would survive! You are brilliant!" he had told her, and picked her up swinging her around.

"OK. To keep Taryln safe, we never speak of this again," she said breathlessly, when he put her back down.

"Agreed," he answered. "There is one, though, who will come. And, that person will be the only one who will be able to touch the book."

"Who would that be?" her Mother had asked curiously.

"Legend has it that this person would be known as the Jewel of Anaerris."

Taylor had seen her Mother look into her mate's eyes, and nodded. She never asked again – at least within Taylor's hearing. It had been a long time since she had thought of her real name, Taryln, but when she chose her human name, now, she was grateful. Now that she thought about it, one more time came to her. When she turned sixteen, her parents had mentioned it one more time to each other. That the person would be was half-Anaerris, half-human, but that the true powers would not manifest until taking a mate. They had explained a bit of everything through the years, but not all. They were killed a week later in an odd freak car wreck that severed their heads – the only way they really could die.

Taylor frowned. She had always believed it to be an accident, but now, she wasn't so sure any more especially with the book right here in front of her. It was hard to kill their kind, but Taylor had never questioned it. However, was it really an accident? Or, were they set up to take a fall? She knew that at some point, she would have to investigate it, but right now, the dilemma of the book was far more important.

No matter what, the idea of touching the book would mean death. There was only one could touch it. This person would be born of the one who had written the book. Only he, or she, would be able to touch it. All others would be killed instantly! But, why could Gem touch it? She was human, right? Yet, Gem held it in her hands without any problem! Taylor's eyes widened in shock. Why *wasn't* Gem dead? A sudden thought appeared within her mind, that she rejected just as fast. No! Her mind and heart just could not accept what it was trying to tell her!

"Who the hell are you, Gem?" she thought. *"What the hell are you?"*

The obvious reason was something that Taylor's vast mind refused to acknowledge. The idea was totally stupid! That's when Taylor realized that the old woman who had donated her library to them could not have been just any old woman! She had to be one of *them*! She had to be Anaerris! All Taylor knew about the book was that it was one of the most famous books in the supernatural world, that it was written by an Anaerris, and that it had disappeared eons ago. Most of them had long stopped believing it existed. And, finally, the Jewel of Anaerris would be the one who could touch it! Yet, now, it turns up in this very library? Her mind finally righted itself, and the truth finally grabbed her. She could not deny it any longer.

"Damn!" she said to herself as she walked back to the desk leaving Gem holding and petting the book with what looked like complete affection! Now, she had to talk to Jaxx. If Jaxxon was her mate, then he would be at the forefront of one of the biggest mysteries of their entire age – and Gem was his destiny! "Damn!" Taylor repeated under her breath.

Jaxx parked his car in the library parking lot, and sat trying to figure out whether he should go into the building, or not. Last night had been momentous – both for him and for Gem. She had no idea that she was his mate, and even he was still having trouble believing it himself! So, how was he going to tell her who he was, what he was, and that she was his mate, when he couldn't accept it? But, still. How was this possible? He was doomed to never have a mate. The Fates decreed it as so. So, exactly what had happened? How could his destiny have been changed? How could he have a mate? Too many questions, and not one, fucking answer! His hands rested on the top of the steering wheel as he lowered his head to rest against them. As much as he tried, the idea of seeing Gem this afternoon was causing excitement to build inside, and he felt his hard-on growing by the second. He needed her. Needed to thrust into her body…to mark her as his, as his kind did with their mates. But, she was of another race! This just couldn't happen, yet it had! He reached down to straighten his cock that had curled around in his tight, black jeans causing him discomfort. His hard-on kept growing. He needed to complete the bond with Gem. He ran his fingers through his hair, and wondered why in the hell the Creator had seen fit to give him a mate now? A mate! After all this time?

His logical mind was trying to drum some sense into him, while his heart told him to take his mate, mark her, and imbue her with his own powers! Then, he remembered the council! Shit! He was sent here to do two things. One, find the Anaerris Jewel, and dispose of whoever it was, and two, find the book, and return it to them. So far, he had been zero for all. He had found neither after five years. The council was on his back, as usual, with orders and demands. He was sent, because he was their tracker – and the best. But, this was threatening his emotions, and it was very foreign to him. Emotions were not something that he understood. As long as his mate was not marked, his body and mind would not – could not – focus. The council had believed, as did he, that he would never find a mate. It was not in his destiny. Well, that was all shot to hell, now! He should report to them immediately, but for some odd reason, he didn't want to do it. His protective side came up to greet him. Jaxx did not want them to know about Gem, because he was afraid they would take their anger and hatred out on her. Sighing, he raised his head, and opened the door. As he walked toward the library, his protection suddenly grew to urgency, and he picked up his pace as he ran up the stairs. Something was wrong. Very wrong. And, Gem was in danger. He knew it!

Unconscious of the turmoil developing around her, Gem put on her white cotton gloves, before lovingly sliding her hands over the surface of the book. There was – *something* – about this book! She didn't know what it was. She just felt drawn to it somehow. Pulling her hands away from it, she turned them over expecting them to have black on them. However, turning them over and over revealed nothing at all. No smudge, no black, not even a tiny grain of gray appeared on them! Strange. Very strange, and no matter how much she wanted, it was a thought that continued over and over in her mind.

"My gloves are totally clean! How could this be?" she said to herself in a silent whisper, repeating many of the same things over and over. "It's so beautiful! It doesn't reflect light; it doesn't absorb light. I've never seen anything like it!"

Gem didn't tell Taylor immediately, and in a way, she almost felt a bit scared. Gem just knew that Taylor would think she was mad as a hatter, or nuttier than a fruitcake. But, she couldn't help it. The book called to her – as if it were hers! She felt something coming from it. A power? She had no words with which to describe the feeling the book was giving to her! Words failed her – miserably! Geez! This book and feeling, combined with her uprooted emotions about the Professor, as well as all those really scary dreams she'd been having all her life, were enough to give her the heebie-jeebies! But, still, she couldn't resist as her gloved hands picked up the ancient book up from its resting spot on the table. She turned it sideways noting it had a lock on it. The lock was most unusual in that it mimicked a very familiar embossed symbol that was on the cover. Gem looked at it, and surprise covered her face as she recognized it! It was the same symbol that was on her....

"Uh, maybe you'd better put it back, Gem! It's the strangest book I've ever seen," Taylor interrupted her thoughts. "At least until we can get an ancient manuscript expert to look at it."

Taylor didn't touch it, and shook her head when Gem offered it to her to put back.

"Come on, Taylor! It's just a damn book! Don't you want to see it?

Again, Taylor was silent, and shook her head, again. Gem huffed at her.

"No!" Taylor whispered.

Gem's eyebrows drew together.

"What the fuck is wrong with you?" Gem whispered to her, then giggled as she repeated, "It's nothing but a damn book! It won't bite, you know!"

Taylor didn't move from her spot; she was frozen. Gem looked down at the book in her hand, then back up at Taylor's terrified face as understanding dawned.

"You know, don't you? You know what the book is!" Gem's voice was low., and almost threatening. Gem watched Taylor's eyes dart to her in terror, while her head shook from side-to-side in denial.

"Of c-course n-not!" Taylor answered shakily.

"Yes! You! Do!" Gem accused her.

"Shhhhh! This is a library, for heaven's sake!" whined a patron, who sat at a table that was across the room.

Gem grabbed Taylor's arm, and towed her to the CCR shutting the door with the book in hand. It wasn't just climate controlled, but it was also sound proof. She dropped Taylor's arm, and turned to her in anger.

"Taylor! I've never seen you so terrified before. What the hell is this thing?" she demanded, holding out the book.

Taylor's terrified eyes looked at Gem. There was only one who could touch the Codex. And, that one was standing right in front of her! She shook her head as the realization hit her. The legend was no longer a legend! It was real!

"Did we get a note about the book, Taylor?"

"Huh?" she asked.

Taylor's eyes widened in surprise. She shook her head as she realized she had zoned out once again.

"Taylor! What the fuck is wrong with you? I said...did we get a note about the book?" Gem asked once more.

"Right, uh...well, now that you mention it, I don't think we did."

"Well, I found it hidden in a spot underneath the bottom shelf in the back of the lowest shelf, covered by other books – as if trying to hide it. Either Ms. Sinclair didn't know about it, or she did, and didn't provide one on purpose."

"Well, that makes sense, I guess," Taylor muttered to herself, while doing her best trying to come to the realization that her best friend in the world, standing before her had to be "The Jewel of Anaerris", the Protector of the book! *THE BOOK!* She couldn't believe it! All Anaerris could sense each other, so why did she not sense Gem?

When the library first came to them, it had also come along with notes about each book. A single letter accompanied all of the books stating that the anonymous donor was sending the library collection to her only living relative, but it had made no mention who the relative might be! As such, when the building was rented to house the library, Taylor and Gem had been the obvious choices to be the librarians due to their backgrounds. Their boss was adamant that the old woman had been an eccentric, and didn't know what she was writing. But, now, it was obvious to Taylor that the relative the old woman had spoken about in the letter had to be Gemma! Taylor also remembered something odd about the day the books were placed into the building. The books in the CCR had been placed inside by someone sent by the donor, until she and Gem had been trained how to handle ancient books.

More unbelievable, it was very clear that Gem, obviously, had no idea who she was. Gem had been left on the doorstep of the Elwood's home. And, it also meant that she had to be protected at all costs – and without her knowledge – at least for the moment. Oh, Creator! Taylor thought. Her friend was in danger!. As long as she didn't know who she was, she might be alright for the time being, but it was only temporary at best. Taylor watched the Anaerris Code allow Gem to caress it gently. Her eyes were fixated on it.

Taylor's musings were interrupted by Jaxx trying to come through the door. Hell! It was bad enough trying to explain that the book was real to Rick, who had been scared all along that it would be found. Taylor had even laughed at his concern! However, what was she going to tell Jaxx? She was his mate! How would he react to this astounding revelation? She walked toward the door, effectively stopping Jaxx from entering.

"*No!*" Taylor whispered to him, dragging him away.

"What the fuck, Taylor?" he asked, keeping his voice low.

In the meantime, Gem hadn't noticed Taylor leaving.

"I'm going to open it," Gem said softly to herself. "I have to open it!"

Suddenly, Gem had to feel the cover with her bare hands. Against her training and better judgment, she removed her gloves, and touched it. Surprise followed her sharp gasp as she watched the book change the instant she touched it! The symbol she had seen before, glowed bright crimson on the front of the book shocking her to her core! She frowned. Why is it reacting to her, now, when it had not before when her bare hands touched it? She shook her head as her curiosity took over. The lock bore the same symbol as the amulet in her blue velvet box! She was sure of it! Suddenly, Gem heard a click, and the lock split, and spread open from the center. However, the symbol had more on it on the front cover. Gem's shaking hands hesitated, before she opened the cover to reveal very thin sheets of shining metal that looked like silver.

"Shit!" Gem exclaimed, quietly as if she were in church. "What is this?"

Jaxx felt Taylor pull him away from the door with her finger on her mouth. He frowned at her, and tried to speak only to be silenced by Taylor.

"Wha…?"

"Shhhh!" Taylor told him, glancing over to make sure that no one could see them.

"What the hell, Taylor?" he whispered.

"It's not possible, but it is! It's her! It's not possible, but it's the Jewel!" she told him with her eyes fixed in a state of awe. She grabbed the lapels of his trench coat, and shook him. "She's the Jewel! *The Jewel!*"

Jaxx yanked her hands off of his coat, and smoothed the lapels back down, while Taylor just stood there in shock her arms at her sides.

"Have you taken leave of your senses?" he asked her quietly. "What the hell is wrong with you?"

"Gem! It's Gem!" she gasped.

"What? What about Gem?" Suddenly, Jaxx felt a sickness invading his stomach. "Taylor! Is she OK? Is she hurt?"

Nothing came from her. He grabbed her shoulders, and this time, shook her.

"Focus, Taylor! What about Gem? Is. She. OK?"

Taylor shook her head.

"It's her! She's the one!"

"The one what?"

"Jaxx!!" Tears were flowing down her cheeks, as she tried to make her words coheren so Jaxx would realize what she was telling him. "The Jewel! I can't believe it! The Jewel! She is the Jewel!"

"Will you stop it, Taylor! What the hell are you babbling about?" Jaxx demanded, this time shaking her so hard, her head bounced forward.

She gulped, gasped, and sputtered, but still managed to keep her voice down to a whisper.

"G-Gem! She's the Jewel! The Jewel of Anaerris!" Taylor stammered. She grabbed his shoulders to shake him. "Did. You. Hear. Me? Don't. You. Get. It?" she kept enunciating, shaking him as she emphasized each word. "Jaxx! Gem is part Anaerris! She is the *Jewel*!"

Jaxx didn't believe his ears, and dropped his hands from her arms in surprise. Was Taylor saying what he though she was saying? No. No way! She'd lost it.

"Taylor! Get a grip! You have lost your mind! For her to be The Jewel, she would have had to have found the Anaerris Codex. I've been looking for it for thousands of years! Seriously? How could she have found it?"

Her tearful eyes lifted to meet his. He waited for her to grin, and to tell him she was just joking. But, she didn't. Her head nodded slightly.

"The Book?" he whispered.

Again, Taylor nodded.

"The Book?" he whispered, dropping his hands form Taylor's arms. "She found it? Gem? My Gem?" he stopped, then continued as he uttered the two words he'd been avoiding. "Taylor? Gem? *My mate is the Jewel of Anaerris?*"

"Yes," Taylor answered with a sudden, quiet calm.

In a move so fast, no human could see him, he rounded the corner, and came to a sudden halt staring through the door at his mate. The woman who had bound him to her forever was reaching for the book.

"If we're wrong, Taylor, she'll die! I can't let her touch it!" Jaxx made a move toward the door, and Taylor stopped him, earning a growl from him.

"No, Jaxx! Look!" she pointed.

Both he and Taylor watched as Gem's bare hands caressed the cover of the book. Jaxx opened his mouth to cry out to his mate to not touch it, but for whatever reason, no sound would come! He looked at Taylor who was also trying to make a sound, but also could not do it. Certain Gem would be cooked to a crisp, Jaxx began to move forward to stop her, before she touched it. But he was was too late. He came to a stop, and waited in horror for her death to come. Instead, they saw a lock appear on the cover, and quickly, Gem opened it.   Both Jaxx and Taylor gasped in shock as they saw very thin silver pages appear. Jaxx had to face reality, because he was just hit with the truth! His mate wasn't just anyone. She was "the one" – the Jewel of Anaerris. Gemma Elwood was the legend – the Protector of the Anaerris Code.

~ 6 ~

**"Geez! I thought that Death would Hurt More!" ~
Gem**

Unaware that she was being watched, Gem stared at the silvery metal pages before her.

"So beautiful," she whispered reverently, still caressing it.

It was so beautiful, and the book called to her to touch it. Her hands reached out, and she stared at the silvery metal pages before her. Her hands automatically began to turn the pages carefully. Strange writing was engraved on each page, both back and front. Her fingers brushed lightly over them. As she looked, suddenly the same nightmare dream she had over the span of her entire life became a...

Waking Day Dream

Gem found herself looking down from that same bluff into the blackened valley below her. As she watched that same river of red flowing toward the large, red and black moon in the sky, she wondered if she could probably reach out to touch it. They seemed so much closer and much bigger than in any of her other dreams. Strange thought when there was a great battle raging below her. She felt something pierce her back, and looking down, saw a blackened spear that sliced through her chest. Her first thought was "What the hell?", and her second thought was she imagined being stabbed should be much more painful. But, it didn't hurt even as she sank to her knees as her life blood poured from her body onto the blackened ground. Like the river of red below, her blood sped toward the precipice, which disappeared as it spilled

121

over the bluff. Hearing a noise behind her, she turned her head to see what it was. Two large men stood behind her…one with red eyes that glittered with the lust of a kill, and a hand on the spear as he shoved it deeper into her body. The other man also had red eyes of hatred as he slit the throat of the one who killed her, then took his head off in one, swift blow with his sword.

She knew she was dying. Nothing could bring her back. He was her love. The love of her life, and they had both risked all, yet, Gem didn't know what that meant. No. It wasn't her love. It was someone else's love. As she fell to the ground, he moved with a speed that could not be seen by her standards. He caught her before her head hit the ground, and cradled her in his arms staring with love from his red eyes. His hair was blonde, his skin darkened by the sun, and his body strong and unending.

"Please?" he silently begged her.

She stared up at him, then felt her head nod slightly. She would be unable to live in this form. She had to change to protect the great secret that only they knew. Praying that this change would not hurt that secret, Gem jerked as she saw his fangs descend, and his head bend toward her neck, sinking them deeply into it. A stinging fire of unimaginable pain streaked through her body. She felt like a fish out of water flopping around. The last thing she saw was his reddened eyes full of terror as his fangs dripped with her blood. Were they too late?

End of Day Dream

Closing her eyes, Gem felt a jerk back into her own reality, and upon opening them, she realized she was not standing on a blackened world of death, but she was in the library.

"Oh, crap!" Gem said aloud. Silently, *"Why the hell did this time feel much more real?"* she said to herself.

She blinked her eyes several times. She'd had the dream so many times, but this was the first time she had it while she was awake! But, why? She looked at the book, which closed with a thump without anyone touching it, and locked itself. Gem stepped backward, and almost hit Jaxx, as she fell to the floor. He caught her just before her head hit, and Gem found her green eyes staring into his brown ones – just as the woman did into her love's red ones in the vision. The only difference was that she wasn't dying, and she wasn't on a blackened world. She was in the library, again, and in the arms of the man that she loved. They stared at each other for what seemed like ages, and she was drawn into his eyes. Into their depths. They were ageless – ancient. She saw...she saw a blackened and scorched ground with two moons shining down upon a world that no longer reflected nor absorbed the light from them just like the book! He held her hand as she saw through his own eyes great pain, hatred, loss, self-loathing, revenge. He stood with a sword in hand. She watched him swing the sword as he took lives of those who had taken innocent lives in such brutal combat – her people. The Anaerris.

"WTF?" Gem whispered.

As Jaxx's eyes bore into hers, he drew back in shock as he felt her mind delve into his. Stunned, he blocked her while trying to figure out how she could enter his mind at all – something that she should never have been able to do! Moments later, he saw her eyes go from her beautiful green to blood red in seconds!   Gem felt rage within her own mind and body. Drawn back into her own reality, she stared at Jaxx, turning to look at Taylor who registered the same shocked look. Gem was confused. Why were they staring at her as if she were an enemy?

She loved both of them very much, so why did they show fear and shock? Was something wrong?

Gem glanced around, but saw no one else near her. Her eyes turned back to Taylor who was still registering shock.

"What?" she asked glancing back and forth between them.

"Your eyes, Gem!" Taylor gasped in a tiny voice, stepping back.

"Huh?" Her eyes? Gem was completely confused, now. She looked at Jaxx, half expecting him to withdraw from her in disgust as Taylor had done, but he didn't. If anything, his eyes softened into love. He loved her! But, how was that possible? OK. So, they'd almost lost control last night, and would have if that damn car had not passed them, but still…?

Jaxx glanced at Taylor quickly, then helped Gem to her feet.

"Taylor, we have to get her out of here, now. She cannot be seen like this!" Then, he turned back to Gem to softly say, "Let us show you."

"I-I don't understand. I don't want to leave! I need the money, and I'm not leaving the library, Professor!" Gem gritted her teeth at him. Who the hell did he think he was? No matter what happened last night, by damn, he did not "own" her, and could not tell her what to do!

"Shhhh," he cautioned her.

"No!" She kept her voice down, but she would not let him get away with it! "I am staying here, sir, and there's not a thing you can say about it! No one tells me what to do – even you!"

Jaxx said nothing, but just stared into the red eyes of his mate, and shook his head.

While Jaxx was trying to keep Gem quiet, Taylor rushed to her purse to drag a pocket mirror from her tote.

Rushing back, she held it out to Gem. Looking back and forth from Taylor to Jaxx, she hesitated taking the mirror for only a moment. She opened it slowly, almost afraid of what she might see. Why she should be afraid, she didn't know.

"You've never been a coward, Gem. Don't start now," Taylor said softly to her best friend.

Taylor was right. She had never been a coward. Afraid, hell yes, but no coward! Taking a deep breath, she closed her eyes, then opened them. She froze. Nope. She was wrong! She had just turned into a coward as she fixed them on the mirror. Her fingers wrapped around the mirror, and her knuckles showed white as she gripped it tightly not taking her eyes from it.

"No!" she whispered. Her eyes were red, but this time, they were worse than ever! They were truly blood red... like... like...well...almost like a...vampire? This just couldn't be right! "Oh, shit!"

Settling into an almost catatonic state, Gem dropped the mirror. She had kept everyone from knowning about her eyes for years, and now? Of course they made an appearance in public! Only Taylor's swift movements rescued it, before it hit the floor and broke.

Both Jaxx and Taylor waited while Gem came to grips with what they knew was a life-altering event just as they tried to cope with it.

Finally, Gem spoke in a whisper.

"I-I don't understand?" she demanded quietly. Almost to herself, she added, "W-why a-are m-my eyes so much more red than in the last five years?"

In seconds, her eyes changed back to green when tears began to fall. Jaxx almost cried himself looking at Gem. Well, he would if he could.

"I have no idea, my love," he told her. Suddenly, what she had said came barreling toward him. "What did you say? What do you mean, five years ago?" he demanded.

"Yeah!" Gem retorted. She stared up at him, her tears drying for the moment. "Why?

"You said they were worse than the last five years? Are you telling me that your eyes have been manifesting red for all that time? When? I mean...what was happening when they turned?"

"Well, duh!" she sneered. For some reason, she was very reluctant to admit to him or Taylor that they turned red every time she was aroused, especially during her recurring dream. So, she just gave him a "it's none of your business" look.

Surprise gripped Jaxx, and he sat back in stunned realization of why her eyes would begin turning. He calculated that they had begun changing at about the age of sixteen. That was the age of an Onaerris when their eyes turned! But, that couldn't be possible!

Gem was very upset, and even the wind beginning to howl wasn't enough to distract her. The wind was followed by thunder and lightning, and heavy rain began to fall. The next lightning struck very close to the building. Everyone had left the building for which the three of them were happy.

"Taylor...,"

"You have to get her out of here," Taylor interrupted Jaxx.

"Done."

"Gem, do you think you can go with Jaxx?" Taylor asked her.

Gem nodded slightly. As long as he was with her, she knew she would be calmer. That just set off another round of tears. Neither Jaxx nor Taylor noticed that the harder Gem cried, the louder and stronger the storm roared outside.

"Can you stand?" Jaxx asked her, watching her nod slightly, helping her to stand. "Will you be OK a moment?"

Gem barely nodded her head once, and he followed Taylor to the desk. The two spoke quickly.

Slowly and careful not to move her head too much, Gem got to her feet...the book calling to her, again. She walked toward it as if drawn, until she placed her hands on the cover. A quiet came over her, and with it, the thunder, lightning, wind, and rain ceased. Gem knew that the book was hers, and only she could control, or touch it. She still didn't know why, just that she could. The rest she knew would fall into place eventually. But, she also knew she had to protect it no matter what. Quickly, she decided that the best place was in its hidey-hole in the CCR. No one but her would know where it was. Glancing quickly at Jaxx and Taylor who were still talking quietly, Gem made her way back to the CCR. After shutting the door behind her, then bending down, she began to whisper to it.

"I understand, now, that you and I are one in some way. I may not know why, but I know that will come when it is time."

She felt a gentle vibration under her hands as if the book was happy. Strange, but she still thought it was all weird. Kneeling, she began to put it into its little cubby hole.

"Now, you stay right where you were. There has to be a reason why you were there in the first place, right?"

Suddenly, the book obeyed her, and jumped from her hands, implanting itself right back into its little hole like magic. Gem frowned and shrugged, but replaced some books in front of it, so that it would not be noticed. Then, she sighed with relief, and walked out of the CCR.

Gem was so focusted that didn't even notice that the door closed behind her without being touched.

Gem slowly walked toward the desk where Jaxx and Taylor were, and they turned.

"Where's the book?" Taylor asked her, a look of fear in her eyes.

Gem frowned. What the fuck was wrong with these two? Gem decided that neither Taylor nor Jaxx should know. The book needed protection, even if she didn't understand what was happening.

"I put it back in the CCR, Taylor."

"Where?"

"Ummmm, well, you see…," Gem began.

"Never mind. We don't need to know," Taylor said. "In fact, don't ever tell us! In the meantime, Jaxx is going to take you somewhere safe, Gem."

"Safe? But, why?" Gem asked.

"Because you have to be protected," Jaxx said to her. Gem still hadn't noticed that Taylor was calling him Jaxx.

"I…don't…know, Taylor," she hesitated. "Is that really necessary? What about Lola?"

"Lola will be just fine with us. Stay with Jaxx, and we'll bring her to you, OK?" Taylor told her. Knowing who Lola was, there was no way that Lola would be apart from her charge.

"But…"

"Gem," began. "You must be protected. You are in grave danger from the council, and if you are left alone, they *will* kill you."

Gem's eyes grew wide with shock.

"You said what? Council? What Council? Why would anyone be after me? I haven't done anything!" she cried.

"No, honey, you haven't. But, Gem…well, we have to talk," Jaxx said to her while Taylor nodded in agreement.

"He's right, Gem. Look. All you have to do is go with Jaxx, OK? He'll explain, but we *must* get you the hell out of here! And, you can't come back to the house. It's far too dangerous."

Gem crinkled up her eyes in puzzlement, feeling Jaxx's hand close around her arm.

"You know something, don't you? About me? Both of you?" she accused them as she stared at them.

"We can't talk here, Gem. They might be able to hear!" Taylor told her.

"They? They, who?"

"Oh, hell, Gem!" Jaxx was exasperated with her. "Come the hell on, will you! I told you! We have to talk, and my home will keep you safe."

"You warded it well?" Taylor asked.

"Naturally. Your house?"

"Only as well as I could, but not enough for Gem. I don't have that kind of power, and you should know that," she answered.

Taylor darted anxious eyes around to see if anyone had come into the library. They were very lucky the Council hadn't discovered her, yet. Obviously years had gone by without a problem, but Gem's life had, now, been changed irrevocably. She was awakened, and even though she didn't know it, she was the Anaerris Jewel. Her protection was absolutely their first priority. She'd have to tell Lola, and let her decide what she needed to do. However, there was no doubt at all that she would insist on being returned to Gem.

"Right. Taylor, your family will also have to come to my house, then. We cannot afford to have them find you as well. I shudder to think what they might do if they find you," Jaxx told her even as she shook her head. "Taylor. Think about the kids! They will not stop until they find out what they want to know. I should know. I was one of the ones who used those same tactics to get information out of others. And, they *will use* your children if necessary!"

Taylor's head jerked in shock. She had heard of the tortures that the Council of Ages ordered, but it never occurred to her that Jaxx was one of those who did it! For a single instant, she thought of dragging Gem away from him, but realized that if she was his mate, he would do everything he could to protect her against them, as well as her friends. And, her childrens' lives were at stake. Meeting his eyes, she nodded.

"OK. I'll get the kids and Rick ready, and we'll get to you tomorrow morning. How much time do you think we have?"

Gem looked from one to the other.

"Time? What does that mean? Time for what? Why?" she asked, but they completely ignored her as they continued to speak.

"They will have felt the awakening of the book. We might have, oh..." he glanced at his watch while ignoring Gem's question, "maybe if we're lucky, forty-eight to seventy-two hours – maybe even less. Oh...and you might go ahead, and get Stan and Stacey as well. They'll be in danger, too."

"Will do. I'll bring them, and the children tomorrow morning."

"What are you going to do?" he asked her.

"Diversion. You have to set up a diversion to protect Gem and my children. Rick and I have that expertise."

"Now, wait a second, Taylor! I'm not a babysitting service!"

"Doesn't matter," she said, turning to Gem and putting her arm around her. "She is the one who must live. Without Gem, everything we have fought for...everything we have died for...everything we have waited for will be lost, and you know it! We don't have time to argue this! Rick knows the risks as do I. We will only just need our children safe, and we can do our job! Gem's safety depends on us!"

"But..." Gem started. She was terrified hearing all this stuff, and not having a clue what the hell was going on right here in front of her. Me? What the hell were they talking about? Keeping me safe? From what? What did they know that she did not know?

Jaxx turned to Gem, and held out his hand. She looked at it as if it were a snake that would bite her! He wiggled his hand at her.

"Come on, Gem!"

Gem glanced at Taylor who nodded vigorously, so Gem put her right hand into Jaxx's left, then looked back at Taylor. She was completely confused, and totally puzzled by everything. What was going on?

"Wait! Before you leave, I need ask you one more thing," Taylor told Jaxx. "Gem, you don't mind, do you?"

"Sure! I mean, after all, it doesn't concern me at all, so where's the danger, right?" she said sarcastically, plopping into a chair.

Now, there was the question of the century! He proceeded to follow Taylor. Gem felt a "pull" from the direction of the CCR. She wanted...how she wanted to run back to feel the book in her hands! But, she bit her lip trying to ignore the pull. It could truly be a big mistake, and there was no doubt that Taylor wanted the book to stay right where she put it! Looking at the two of them with their heads almost pressed together, she watched them whispering, but about what? Narrowing her eyes, she huffed, when she finally saw him walking back to her. She leaned back in the chair, folded her arms across her chest, and pouted.

"Ready?" he asked.

"Well, I don't know, since I don't know what the hell is going on!" she told Jaxx who practically yanked her out of the chair, and led her out the back door. Just before he opened the door, she stopped and gripped his arm stopping him from turning the knob. "But, you will tell me what's going on, right?"

Jaxx just looked at her without answering.

"Let's take your truck. You drive! By the way, it's faster than it looks." For a moment, he was quiet. "We have to talk, Gem. And, yes. Not just about last night, but what is happening. The only way you can be safe is for you to know it all – even though we just discovered a few minutes ago who you are. And, before you ask," he continued seeing her mouth open to ask another question. "Taylor, Rick, Stan, and his mate know everything."

Mate? Did he just say that Stan's wife, Stacey, was his mate?

"Mate? You mean wife, right?" she asked.

Barring the fact that Jaxx didn't answer her, again, he said nothing, but quickly ushered her out of the building. When they reached the truck, Jaxx insisted that she drive once more. Sighing, she knew she had lost the argument, and climbed into the driver's seat with Jaxx following into the passenger side. Last night seemed years ago, and she knew she must look like a total freak with her eyes washing away her mascara letting black streaks flow down her cheeks. She brushed her hands across her cheeks starting underneath her eyes. Yeah. Like that was going to help. But, at least driving was something to do while she pondered everything she *didn't* know! And, also, what she did. Her eyes, for one, turning red. It would seem they turned that way during extreme emotions. Wait! Did that mean her eyes were red last night? Now? How could he have seen them? There was little light that night, and the two of them were in the throes of sexual desire. Would they have noticed if she did or did not have red eyes as involved as they were?

Suddenly, a huge burst of lightning almost blinded them, which caused Gem to swerve. That was followed by a boom of thunder that sounded like an explosion. That's when they realized that the storm had intensified, again. Gem's eyes dried instantly. She was getting damn tired of these storms!

"*Faster*! It's catching up to us!" Jaxx yelled.

Gem nodded, and floored the truck. Gem caught her breath as she was suddenly pushed back into her seat at the sudden acceleration!

Jaxx pulled out a box, as Gem turned the truck onto his drive.

"Open the gates!" she yelled.

Jaxx pushed a remote that he always had with him, and used it to open the large iron gates that prevented entry into Jaxx's Mansion. They weren't going to make it, and he knew it. She almost made it through the gates, when a bolt of lightning struck the back of the truck with such force, it tilted forward. Suddenly, it was rolling over and over back to front, turning sideways, and continuing onward until it came to a rest on its top. Naturally, the truck was far older, and had no seat belts, so Gem flew out the door into the air. A huge wind suddenly appeared, blowing her away from the truck, and upward as if it had a mind of its own.

Gem felt her entire body being torn in different directions. She knew, without a doubt, that she was dead. In a split second, her life passed before her eyes. When it got to the book, she felt something strange inside of her.

Now, even though the wind whipped her from side to side, she was at peace. And, she remained in that peaceful state even while the wind threw her into a tree, impaling her through her chest on a tree limb.

Jaxx rubbed his head. "Damn!" he muttered.

He looked around. He was still inside the truck. Bringing his hands down, he saw that they were sticky with blood, even though his wound had already healed. He breathed deeply even though it was not necessary. He shook his head of the cobwebs that had imbedded themselves into his brain, then looked at the driver's side. He sprang up, and hit his head on the roof of the truck as he scrambled out of it.

"Fuck!" he yelled, as he felt a knot form on his head. Even though he knew that it would disappear in a few minutes, it still didn't minimize the pan of it.

Desperation was on his face as he looked around for Gem. Where was she? He couldn't find her!

"Gem!" he yelled. Nothing. No answer. His eyes easily saw into the night's darkness without a moon to help. He scooted around in the area, until he finally propped himself up against his massive oak that was beside the drive. Suddenly, he felt something wet dripping onto his shoulder. He brushed his hand against it, not paying attention to it. He rubbed his face, feeling sticky wetness. He sniffed. Rain didn't smell like iron! Jaxx's stomach did a flip as he saw what was on his hands. Blood! He closed his eyes, afraid of what he would see above him. Gathering his strength, he stood away from the tree, and looked up into the tree. His eyes widened as he realized what was above him.

"Oh, my CREATOR! *Gem*! NOOOOO!!!!!" he screamed.

In seconds, he sprang to the branch just below the one that impaled his mate.

"Gem!" he cried, tears sliding down his cheeks. He had never cried in his entire life, but he did, now. After careful deliberation, he realized there was no way he could remove her from the branch without doing a lot more damage to her body.

In tears, and knowing there was not other way, Jaxx slowly slid his mate off of the branch until she was finally free of it. Of course, she wasn't breathing. She was dead. Tears in his eyes, he held her as he leaped from the tree, then slowly carried her up the drive, cradling her lifeless body gently in his arms. Opening the front door, heedless of the blood flowing onto the stone floor, he carried her into the library, where he laid her down on the long red velvet sofa. He stared down at her for a very long time, before he took the throw from the back of the sofa, and covered her with it. But, he left her face uncovered. He needed to look at her. A tear slipped form his eye, and ran down his cheek.

None of these storms were normal. Jaxx knew the penchant of the Council to punish others in an attempt to draw out those they felt had overstepped the restricted bounds that they placed on their kind, but he refused to believe that Kulana and Faerron had anything to do with this! It just wasn't their style! Kulana was the head of the Council of Ages, having been voted into the position by both the remaining few survivors from Anaerris and Onaerris. That was just about seven thousand years prior. Then, Faerron and she had become mates five hundred years afterward, and he, too, was voted into office. But, Eloran? That was an entirely different story. He'd coveted being the leader of the council almost from the first day it was created. Kulana had been voted into the position by only two votes, but still, it defeated Eloran.

He'd never forgotten it, and he certainly never had forgiven it either! His mate, Delinear, was just as evil as Eloran, and it didn't help matters that she was an Anaerris! Worse? Almost half the council members were followers of Eloran.

Slamming his hand into the mantel once again, he broke off a piece of the mahogany, making a vow then and there. He knew Eloran was behind all of this. Jaxx was certain of it. Eloran had murdered his mate! That was a mistake that he should never have made. Jaxx was older, stronger, and smarter.

The truth was that Jaxx, himself, had been the first choice for leading the original Council of Ages, but the only reason that he had not become leader of the Council of Ages was that he didn't want it. His colleagues had tried to reason with him, but he had refused, then tried to leave. Instead, Kulana had been forced to stop him by a vote of the Council, and he had been "blackmailed" into becoming the Council's enforcer and tracker. Jaxx never wanted to be part of the council, but the Council struck a deal with him, which he had been forced to accept, and he had been doing their bidding ever since. But, no longer. Since he had now found his mate, he was no longer bound to his agreement. And, that deal had only consisted of the stipulation that he would not take a mate in any way. But, Kulana had been very devious. She had never stipulated he would *never find* a mate. A loophole, as it were. But, quite frankly, and honestly, Jaxx had never even entertained the idea that he would find a mate. As one of the oldest still left alive, he'd lived so long, even he didn't remember his own age! It had been thousands of years, and he had convinced himself that there was not a mate for him.

Well, that just flew out the window! The Council had destroyed his mate, and according to the Onaerris code of honor, he demanded, and it would be perfectly legal, in destroying the one, or ones, who had killed Gem! He would kill them, first, then he would try to find a way to kill himself! He refused to live in a world without Gem. It was a "mate thing". If one died, soon thereafter, the other would follow. It was the only time that one of his kind could die, and he planned on following Gem quickly. He turned, putting his arms behind his back as he walked over to stare at Gem's beautiful face.

"The possibilities, Gem! I dreamed of having a life with you forever," he whispered, as he sank to his knees, putting his head onto her lap. Silently, his shoulders shook as he cried.

He didn't know how long he lay there, but suddenly he felt a slight twitch. He raised his head to look at Gem. In total shock, he realized that Gem's color had paled to the color of an Onaerris. Her features were perfected. Her skin was pale, her red hair had turned a darker auburn.

"What the fuck?" he whispered.

That's when he saw one of her fingers moving! It was not possible! Even if she was the Jewel of Anaerris, she was also half human! She had no powers! She couldn't heal herself! Jaxx remembered the previous year, Gem had cut herself on a piece of metal, and had almost lost her life. So, how could she be alive after being impaled? He watched the finger for a while, but it didn't move again. He stood. He needed a cup of coffee. Blood was needed for his life to continue, but he also liked certain human drinks. Coffee was one of these. First, he stepped to the refrigerator, and pulled out blood to let it warm to room temperature, while he put his K-cup in the Keurig coffee maker for a single cup of coffee. Frustrated and sad, he didn't give his blood time to warm, because he wanted to be with Gem. So, he drank the blood down quickly, picked up his coffee, and went back into the library, sitting down in his large wingback chair. He just stared at Gem, waiting with hope that he would see a small movement of any type. He was sorely disappointed.

His coffee downed in one gulp, he rose, and returned to Gem's side. He brushed her beautiful red hair from her face, leaving a streak of blood on her cheek, and bent down to kiss her lips. Briefly, he wondered if she looked more like her Mother or her Father. Anger welled within him, and he tasted poison from his fangs as they descended. The body of his mate. Never would he know the pleasure of being inside of her. Never releasing his seed into her. Never to spend his life with her – to give her his immortality. That chance had been last night, and he hadn't taken it! If only he had not stopped after that damn car had passed! He would have completed the Blood Chain, and she would be immortal! Gem would be with him forever. His head fell forward into his hands, and silent pink tears flowed down his cheek.

Gem didn't understand what was happening to her. Inside her body, she felt her heart slow then speed up so fast, a Doctor could never hear where the beat stopped and started again. Finally, her heart began to slow, only this time, it stuttered until it stopped. She waited for death. It didn't come.

"What the hell?" she wondered.

Inside Gem felt a tightening of her veins as her blood rushed from her. Whatever was making her chest hurt had been removed. Even though her heart no longer beat, pain began to burn inside of those veins. The pain increased dramatically in seconds, and she wanted to scream, but couldn't. If she wasn't alive, then why was she in pain? She always thought that death would be peaceful, but that wasn't what was happening. Struggling to breathe, she realized she didn't need to do so! Just another *"what the hell"* moment. It didn't matter, because she could not move. The pain moved around the massive hole in her chest, but the hole didn't hurt! Damnit! It felt as if a zillion needles were punching into her skin all at the same time, while inside she felt as if knives were tearing into her veins. Someone was slicing her open over and over again without stopping. Still she couldn't scream.

"HELP ME! PLEASE! SOMEONE HELP ME!" she cried, even knowing no one would hear her. Somewhere between the pain, and what was assuredly death, Gem awoke lying on the pink beach in her dreams with the peach sea letting the soft water move over her nude body in gentle waves. Well, this was different! She'd never been naked in her dreams before, so this dream was definitely different! But, for whatever reason, she didn't care! The water was so soft – like the caress of a feather. She sat up, and looked around. Two moons, as always, one white and pink, the other red and black, were shining above her large and bright! A brilliant, and quite large, pink sun was shining behind them. She looked toward the horizon, and noticed the peach sea just flowed toward the two moons appearing to drop off in the distance. It reminded her of an infinity pool for oceans! She cocked her head.

"It's an infinity sea!" she giggled. Then, turning her head, she noticed huge spires far across the sea rising very high above the trees and other flora and fauna. Each was a different color. Beautiful, shining like jewels. The pink sun caused flashes of tiny lights on the jewels which blinked constantly. They were beautiful, and instinctively, she knew it was a city – a massive city unparalleled anywhere in the galaxy. The Galaxy. Well, she was in a dream, after all, so that's what she was going to call it!

Doggone it, though! She couldn't think of a name for it! Well, she'd get back to naming her own galaxy later, and laid back down on the soft sand, and sighed as she stared at all the beauty around her allowing the water to caress her, again, and she closed her eyes.

~ 7 ~

***"Life Continues, even when You are in Your Own,
Personal Hell!" ~ Jaxx***

Gem opened her eyes to the same, horrific dream she had been having as long as she could remember. However, this time it was even more real than it had ever been! She stood on a blackened bluff high above that massive deep valley with a river of blood flowing toward the blood moon just as it always did. She cocked her head. On the other side of the valley, maybe gorge would be a better word for it, stood a spire, but just one. It was no longer shining like a jewel, but looked like a burned out hulk of wheat. Her eyes widened as she realized the deep valley wasn't a valley at all, but what was left of that beautiful peach sea that had caressed her body! But...the water was gone! The depth of it was unbelievable! And, the spire was all that was left of the City of Spires! How did she know the name of the city? And, what could drain an sea? Maybe some massive tectonic upheaval, she assumed. But, it left nothing? And, what about the blackness? It neither absorbed nor reflected light.

Gem had sudden clarity of the situation. The battle below her was huge. It was a massacre of proportions that she could never believe in a conscious state. She had the feeling that she was waiting on something – or someone. Her people were being massacred! She barely had time to wonder where she was when, she felt the same prick as so many times before, and looked down. For the first time, she realized the rod that pierced her body had an eerie, black glow! Her eyes traveled up to meet the eyes of the one who had killed her. He stood with his face in the dark, and bright red eyes staring at her through the visor of the helmet he wore, which was part of his armor. As her

141

knees buckled under the pain, she watched him scream. Gem stared at him as he, too, sank to the ground, following her own descent. Red liquid like lava spewed from his wound, and it covered her face as it sprayed from his body. She watched his severed head fall onto the ground, rolling at her feet. Before she fell backward, she stared at the head, then looked up to see who had killed her killer. As in all her dreams, his eyes were horrified as he realized she had a spear sticking out of her chest.

"NO!" he yelled, and caught her just before she fell onto the charred ground.

Gem tried to say his name, but her voice froze.

"No!" he cried, again. He held her gently, and his hand stroked her face, bloody tears streaking down his.

This was the man she loved more than life itself. No, not Gem. Whoever's memory she shared! The woman had refused his gift more than once, but now, she couldn't bear to be away from him forever – to cause him more pain. He had told her that he would find a way to join her if she ever died. She couldn't have that! No! No movement was possible, now, and her voice was gone. A question shone in his face that begged her to please let him do it! There was no way Gem could refuse him, so she barely nodded looking at him.

Crying pink tears, she was hoping it wasn't too late. Gently, he pulled her to him, burying his face into her neck. He opened his mouth, letting his fangs descend. Tears flowed from her own eyes. Gem could actually feel the prick of his bite, his mouth suckling what little blood she had left, draining her. As the blood flowed into his mouth, she began to get very sleepy, until her eyes closed, leaving the land of the living, and joining the land of the dead. Her last breath taken, she died in his arms.

As always, she awoke naked in his bed of crimson sheets – cradled in his arms. When he realized she was awake, he looked into her eyes with his red ones. She had made it! Thank the Creator! His mouth descended to hers as his hand came up to caress her bare breast and nipple. A wave of pure power and fierce desire took her by surprise. His mouth demanded hers open to his, She opened it for his tongue to dart inside it. His fangs scraped her lips, but it didn't hurt! She pressed her mouth even tighter against his, feeling her own fangs as her tongue and his dueled, until one would dominate. She sighed in pleasure as he won. But it just wasn't enough! She needed him inside her! Now! Pulling him on top of her, she spread her legs to cradle his hips between them. He didn't wait. His hips drew back, and he plunged his cock deeply into her, straight to her womb! The fierceness of his movement would have killed a human, Gem thought.

Strange. In the other dreams, during sex, Gem only saw it from an objective point of view. She didn't see anything, either, but she knew it was happening. But, this time, when the woman cried out, so did Gem, and she felt his massive cock moving inside of her fast and hard. When she tightened around it, she felt his hot seed erupt inside her womb! But, he did not stop, and continued to pound into her body. Her new, transformed body. Meeting each thrust with her own, her own red eyes stared into the mirror above his bed – their bed. She clasped him harder when she felt his semen flood her once again. She was ecstatic, when she realized that everything was still within her. She had a secret that only he knew, but Gem couldn't figure out what it was. Whatever it was would send them on a journey of hiding from the Council. But, what was it? What was the secret? And, as always, that was where the dream ended.

"*Crap!*" Gem said to herself. Then, she yelled as she demanded to the Cosmos, "*Why give me these dreams if I can't understand them?*"

Again, she passed into the darkness reserved for those in death.

Hours passed, before Jaxx finally notified Taylor. She read him the riot act, even while she was crying hysterically. She was beside herself with grief. But, there was nothing she could do any more than Jaxx could. Day turned into night. Almost twenty-four hours had passed. Earlier, he had carried her up to his bed, cleaned her up, tended to her wounds. Then, he pulled out one of his black t-shirts, and placed it over her head. It was long enough to cover her modesty as he pulled the red sheets over her.

He climbed into the bed to hold her cold body. Even though he had seen no other movement, he still hoped.

Closing his eyes, Jaxx's mind wandered back to his beginnings. Well, he really didn't know how he was made, but technically, the Creator made them as well as humans. All he knew was that he had always been. No childhood, no growth. Nothing more. What he did remember was the pain of the war between the Onaerris and the Anaerris.

The King of Onaerris desired the planet of Anaerra, because of its beauty. His own planet was volcanic, hence the red color of it. It was a combination of lava, flame, and blackened soil. Humans would have called it Hell if they knew about it. To him, it was his home. But, when the war began, both he and his brother, along with a few Onaerris and Anaerris, including Kulana, conspired to stop the destruction as best as they could. But, the Onaerris leader, Gwalese, had an obsession to take what he felt should have been their birthright. Legend had it that their kind had originally been banished from Anaerris, because they were abominations in the Creator's sight. Neither Jaxx nor Kulana ever believed it, nor had many others of both races. They believed that the two races were separated, because of their physical differences. Where Anaerris needed cooler temperatures, his kind needed extremely hot conditions. Onaerris drank blood to survive, while the Anaerris drank the cool, peach waters of their world. Neither went hungry. For eons, the Anaerris supplied the Onaerris with their rejuvenating blood while they, in turn, provided strong metals and jewels from their world to build the beautiful jeweled buildings of Anaerris. It had served all of them for time immemorial. For whatever reason, though, the leader of the Anaerris, Sitla, had decided to change the terms of their agreement, and began to limit the blood to the Onaerris. Of course, Gwalese retaliated with a limited supply of the metals and jewels. No one ever knew what the problem was between the two, but the disagreement escalated until war was declared by Gwalese, who was determined to capture Anaerra and its people, then take their blood and planet from them by force.

The Onaerris attacked the Anaerris in a surprise coup. But, the goal was thwarted. When they arrived, Anaerris was already a blackened wasteland. The ocean had been completely drained, and the land burned beyond recognition. This inflamed Gwalese even more, and he ordered that his people were to seek out all Anaerris, and drain their bodies of blood. The stench and burned land rose to the point that even the Onaerris became sickened. A group of Onaerris renegades had banded together with a group of Anaerris to try and save both their species from the certain extermination of both Gwalese and Sitla. At some point, Sitla's daughter, Kulana, began to change her viewpoint. Since no Onaerris or Anaerris could procreate, Kulana had made Jolinaer part of her family. And, because Jolinaer considered Jaxx a brother, they accept him as well.

Jaxx and Jolin had always considered themselves brothers, since they were both charged with specific duties. Jolinaer was the Herald of Onaerris, and because his heart was softer and kinder than most Onaerris, Kulana had deemed him as the envoy to Anaerra representing his people long ago. On the other hand, Jaxx was *the* Enforcer – the one who was charged with tracking and punishing those who would dare to go against the Onaerris. He had reveled in it, and was merciless when he found his prey, killing them without trial or explanation. Whether or not he liked the Council, he was a violent being. Kulana had hated Jaxx's job, and tried to get him to stop. But, he had grown to love his position within the hierarchy too much to bow to Kulana's desires. When Jolinaer had begged him, he looked upon his brother as weak.

That was until Jolinaer had disappeared just after the attack on Anaerris. Jaxx had seen him twice before with a red-haired beauty. The first time he saw her from afar. But the second time, she was just a short distance away, and he had met her. Jax remembered it well. Jolinaer had called him to meet in secret, and while the beauty was there, it was Jolinaer who told Jaxx that he was leaving the realm taking with him – his mate! Jaxx had been stunned as he had looked toward her. He narrowed his eyes at his brother.

"What the hell do you mean you're leaving with an Anaerris? When did you get a mate? We're in the middle of a damn war, and you want to desert the rebellion?" Jaxx had yelled, and had looked upon the female with disgust. "And, with an *Anaerris* female?

Jolinaer had placed his hand on Jaxx's shoulder, and introduced Analyse.

"Brother. You know me well. Do not believe the reason for this war brought about by Gwalese. It was never about blood, but about something more," he began.

"Really?" Jaxx's lip turned up into a sneer. "They broke the contract with us! They deserve to die!"

"Oh, my brother. You are so wrong," Jolinaer had said as he looked back toward his mate who nodded, then turned to speak again. He had produced, and held a small, oblong crystal jewel from beneath his shirt. "Gwalese attacked because of this."

Frowning, Jaxx asked, "What is that?"

"This is the most dangerous thing that has ever been created, Jaxx. Not to just both the Onaerris and the Anaerris, but to the entire universe," Jolinaer had explained to him. He handed the jewel to Jaxx who took it automatically. Then, his brother charged him with a warning. "Protect this with your life, my brother. This is what Gwalese wanted, and it was my fault. I let him know about it. This is the reason for the war."

Jaxx turned the jewel over and over in his hand, then looked back up at Jolinaer, his face a question.

"Just a crystal?" Jaxx had asked, again, before he frowned, knowing that there was more to it than just this ball of rock. "OK, so how about telling me what this really is?"

"What you hold in your hand," Jolinaer had told him, "contains the entire peach ocean of Anaerra, and it's the key to Terraforming Anaerris."

"What!?" Jaxx had gasped in shock.

"Terraforming, Jaxx. That crystal can Terraform any planet. Within it lies the peach ocean – all of it! And, it *will kill* the indigenous population along with the flora, fauna, and wild life on any planet if it is unleashed."

Jaxx had almost dropped the thing on the ground at his words. Luckily, Jolin had caught it before it hit the ground, handing it back to the reluctant Jaxx.

"This is strictly forbidden by the Creator!" he growled in a low voice. "How did this thing come to be? Where did you get it, and no," he shook his head. "It cannot be true! It is just not possible!"

"Jaxx. Listen to me," Analyse told him. "It was designed by an Onaerris, and an Anaerris built it. These two were both traitors to all of us! They wished to rule all, and to change the face of the universe against our Creator."

"Huh? Who did it? Which two?"

"Jaxx," Jolinaer said, again placing his hand on Jaxx's shoulder. "Have I ever lied to you?" Jaxx shook his head as his brother continued. "It is the truth, but I cannot tell you who it was. To do so could easily put everything in danger in the universe! This is why Analyse stole it – to keep it out of the hands of Gwalese!"

He had swept his other hand toward the land around him.

"How did you find out about it? No! Wait! You mean that Anaerris was…I mean, the peach ocean…I mean…it's inside…?" Jaxx stammered in shock, finally coming to grips with what they had tried to tell him. Almost to himself, his voice a whisper, "How can it be possible?"

"It matters not how we discovered it, my brother. The point is that we have it. We are entrusting it to your care, my brother, because you are the only one we can possibly trust to keep it safe! Understand me, now. Protect this with everything that you have. You are the only person who can do this. Within it is the knowledge that will change the face of any planet. Be careful with it. Take it to a new world, and hide it. Do not ever let it out of your sight. When the time comes, one who will have the power will be able to use it properly."

"Who?" Jaxx just had to ask the stupid question.

"I cannot tell you, now, but until that time, it must be kept in secret. Do you understand?"

Jolinaer's voice had become impatient and desperate.

"No. I don't understand, but I do understand Terraforming, Jolinaer," Jaxx had told him, then nodded. "So, this is what Gwalese was after, and the real reason for this war? While you and I have always been of the same views, Jolin, until this war, we were against one another. But, I cannot deny what is before me."

Jolinaer glanced once more at the red-haired beauty. His head jerked up at her soft voice.

"Again, I cannot tell you who told me about it, but once I was informed, I stole it from our archives, Jaxxon, before it contained the ocean, and definitely, before the traitor knew it was gone."

"So...just what can you tell me? The name of the traitor?"

"Yes," Analyze began, only to show a saddened face to Jaxx. "I am sorry, Jaxx. It was Delinear."

"*Delinear?*" If any name had been least likely to hear coming from her mouth, it was his own mistress!

The beauty nodded.

"Yes. She had placed it there, believing it was safe and no one knew of it. Yet, what she did not know is that I discovered her intent, thanks to another who happened to see her, and who brought it to my attention. I followed Delinear, until I saw where she had hidden it within the archives, then retrieved it. To my shame, later, I accidentally turned it on. I watched in stunned disbelief of its power! It did not take long for me to figure out what it was! I thought quickly, and the only way to make sure death of our people would not follow, because of the crystal, I ran down to the beach, and used its power to drain the peach ocean. It finished just before we were attacked."

"Wait! *You* drained the peach ocean?"

"Yes. It took quite a while, and no one noticed at first. Until the last drop was taken, it was impossible to tell the people without revealing the reason. So, I panicked! I also knew that Delinear was involved with Eloran. The two of them were evil incarnate, but I never thought that they would betray not only our world, but his, and the entire universe!"

She looked at him as she slowly moved forward. Then, she stopped directly in front of him. "Jolinaer trusts you above all others. Please, Jaxxon? You must hide it, and make sure it does not come into their hands, again. If they get it, they will destroy this world, and more probably, the universe! And, then, they are going after the Creator! This cannot happen!"

Jaxx just stared at the beauty, then slowly looked down at the crystal. It was beyond his mind that he was holding an entire ocean in his hand. The peach ocean was virtually bottomless, which was ridiculous, of course. It was simply of a depth that rivaled no other.

"How could they destroy the universe? After all, we are powerful beings, but not that powerful! And, we are equal in powers, so how could it work?"

"There is one thing that they do not know. The crystal cannot be used without the 'key', and the key will remain a secret until it comes into contact with...well, something else, which I am not prepared to talk about right now. Anyway, the key must be used in conjunction with the crystal, and only when they come into physical contact. Without the key, we can not rebuild Anaerris. Like the last time, only not following the Evil One."

"But, that's nothing new. It's the very reason we screwed up, and were thrown onto those worlds – because we blindly followed the Evil One."

"Yes. But Delinear and Eloran want to *have it all*! They will enslave the countless beings all over the universe, but only after having disposed of the Creator!"

"Damn! As if they could!" Jaxx had said, when he realized what that meant. The realization that they could actually do it was unthinkable. He looked into her eyes, then back to Jolinaer. His decision was made, and he nodded.

"You have my word, Jolinaer. I will do as you ask. I will take this crystal to another world, hide it, and will make sure that it is safe."

"Thank you, my brother." Jolinaer breathed a sigh of relief. He had known that his brother would not fail him.

"Will I see you again?" Jaxx asked, and as an afterthought. "Do you know where you will go?"

Slowly shaking his head cautiously, Jaxx narrowed his eyes. He was lying! He did know where the two of them were headed! "I do not know. Perhaps one day, far into the future, but for now, we must both flee."

"Then, I shall miss you, brother," Jolinaer repeated. He and Jaxx had grasped his forearm in the age-old way of welcome and goodbye. Then, tried one last time, "You cannot tell me?"

"It is best you do not know, my brother. At least, not at this moment. But, when, in the future, you hear of legend or myth, be certain that the one of whom they believe is myth, is quite real! And, when the one comes, you will be charged with protecting her."

With that, Jolinaer dashed in an instant to his mate. Jaxx's mouth had dropped. It was the first time that he had seen a Vorc'ara form.

He started to lunge at Jolin, but before he could reach him, the two of them jumped through it. It closed in an instant, leaving Jaxxon gaping in surprise. Only leaders of the Anaerris had the ability, and that fact had been a deep secret between them for years. It was rarely spoken of it, and to his knowledge, only he and Jolinaer even knew of the ability. It was then that Jaxx had realized that Jolinaer's mate had to have been of the royal house of Anaerris, and it brought him to his knees in shock as he realized who she had to be! Analyse! The daughter of Sitla! He would never have believed it. Ever. As he watched the Vorc'ara close, he stared down at the crystal within his grasp. This little thing was capable of destroying entire worlds! But, not without this "key" that they had told him about. His head shook in disbelief! He remembered looking around him to make sure no one was around, then placed the jewel in his shirt. He had to keep the key and the crystal from ever coming together! As he turned to try and figure out what he was going to do, he heard a noise, and turned. Shocking him, he saw a Vorc'ara form in front of him, and knew that Analyse had sent it to him. He turned his head side to side quickly. Yes, it was time to leave. Seeing no one was watching him, he knew that this age was over, and a new one was beginning. So, Jaxx stepped through it landing him on a planet known as Earth over twelve thousand years ago.

For years after he came, Jaxx had wished that he had not been given the crystal, even though he continued to protect it. Like him, though, a few others of both races who were also against the war, had eventually found their way to Earth not long after Jaxx. In a very short time, they realized that the powers that they had on their home planets were much more powerful on Earth. Along with Jaxx, each had taken on a persona of an ancient god in which the humans believed for thousands of years. When

Azor decided to step down as a god, Jaxx took on the persona of Poseidon on a relatively large island in the middle of the most recent ocean the natives called Atlan. It was there that he had placed the crystal in a statue that the people had created to honor him. He never really understood why they made Poseidon into an old man with long, white hair and a long beard, then portrayed him as half-fish and half-man. Unfortunately, as time passed, their own arrogance made them believe that they were truly gods, and above the humans on the planet – Jaxx included. When they realized they could do just about anything to the people on Earth, they did what they wanted with them – anything they wanted with them. And, with the discovery that they could impregnate human females, they went wild, and the women gave birth to creatures called Nephilim. Some were hideously deformed, some were giants, and still others were the image of a man, with power of the "gods", and later, called fallen angels.

After their arrogance reached magnitudes that were unimaginable, each decreed a statue in his, or her, own image be created depending on what territory they ruled. While benevolent, but violent when needed, Jaxx ruled with an iron hand. He made plenty of mistakes, but humans had gotten the idea that he had five sets of twin boys with a human woman. Of course, that was simply a made up story by his best friend, Stanorak, and the first Poseidon, Azor. But, in truth, the five sets of twins that Azor's wife bore, were the ones called "demi-gods". After Stanorak had decided to go away with his wife, they came up with the story that he had been killed in one of the many Atlantean wars. At the same time, Azor was killed in a very strange freak accident caused by tornadoes, and his human wife, Cleito, had been inconsolable. In time, she died from a broken heart. Jaxx took Azor's children into his home, and adopted them as his own sons. He had them trained to be the mightiest of warriors, and no one dared go against them! All ten of them were of a much larger size than a normal human due to their heritage, and once they had proved their loyalty, they were each given territories to rule in the name of Poseidon. He had further promised all ten of them that he would look after their progeny for all time. And, there were just too many of them, now. So, even though he still watched over them, he had decided it was time to let them go their own way.

Unfortunately, the crystal cracked during one of the frequent earthquakes, and in consequence, it created the greatest flood that had ever been unleashed on the face of the planet. The entire peach ocean of Anaerris, which was a heavy water, was dumped into the salty ocean of Earth, creating a huge, worldwide earthquake. In consequence, that let loose the waters that were under the Earth, and also affected the Earth's climate sending a deluge of rain that lasted forty days. All of it mixed together, and became the Great Flood of legend. The almost destruction of the planet along with the humans was the result. Only a very few humans survived thanks to the Creator who had stepped in and given instructions to one of them on how to build a gigantic ship. The Ark was what humans called it. While the man's name was different throughout all the world's myths, the fact was there was only one man and his family.

Even though Jaxx had managed to rescue the crystal, the damage had been done to Earth. The alien waters had mixed with the oceans, and had provided conditions which actually made the humans stronger, but their lifespans had become much shorter. At first, some humans lived for hundreds of years, but in time, that changed, and they settled into a life longevity of just a couple of hundred years. Later, thanks to the slightly thicker peach ocean, the conveyor belt that controls the jet stream in the Atlantic Ocean bringing warmth to the northern sections of the planet, Earth alternated between small ice ages and warming of the climate. This had caused the humans longevity to plummet to about one-hundred and twenty years. Other things like illnesses and plague reduced their longevity to no more than thirty-five years for eons. Therefore, they would marry at a very young age, produce children, then die around their thirty-fifth year.

Once the waters receded back into the bowels of the Earth, the planet's oceans remained twice as big as they had been prior to the flood. The "gods" ceased to be real to humans after this, fading into mythology and legend, and the fallen had blended into the world of humans. A council was created of the remaining Anaerris and Onaerris – both understanding it was necessary for their few numbers to survive. Jaxx had become their tracker and enforcer, but without the need to destroy humans. There he had stayed, until now, and his sole job was to maintain a strict code of ethics for all of them. And, if any deviated, it was his job to destroy the perpetrator.

When the Council was created, Jaxx turned down the leadership. The next candidate was Kulana – a good and fair man. He knew his honesty, and he took no bullshit from anyone! He was Onaerris, and had found his mate long ago, but he never told who she was. And, until Jaxx saw Faerron open a Vorc'ara in front of him, he hadn't known who she was.

Pain gripped his soul, as the past fled his mind. He turned to stare at Gem. The loss of his brother had saddened him greatly. However, that was minor compared with the loss of his own mate laying so still on the red velvet Queen Anne sofa in the library. For the first time, he knew why his brother risked it all to be with his mate. He would have done the same thing, and he would do the same with Gem if she had lived. Tears slid down his face at her death. He would go to the Council, tell them the truth, then take his leave and vanish from the face of Earth.

~ 8 ~
"We Have Tracked that Abomination through the Storms" ~ Eloran

Ten, and very bored, Council members, sat around a half-moon table watching two of their leaders arguing with each other. While some were discussing other boring business, another leaned back in his chair, eyes closed, contemplating his own years fighting that damned council. In all these thousands of years, they still couldn't agree on anything! Logic should follow that if they hadn't done so in all these thousands of years, it sure wasn't going to start now. He cracked his eye open to a slit to see the two men standing in the center of the room. He yawned, and closed his eyes once again.

Across the center table, another man just looked annoyed, while the man opposite snored loudly! The two leaders,representing both Anaerris and Onaerris, continued to argue, unaware the others were not bothering to listen, because they were so used to it. They just no longer cared!

The Council of Ages represented an even number of both Anaerris and Onaerris, plus the two leaders of both. And, perhaps, thought the man sitting with closed eyes, that's where they had gone wrong. Because there were an equal number, they could never break a tie. He huffed.

Kulana was Anaerris, and the elected head of the Council of Ages, while his counterpart was the man from Onaerra, Eloran. He was a particularly hateful being. Again, the man opened his eyes, and stared at the two men. Considering them both, he noted that Kulana stood six-feet, seven inches tall and sported hair so white, it put to shame any other white. Brilliant peridot eyes shone like jewels, while rivulets of tiny diamonds streamed down his white hair, which dropped from a simple, silver band encircling his forehead. The only other jewelry he wore was on the middle finger of his right hand, where a circlet of pink and white sapphires glittered incessantly with every movement he made – a gift from Faerron upon their mating.

In contrast, Eloran was dark-skinned. A human would say that he his skin was olive. His most striking feature was that he was completely bald, and his head shone as if he polished it on a daily basis. His eyes, at the moment, were bright red, while normally black. Figures! In fact, from time to time, Kulana had wondered if he didn't polish it! He sure would not be surprised if he was right! Like Kulana, he sported a circlet around his forehead, but it was coal black without a sheen. A matching ring with a black diamond adorned the first finger of his right hand, which was currently pointing directly at Kulana.

"You are claiming nothing!" Kulana accused his nemesis.

"No, I am stating *facts*! We sent Jaxxon on a specific mission, and nothing has happened in the last five years! And, on top of that, he is nowhere to be found! So, where is he, Kulana?" demanded an enraged Eloran. "I know you know, so answer the Council!"

Eloran slammed his hands down on the flat surface, leaned forward in a threatening stance, and gestured with his right hand toward a hologram that rose above the table in front of them.

"How should I know? He will report back when he has something concrete!" Kulana said as she slammed her fist down on the opposite side of the table. "For the Creator's sake, Eloran! You know Jaxx! You know how he works!"

"And, your point would be...what?" he asked in a snide voice while throwing his arms out in a sweeping motion. "That Onaerris bastard has been nothing but elusive! Jaxx has been gone for almost five years, and we have heard nothing! Do you hear me? Nothing!" Eloran yelled back at her, as he slammed his balled fists onto the table, again.

"You know as much as I. He has narrowed the place to a region in Colorado, in case you have missed the HG in front of your face! I have told you over and over that it's going to take a lot time!" Kulana breathed deeply, and rubbed his neck in frustration. Eloran had been fighting him as long as he had been leading the Council. And, it didn't matter about what! Just anything and nothing! And, Kulana was really getting pissed about it! No matter what, he had to delay for Jaxxon as long as possible, but he feared that his time was just about gone. Hell! He needed a new tactic. "Eloran, you knew this from day one, so you have no reason whatsoever to whine!"

"Whine? Whine?" he yelled in disbelief, as he stood up straight. "That's what you think I'm doing? Whining about a bunch of bullshit? After 5 damn years?? Well, five years is five years too long, and I'll wager the rest of our colleagues would agree with me, not you!" he yelled. Turning to address the Council, he shouted, "I demand a vote – now!"

Kulana shook his head, and uttered an oath underneath his breath. But, there was nothing he could do. When a council member called for a vote, it had to be done. Kulana glared at Eloran for a long time, before finally looking at the Council. If only he could find some way to stall for time, but there was no more time. He turned to look at Faerron, hoping that she would have an answer. A simple nod told him he didn't. Both of them had been desperately trying to hold onto the leadership of the Council, while they had kept them in the dark about the additional job that had been assigned to Jaxxon by Kulana. He almost shook his head, because neither of them ever understood why Jaxx had always been adamant about taking a human name, but maybe it had been a smart move. Probably what was keeping Eloran from zeroing in on him. Neither of them had heard from Jaxx in the last week, and that was very troubling. Something had to have happened to keep him from contacting them. He was always right on the money, and reported without fail. Kulana had no idea why he hadn't. Right now, with Eloran calling for a vote, neither of them had a choice.

After one last glance at Kulana, Faerron lost it. Was he ever glad that she did!

"That is *enough!*" She looked around at all the council members who served with them. "I am the elected keeper of records, and the records were specific to the mission to which Jaxxon was directed. It was unanimous, and it has not been forgotten!" She turned. "Eloran, we will not vote. We agreed to give five years, and *three months*. That was the *original* vote that we all agreed would stand. That leaves him at least two more months to complete his mission! And, he will be given that two months whether or not you like it! The rules stipulated that if any vote be unanimous, that vote would stand for the entire time agreed upon by every member of the Council!"

"You are a fool, Faerron! Just because we all voted to give him the task with that time frame, does not mean that we should hold ourselves to it! We are the Council of Ages, and as such, we have all the rights to change the terms if we so choose!"

Those words pushed Kulana beyond his patience, and he answered with a booming voice.

"HOLD!" he declared, using his given power to freeze anyone around him. "It does not matter what our 'rights' might be, Eloran! Since we all agreed, that does not apply. Faerron is right. And, since the time frame has not yet ended, then the terms cannot change – even by a new vote! You should know this! Or is your desire to seize power more important?"

And, there it was...out in the open! Faerron stood straight with her arms folded, and smirked at Eloran. Her mate was the leader for a reason, and seeing Kulana exercising his powers over even Eloran was giving her great pleasure! Eloran stared at Faerron, his eyes raking down her perfectly proportioned, five-foot seven-inch tall body, black hair, and red eyes with ill-conceived lust.

"Fuck you!" yelled Mallorick, an Onaerris Council member who could not move because of Kulana's power, but still had the use of his mouth. "I demand that you let us go, now!"

"Only if you proceed in the correct manner!" Kulana commanded.

There was not a word said after his declaration. As he looked at each Council member, he finally nodded his head once. No answer was tantamount to an agreement, so he unfroze them as he raised his hands, but he still kept their feet solidly frozen.

Eloran shook his arms, and turned his head to look at Kulana. Anger roiled from him, and he didn't try to hold it back. He was angry!

"I do not have to bow to your insolen..." Eloran began, only to be silenced by Kulana.

"SILENCE!" he roared.

Kulana walked around the table along with Faerron who took his hand. They stared at each Council member. Because he was Anaerris and she was Onaerris, their bond and their powers were much stronger than any of the others. Except for two others, none had a mate. Luckily, those two were mated Anaerris, Lenoria and Baerra, and they were on their side. They turned to grin at Eloran. None of them wanted him here, but he had been elected fairly. It gave them sheer happiness that he had been put in his place!

"Two months. These last two months were given to Jaxx, and that was the Council's agreement. And, in case you don't remember," Kulana warned him.

"And, if that two months goes by without hearing from him?" Eloran demanded. He wanted a firm vote on this, but he knew he was not going to get one.

"Then, we will take action. But, not until then!" Faerron stared at the other members. "What say you? Eloran called for a vote. You all know the rules, or will you go against them? Will you give the two months agreed upon over five years ago?"

Lenoria and Baerra answered immediately, and together.

"*Parrinea*," they said.

"*Parrinea*," the other two from Anaerra stood to agree.

"*Sarran*," Eloran loudly exclaimed.

"Sarran!" voted Delinear who was the Anaerris mated to Eloran

"I vote *Parrinea*," Faerron said..

"I also vote *Parrinea*," said Kulana.

"*Sarran!*" came the loud voice from Imaerra with Quazer adding his own thumbs down vote.

The same vote of five to five stayed the same – always. All ties ended with the yes votes winning in every case! Idiotic, to be sure, but that's the way it had always been. Eloran was trying to find a way around the rules, and if he kept on like this, it probably would change at some point in the future.

"Not so fast! What of the Jewel of Anaerris?" asked Delinear, not giving the two on the Dais a chance to respond.

Faerron turned to her with a frown that even the bravest would have dared not dispute.

"Delinear, it was not his task to find a *mythological* being that does not exist! You are not a human who is so easily swayed by such idiocy! His task was to find the codex, and bring it to us. We did not give him the task of of finding the Jewel of Anaerris – even if the Jewel *was* real. This, you all know."

Looking around, and no one else speaking, Kulana declared, "Now that we are all in agreement, we will meet here in two months. You are all dismissed!"

There was a rustling as all Council stood, and one by one left the room leaving Faerron, Kulana, Lenoria, and Barrae. Just as Eloran walked out the door, he turned on Kulana, his red eyes flashing hatred.

"You have overstepped your power, Kulana. You are warned. Your leadership has become precarious. Watch your back, because you just might find yourself without a position...or...your life!" he added, before he slammed the door behind him.

When the door slammed, Faerron turned to the others.

"Jaxx must be warned that the Council is teetering on takeover. We've known this was coming for a long time."

"You think Eloran would try to mount a coup?" Lenoria asked.

"Of that, I have no doubt," Faerron told her without hesitation.

"Then, contact Jaxx immediately. He must be warned," Kulana said, and they left the room.

The five Council Members who had defied Kulana, gathered together later that day.

"OK. We have to find a way to get to Jaxx before Kulana does. Either Kulana knows where the Terraforming crystal is, or he considers it immaterial. We need to get it back! How Jaxx managed to hide it from me...."

"You mean us, don't you, Eloran?" Delinear frowned at him. After all, it was she who had designed and built it.

"What? Oh. Right." Whew! He almost blew it! "You are right, my mate. As I was saying, we need to get that crystal back! Since we lost Anaerris, this planet will have to do. We can change Earth to our tolerance. Once we have eliminated the human vermin, we will branch outward, and eventually, rule the universe!" Eloran paused. "So, anyone have any ideas?"

"I do, Eloran," Delinear said.

"And?" Eloran was impatient.

"You see, Jaxx and I had an, um, *previous* arrangement, which you all know. What you do not know is that he gave me permission to enter though any ward he might cast! What if he forgot to remove that permission?" Delinear revealed to them.

Eloran's right eyebrow went up, and his upper lip lifted in a sneer.

"Oh, really?"

"Oh, yes! Jaxx could never turn my advances away – just as you cannot, my mate. He and I have a 'connection', you could say. I don't know why I hadn't thought of this before now," she lied. Oh, she had thought of it, but was just waiting for the right time to throw it out there.

"You think that you can get us past his wards?"

"Isn't that what I just said? He could never get enough of my, um, body!" she grinned wickedly.

"Well, done, my mate!"

"What about the storms I created to find him. The ones that led us to his location?" asked Mallorick. "Should we not continue them?"

Eloran shook his head.

"We already found the little abomination by using them. Cease them. He does not scare easily, and probably has already figured out that we sent them. We don't need to push our luck, and he never has een scared. And, it is obvious that while your storms have succeeded in finding him, they did nothing at all to find out what he has discovered," Delinear told him. Then, added, "*If* he has discovered anything in the first place! "

"What?" Eloran was irritated.

"Well, I have been monitoring that tiny bitch, as you know. Since Kulana does not know I found him, this could be an advantage."

"Well? Go on! I haven't got all day!" Eloran was exasperated.

"There's a woman..," Imaerra barely said the words.

"A woman?" Delinear was truly surprised.

"Yes. Human. The storms are how I follow the little bitch who is always with her, and I've seen him with her on a consistent basis only recently."

Eloran's brows drew together. "Mate?"

"I don't know, but it's obvious that he cares about her. However, I have seen no evidence of their being mates," Imaerra told him.

"Well, that's too bad. If she were his mate, we could really force him to do our bidding. Be that as it may, if we can't convince him," he stopped as an idea came to him. He rubbed the back of his head, then said, "Imaerra, prepare to kidnap the girl, and take her to the island.

Bring her to me immediately upon your arrival," Eloran ordered.

"As you order, my lord," Imaerra answered, and the four faded out of sight.

"Gem? How...?" he said in disbelief, as Jaxx watched her eyes fly open.

Consciousness suddenly grabbed her. Of course, she didn't hear him. She was locked inside her body in tremendous pain. What the hell had happened?

"*SHIT!*" she thought to herself. "*My chest is on fire!*"

She began thrashing and screaming. Someone was holding her down, but she still almost threw herself from where she was laying.

Jaxx was astounded at her strength! He had to use a great deal of his own to keep her from flinging her body into the floor. For a minute, he had to wonder what kind of mate had he been handed?

For over two hours, he held her as still as he could until, finally, her body stopped shaking, and only jerked now and then. He had heard bones crack as they rearranged her ribcage to normal, and squishy sounds as her insides were being repaired, but at least, now, her cries had ceased.

Finally, when she was completely still, and she appeared to have blacked-out again, he inspected her wound. Surprise gripped him! It almost totally healed. Except for a large, red, and angry scar, it had healed well enough for him to put her in the shower. Her clothing was bloodied, and torn beyond repair. He carried her to his bathroom, and stripped off her t-shirt. Quickly divesting himself of his own clothing, he carried her into his large shower, which had multiple heads positioned in every angle.

Blood ran down the her drain from both of them, and he could see her wound much better. It was, indeed, almost healed. A few more hours probably. Most likely by morning her skin would be perfect once again. He cleansed her body gently with soap. She moaned as if she was being soothed by the warm water. He laid her down on the soft mat that he had in the bottom, and cleaned himself as well. More "happy" moans came from her. After he had them both clean, he turned off the shower, and wrapped her in warm towels from the towel warmer he kept in his bathroom. The warmth drew a deep sigh of relief from her lips, and she fell into a welcome sleep. He used his tremendous speed to change the sheets on his bed, and placed her on them. He pulled on a pair of briefs, and grabbed one of his black t-shirts, which he drew over her head. It was so long, it fell past her hips, and almost to her knees.

He climbed in next to her, and pulled her into his arms to hold her. A deep sigh came from her, again, and he held her the rest of the night just feeling her chest move up and down, while her cool breath drifted across his face as soft as a sigh. He closed his eyes, and began to meditate for the first time in thousands of years.

Brilliant moonlight was shining into Jaxx's bedroom. Gem moaned a bit, and carefully opened her eyes. Well, actually, she had to fight to do so, because she really, really didn't want to open them. But, forcing them open was her only choice, and when she did, her gaze focused onto a ceiling that was obviously hand-carved. It was beautiful, but the light from the window was really hurting her eyes! She could see every little indentation and shadow. Blinking against the brightness, Gem tilted her head sideways on the pillow, then turned her head toward the window noticing the light from the moon. It was still night? But, how could she see as if it were daytime? She felt her heart speed up, then began to calm in the next second. Whatever was going on, she would deal with it in the morning. Gem was unbelievably tired. Sighing, she snuggled deeper into the soft, satin sheets. She turned on her side, closed her eyes, then felt arms around her that were giving her warm and wonderful ideas. She yawned, and cuddled even closer. Her eyes closed, then flew wide open as she realized that Jaxx was holding her against him – in bed! Gem whipped her head around to see him, and to give him a piece of her mind, but words died on her lips when she saw that Jaxx's eyes were closed, and he was breathing lightly. Must be asleep. That's when the events of last night came barreling across her memory like a pyroclastic cloud after a volcanic eruption! Quickly, she pulled up her black t-shirt to look at her chest. There was a circular area that was slightly pink as if it was new skin, but that was all. She had to have been out for weeks! She even dreamed that she was dead! And, that dream had been wonderful! She'd met her parents! Her real parents! They were kind, but a bit unusual. Both of them had red eyes like she had at the library, and her Mother had red hair just like Gem's! Now, she knew they had spoken to her! But, as hard as she struggled to remember what they said, she couldn't remember a thing! The dream had been strange, to be sure, but now that she was awake, she found it hard to keep and capture the dream. In fact, it had already faded away.

Gem sighed, and decided she wanted to take a shower. It was obvious that Jaxx had already bathed her, since no blood was on her. Her cheeks heated up at the thought he had seen her naked! But, then, he had seen her mostly naked in the truck when they had almost had sex. Slowly, so as not to disturb Jaxx, she moved to get out of the bed, when she felt his arms tighten around her like a vice! Her head jerked toward Jaxx only to find his incredible dark brown eyes staring at her. Her breath quickened.

"And, where do you think you're going?" Jaxx teased.

"Huh? Oh, well, I-I was going to take a shower," she muttered.

"Nope."

"Excuse me?" she answered him irritatingly.

"I said, nope. You are not getting out of this bed, nor out of my arms, until I have thoroughly fucked you," he told her.

Her mouth dropped in surprise. Did he just say fuck? Oh, damn! Just the word made her wet between her thighs! Not just wet! In seconds, she was soaked!

"W-what did you s-say?" she stuttered.

"You heard me. I'm going to fuck you, now. We didn't get to do it in the truck, but you are in my bed, and that is what we are going to do," he explained, then tightened his grip on her. His eyes softened. "Gem. You died."

"What? No, I didn't! I'm right here! I didn't die, I...uh...," she stuttered, again.

Wait. Did she die? She obviously had a hole in her lower chest the size of a large melon. It had been all the way through her body! She had been impaled on a damn tree limb! She looked down at her chest, again. No doubt about it. There *was* a pink area the size of a melon! Her eyes darted back to Jaxx who had not moved his own eyes from her body. She looked back, following his gaze, and realized her entire lower body was bare! Her red curls were riotous hiding her sex. Her eyes raised to his. He had a smirk on his face as he realized she knew he had been looking at where he intended to put his huge cock in minutes! Her face reddened deeply, then her eyes met his, and she smirked even more than he.

"So…I can't take a shower?" she smiled.

"No. Not until I've placed my hard cock right in here," he told her letting his fingers slide underneath as his hand plunged two of them deep inside of her. "I want…no…I need to release my seed into you!"

Gem gasped at the intimacy of the act.

Jaxx could smell her arousal, and it was something that he wanted to attack with vigor.

"Oh, Creator, Gem!" he said as he moved his fingers in and out of her slick channel. "You're so wet!"

In response, Gem reached down, and placed her hand on his hard-on. Even through his briefs, she could feel his hardness, and they were quite damp at the top with his own brand of wetness. She could smell it! For a moment, she stopped rubbing him in surprise. She could actually smell his juices oozing from him – and, they smelled wonderful! But, she put that on the back-burner for the time being. She'd figure it out later. All she wanted, now, was to be underneath him as he slammed into her body until his hot seed spurted into her womb! It was all she could think of at this moment! Her hand pushed aside the band of his briefs, and her hand wrapped around his cock. So smooth! So big, so hard! Like steel encased velvet! She tugged at his briefs.

"If I'm going to lay here part naked without panties, I demand that you lay next to me without briefs!" she told him.

In seconds, he removed them, and flung them to the floor. Then, he yanked his t-shirt off her, which followed his briefs. His fingers still plunging in and out of her, he looked at his mate lovingly. Her large breasts, bare to his gaze, were his undoing. Before he opened his mouth to suckle one of her nipples, he moaned under his breath knowing she could hear him.

"I'm the luckiest damn, fucking bastard in the world!" then, his tongue flipped out to lick the hard, pink bud that stared him in the face.

Gem cried out at the touch of his tongue and mouth. His fingers were playing havoc with her sex while his thumb lazily caressed her clit. He suckled and pulled on her breast transferring to the other one after having lovingly poured his attention onto the first. Gem's hand stayed locked onto his cock. It continued to grow, and get impossibly harder! His slit was oozing with more and more liquid, and she spread it over the head as she gently massaged it into, and downward, ending at the base causing him to moan deeply with longing. Suddenly, Gem's body convulsed into ecstasy as she felt her orgasm hit.

"Jaxx!" she cried, feeling her body release more juices than ever. *"Please!"*

Removing his fingers from her body, he slowly slid over her, pressing his cock at her wet center.

"Are you ready for me, now, Gem?" he whispered, while moving his own wet tip against her wet core.

"Yes!" she cried, feeling him rub his cock against her opening. "Fuck me!"

Just as he began to push into her wet heat, he heard a sound that he had not heard in at least five thousand years. He closed his eyes in frustration. It could mean only one thing. Talk about damn bad timing! He planned on giving Kulana a piece of his mind! Interrupting the bonding of mates was strictly forbidden.

"Shit!" he muttered, as he left Gem to put on his clothes.

"What?" Gem stammered in surprise.

He had moved so fast, she hadn't even realized he was out of the bed until he was standing before her fully clothed.

"I'm sorry, love, but a situation has arisen that I must go take care of!" Seeing her frown, he continued. "Let me put it this way…my employers are downstairs, and I have to attend to them."

"You have to 'attend to them'?" Gem said. "Who even talks like that?"

Before she could breathe her next breath, he was gone. Sitting up in the bed, she was really irritated. That was the second time they had almost had sex, and again, had been interrupted!

"Damnit all to hell!" Gem muttered.

She sprang off the bed so fast, it startled even her, and her mind wondered what the hell was happening. Her anger, however, overrode that thought. She stomped into the bathroom, into the shower, and turned it on hot. Then, Gem sat down on the warmed floor leaning her head against the tile. She let her mind drift for a moment, until her eyes flew open in total shock as she realized what had happened.

"I *died*?" she gasped in complete surprise. How in the hell was that possible? She was alive? When one died, one didn't come back to life. She slid her hands down to her chest, and rubbed it against the still pink new skin where she had healed. "*I really was dead?* No. Not possible, because I'm alive!" She frowned, then asked, "Aren't I?"

At that point, Gem knew that she was not, and could not, be human. And, if she wasn't human, then…*what* was she?

Forget about angry! Jaxx furiously stomped down the stairs. Even though he still had not figured out how, or why Gem was alive, the fact was that they had been interrupted – again! And, he had been so close to plunging into her heat! Even now, his hard-on was still hard! How dare Kulana interrupt his bonding with Gem! In the back of his mind, he knew that he should have told Kulana, before mating Gem, but he had not even explained being mates to Gem! And, he really resented not being able to do other things to her, before they mated. He was fucking pissed – royally pissed! She was his damn mate, whether or not she knew it! As Jaxx slammed open the Montgomery library's double doors prepared to give Kulana a piece of his mind, he came to a dead halt, his anger forgotten for the moment. It wasn't Kulana as he had thought, and the surprise showed on his face, before he could speak. Shit, shit, shit! It was bad enough if it had been Kulana, but this invasion was not only bad, it should never have happened! Not with his wards!

Before he could say a word, the tall, brunette and extremely buxom woman, spoke.

"Hello, Jaxxon. How are you, my love?" she asked, pursing her lips, smacking her lips in a kissing sound.

Glancing toward Eloran's sharp jerk of his head, Jaxx knew he was not at all happy with her greeting.

"Eloran? Delinear? Imaerra? Mallorick?" he demanded. "How in the hell did you get past my wards?"

Delinear flounced toward him sexily, swinging her hips from side to side in an exaggerated movement, and her dark brown eyes said "sex" with every glance. There was one thing about Delinear that no one ever missed. Her wardrobe was always extremely revealing, and right now, she wore an almost see-through, blood-red robe of netting, which was fitted to her form, making no attempt to hide her huge globes with their rose-colored nipples positioned in such a way, that he could easily see the hard tips. Her hands reached out, and began to stroke his chest. She had to fight to hold back the drool that threatened to escape her red mouth! Jaxx was still the best looking and sexy Onaerris that she had ever seen! Their sex had been legendary, and everyone on both their worlds had known it! And, even though she was now Eloran's mate, she still desired Jaxx, and her body registered that fact, even knowing that Eloran could smell her arousal. Hell! He had fun on the side, too! She wanted to strip right there, and wanted to beg him to take her in the brutal manner she so loved – right in front of everyone, too! It wouldn't be the first time.

"Jaxx," she said in a deep, sexy voice. "Surely you have not forgotten that you gave me permission to enter any of your wards whenever I so desired? Remember? It was after sex the second time?"

Shoving her hands away from him, shock widened his eyes. And, Delinear gave him a "I want you right now, right here" look. Hell! He *had* forgotten! He would have to remedy that immediately. Just as he started to expel her, and her companions, his front door banged open, and in darted Taylor and Rick accompanied by Stan and Stacey Tamson. They came to a halt at the sight of the four council members.

Stan strolled up to Jaxx with a frown.

"What the fuck are they doing here?"

"I don't know, but..." Jaxx growled, and was interrupted for Taylor to put in her two cents.

"How did they get in here, Jaxx?" Taylor demanded. "You warded the property against all of them, right? So, how the hell did they get in here?"

"I did. But, I forgot one important thing," he said, ignoring her question.

"However, I intend to take care of that right now!" he said.

"Uh-uh-uh!" Delinear said to him, wagging her finger. "You will hear us out first."

"And, what makes you think that I will do that?" Jaxx snorted.

"Because you are our enforcer, and you have an obligation to the Council, and as I am the overseer of the Onaerris, and your superior, I can demand anything I wish from you!" Eloran finally spoke.

Jaxx turned, and glared at Eloran. This guy was a real prick! He had never liked him. It was one thing to be summoned to the council, but for any of them to show up at his home was supposed to be forbidden. That was why he had been given the ability to ward his property.

"First, you have no rights in my own home. You invaded it, and I have every right to kick your sorry asses out! Second, I have nothing to say to you, nor do I need to listen to you – let alone obey your commands. You have overstepped the bounds of the council just by being here, as well as our agreement," he told Eloran. Turning to Delinear who was still far too close to him, "And, you will never be allowed to darken my life or property, again."

"Wait!" Mallorick said. "Do not be so hasty."

Jaxx backed toward Taylor and the others, and glared. Then, suddenly he realized that they would only have come here if they were after something – or someone. If so, he needed to know what they were wanting. He turned to Taylor and Stan who nodded slightly once, as if they could hear each others' thoughts.

"OK. What do you want?" he demanded, again, his hands crossing in front of his massive chest. "You have only ten seconds!"

Eloran put his hands behind his back, and began to pace ignoring Jaxx's glare as well as his time limit demand.

"We felt it...the Anaerris Code has been found." He whirled on Jaxx. "And, we also know that the Jewel has also been found. What do you know of this? And, do not lie to me! I will know if you do."

"Yeah. Sure you will, you bastard!" Jaxx thought. Aloud, "You are the liar, Eloran!"

OK. So, Jaxx was a master at lying, but that did not mean he could not lie by telling the truth!

He frowned as if he were thinking, shook his head, and aloud said, "Strange. I have neither felt or heard it."

"Be careful of lying to the Council, Jaxxon." Eloran asked him. "Are you sure about that?"

Jaxx knew that for some reason Eloran was trying to trap him.

"I am," Jaxx yawned as he told him without covering his mouth. He was getting bored.

"I haven't, either," Taylor agreed. "Stan?"

"Nope." Stan rolled his eyes upward as if he was thinking, and doing a very poor job of it. "Nope. Nope. Not a thing," he added, crossing his own arms over his own massive chest, while standing defiant.

Jaxx looked at Taylor and Stan, then turned back to Eloran.

"Why don't you quit lying, and tell us what you are really here for?" Jaxx demanded.

"You have not lost your instinct," Imaerra told him.

"We are here to tell you that the council is demanding that you hand over the jewel."

"They want the Jewel?" Jaxx never saw that one coming. They all knew about the myth, but only the five of them knew that the myth was real. That meant that Eloran was fishing for information. If the Anaerris Code

was real, then so, too, was the Jewel. More than that...how would they know he knew? Jaxx didn't want them to know the facts, so he decided to bluff.

"Lie, Eloran! Do you think, for one minute, that I do not speak with Kulana? I know what goes on inside the council. Everything! I also know that you seek to unseat her."

Eloran snorted, and frowned, then grinned as Jaxx turned him onto a different path. Both he and Jaxx were of the few who had come through the Vorc'ara together. Afterward, Jaxx had disappeared, until the Council was formed.

"For the Creator's sake, Eloran! Are you fucking insane?" Stan finally opened his mouth. "Kulana's power exceeds that of yours! How did you not know that everyone knew about your intentions to unseat her?"

Taylor added her two cents worth.

"Eloran, you do not speak for the council. You may be a member, but it is not your place to do speak for it! Only Kulana can speak for the Council! You think we did not know this?"

"Ah, but that is where you are wrong, Taylor. I have every right! She has betrayed us!"

Lola sat on her haunches listening at the library door. This was bad. Very bad. If they had felt both Gem *and* the book, then it would only be a matter of time before they figured out who Gem was. That was something she could not permit! Standing on her tiny little legs, she rocketed up the stairs to find Gem, following her scent. She halted outside the master suite, and rolled her eyes. Of course, she'd be in his room! Now, how was she going to get into the room? Lola kept forgetting that she didn't need anyone to open the door. In fact, there were times she felt she was going dog! Shaking her head, she began to scratch at the door, because she didn't want to reveal to Gem exactly who, and what, she was, by using her powers – at least not yet. That conversation was coming soon enough. At that moment, her pet opened the door, and Lola began to dread that moment of truth!

~ **9** ~

"When you've lost it, believe me! You're mind will do crazy things!" ~ Gem

Gem slowly raised her head from her desk. Disoriented, she looked around her surroundings, frowned, then she blinked several times. She was in her house? Surprise gripped her for the moment, before she saw Lola on her lap. She took a deep breath of relaxation when she saw that Lola was just fine, and snoring away happily with her cute little pug snore. Blinking, again, she looked down at the desk, and saw her computer in front of her. Everything was the same. Her house was OK, her pug, and everything else was the way it had always been. She looked back at her computer, and saw the last line she had typed.

She stomped into the bathroom, stepped into the shower, and turned it on hot. Then, Gem sat down on the warm floor leaning her head against the tile. She let her mind drift for a moment, until her eyes flew open in total shock as she realized what had happened.

"I died?" she gasped in complete surprise. How in the hell was that possible? She was alive? When one died, one didn't come back to life. She slid her hands down to her chest, and rubbed it against the still pink new skin where she had healed. "I really was dead? No. Not possible, because I'm alive!" She frowned, then asked, "Aren't I?"

At that point, Gem knew that she was not, and could not, be human. And, if she wasn't human, then...what was she?

She flopped back in her seat. Seriously?

"Are you kidding me? All of that was nothing but a *dream* about writing my book?" she cried, startling Lola, who looked up at Gem with a distinct frown, accusing Gem for daring to wake her from her nice, cozy sleep! "What the hell?"

Lola pawed at Gem in concern, who picked her up – just what Lola wanted, of course. Gem buried her face in Lola's soft fur, and began to cry. What the hell was wrong with her? If it was all a dream, why couldn't she have just gotten to do the one thing she wanted – to have hot, steamy, raucous sex with Jaxx! Even now, her womb clenched with an urgent need to be filled.

But, if it was all a dream, why was the desire so real? The book? It couldn't be real, right?

Curiosity always seems to kill the cat, and this time, Gem's curiosity just might kill her. She had to know, for sure, that it was all a dream, so she jumped up grabbing her jacket, purse, and truck keys, and ran outside to be confronted by the old rusted truck in front of her. Lola was on her heels, when she stopped in her tracks, causing Lola to run into her legs, and fell on her little butt. Getting up, she shook her tiny body, then glared at Gem, who didn't pay any attention to her. Maybe, just maybe the book wasn't real, either? Had she made up all of it for her book? Grabbing Lola, and jumping into the truck, she sped toward town, and the library.

Fumbling a bit with the lock, Gem finally opened the library doors, and ran to the CCR. She unlocked it, ran inside, and pulled out the books from the cubbyhole. She used her flashlight, and thrust her hands into the dark space. Surprise dawned when she found a book really *was* there! It came loose immediately upon yanking on it. Just like before, she was able to open it, and there were the silver pages. The text was completely illegible. It seemed written in some sort of glyphs, but none like she had ever seen.

Looking through the book while sitting on the floor, Lola plopped next to her and pretended to sleep, again. Gem sighed, and looked down at the page in front of her. Startled, she saw the words wiggle and morph into legible words! She *could* read them! Excited, she leaned down further. Automatically, she had cradled the amulet in her hand, which she had put on earlier in the day. She didn't even notice.

That's when she stopped. She looked down in surprise at the amulet hanging on an unusually strong chain. Puzzled, Gem knew the amulet still sat in the blue velvet case, so how was it around her neck? She had never found it after the fire; never removed it; never went to Taylor's house to stay, and never put it in the side table next to the bed? That meant she could not have put the amulet on her neck earlier. The logical conclusion would have to be that the amulet allowed her to read the book. She removed her hand from it, letting it dangle away from her skin. Gem looked at the silver pages again. They were, again, illegible! She grabbed hold of it in her hand, and again, she could read the words!

"Holy shit!" she exclaimed, as she dropped the amulet, again. The amulet was the answer to reading the codex? That was great! She'd just go home, and write that into her story! Gem stopped as realization grabbed her attention. And, then, anger raised its ugly head!

And, that anger blurred her vision! Jaxx was in such trouble! She knew, for a fact, now, that none of it had been a dream! Still, her thoughts were jumbled as she wondered how he had managed to rebuild the house, and put everything back the way it was! She shook her head, again, because that was totally ridiculous. Then, her brain scrambled, again. No matter what, she was going to rip him a new one! She slammed the book shut, put it back, then she and Lola went back to the truck after locking the library doors. Just as she stepped into the truck, her vision blurred. It was like looking at the world that was drawn in chalk. Now, where was it that she had seen it before? Her brain felt like scrambled eggs. A light bulb appeared over her head. She looked up at it.

"Right! The chalk drawings were on the sidewalk!" She remembered a woman, man, and two children jumping through it! Then, she had jumped through after them. "No, that's not right. It was a movie! That's it! Now, what was it called?" She tapped her head. Then, another light bulb appeared above her head. She grinned at it, and said, "Thanks! It was Mary Poppins!"

The blurry vision passed, and again, her face crinkled up in total anger. Her plans had changed. Suddenly, the speed of the truck was excessive through the town as she sped straight to the Montgomery Mansion. And, she was there in almost an instant.

"Wow! Cool!" she murmured.

She rolled down the window, and pushed the button.

"Yes?" Yep, that was his voice! Good!

"Professor?" Gem demanded.

"Who is this?" he asked.

"It's Gem Elwood, you bastard! Open the damn gates – now!" she ordered.

Immediately the gates swung open.

"Good thing he did it, or I would just have to go through my wormhole!"

She didn't waste time, so, she picked up her adorable and cute little truck, Lola, to the front door. When she got there, she wasted no time using the knockers. They were really, really big knockers!

"Gee, what big knockers you have," she muttered to the doors to the really, really big castle.

Finally, the massive doors swung open, and she stalked inside, brushing past the knight in shining white armor, who opened them. She whirled to face the knight, her blurry vision returning. When it cleared, Jaxx stood there.

"OK! What the hell is going on?" she demanded, as Lola leaped out of her arms! Gem balled her fists as they settled on either side of her hips.

"Excuse me?" Jaxx asked. "Is there something you wanted, Ms. Elwood?"

Why the hell did he act as if he didn't know her that well.

"Ms. Elwood? You call me Gem, so don't give me that! And, stop trying to change the subject! I don't know how the hell you did it, but I'll be damned if you think you'll pull the sheep's wool over my eyes!"

The Professor looked at her in puzzlement.

"You know exactly what I mean! I just came from my house, so how did you rebuild my house exactly the same, replace the same furniture, fixing my truck, and everything else you did? So, just how the hell did you manage that? And, don't even think about lying!"

"Excuse me, Ms. Elwood, but I really don't know what you are talking about, Ms Elwood. Would you mind explaining *what* you are doing in my home, Ms. Elwood?"

The blurred vision hit her again, and for a moment, she thought maybe she was asleep, and all of this was a dream, but there was no denying the necklace with the amulet was still around her neck, and that it was his undoing. She took the few steps that brought her almost up against his body. His tall, lean, hard body. Why was he wearing his armor without his helmet? His scent was almost more than she could take, but Gem wasn't going to give into his obvious desire for her...uh, her desire for him....

"Yeah. You know where you went wrong?" she pulled her necklace out waving it at him. "This! This is what you didn't count on, you jerk!"

He frowned, as he realized that the amulet was....

"NO! It can't be!" he whispered. "What the fuck are you doing with that thing?"

"I KNEW it! I knew it! You are a jerk! How in the hell did you do it?"

She reached out and tried to push him, but he didn't move. All he could do was stare at the amulet.

"Shit!" he said.

"Y'a got it boody! You are in deep, dank sheepish!" Gem slurred back at him. She didn't even notice. "Whach made y'a tank you cood'a get away whis it?"

"Actually, it was pretty easy," he said, grinning, but his voice sounded like a pre-programmed robot.

In fact, Jaxx's body almost resembled a steel post in his armor. If Gem had to use a word for him, she would call him a "stiff"! Ha! That was just so funny! After a few minutes, he began to look like a mannequin. She poked his right cheek. It felt like he was made of wax!

"Jaxx?" she asked in surprise. No answer came. "Jaxx!"

Again, no answer. What the hell was going on? Her eyelids began to droop, and her vision became even more blurry than it had earlier. She was suddenly, so damn sleepy! Gem had no idea what to do, but finally, she walked past the "stiff" to the sofa, and lay down. She'd just sleep a few minutes, then maybe she could figure out what was happening.

"Lola, come here," she said, turning her head.

But, Lola was frozen – just like Jaxx. Trying to get up, Gem failed miserably. Her last conscious thought was that everything seemed to be a sketch, and was in black and white. With that, her head fell back on the sofa, her eyes closed, and she slept.

Death, darkness – and cold surrounded her. It was just too hard to fight against the sleep that had taken her. Gem's desire was so strong not to wake, it was like swimming upward in an ocean. One could just see the light, but could never quite reach it – and the urge to give up, and let the depths take you deeper was beckoning her to let go, and sink into its cold, dark arms below forever. Slowly, Gem forced her eyelids open. Looking around, Gem realized she had fallen asleep in the shower! Blinking, it took her a couple of minutes to realize that this was the real world, while the other world had been the dream. She shook her head in anger. Seriously? What fate made her have a dream that wasn't real, but felt real, only to wake up in another world that was real, but felt as if it wasn't? She doubted anyone would be able to follow her train of thought on that one – including herself!

She hopped up, then dropped back down on Jaxx's giant, twenty-foot bed. Her mind wandered to why Jaxx would even need a twenty-foot bed? Unless he had company. Maybe multiple company in it?

"OK. Ewwww," Gem muttered wrinkling her nose, she looked at the bed, again.

Shaking her head, she realized that it wasn't a twenty-foot bed, but it was a king bed. Why was she even wondering about how many women had been in this bed – his bed – in the first place? What had happened between them – well, almost happened – again – came back to her. Her womb and channel clenched tightly as she remembered how she had felt his cock enter her opening. Her body released liquid excitement just thinking about it! And then, she remembered that he had become angry at something he had heard, dressing faster than she had seen anyone dress. He had actually told her to stay in the bed, just before he ran from the room!

Whatever his reason, she sighed. Right. Sure. She was going to stay in the bedroom without Jaxx making love to her! She needed him more desperately than before he left! If he thought she would follow his rules, he had another thing coming!

Standing, she looked around the room, noticing that the walls were Mahogany – at least that was her "guestimation". Antique furniture dotted the room. A wardrobe, a Highboy chest, and a Bombay dresser with an extremely ornate mirror, hanging on the wall above it. The hardwood floor was covered with a salmon colored oriental rug with intricate flowers and leaves, scroll work, and a medallion in the center in a multitude of beautiful colors. The ceiling was obviously hand-carved, and laced in scroll work, flowers, and leaves. Her eyes lowered, again, and she saw three doors to the room. One to the right of the bed on the opposite wall; two on the opposite wall from the foot of the bed – one of which led to the bathroom, and the other to the closet.

Gem decided that she needed a shower – for therapeutic reasons! She was so damned aroused, she tried everything she could think of for release! She used her own fingers to pleasure herself, even using her imagination as if they were his. But, no amount of fast movement helped. In fact, it made her worse! She needed hard – very hard! She grabbed the hand-held shower head, sat down, and turned it to a stream. Leaning back against the backrest built into the shower, she let the stream hit her clit, as she imagined Jaxx's pumping cock inside her!

"Harder, Jaxx! Harder!" she cried aloud to her imaginary Jaxx. She was panting and feeling her excitement soar with the water flooding her sex. The position of the water slammed harder onto her clit, until she felt her climax. In truth, her channel continued to clench and throb, and she had several climaxes, which even made her pee a little bit, but at least she had some sort of short-term release!

"Yep! That did the trick – for a while, anyway!" Gem murmured to herself.

When she stepped out of the shower, she poked her head into his almost certain that Jaxx would be waiting for her. But, he, still, hadn't returned to the bedroom.

"Hmph!" she muttered angrily, and stomped back into the bathroom to dry her hair.

Gem walked to the large, gilt framed mirror that hung over the two sinks, which were sitting atop a solid, green marble top over a white cabinet. Jaxx had already made sure that one of the sinks was hers. Many products adorned the cabinet for her, exclusively, along with everything a woman would need for face and hair. She really blushed when she saw a box of her favorite tampons sitting on top of the counter! She had never even let her Dad see her feminine hygiene products let alone anyone else! But, to think that Jaxx knew her brand was overwhelming, until she realized that he had probably asked Taylor. Damn her! Breathing deeply, Gem just sighed. Well, there was no getting away from that embarrassment, then realized that an adult male should know what women use. Periods were not exactly a secret in this day and age. She was just glad hers wasn't due for the next three weeks! Hopefully, she'd get some action before then! She grinned at herself in the mirror.

After toweling her hair dry, she picked up the blow-dryer, and began to dry her hair. While she was drying it, her mind wandered. The heat from Jaxx's body as he lay on top of hers, had scorched hers. Gem took another deep breath as she remembered the luscious smell of his male body. Clean, musky, and all male. Gem took another breath, then another, drugging her senses with his scent. It was as if her sense of smell had suddenly become even more acute. And, his was everywhere!

Gem heard what sounded like a scratching noise at the door to the bedroom, and she slowly walked toward it! He can't even walk into his own fucking room?

"WTF?" Gem whined. What a bastard! That was it! Gem stormed toward the door when she heard another sound out in the hall. She stopped. Listening, the noise came again. Hmmm. Jaxx wouldn't scratch! So, she opened the door carefully, her eyes widening in surprise as she saw who was standing in front of her! Her two bags and Lola were sitting outside the door. Looking up and down the massive, and long, hallway that extended in each direction, Gem saw no one. She turned her head to look at Lola again. But, who had brought her case? She stared back at Lola with narrowed eyes.

"Lola? Did you bring...? But, how did you get here?" Her eyes wide, she added, "Oh, for goodness sakes, Gem! Of course, Lola didn't bring the suitcase!" Shaking her head, Gem, said to no one, "Who's the jackass now?"

She stepped outside into the hallway, grabbed her bag, and darted back into the room, allowing Lola to follow her. She shut, and locked the door. She had to get dressed. The urgency in Jaxx's voice convinced her of the rush.

Plopping one of her bags on the bed, she opened it. Her workout clothes were in it along with several pairs of jeans that she had bought after the fire. A few light sweaters, panties, bras, and socks as well. The other bag held her makeup, toothbrush, and other toiletries. She was definitely going to have to thank Taylor. She looked down at Lola.

"OK. Lola. I'd better get dressed before Jaxx comes back, right?"

Lola cocked her head sideways, and it seemed to Gem that Lola gave a slight nod. There were so many ridiculous ideas running through her head, Lola was just one more weirdness that she just didn't need right now. Later, then. Right now, she knew she had to get dressed and get down to the library. No matter what Jaxx had told her, there was no way she was not going to go find out what was happening. From her case, Gem chose a pair of dark blue skinny jeans and a Kelly green sweater. She reached in to grab a pair of matching green panties, when her eyes saw the blue velvet case. Huh. Taylor must have found it in her bedside table. She lovingly picked it up, and turned it back and forth, the dream puzzling her even further. She didn't need the amulet to read the glyphs, of course, so why did her dream suggest that she did? On a whim, she took it out of the box, and put it around her neck. Then, turned, she pulled out her makeup, applied it, pulled her sweater over her head, then put on a pair of high-top black boots that easily went over her jeans. Gem turned, and left the bedroom with Lola's tiny little legs scampering quickly to keep up with her pet. The carpeted staircase rendered their footsteps silent, and the two started to walk lightly down them. As they got closer to the library, they heard several loud voices. Stopping to look at Lola, who looked back at her, Gem shrugged, then they continued down even more carefully. She and Lola tried to be as quiet as possible. When they reached the last stair, the voices were really angry all the way around. She heard Jaxx's voice accompanied by Taylor's. And, yep. That was also Rick, Stan, and even Stacey. But, there were other voices that she had never heard before, and that made her tiptoe to the sliding pocket door that closed the library from the living room. Lola came to a stop at her feet, and pressed her ear to the door. Looking down at Lola, she placed her own ear to the door. Raising her eyebrows. She couldn't catch every word. She needed to open the doors just a tiny bit. Quietly, she slid the doors apart just enough for both she and Lola to finally hear everything that was being said.

"What the fuck are they doing here, Jaxx? And, for the love of the Creator, *how* did they get in here, Jaxx?" Taylor demanded. "You warded the property against them, didn't you?"

"I did. But, I forgot one important thing. However, I intend to take care of that right now!" Jaxx said.

"Uh-uh-uh!" Delinear wagged her index finger back and forth at him. "You will hear us out first."

"And what, exactly, makes you think that I will listen to you?"

"*Can't say I blame him, either! What a bitchy...bitch!*" Gem thought

"Because, you are our enforcer, and you have an to the Council, and as I am the overseer of the Onaerris, and your superior, I can demand anything I wish from you!" an unknown male voice said.

"*Enforcer? What the hell does that mean?*" Gem asked. So intent was she trying to figure that out, she realized that the voices were becoming even angrier. She had become distracted, and lost her place in the drama unfolding in front of her. "*Oh, hell! Get your head in the game, Gem!*" she admonished herself, then she listened carefully – well, as carefully as one could listen through doors.

Concentrating on keeping her ears open, Gem heard a tiny little laugh that sounded suspiciously like the woman was grinning. Jealousy reared its ugly head! She just had to get a look at this woman who had been with Jaxx previously. Quietly, she moved to put her fingers on the slide indentation of the door, and gently opened them a bit larger, leaving just enough of a crack to let her see into the library. She looked through the crack, and saw more people in the room than she had thought.

Four people, besides Taylor, Rick, Stan, and Stacy, stood in dark blue robes similar to a judge's robe. Three men, and two women were standing in a slight arc facing the others. She saw the women, and her mouth dropped open. One man and woman were as dark and tan as Jaxx, while the other couple looked as if they had been in they hadn't seen the sun in years! But, the tan man and pale woman, who were obviously a couple, captured her attention most. But, her clothing?

"Holy shit!" Gem told herself with her mouth dropped. *"What the fuck is she wearing? I mean isn't she wearing?"*

It was red as blood, and made of net! Her entire outfit was like a net robe! Nothing was left to the imagination! Everyone could see her nipples poking out of the netting, and her figure was lean, and perfect! And, the "fur" at the apex of her thighs were curly and easily seen!

"Damn her!" Gem almost muttered aloud.

And, worse, it was obvious that, while she had a thing for Jaxx, the man by her side was hers.

The woman was beautiful! Not just pretty, but she was a true beauty. With her skin as pale as milk, her coal black hair hung down to her waist as smooth and straight without a hair out of place! She was just like a woman out of a 1940's pin-up! Would someone please tell her why it is that all these "other women" had big tits, small waists, perfect butts, and gorgeous hair, while Gem had only the big tits? Shaking her head, she also saw that the woman was tall – perhaps five-foot seven inches with coal brown eyes, and from what she could see, she glided easily as she approached. How in the Hell could she compete with that vision of beauty? Depression set foot in Gem's mind. Why would any man look at her unruly red hair, with her tiny frame, and hair the color of Lucille Ball's, when he could have *that* in his bed? To be thrusting into that body? But, to all intents and purposes, her face looked – hard...as if she had lived a hard life.

Gem looked down when she felt Lola at her feet. Lola was being very quiet, and peeking into the room just like Gem. Lola lifted her head, and stared at Gem. Then, the two of them looked back into the crack. Whatever was happening, it was terribly important. At least, it sure seemed that way!

The beauty reached touched Jaxx's face, and planted a kiss on his lips, while her hands stroked his chest! What a bitch! Gem tried to separate her feelings from her logic, but it was too hard. Worse? It took all she had to not burst into the room, and kill her with her bare hands! Bringing herself to a surprised stance, she wondered where that thought came from, because she had never had a desire to kill anyone! E-VER! Whoa!

"Jaxx, surely you have not forgotten that you gave me permission to enter any of your wards whenever I so desired? Remember? It was after sex the second time?"

Gem had to stop herself from running to the room, and slamming her fist into that pretty face of hers! Why was she so passionate about this? Still, Gem managed to bite her tongue, and continued to listen. Better to get all the ammunition that he could get, before she flew off the handle!

Jaxx's anger narrowed his eyes as he jerked her hands away from his torso when she slid her hand closer to his crotch. He pushed her away – violently to the point where she stumbled backward, and the man caught her.

Hmmm. The man. He looked...evil. Gem couldn't think of another description! His hair was also coal black and almost glowed with a sheen. It was slicked back so tightly, Gem wondered if it hurt! Letting her eyes travel up and down his torso, he was very thin. He had to be no less than six-feet, eight inches tall. He had the strangest eyes she had ever seen. They tilted just slightly up, and his eyelashes and brows were also coal black. But, his eyes were the color of a bright blue. A stark contrast to the beauty standing beside him.

A huge crack startled Gem, bringing her back to the conversation going on inside. She peeked, and saw a huge, red hand appearing on the left side of Delinear's face. Gem had to hold back her laughter, but she still couldn't stop the huge grin that appeared on her face, because Jaxx has just slapped the naked woman!

"That's showing her!" Gem almost giggled out loud, but caught herself in time.

Delinear stared at Jaxx in shock. It was apparent that she never believed he would strike her. Her! Delinear of the Anaerris! The most beautiful woman in the Universe, self-proclaimed, of course, and he had struck her? Her face screwed up in anger, and when she screamed, she sure sounded like a...like a...Gem tried to think of the right word.

"Banshee!" That was the word, Gem thought! She screamed just like a Banshee!

"You son of a bitch!" Delinear yelled at him.

"Yeah? Well, I'd rather be the son of one than one!" Jaxx said to her.

Behind him, Taylor and Stan roared out loud while Rick just grinned big, and Stacey bent over holding her stomach as she laughed, because it hurt so much!

Gem almost laughed out loud, too. She pumped her fist into the air and mimed "YES!", but she managed to keep silent. A little sound came from Lola, and strangely, it sounded like a giggling snort!

Delinear lunged at with him with claws extended only to be jerked backward, landing on her ass – again, which just elicited another silent laugh from Gem, as well as out and out laughter of her friends.

"ENOUGH!" the tall man shouted, his voice causing the entire building to shake. "I will not tolerate this any longer! The Council met, and it was decided that you have had enough time, and that two extra months would not make a difference. Therefore, you are recalled to the Council of Ages to address us and to explain why you have not completed the task that was assigned to you!"

Jaxx narrowed his eyes. Finally! They were caught in their own lie! He had dreamed of this happening for eons, and now, thanks to the warning from Kulana and Baerra he had mentally received a few moments ago about the approaching coup, confirmed everything he and the others had suspected. Jaxx had little time to prepare for what he would say, so he decided that the best thing to do at the moment was bluff.

"No," Jaxx snorted.

Silence greeted Eloran, and the others dropped their mouths in shock. Jaxx was defying them? No one defied Eloran! When his voice finally returned, he ground out the words in what was meant to be authoritative, but in reality, it came out stunned and shocked with a high squeaky voice.

"What?" Eloran squeaked. "You dare defy the Council of Ages? You know the penalty for this! And, still, under penalty of death, you defy the Council?"

"No. I defy only four Council members, Eloran." Jaxx pointed to all of those standing before him, and snickered at the one still sitting on her butt.

"How dare you!" Delinear yelled as she jumped to her feet. She was at Eloran's side in an instant opening her mouth to speak. Before she could get any words out of her mouth, Jaxx beat her to it.

"Of course, I dare. Have you forgotten the agreement signed by each of you? The one I have right here in my pocket?" he bluffed, patting his back, blue jean pocket.

"What agreement? We never signed an agreement," said Imaerra.

"Excuse me? There was no signed agreement, therefore, we can recall you!" Eloran agreed.

"Really? Well, isn't that interesting, Taylor?" Jaxx asked, pulling paperwork and waving it in the air.

"Sure is, Jaxx! You showed us that document when you first appeared in town, to identify yourself, and your reason for being here!" Taylor bluffed right along with him.

"Hey," Stan began, "isn't that the document you showed me when I was in the middle of a car job?"

Taylor, and Stacy snickered at Stan's comment.

Stacy couldn't help it. It just popped out of her mouth!

"Well, it was a job, but it was a bit private even if it was under the car!" she laughed, hearing Jaxx and Stan snicker even more. Taylor let out a huge, hearty laugh grabbing her sides in laughter. "And, you, my dear, couldn't take the time – uh – you were too busy to read it, so Jaxx showed it to me," Stacey grinned. "He was very patient, and when I stopped 'helping' you and crawled out from under the car, I saw it myself!"

"That's right! I was a bit too 'busy', my love," he said, trying to keep from laughing. "I had no idea that Jaxx had shown it to you?"

"He sure did!" she responded with slightly narrowed eyes crinkled with amusement, telling him she knew he was trying to keep from laughing at the lie.

Rick was just standing there with a huge smile on his face. He nodded agreement.

"I saw it as well," he offered, noting the bluff, but not giving it away.

Jaxx nodded in satisfaction as his friends backed him up on the lie.

"So, as you see, I have the proof, and three witnesses who saw the document that I was given by Kulana. Do you really want to go so far as to call *her* a liar?" Jaxx asked. Eloran and Delinear said nothing, but scowled. They knew it was a bluff, but they couldn't prove it. "Good. That's settled. I have two more months to find that damn book – by law! I will report no findings, until I stand before all ten of the members of the Council as I said earlier. Is. That. Clear?" He enunciated all three words.

"Bullshit! I will believe no word of an Onaerris!" Delinear sneered, while ignoring Eloran's frown. No. She didn't believe him any more than any other Onaerris. Or Anaerris, for that matter! She was the only one she could trust!

"But, you are Anaerris, and Stan is Onaerris. Does that mean that you would call him a liar?" Jaxx's eyes narrowed in danger. "If so, then your little group is in serious trouble, and the Council will know."

His look had terrified everyone, but Delinear was not phased one iota. She continued.

"I do not care whether Stan is Onaerris or not! Anyone who stands together against us is our enemy!" she yelled.

That was all Jaxx needed to hear!

"You have just admitted your own intentions, and have betrayed the Council. I assure you that Kulana will have my report today!" Then, he finished. "Delinear, here this, and heed my words! I hereby revoke my invitation to you in any domicile in which I reside from this point forward and forever! And, it includes this current location! You understand the consequences if you dare try to stay! You are no longer welcome here, so I suggest you get your *fat ass* out of my home, now, or you will burn."

Taylor laughed. "Good one, Jaxx!!" and she and Stacy knuckled bumped each other.

"You cannot revoke my right," she demanded, ignoring the others. "It is impossible!"

"Can I not? That is not true, and you know it. There's always a loop-hole, and you just invoked it! Because you have called me a liar, you are no longer a friend. You have also told me that I am your enemy, making you mine, and thus, unwelcome," he told her. "You'd better leave, before you begin burning, Delinear."

Delinear waited a few moments, then laughed heartily when nothing happened. Jaxx was about to wonder why it didn't work, when Eloran began to slightly double over in pain.

"See? I am still important to you, or you revocation would have worked, Jaxx!" she laughed.

Jaxx walked over to the fireplace, and stood with his feet spread, and his massive arms thrown across his chest. He showed no expression. He was clearly waiting for something.

Suddenly, Eloran screamed so loud, Gem had to put her hands over her ears! Gem shifted her eyes over to him, and saw that his skin was glowing bright red, and tiny jets of flame covered his body, and he faded away. Following, each butt-ass Council member, in turn, began to scream as they faded into nothing.

"You have not heard the last of this,!" screamed Delinear as her body caught fire, and she, too, faded out of sight.

Jaxx let out the first, real, laugh he had had in at least eight thousand years!

~ 10 ~

"Nothing so satisfying as being able to put a bitch in her place!" ~ Jaxx

Followed by the others, their laughter reverberated throughout the house, and it was like a cleansing that it had been craving. Taylor was wiping tears from her cheeks that had found an escape route from her eyes. Stan was laughing uproariously, while Stacey lay down on the sofa, because she was laughing so hard. Rick stood at the fireplace with a huge grin on his face, and tried to hold back his own laughter, which was unsuccessful, of course!

No one knowing that she was out in the hall, Gem sank down on the floor, laughing hilariously as quietly as she could, while Lola fell on her back, and quietly snickered with little pug snorts beside her. There was something so damn satisfying hearing Jaxx put those Council Members in their place! Especially when that bitch couldn't believe that Jaxx would not take back his "invitation".

As the laughter calmed, and Taylor spoke – well, correction. She stammered and stuttered through her laughter.

"I-I c-c-can't b-b-believe that you put D-Delinear in her place, Jaxxon!" Taylor said gasping between giggles.

"Yeah. What she s-s-said," Stacey laughed while pointing at Taylor. "B-but s-sl-slapping Delinear? OMG! That was the best freaking moment E-ver! Why didn't we get that on Video? Talk about priceless!"

"Jaxx," Rick began, "what the hell ever prompted you to ever want that bitch?"

Jaxx's eyebrows went up at the question. What should he say? It was her body, and the sex was awesome?

Because that was the only reason that he could remember. And, he had to admit, now, that the thought that he had been inside her body made him sick to his stomach!

"Oh, come on, Rick! Don't tell me that if you had a chance, you'd take a piece of that body. She was always offering it to Jaxx! I mean...she had it bad for him back then!" Stan commented.

Rick looked at Taylor's narrowed eyes, grinned, then answered Stan.

"Stan, if any woman, bitch or not, had offered me that body, then, yeah. I'd take it! It's not my problem if the cow offered the milk free!" Rick hooted loudly.

Taylor glared at her mate, but it didn't hold, because his statement was so like a man! She doubled over as she broke into another bout of laughter.

Jaxx slapped Rick on the back, and laughed with everyone else.

"Cow! "he laughed. "But, why go around insulting bovines?" he added.

Laughter rose even louder, but soon, died back down, again.

"Trust me...Delinear would get an academy award for her performance! All of them! I still can't believe that I didn't realize what her original goal was."

"Which would have been???" Stan asked him.

"For us to mate, of course. She has always had an obsession with me, so when she offered, I gave in to her," he told them, then waived Stacey silent before she could speak. "I know, I know. Stupid is as stupid does. Just because we live long doesn't mean that we don't make idiot decisions sometimes."

"Then, w-why leave it where she would be able to invade your w-wards?" Taylor stuttered, swiping the tears from her cheeks, once again.

"Honestly? I had forgotten I did, Taylor. Again, I know it was a dumb thing, but she was nothing to me. It didn't take me long to figure her out. Once I did, I left, and this is the first time I've seen her since then." Jaxx paused before continuing in a solemn tone. "Besides...now, I have real, true love for the first time in my life, and Gem is the only one that I will ever want by my side throughout the ages."

The hurt that had set into her heart at his words concerning Delinear, morphed into relief and happiness. Gem realized she was still eaves dropping, so she motioned to Lola, and both of them quietly left the area. She needed to walk; to clear her head. She turned and the two of them sped down the hallway through the kitchen, and out the back door.

For ten minutes, the two companions walked silently through the woods with Gem not really caring about where she was going. She just needed to catch her breath, and try to figure out how she would explain why she was eavesdropping. She'd never been good at lying, but she certainly was going to try. Gem neared the stone fence that separated Jaxx's property from the road outside, when she heard voices. She looked at Lola who gave her a nod. Wait! What? She did a double take frowning at Lola who just looked at her, so Gem shook her head, and quietly approached the wall. Leaning with her back against it, she realized that she was listening to the same people who had just stood in Jaxx's library! Wait a minute! His place was "warded", but did that mean he was involved in the black arts? No. No. She refused to believe it, but what else would explain how their bodies burst into flames, then just vanished! Nope, nope, and nope. Didn't happen. It had to have been a dream! Man, but she was slow on the uptake! The voices butted into her thoughts. They sounded as if they were about to hatch an evil plan! She shook her head. Did she really, just seriously say that to herself? This all seemed as if it was a bad excuse for a made for a B movie!

"Did anyone ever tell you what a dumb-ass you were, Delinear? Oh, wait! Jaxx just did!" the male voice guffawed while the other two laughed as well.

Gem shook her head. She had not paid any attention to the names of the other two people with them. Since they had really said nothing specific until now, the voice who had just spoken simply had to belong to one of them.

"You *fucking bastard*, Mallorick!" she heard Delinear yell. "How *dare* you speak to me like that!"

"Really? And, what are you going to do about it?" the voice that belonged to Mallorick asked with contempt.

Gem heard a shuffle, then a muffled "Aghhhh"! She decided to take a chance, and peep through the fence bars.

"That is enough!" Eloran said, grabbing Delinear by the scruff of the neck as if she were a dog.

"Well, it didn't work. Delinear overestimated Jaxx's attraction to her!" Mallorick answered.

"No. What made you think he would still prance around you like a dog in heat?" Eloran asked, his voice dripping with sarcasm.

"Watch your mouth, Onaerris," she told him, then whirled on Eloran. "Be careful what you say to me, Eloran! I am not tolerant – even of you!"

"And, what? Kill me? Really, *Anaerris*!" Eloran imitated. "You are too vain to realize that you don't have the effect on most men that you think that you do!".

Gem heard what sounded like a slap. Her hand flew to cover her mouth trying to keep her giggles from being overheard. She looked down at Lola who seemed to be giving her a "shut the hell up" look.

"OK, so. Now what?" the other female voice answered.

"What do we do, Imaerra? First, we need to get ahead of the game, before Kulana finds out that we not only went against council rules, but we lied to her and Jaxx. Thanks to you, our secret is out, Delinear. Your temper has always been your downfall, and now, I have to do damage control! Kulana and the Council will never believe us. Second, it's time for us to find a secure location. Our time on the Council is at an end."

A slight gentle wind was felt by Gem, and she peeked through the stone fence posts. They were gone, and she sighed in relief. Turning, she shuffled into the woods that were on the property. Gem had lost all sense of time, and she guessed that she and Lola had been walking for about an hour. Suddenly, the two came upon a very small clearing that had a little woodshed sitting in the center of it.

Gem noted that the small building didn't look as if it had been used in years. It was badly weathered, and the paint that had once been red was almost totally gone, now. The roof was standard, and several shingles were missing. The padlocked door was enhanced with a combination lock like the ones she had on her lockers in school.

"That's weird, Lola? Why lock a door when there is nothing inside it? Well, maybe there are expensive tools, but why would someone leave them in a dirty and run-down building?"

Lola was having the exact same thought, and just cocked her head at her pet. The logical answer was that there was something inside it that Jaxx did not want found, and it was at least deterring one from entering.

Gem placed her hand on the lock, and the hook just popped open. She turned to Lola.

"Well, I didn't exactly unlock it, right, Lola?" Then, with a sneaky expression, "Want to see what's inside as much as I do?"

Lola's silence and cocked head indicated she agreed, so Gem removed the lock, and opened the door, which groaned with a loud squeak. She and Lola entered the dark building. She jumped when the door slammed shut behind her. She also heard a *click,* and turned to open the door again. Only it was locked.

"Hmmm. OK. If we can't get back out, there is only one way to go. Forward!"

A few steps into the building was all she could take before darkness enveloped her. It was so black in the little shed, she stopped dead still.

"Now, what, Lola? I don't have a flashlight...."

She snapped her fingers when she remembered.

"Wait a sec!" and, digging into her pocket, she fumbled around until she found what she wanted. She pulled it out. It was her small, quarter-inch flashlight with a high beam. She had almost forgotten she had put it in her pocket for an emergency that she used to find the book in the CCR! It was a security blanket for her in case she needed to unlock her door to her house in the dark.

She turned it on, and it flooded the little shed with light. Gem pointed it, and made a circle. She heard a rustle ahead of her.

"Lola? Lola, what did you find?" Gem demanded.

"Woof!" Lola said to her, and her light showed Lola taking off at a run with Gem on her flank.

"LOLA! Come back here!" she shouted. Somewhere in the back of her head, she registered the fact that this place was much larger on the inside than the outside, and she had a Dr. Who moment, remembering the Tardis. It had the same oddity about it. Now, what was that called? Gem forgot what the scientific name for being larger in the inside than the outside. Still, though, she continued to chase Lola, having no idea where they were going!

Suddenly, Lola came to a complete halt! Thanks to Lola's Fae eyes, she could see everything before her! Never in her entire, long life as a Fae had she ever seen anything like the scene before her eyes! She heard Gem panting from the exertion as she brought up the rear – and almost tripped over Lola!

"Lola! What the hell were you thinking? You scared me to death! Don't you ever do anyth…!" Gem started to admonish Lola for running away from her, when she glanced out of the corner of her eye, and realized that they were both standing on a ledge. She grabbed Lola, and backed up against the wall feeling her heart beating so hard, it was about to pound out of her chest! OK. She was afraid of heights! But, Holy Moly! Below her? Blackness! She sank down onto her butt immediately, and Lola climbed into her lap to lick Gem's face. Moments later, an audible "click" was heard, and one by one, lights clicked on to light up the tunnel behind them, and then, the space below them. When enough had lit the room in front of her, she slowly stood with her mouth dropped.

"Lola?" she asked. Realizing her little dog was not much of a talker, Gem set her down. It wasn't a ledge she was on, but it was the top of stone stairs that led down into the most amazing room she had ever seen – a room in a cave! A huge cave – maybe about the size of a football field, and at least as high, was in front of her!

This "room", for lack of a better description, had three sets of staircases: one on the left that led upward to a clear landing that led down to a lower landing, before they wrapped around the left side of the cave, while the right set of stairs led down to another clear landing wrapping around the right side of the cave. The left side had three doors, while the right had only two.

The stairs in front of her wound in a very wide twist as they descended into the "great cave room". She heard little nails on the stone, and realized that Lola had already started down the steps. Gem ran after her.

"Lola! Stop! Wait!" she yelled, which was really dumb. As if Lola would stop!

Gem never liked to go into the unknown, but Lola was always eager to explore new places. Gem just wasn't the kind to leap before she looked. But, she was beginning to rethink that position, now. She followed Lola down the stairs, until she reached the main level. Lola had beat her, of course.

When Gem's mouth had successfully closed after looking around in awe, she looked to the left. To the far end of the room, a giant fireplace – large enough for her to stand upright inside – stood encircled by a cacao colored, leather sectional sofa flanked by two tan, leather recliners. A large, flat top rock in the center served as a coffee table, and set on a rock pedestal. Not a bad idea, either. No coasters needed. Caves always had a tendency to have a lot of moisture, so the stone was a good call. Two tiled and metal (must be aluminum) end tables were placed strategically with one between both recliners, and one at one end of the sectional. Lights were provided by Tiffany lamps that sat on both tables.

A huge, 70" flat screen TV had been installed over the fireplace. Gem wondered where the hell he'd gotten it, and wouldn't it be hurt by the humidity of the cave? That's when she realized that there was no humidity! She wondered how that was possible. Her eyes continued to cross the room, and she saw a huge mahogany, divider had been placed to divide the "media room" from the next part of the cave.

After she had walked around for a few minutes, and years later she wondered how she had missed it the first time, there was a waterfall. OK. That was a mild term for it. It was in the center of the cave, and fell from...Gem's eyes darted upward until she was craning her neck backward to see the source. Her mouth opened in shock. The water was flowing from a relatively small hole in the rock roof that was at least one-hunded and fifty feet high! It cascaded down a succession of rocks that fit together to keep the water flowing downward,which kept it from splashing onto the floor. It emptied into a large, twenty-foot, semi-round hole in the cave floor! For the life of her, she couldn't figure out how it was circulating! The pump would have to be massive! What was even more amazing was that it made very little noise! And, the noise it did make was very soothing.

Shaking her head she looked to the right where a massive kitchen stood in gleaming stainless steel, glass, and stone. She looked for the bright light that illuminated it, but could find none! It was outfitted with everything known to mankind – or womankind – who loved to cook. Since she did like to cook, she was drawn to it. Gem walked to the kitchen, and just stood. A twelve-foot bar of stone and black granite stood in front of her, which looked for all the world as if it had been hand carved! And, the black granite top sported a large, stainless steel sink that was set deeply into it. The granite overlapped the rock, forming a breakfast bar complete with no less than six stools covered in black vinyl with black frames. Or was the fabric actually leather? Everything else was top of the line, and the most expensive of everything. Yep. Leather it was!

Gem also saw several kinds of appliances on top of it. She raked her fingers along the smooth, cool granite as she walked around the bar to the kitchen. The back side of the bar had two dish washers that had been inserted into the rock?

"How the hell?" she wondered, then turned.

The kitchen was in a "U" shape with two of the largest side-by-side refrigerators she had ever seen in her life! To the right of those was a triple sink and then two, large wall ovens – again, set into the rock wall! To the right was a gigantic oven complete with large grill, and eight burners. The glass, black, and stainless steel cabinets completed the kitchen. That's when she realized that there was a large, hanging wine cabinet over the bar with stemmed glasses for all types of different drinks.

Gem stepped onto one of the bar stool's foot rest, and plopped down on it. She put her head in her hands as she continued to look at her surroundings. How was this possible? She looked up to the landings, and presumed that was where the bedrooms were. Maybe an office? Jaxx's bedroom?

"OK. Don't go there unless he's with you, Gem!" she said aloud.

The waterfall was very relaxing to hear, because it appeared that Lola had curled up next to it, and was snoring happily as she slept. A small smile escaped Gem's lips. It would seem Lola had made herself at home in this monstrous cave. Gem stood up, and walked to the media room. She watched some TV for a while, and then, decided to take a nap. She lay down on the sofa, and in seconds, Lola had jumped up onto her legs, so she could wiggle between them and the sofa back. There were several throws, and Gem covered the both of them up with one of them. Listening to the soothing sound of the waterfall, Gem fell sound asleep, and for the first time in her life, she had not one dream.

Jaxx was frantic. Gem had disappeared! The five of them searched the house from top to bottom, and finally they searched the grounds. It took them hours, and finally, they entered the clearing with the shed. One look was all it took to see that the door had been breached. He had an epiphany!

"Wait here," he told the others. "If I'm not back in an hour, I will have found Gem, and well...."

"You're going to mate her, right?" Taylor asked with a smirk on her face.

"Yes, I am. I can't let her go around without my protection any longer."

"OK. Go get your mate, buddy!" Stan slapped Jaxx on the back grinning like the Cheshire Cat in Alice and Wonderland.

When he walked into the shed, the rest of them laughed, turned around, and slowly strolled back to the house. There was no reason for them to wait for Jaxx, let alone Gem. They'd be gone for a while...quite a while!

Jaxx walked into the one place on Earth that was his, and his alone. No other could cross the threshold, and if they did, they would die – even his own kind. But, there was one person who could cross it. His true mate. Only she could enter his warded thresholds, and survive. It would be as if it were he that crossed it.

Entering, he searched quickly for Gem. He didn't see her immediately, but he did hear a little snore. Following it, he found Gem sound asleep on the sofa, and Lola was snuggled up against her, snoring her little pug snore. He was unsure how Lola could have entered, but he assumed it was because of the close ties the two of them had...or maybe dogs were immune to wards. That was a frightening thought, and for a moment that worried him, until he realized that it was just fine, and OK, since she was so protective of Gem. Hmmm. Perhaps they did have the ability to bypass wards.

Noticing that Gem shook a little, he assumed she might be cold, so he built a fire in the gigantic fireplace, then sat on the stone table, and stared at Gem in her sleep. She was a true beauty. Her face was scrubbed clean, and she was innocent in her sleep. Jaxx's mouth quirked his mouth at how her face would look in sleep having been made love to numerous times! And, now, he was ready to find out!

He stood, and kneeled by the sofa. Like Prince Charming kissing Sleeping Beauty, he leaned over and pressed his lips to hers. In a few moments, he felt her lips move against his, and he deepened the kiss.

Gem's eyes flew open when she felt lips on hers, and stared straight into Jaxx's eyes. His lips left hers, but stayed close, so he could slam his mouth into hers again. Her eyebrows went up, and then, a groan that came from deep inside her escaped, and she threw her arms around his neck pulling him to her. Their kiss was not slow or gentle. It was fast, and filled with desire! Just what Gem wanted.

Neither knew how long they lay locked with their lips against each other, but finally, Jaxx raised his head, when he heard a huffing sound. The two of them looked over at Lola whose head was peeking up from between her nice, cuddly place next to Gem, and was glaring at them with a "get a room already" look.

"In other words, Lola is claiming the sofa, and she's telling us to 'get lost'," Gem laughed as Jaxx pulled her to her feet.

"Let me show you my place," he whispered into her ear.

Gem's stomach plummeted to her feet! Just his words could cause her to orgasm! The wetness that suddenly appeared and drenched her panties was testimony to it! Gem turned to give Lola a kiss on her little head, leaving a very happy, and contented Lola snuggling down into the sofa in front of the roaring fire that Jaxx had built. Gem let him lead her to an arch that was just off the kitchen, and down a long corridor. She heard it, before she saw it. Waves upon crashing waves were just ahead. Quietly, they exited another arch, and into....

"Oh. My. God!" Gem breathed quietly as she beheld water. Lots of water. Not just water, but an entire ocean? Her mouth hung open for so long, her mouth became terribly dry.

Gently, Jaxx reached over, and shut her mouth with his hand, and she licked her lips trying to put moisture back into them.

"What do you think?" he asked.

All Gem could do was shake her head.

"Don't you like it?"

Gem nodded her head.

"How?" she whispered. " I had no idea that this kind of thing could be underground!"

"Actually, my love, it's only one of such caches all over the Earth," he told the stunned Gem.

"But, how?" she repeated.

The moment had come that he had been dreading. He had to come clean, and tell her who he really was. Would she shrink from him when he did?

"It's a really long story, Gem," he told her.

"Well, I'm not going anywhere, so give it up, Jaxx!" she demanded.

Well...when your mate demanded something, you gave it!

She stamped her foot!

"Who are you, Jaxx?" she asked, then whispered, "What are you? I'm not going to ask, again, so if you don't tell me what's going on that includes *my life*, them I'm gone!"

Jaxx took her hand, and led her to the pure white sand closer to the ocean. He waved a hand, and a large blanket appeared, a bottle of wine, and some cheese and fruit. He looked at her surprised eyes, grinned and sat down, motioning Gem to do the same. She carefully sat down, keeping eye contact with him at all times. And, it was then, she knew her life was about to change.

"Gem, I'm not from here."

"No kidding! So, where are you from?" she almost snarled. "What are you? A magician?

"No, of course not!" he began, putting up his hand to stop her from asking the obvious questions. "Please, let me finish."

Gem squinted at him in annoyance, but didn't say a word.

"I am very old, Gem. I am older than this planet. Older than the Universe. And, even before this Universe ever existed."

Gem opened her mouth in disbelief, then tried to speak, but she couldn't.

"Long ago, our Creator designed angels. As eons continued, He decided to put a group of beings above us. He was lonely, and wanted beings of his own kind."

"You mean humans?" Gem finally was able to grind the question from her lips. "You're a-a-an angel? Holy shit! I-I mean, Wow!"

He laughed.

"Yes. Unfortunately, I was fooled by one particular angel, as were others, and we joined him in rebelling against the Creator. He cast us from the great expanse, which is what we called it, onto a moon in the newly formed Universe called Anaerra. Within a few thousand years, we were split up onto two moons. Our kind, my kind, survive by drinking blood."

Gem interrupted. "Y-you mean like a-a v-vampire?" she squealed.

"Well, truthfully, the legends about vampires are true, only what many don't realize is that we are angels – fallen, to be sure – but, still angels."

"Holy crap!" she exclaimed then asked herself, *"Seriously Gem? That's all you can come up with?"*

"Yes, well, my moon was called Onaerra. Where Anaerra was the most beautiful place in the Universe, Onaerris was the opposite. It was volcanic in nature." He watched her mouth drop. He watched Gem lean back, and waved his hand for pillows, then continued. "For eons, we provided the Anaerris with precious jewels to build their massive spires! In return, they provided blood for my kind to live," he paused. "You OK so far?"

"Huh?" Was he kidding? The man she loved was an angel vampire, and he asked if she was OK? "Not really, but continue."

"So, many, many hundreds of thousands of years later, the Anaerris, for some reason, stopped providing us with blood, causing a great deal of pain and suffering for my people. Unfortunately, our leader was so corrupted by the lack of blood, he decided that we would invade, and conquer, Anaerra. By the time we did get there, everything was dead...and the moon was completely unliveable. This made our ruler even more angry. There was a great battle to the death. We have special weapons that are the only things that can kill us, and we used them. Blood from both sides filled the moon generously. After a while, my brother, Jolinaer, turned his back on his own people. And, he took a mate. An FYI...angels could not procreate with each other. There were never children. Anyway, the short of it was that several of us on both sides decided to stop the bloodshed. A crystal was given to me, which held the great peach ocean of Anaerra, and..."

"Rewind, and back up, Jaxx! An ocean was put into some crystal? That must be some crystal!"

"You bet. It's about the size of your beautiful hand!" Jaxx took her hand and kissed it, making Gem shudder.

"Now wait a minute! You are saying that an entire ocean was placed inside a crystal that fit in you hand? Come on, Jaxx!"

"It's true, my love. Now, let me continue!" He grinned when she stuck out her tongue in a juvenile move, but with a smirk. "My brother and his mate, who was Anaerris, entrusted me with that crystal, and I came to Earth, at their request, along with several other friends...Taryln and Stanarak, to name two of them. Jumping forward, the lot of us set ourselves up as gods to the humans. Stanarak, and I guess you have already realized that it is Stan, became my second in command on Atlantis, where we settled, then...."

"Atlantis??" squeaked Gem.

"Yes. It was real, "he told her, answering her next question. "Anyway, one of our own found a human female, Cleito, and married her. She actually had five sets of twin children! We were all shocked that we were compatible with humans, and that for the first time, we could procreate! Many of us went a little nuts, and had tons of kids, then...," seeing her eye narrow in anger, "and, no, Gem. I never had another woman, so get that idea out of your head right now! Now, as time went on, I replaced Azor, who held the title of the original Poseidon, and took over the persona. I ruled the Earth's oceans. I put the crystal in a statue, made in my honor by my subjects, then an earthquake hit Atlantis, the first of many. The statue toppled with subsequent quakes, and the crystal cracked, pouring the entire peach sea into the

Atlantic, causing the immediate rise of the oceans, and inundating Atlantis. In the process, the pressure on the Earth's crust increased due to the peach ocean, and massive earthquakes resulted, followed by massive rain for about forty days. When the fountains of the deep opened up, and released the interior oceans and lakes, the gaps left inside the Earth, later also served as a 'drain'. Many caverns either collapsed, remained intact, or new ones were formed. This one you see before you is one of those that remained intact, and this is just one such ocean. Unfortunately, afterward, the drains were not as large or numerous, so, the oceans of Earth rose many feet even after draining into the fissures and caves," he told her. "By the end of this, and after what water did drain away, the entire topography had changed. Ages went on, gods fell by the wayside, and we just began to blend into the human population. Some of the past ice ages were actually due to this mixing of the oceans. This fountain is a filter that I perfected after thousands of years."

"Wait a sec! Are you telling me – that is the ocean – *the Atlantic Ocean* – flowing through the main room?" she asked as her voice raised a notch higher.

"I tell you that I used to be Poseidon, ruled Atlantis, caused the Flood, survived the Flood, and *that* is what you got out of all of that?" he smirked. She stuck out her tongue, again. And, what a beautiful tongue it was! He almost leaned forward and grabbed it with his mouth! His arousal was already huge, but, instead, "Pretty much, and it's filtering out the peach ocean from the waters of the deep," he answered her question.

At that point, all she could really register was that she was in love with the god, Poseidon!

"*Poseidon.* Where is your pitchfork?" she laughed.

"It's a *Trident!*"

"Pitchfork; trident; it's all the same!" she giggled.

OK. He'd play along! "Well, it's actually in my bedroom. I keep it to remind me that arrogance leads to destruction. I'll show it to you. To continue, you see, the peach ocean is more dense than the waters of Earth. As I said, I established a type of filter that is filtering the peach ocean from Earth's oceans, and that is what is happening as it flows into the cave. There are two 'drains' underneath. One filters off the denser peach ocean while the other flows back into the ocean itself. In other words...I'm separating the oceans. It was not for the peach ocean to join with the Earth's oceans. They are not compatible. As I filter it, that is what is causing a lot of weather anomalies. Unfortunately, it's possible it will take another fifty to a hundred years to completely be separated. It's been filtering for at least six thousand years so far. It's almost done."

He watched several emotions alternately flash in her eyes.

"I don't know what to believe, or what to even say. I mean...what can I say about this whole thing? I stumbled into all of this supernatural stuff, and wait! You said I died? So, how am I still here?" she asked him.

"Ah, my lovely, sexy little Gem! There is a very logical reason why," he began.

"And, that would be…what?" she asked.

"Why, Gem! Have you really not figured that out?"

Oh, she had, and she had discounted it immediately. There was no way she was one of them! Nope. Not happening. So Jaxx did the only thing he could do.

"You are one of us, Gem, or more accurately...you are the legend of a prophecy."

Gem's eyes were wide with wonder, terror, and surprise. She turned, and her eyes met his, her mouth gaping, and her head shaking.

"Come on, Gem! You are one of us. You are obviously not human. How else do you explain that you were impaled one minute, and the next, you were completely healed?"

OK. When he put it *that* way, Gem still hadn't been able to accept it. Oh, piddle! She needed a distraction at the moment to keep her from dwelling on the facts.

Frustration at not having Jaxx inside of her yet, grew in seconds. The ocean forgotten, on purpose, she took a step toward him.

Jaxx couldn't wait any longer. His cock was hard, and ready. He yanked her into his arms, and slammed his lips down on hers in another erotic, sensual, and exciting kiss.

Gem melted into his embrace feeling moisture pool in her panties, and they were wetter than ever. She reached around his neck to pull him tighter against her. She felt his huge erection grinding against her stomach, and pushed back against it, undulating her own body while she groaned in deep desire.

Jaxx broke off the kiss.

"Now, Gem. I can't wait any longer."

Gem nodded as he picked her up in his arms, and ran at his preternatural speed to one of the doors on the lower landing.

He placed her on his huge bed that was twice the size of a normal king – she really didn't want to think about why – and climbed in next to her. Gem stretched like a cat in heat. And, in truth, that's exactly how she felt! She felt as if she was in heat. She pulled him onto her body, and he slammed his mouth into hers again and again. His tongue dove into her mouth, letting his hand cup her breast. When she felt his fingers pinching her nipple, she arched hard against him.

Jaxx was in heaven! Her nipple was hard under her bra, but he could feel it easily. He needed more. He needed her naked under him. He needed to slide between her legs, thrust his extremely hard cock into his mate, and release his seed into her womb.

In seconds, his hand found its way underneath her shirt pushing her bra out of the way so that he could feel her naked breast and nipple. He groaned as he felt the bud harden at his touch as he gently pulled, and flipped it.

"Jaxx!" Gem cried.

He raised his head, and his bright red eyes glowed as they stared into hers. Gem wasn't scared at all. His red eyes were a huge aphrodisiac!

Panting, Jaxx begged, "Tell me, Gem. Tell me what you want. I want to hear the words from your lips."

"You mean you want dirty talk?" she teased him.

"Very dirty talk," he grinned back at her.

Gem craved to feel his hot, naked chest against her soft breasts with their hardened tips. Her panties were thoroughly soaked, and could no longer hold her juices. She felt her womb clench, pumping the precious liquid from her body, and down her thighs. The wetness poured even more heavily as her womb prepared her for his entry into her body. She desired him; ached for him. Needed it like she needed to breathe!

"Jaxx! Touch me, please!" Her tone was desperate for his touch.

He pulled back, looking into her eyes heavy with desire.

"Where? Where do you want me to touch you," he asked breathlessly.

"My clit! OH! Please! Touch my clit!"

His cock grew even larger as he heard her use the word, and he could feel his own liquid flowing from his tip. He so wanted her to suck the droplets.

"You need to know, Gem, if I touch your clit and feel your wetness that I can't stop?"

She nodded her head.

"I understand!" she whispered. "But, I don't want you to stop. Take me! Make me yours!"

Jaxx backed off, and released his claws. Her eyes widened when she saw them extend from his fingers. He gave her a very devilish grin, and watched in wonder as he used them to rip her clothing from her body without scratching her. He grabbed her panties tearing them into pieces, until she lay naked before him. His red eyes raked over her nude body, lingering on her breasts and red pubic hair that hid her sex from him. He lay beside her, and his mouth sank down onto one of her nipples, licking and suckling gently.

Gem arched against his mouth! Nothing was as decadent as lying naked in front of him while he was still clothed! She had never felt anything like this! Each suckle combined with each lick of her hard nipples sent waves of throbbing through her womb! Liquid fire poured, and she squirmed against him, begging him for entry.

There was no way that Jaxx could hold back any longer. He needed to feel and to see her opening soaked with her juices, so he reached down.

"Spread your legs for me, Gem," he murmured softly. "I want to see your pussy! Feel it! Taste it!"

Without question, her legs drew upward, and she let her knees fall apart, opening herself to him. He began to suckle her other breast as his fingers slowly circled her clit, pinching it between his thumb and forefinger with just the right pressure, causing her to yell out his name. It was swollen with need, and he felt her muscles contract. Jaxx slipped one finger inside of her, and Gem scream his name, when two more joined the first one as they sank deeply within her. He moved them in and out without stopping, feeling her clutch them, and throb against them, while her body softened for his cock. His cock was hard, and he felt explosive at the thought he would be ramming it up her in minutes!

"Gem! You are are so fucking wet!" he moaned against her nipple, his breath causing her to squirm with need.

Raising his head, he looked at Gem. Her eyes were closed, and her moans came quickly along with her breathing.

"Open your eyes, Gem. Look at me," he demanded. "I want to see your eyes when I take you!"

Her eyes opened, and he caught his breath! They were a beautiful red, now, filled with desire.

Gem was panting and forgot to breathe at his words. That's when she realized that she didn't need to breathe at all.

"I want to put my cock inside of you," Jaxx whispered.

"Yes!" she cried quietly.

"Thank the Creator!"

In seconds, he was nude. He climbed over her, and pushed her legs apart.

"Wrap your legs around my waist."

Gem did as he asked, and in one, swift thrust, Jaxx buried himself inside of her, hearing her scream his name. Because he was so large, her slick channel needed time to fit him. He stayed still, but his lips came down on hers, filling a lustful need within his own body. He never knew what he had been missing! His mate was beautiful, smart, a bit funky, and had a true, loving heart. Her green eyes attested that she was Anaerris, but her red eyes told him that she was something else. But, what? Well, he'd figure that out later. In the back of his mind, he wondered if she could be a combination of the two races. As far as he knew, none of them had the ability to procreate, but he pushed that to the back of his mind as he felt her walls begin to squeeze his cock. Jaxx lost all thought as he began to move slowly in and out of her. His need to release was great, but he wanted it to be memorable! Once his seed was planted into her womb, she would be his mate forever. He didn't stop to wonder if she was as immortal as he was, and in truth, it didn't matter at all. All that was needed at the moment of their first coupling was his release, and he would share his immortality with her. His only regret was that he was sterile, and his seed would not produce their child. He wanted to impregnate her desperately.

Gem couldn't believe this was happening to her! She had never dreamed that she would lay below a man, and feel him move inside of her! But, here he was...Jaxx...the most perfect specimen of a man she had ever met! Her slick sheathe contracted around his cock, and squeezed it tightly. She heard him moan loudly, and she followed as she screamed his name several times. His strokes became more frantic. Gem felt him move all the way out, and slam back into her. She needed his seed! Now!

"Jaxx!!!" she cried. "Please! Please!"

"Oh, Gem!" he cried, feeling his imminent orgasm.

"Fill me!"

Speech was forgotten as he slammed and pounded into her body with such force, she inched toward the headboard with each desperate thrust. Suddenly, Gem felt her womb tighten and throb hard, and she felt her first orgasm burst forth.

Jaxx's balls tightened, and he felt his seed flow into his cock, exploding his semen into her body. With each thrust, more seed was propelled into her.

Gem's body felt the huge, violent jets of hot semen deep inside her. She thrust upward as he thrust downward, causing their naked flesh to slap in union which echoed throughout the room.

"Oh, Creator!" Jaxx cried.

She grabbed his ass, and squeezed it as he pounded away inside of her. She had never felt such desperate need! Over and over he slammed into her. That's when she felt it. A change not only in her own body, but in his. With his last thrust, he collapsed upon her, but held himself up to keep from crushing her. Her red eyes flew open, and met his red ones. She was filled with thoughts not her own, and she felt hers fill him as well. Ancient thoughts flew through her mind of beauty and war and the end of a world and an entire race of people! He saw her eyes fill with water, tears flowing down her face.

Jaxx had forgotten that once they were mated, she would receive all of his thoughts, and he, hers. What a stupid thing for him to forget! He watched her eyes open wider and wider, and tears filled his eyes at what he knew she saw. He should have told her, before he took her! That was his responsibility, and he had failed. He hung his head in shame, then rolled off her onto his back, his erection still large, but his balls empty for the moment. He flung his arm over his eyes.

"I'm sorry, Gem," he told her, shaking his head. "I should have explained."

Gem frowned.

"Sorry? For what? Fucking me?" she said angrily, and started to get out of bed.

As if he made no move at all, Jaxx penned Gem's body underneath him slamming his mouth into hers. His mouth was brutal against hers, and her hands rose to his head to press him even closer! She never wanted to be anywhere else but right here. He tore his mouth from hers, and stared into her eyes. He wanted to make sure she understood what he was about to say.

"Do not *ever* say that we fuck, again! We made love. Lust-filled, yes, but it was still love. I did not fuck you!" he told her, slamming his mouth against hers, again. This time, though, he relaxed his lips, and his kiss turned into one of tenderness and love. He raised his head to look at her stunned face.

"You are mine. I am yours. You are my mate."

She turned her head in surprise.

"I'm your what?" she almost yelped.

Jaxx grinned with tolerance.

"My mate. You see my thoughts, right?"

She nodded.

"And, I, yours."

"I don't understand."

"There are three stages to our kind of mating, my love. The first was when I poured my semen into your womb. We are connected together physically, and you now have my immortality."

"Immortality?" Gem parroted. "What do you mean by that?"

"It means, like me, you will live as long as I."

"And, how long is that? Just how old are you?"

"I'm old enough that I do not remember."

Gem gaped before she stuttered.

"A-and t-the second?" she stammered, still trying to process what he was saying.

"The transfer of our minds to each other, which, as you can see, has already been done. It's unusual for it to happen during intercourse, though. I don't understand why. But, regardless, we are connected mentally."

"And, third?" Gem was almost afraid to hear the answer to this one. She was right.

He closed his eyes. This one wasn't going to be easy to tell her, and he figured the best way to tell her was to just blurt it out without thinking about it.

"Blood," he answered.

~ 11 ~

"Mating with a fallen angel? Who'da thunk? Right? Not Me!" ~ Gem

Gem shot bolt upright at the word.

"Blood? What? You are a vampire!" she finally asked, having had the question on her tongue for the last few days. "Are you going to drain me? Are you going to drink my blood?"

"Huh?" he asked stunned.

"A bite! Isn't that what you – mean?" she ended in a whisper. She was almost afraid of his answer, yet excited at the same time, so she just had to joke about it.

"Yes, but the bite won't just come from me, Gem. It will also come from you!" he told her watching her mouth drop, and her head began to shake. "Yes. Now, Gem, tell me what your mind sees," he ordered.

"But, I…"

"Please?"

"Weeelll, OK. But, whatever happened to the relaxation stuff after sex?" she muttered.

"Permanent bonding will not be completed until all three of the steps are finished. It will come as soon as you accept my thoughts. Now, close your eyes, and I'll walk you through it, and what it means," he told her. "Now, my love, tell me what you see."

Gem shut her eyes, and her thoughts began to arrange into a pattern.

"Hmmmm. Let me see. Yes! I see…a beautiful landscape," she began.

"Tell me."

"Well…I see three planets?"

"Moons," Jaxx corrected gently.

"Whatever," she snipped. "Well, one of the plan...I mean, moons...is streaked with pink – uh, well, it looks like pink or lavender ice, while the other moon is mostly black and blood red."

"Go on."

"OK! OK! Stop being a nag!" she grinned. Jaxx said nothing. "Now! Let me see.... It's covered in aqua and green, and...a peach ocean!" she exclaimed, opening her eyes in shock. "Are you telling me that is what the peach ocean looked like?"

He nodded, still not speaking. Gem closed her eyes, again.

"It's so beautiful!"

"It was – once," he answered with sadness. "Go on."

"Spires! I see spires of every shape and color! Like jeweled structures! Blues, pinks, reds, greens, silvers, golds, purples, and several other colors that I have no name to give them! Each vary in height. Some reach high into the sky, and beyond the clouds, but beautiful all the same. There are rolling hills with lavender grass – or what looks like grass!"

Listening to her describe it, he felt the nostalgia combined with anger and longing. She continued.

"I see some type of conveyance. It looks like a glass tube that encircles the city of spires as if it were a roller coaster."

She turned to him in shock, her eyes flying open. He didn't need to see her reaction. He knew it.

"Where?" she asked, stunned by what she saw in his mind.

"What you are seeing, Gem, are three moons – Anaerra, Onaerra, and Domaerra. But, your dream is about Anaerra. It was, once, the gem of the Milky Way Galaxy long ago, and it was a place of peace, learning, and cooperation for eons – much like your city of

Alexandria, Egypt, and it's magnificent library. In fact, it had been a center of learning for so long, even I don't remember how old it truly was. It was before the banishment, obviously."

He stopped to look at her as her eyebrows went up in question. She almost said something, but stopped waiting for him to continue.

"There were three moons, which circled an ancient gas giant planet that has no name."

"Why?" Gem asked him.

"Huh? Oh. Well, I don't know. Just never thought about it, I guess!"

Gem tipped her head sideways, and gave him a "your giving me a load of crap" look. He ignored it. So, she asked the next obvious question.

"What? You mean, like it was a potential sun like Jupiter was in the movie, 2012?"

"Well, that's a fair appraisal, I guess."

"So, why were they so different?"

"Domaerra, the lavender and white moon, literally is made of a lavender ice. The lifeforms on it, if they still exist that is, were quite docile when we were there. Been a really long time! They have no animosity or anger in them. Their looks were quite different than the humanoid forms that were placed on Anaerra and Onaerra, because they were indigenous, whereas we were not."

"They sound really interesting. So, what do, uh, did, they look like?" Gem was really curious, now.

"Hmmm," Jaxx began. Gem could see that he was trying to figure out how to tell her. "I guess, the closest resemblance on Earth is the platypus, but with a body that stood upright, covered in lavender-pink fur, and they were only about two and a half feet tall."

"You mean live stuffed animals?" Gem asked in surprise with a little giggle. Jaxx smiled.

"Yes. You could say that they are like that, except that they have pale eyes, and without the benefit of pupils, they could see extremely well. Oh...and they had extremely long nails which could slice through anything easily. They were designed to slice through solid ice without effort in order to eat the creatures in the ancient frozen ocean that were under the ice. In addition, their bills were also very sharp, and could 'drill' into the ice quite easily as well."

"Sounds like they might have been a cute pet animal," she grinned even larger at the vision that popped into her mind's eye.

"Close enough, but they are not pets. Never could be. They were sentient beings, who were kind, and loved everyone, thus, we were forced to leave them alone. The Creator ordered it so."

"OK. So, what about the red moon?" she asked.

His red eyes stared into hers with such great sadness, Gem felt deep sympathy.

"I was placed on Onaerra. There were no indigenous beings there, just as there were none on Anaerra. Many thousands of eons later, we were basically divided based upon our physical characteristics, and my people were 'dumped' on Onaerris. The rest were lucky, and allowed to stay on Anaerris." The memory of why caused Jaxx's face to briefly morph into a sadness that he knew would always be with him. Gem saw that brief look, but let it go...for now. He continued. "The moon was the antithesis of Domaerra. It was hot. Volcanic hot. Lava dotted the landscape with little land for us to live. The majority of it was blackened lava. But, unlike on Earth where lava eventually springs up new life, on Onaerra, it did not. And, last, there was Anaerra, also without indigenous peoples. It was a true jewel of the universe, with its peach ocean, jade and purple grasses and mountains. The climate was beautiful. Never too hot or too cold – a mild and temperate climate."

Jaxx threw his arms behind his head on the pillow, and stared at the ceiling as he spoke, his mind taking him back as if it were yesterday, instead of thousands of years ago.

By this time, Gem was so fascinated, she forgot all about their nudity as she sat cross-legged on the large bed. She propped her elbows on her knees, and put her head in her hands. Then, a thought occurred to her.

"Wait. You said that the Domaerra's beings were indigenous, but you guys were not. So...how did all of you come to be on the other two moons?" she asked.

Without answering her question, he continued.

"It's probably a story that you, and others on Earth, will recognize. We were a violent race, and believed that we had been short-changed by the Creator, long before we ended up on Onaerris. When we, uh, broke the rules, we were thrown out of paradise, and onto Anaerra. Those who had been given the moon of Anaerra, were not punished as badly as we, because they were not quite as bad. Conquering other worlds was our biggest desire, and our fangs made doing so, quite easy. And, we did it quite well, before we were 'dumped' on Onaerris with no way off of it. Our ability to leave the moons was ended, but every day we were bombarded by the beauty, and coolness of Anaerris, which we saw every day above us. We desired, more than everything else, to take Anaerris. We were angry, jealous, and hate was deep within our souls, Gem. So, we waited countless eons for our chance to kill and destroy. After all, why should the Anaerris have the best world? They were the same as us."

"Uh-oh!" thought Gem, as she began to realize what, and who, he was talking about when he had said "Creator". She gulped, and pushed down her rising panic,

hoping that she was wrong. *"Yeah. Right. Keep thinking that, Gem,"* she told herself knowing, but trying to ignore the outcome.

Jaxx kept talking not noticing Gem's hesitation.

"The Anaerris evolved into beings who desired knowledge above all else, while the bitterness and anger of my people increased exponentially over the endless time that awaited us. At some point, and no one knows why or how, the discovery of ancient documents changed everything on Anaerris. They buried themselves deeply in these documents, studied them, and they learned much. Eventually, a select group were given the right to leave their world, but only to select worlds and other realms – one of those being Earth. Until, finally, our chance came. One of the Anaerris was in the select group, and she betrayed her own world, because she desired to become Onaerris."

Gem began to frown. A traitor? Who….

"Delinear!" she exclaimed.

There was a catch to it. She just knew it! She didn't have to wait long.

"Yes. I was right with my people. I had the same hate and anger toward the Anaerris. But, that changed, and to my undying shame, and a few others of my kind, we did not stop the invasion. But, there was nothing left at all, except a river filled with the blood of not only Anaerris, but Onaerris warriors. We fought for well over a thousand years on the blackened land, but in the end, the Anaerris could not stand up to us."

"Why? Why would you want to kill them?" she asked him sadly. A new thought came to her. "The peach ocean? You made no mention of it. What happened? I mean, how could an *ocean* disappear?"

"I'll try to answer your questions in order. Because my people are lovers of blood. Blood lust is what feeds us, and drives us to attack. We need blood to live, and are unable to live without it," he answered. "Look. You know of Earth's mythologies? Gods, and other mythical creatures?"

She nodded, not getting what he was saying.

"As I said before, one part of those myths is definitely a fact. We would be referred to as the 'Fallen' in your language," he began, when she stopped him.

Leaning on her elbow, she turned toward him.

"Hold it! The 'fallen'? As in 'angels'? Those fallen?" Her voice was stunned. "Are you telling me, that you followed *Lucifer*?"

"Yes. You see, on our moons, our magic was prohibited by the Creator, and because the radiation from that sun, stopped our abilities. The Anaerris were also severely incapacitated as well, but not completely. Anyway, during the battle, some of the other Onaerris and I began to realize that the Anaerris were no threat to us, as we had been led to believe. Along with some others from Anaerris, we joined those who also wanted no part of war. Together, we plotted to end the invasion," he told her. His eyes glassed over as he remembered the sacrifices they all had made.

As he told her the story, the pictures appeared in her own mind.

"Go on," she urged. This was far too interesting to her. Strange? Surprising? Yes, but fascinating!

He looked at her, seemingly oblivious to her naked body as well.

"Right. There were six of us who were the leaders of the rebellion. They were..."

Gem interjected, because she knew exactly who two of them were.

"You, Taylor, Stan, and who else?" she asked him.

Jaxx smiled at her. She was intuitive, too.

"Kulana and her mate, Faerron."

"But, that's only four, Jaxx. Who were the other two?

"The last two were a shock to me, because none of us knew who they were – not even Kulana or Faerron. I certainly was not prepared, nor would I ever have believed it was possible," he began, surprised by his own words. "Our greatest warrior of all, Jolinaer, fell in love with the daughter of the great house of Anaerris, and she with him. Analyse was her name. Their love bridged the gap between all of us, and it was they who actually started the rebellion, together. It was not until a while later that I learned of the identities of who actually started it. But, still they helped found the movement to forge an alliance. Together with a few others from both moons, we put our plan into action to end the war. Unfortunately, it would leave most of the Anaerris and Onaerris dead." Jaxx's voice was quiet with remorse. His sad eyes raised to hers. "We were too late to stop the massacre."

When she sat up suddenly, her heavy breasts slightly bounced. His hungry eyes stared at them, as his hands rose to cup one of them. But, she wasn't having it. Nope! She grabbed his chin, and yanked his eyes up to meet hers. They were green, again.

"No. You don't get to fondle my boobs! Forget them for the moment!" His eyes darted back up to hers. "How did you plot all of that? I mean...if you didn't know who the leaders were at first, then how…."

He battled his libido trying to keep his eyes on hers.

"It isn't the how, Gem. It was the who, and the why," he told her, gasping as his need gripped him, his arousal growing by the second. "Let's talk about this later, Gem. Your arousal smells so good to me! I need you, again," he told her, pulling her head down to place his mouth onto hers.

A thought entered her mind, and she pushed him away from her.

"Wait a second! Let me get all this straight. I am your 'mate', whatever the hell does that mean? We had sex..."

"Made love..." he interjected.

"...whatever. I want to know the rest."

"Later," he whispered dragging her lips against his. His eyes raked over her gorgeous, nude body, and he pointed at the lower half of his male anatomy that was quite large. "Gem, I just can't concentrate until I have you, again, see?"

"But…," she began, before his soft lips silenced her.

Gem was scared. She didn't want to be "mated", or connected to anyone, and yet…she couldn't deny that she was crazy about Jaxx. But, did she love him, or was their monster sex-a-thon the reason? Even now, she was ready for him. Her body let loose a flood of their precious liquid onto the sheets. She wanted more of his seed within her just as much as she knew he wanted to spill it into her. Once made, it would be forever.

Jaxx pulled her down onto his chest, and she automatically straddled his massive manhood, her wetness sliding along his massive cock. Gem's sex was so sensitive, that she couldn't resist him any longer, and her tongue darted into his open mouth as did his into hers. She felt him grab her ass, and lift her up gently. Without thinking, she automatically impaled her wet channel onto his massive hard-on, and began to move up and down slowly. She removed herself from his body, and slammed herself back down onto his cock. She felt her breasts bounce hard as she picked up speed. She felt Jaxx grip them, and gently rub her hardened nipples with his incredible hands and fingers! She needed more, so she leaned down over him, and brushed a nipple at his mouth.

He opened it, grabbed the hard bud, and began to suckle her.

"More, Jaxx! Harder!" she gasped in pleasure.

Jaxx had no option but to obey her, and do exactly as she had requested. He sucked the nipple deeper into his mouth. The taste of her drugged his senses along with her moving up and down hard and fast on him! He felt his hips slam his cock deeper as she came down on it, and the slapping of skin sounded in the room so loudly only egged them on to more.

"Gem! You taste so good!" he told her, before grabbing the other nipple and suckling it.

"You feel so good inside of me, Jaxx! Harder!" she begged, again.

Jaxx obliged his mate, and rammed himself even harder into her body, convinced that she would be black and blue after he was finished, but he didn't care! It was time to share their blood, and he felt his fangs descend.

Gem's eyes grew wide as she watched his fangs descend from his mouth, and she stopped moving. She gasped as his mouth gripped her nipple. Surprised gripped her.

"Demon?" she gasped, as she felt the points gently scrape her breast. "Y-you really are a Demon?"

His bright red eyes held her gaze. His mouth drew back over his fangs in a smirk.

"A bit more like an angel who fell into becoming a demon! Do you object to me? To all intents and purposes, I am a demon, and this demon wants to mate with you!" he told her, as he thrust up inside of her. "You are my mate – my other half – my wife. So, what are you going to do about it, mate?" he whispered against her breast, his eyes staring up at her. "Well?"

Shouldn't that scare her? But, instead, his eyes and fangs just made her hornier? She didn't stop to ask why, slammed onto him harder, which made his fangs continue to scrape her breast gently. It was the sexiest thing she had ever seen, or felt! His eyes were red, his fangs were snow white, and very long. Suddenly, she desired nothing more than for him to sink them into her anywhere he wanted!

She leaned down to his ear.

"No! I am your mate, Jaxx! I understand, now. So, bite me, already!" she whispered to him. "Bite my tit. I want to feel your fangs pierce my flesh! Take the blood I give to you freely!"

Jaxx looked into her red eyes. Did she not understand? He suspected that she might be like him in some way. Unlike him, though, she was obviously only half-Demon, but there as no denying that she was also an angel! He had no idea what that entailed at the moment, but he needed her fangs in him as well. But, they had yet to descend. So, while he waited for them, why not bite her? Nothing gave him a greater desire than to sink his teeth into her white, delicious flesh, while he shot his seed into her body!

"Please!" she begged again, and held one breast to his lips.

He couldn't resist, and he began to suckle her nipple, again, gently. His hips came up harder with each thrust. Her pussy was drenched in their juices, and his seed drove him harder and deeper into her slick sheathe. And, then, he opened his mouth, and sank his fangs into her breast deeply. Her blood leaked into his mouth, making his cock slam into her body with gusto! He heard her scream his name with each suckle of her blood, as they each met their thrusts with such force, the bed sounded as if it was going to collapse.

"Jaxx!!!" she screamed.

"Gem!!!" he screamed, but was unaware that he did.

Gem didn't know she could behave with this abandon! It both excited, and shocked her when she felt his fangs sink into her flesh, and began to suckle not only her nipple, but blood from her. She flew into a animalistic frenzy when she felt his cock slam even harder into her, and his suckling scorched her skin with each suckle. That's when she realized that something was cutting into her lower lip drawing blood. Her tongue slid over her own fangs! Surprised, she stopped moving, and he opened his eyes. Her fangs had descended! Thank the Creator! He didn't know if he could wait!

He stopped sucking her blood, allowing a small trickle of blood from both wounds to slide down her breast. Taking his finger, Jaxx stroked her fangs. That did it! She began to move frantically.

"Gem! Bite me...here," he told her pointing to his carotid artery.

"But, won't that..." she began.

"It's what Demons do, Gem, when they mate."

"But, I thought they did that to humans to drain them? And, I'm not a demon!" she disagreed while panting like some animal.

"Oh, my sweet, Gem. You are also part Demon!" he stroked her fangs, again, illiciting a loud groan from her lips. I'll tell you the rest, but right now, mate with me! Drink from me, Gem! Make me your mate!" he begged her. He was desperate for her to say yes!

Despite her horror over his words, she knew she wouldn't stop! Of her own accord, as if she had been doing it forever, Gem draped her head into his neck. Her red hair spilled over his neck. She could smell the blood, and feel the pulse where it was strongest. She licked her lips and fangs, needing his life source desperately. She opened her mouth, and pierced his artery. A flood of sweet cinnamon bathed her mouth as she tasted his hot blood. She moaned. He continued to pound into her, and she met his thrusts equally as she drank from him, making him her mate forever. It was instinctive, and the best food she had ever had! She needed to feel his fangs in her neck, and wasn't disappointed when she felt two sharp pricks, and then, something happened that gave her nothing but the most physical and mental joy she had ever had as he drank her blood. The merging of their minds became total just as he had said would happen. She knew everything he had ever known. His age, what he had seen, what had happened, both bad and good, and it awakened memories within her mind that she knew had been passed to her by her real parents. This, she shared with her mate as well as her life blood.

In moments, her womb flooded with something else. Something she had never felt. It was hot, thick, and it felt as if a dam had broken, letting loose all the liquid in her body.

"Gem!" he yelled. A very strange pain gripped his balls, and they filled, until it felt as if they would burst under the pressure! When they let loose, it was like a pressure washer that had been turned on high a thousand times over. He shoved his cock deeper and deeper with each release of his seed. He desperately drove on to reach her womb!

Surprising them both, Gem felt Jaxx pierce her cervix, and enter her womb! She jerked when she felt his cock touch the inside of her womb, only driving her to demand more! She began to slam herself even harder onto his cock. They both released their necks at the same time, their wounds healing immediately

"Fill me! Fill me with your seed!" Gem ordered, throwing her head back in ecstasy.

"I don't understand how I could be inside your womb, but it's the most amazing feeling I've ever had. It just feels so right!"

"I know!" she gasped, allowing her fangs to draw blood from her lip.

He lost all track of time as he pounded into her womb for a very long time, his balls continually filling with each thrust until they stopped. Finally, he felt the last drop burst from him, and Gem collapsed onto his chest feeling a massive amount of fluid flooding through her channel, even though he was still inside of her. Suddenly, she was completely exhausted.

"Jaxx, I love you!" she whispered to him in surprise.

He smiled deeply when he saw her eyes close as she entered the Dreaming. She was in for a huge surprise!

"And, I love you, too, my mate. Close your eyes, now, and sleep, my love. When we awake from the Dreaming, our mating will be completed, and a whole new life for both of us will begin."

"Hmmmm? The D-d-dreaming?" she whispered, while she fell into a delicious unconscious state.

A tiny smile lifted her lips, and he kissed her forehead as he, too, fell asleep. The only time a Demon would sleep was after he mated with his one, true mate. They would experience much more in the "Dreaming" that would befall both of them. Still inside of her, they both fell into a very deep sleep, and he began to share with her his life through a mind-link that had formed between them. When they awoke, they would feed from each other, and then would continue to do so for the rest of their existence together, sustaining them both.

Gem was dreaming beautiful dreams. She had never experienced anything as magnificent as the sex she had with Jaxx! Was that a dream, or was this? It didn't matter. She was sated, and relaxed as she had never been!

Suddenly, she was standing on the lavender, rolling hills of Anaerris.   In seconds, arms wrapped around her, cupping her breasts. Looking up into the sky with two moons above, she sighed. Then, she looked down, and her eyes widened in shock! She was completely naked! Out in front of the Creator and everyone to boot! And, Gem didn't give a damn about it! She felt his hardness rubbing against her crack, and pushed her hips against him. She placed her hands over his, feeling him caress her nipples lightly, exciting her all over again!

"Jaxx," she breathed. "How is this happening?"

"It is called the 'Dreaming', Gem. The time when you and I will seal our bond forever." He frowned. He hadn't considered even asking her. He had just assumed that she had agreed! But, she hadn't. "Gem, I know I never, officially, asked you to bond with me. I am truly sorry. I was so excited to be with you forever, it never occurred to me that you might not feel the same."

Slowly, Gem turned making sure she remained in full contact with his body. Her curls pressed against his cock, and she flexed to push against him. She wanted him to know that this was what she wanted, too.

"I want this, too, Jaxx. I don't understand why, but I do!" She reached up to kiss him, pushing her hard nipples against his bare chest. Then, whispered, "How can this happening? And, can we make love here?"

He laughed. She was so eager to have him inside of her again – and he wasn't about to disappoint.

"We can do anything we want to here, Gem. Your mind is joined with mine, and you are with me at a time of peace. Tell me what you want me to do?" He wanted to hear it from her lips. "Here, we can say and do anything at all."

"Really?" she asked him, a slow grin appearing, her fangs descending.

"Really," he whispered back to her. "Any fantasies can be realized in the Dreaming."

"Oh! Well, then...I always had this one since we met?" she began in embarrassment.

"There is no need to be embarrassed here. Now, what would your fantasy be?" he urged her. "Ask anything of me."

"I want – uh – well, you see...um...I want you to – um – lick me?" she finished softly, her face beet red.

He grinned wickedly at her, and she knew he wanted her to say it.

"*Where* do you want me to lick you?" he asked softly with a conceited smirk.

"You're really going to make me say it?" she asked, and playfully slapped his arm.

"What do you think? I want to hear you ask for it," he laughed with his lips trailing up and down her shoulder.

"Well, uh, I-I want you to lick my pussy," she finished, her voice almost too low for him to hear, but he did.

He wrapped his arms tightly around her drawing her to the ground. The soft grass felt like velvet to her back as he laid her down.

"While this is happening in our minds, I can assure you that when we awake, what I am doing to you, now, I will do to you, then. And, I will eat your pussy as much as you want my beautiful, sexy mate! I want to taste you! But, on one condition?"

She panted in anticipation.

"Anything!"

"My fantasy?"

She smiled. "What is it?"

"Will you suck my cock?" he whispered.

Juices poured from her when he said it, and her mouth watered. She wanted to suck him. To lick his slit as it oozed his liquid. She wanted him to explode inside of her mouth. To taste his essence of love!

"Deal!" she agreed with her own smirk.

Slowly, Jaxx lay down onto her body, kissing her deeply. Next, he moved down to her nipples, and grasping one in his mouth, he sucked hard. His fangs descended, and she arched hard under him. In seconds, she felt his fangs bury into her flesh on either side of her nipple, and her blood flowed into his mouth, again. She was so excited, she moaned and wiggled under him, needing him inside of her.

"Not yet, my love. I am going to feast on every part of you," he told her.

The wounds healed as he moved downward, burying his lips and face in her curls that hid her sex. then, Jaxx slipped his hands between her thighs. "Open your legs to me, Gem."

She gasped, and eagerly opened her thighs. His face and mouth slid underneath her as he placed his hands under her hips lifting her to his view. For several moments, his eyes feasted on her shining, wet, and swollen sex.

"Your pussy is so beautiful, Gem!" his voice was almost reverent.

Bending his head, Jaxx's tongue flipped out and licked the juices that coated her wet, ripe, and swollen bud, before it dove inside of her. Gem cried out as her eyes focused on the two moons above them. She was laid out nude with her lover and mate between her legs. Anyone could come along and watch them, but she didn't give a damn! Let them look! She'd relish in having sex with Jaxx in front of thousands, just so they could see that he was hers, and they would be out of luck! Seconds later, she felt a little sharpness on either side of her entrance, and she wanted something else!

"Bite me!" she cried softly.

He raised his head. If there was never a more sexy sight than seeing his face shining in the moonlight dripping with her juices, she couldn't think of it! He began to slide upwards toward her breasts when Gem stopped him.

"No. Not my breast!"

"What? Where?" he asked.

Gem was really surprised at how totally clueless he was aboutwhat she was asking.

"Bite there," she told him, putting her fingers on her opening. "There! Bite my pussy!" she groaned. "I want to feel your fangs sink into me. Drink from me!"

Jaxx's eyes widened. Then, he grinned as his head slid back between her legs.

"If that is what my mate desires, then who am I to deny her?"

He grinned devilishly. Positioning his mouth on either side of her entrance, his tongue slid into her channel, and he bit into her wet pussy. He felt Gem jerk as she felt his bite, and she screamed out his name. Suckling her, and diving his tongue inside of her, he drank. He had never tasted a more delicious drink in his life! With each suck, the liquids of her body flooded his mouth and mixed together with her blood. The taste was tangy and sweet, and his balls began to fill quickly with each delicious sip. Her moans of excitement only drove his lust higher – and that is what it was, now. Pure, unadulterated lust for his mate!

Lust is a very odd emotion. It is never satisfied. It destroys relationships and marriages; it drives people to kill; people would risk everything just for that single, momentary, lust-filled moment of sex; others would dare so right out where everyone could see them, because they are in a haze that blinds one to everything and everyone around them. And, yet, in a loving relationship, it only cements that love even more, because they are "official", which is a moot point, but true.

And, until this very moment, Gem had never really understood the word! Watching her mate drink from drink from her caused more wetness to flow! Lust engulfed her mind with all manner of carnal thoughts. His bite combined with his suckling, served to throw her into a phase of desire where she cared about nothing, but feeling the sensations his mouth was giving her! A change began to happen to her. She could feel it. Unknown to Gem, a deep, crimson red filled her eyes instead of the red of Jaxx. Her own fangs descended, and she felt a strength within her limbs that was unbelievable. It grew with each suckle, until she cried out his name in a deep husky voice, surprising Jaxx so much, he withdrew his fangs, licked the wounds, then lifted his head to look into her eyes! He breathed in sharply at the sight of her face! It had changed into – well, he didn't know what it was, but he did know that she was wrapped in as pure a lust as was he! But, she looked like an angel! Her eyes were a deep, dark crimson red – like a deep, red wine! A very naughty, sexy angel!

His balls continued to distend, causing great discomfort between his legs, he kept readjusting his own legs in his lust-filled body, while they continued to grow to a size that should never have happened. Gem reached down, and pulled him up to her mouth in one fast movement. And her eyes changed to pure black – even the whites! For the life of him, he had never seen anyone's eyes change to that color.

She stared into his red eyes with her black ones as she kept his face cradled in her own two hands. She was beautiful! Her face was nothing less than an angel's, even though her eyes were that of darkness! It was such a turn-on that he licked his lips, and curled them upward into an evil grin.

Gem savored his eyes, and the lust she had been in had magnified in that instant by one hundred percent! Her womb clenched, her channel squeezed tightly against nothing, and her body flooded with heavy juices that flowed from her! She needed him inside of her; needed his cock pounding hard into her womb!

"I want to taste us on your lips,!" she commanded him. Her breath stopped as his eyes met hers.

Well, she didn't have to ask him twice, and he slammed his mouth onto hers. There was nothing gentle about this kiss. It was wild and unrestrained – a kiss from an animal! And, she loved every second of it!

Their desperation to taste each other in whatever way they could was explosive! Then, Gem flipped him over without any effort at all, and in seconds, her mouth closed over the head of his cock suckling hard. The flavor of his cinnamon liquid in her mouth drove her even higher than ever! It was so delicious! She knew that this was not real, but it sure felt like it! Changing positions, she laid between his legs, cradling his shaft in her hands ever so gently.

Her black eyes stared into his, and her mouth turned up into an evil grin that even shocked him! Shocked and excited him even more! His balls filled even more as she suckled him! He was so full, the pain was unbearable! Jaxx couldn't wait much longer to empty them into her deliciously hot, wet pussy! Jaxx knew if she didn't move her mouth soon, he would explode all of it into her mouth!

Gem felt his thoughts. She licked her lips slowly, and her tongue leaped out to lick the swollen head of the organ she wanted inside of her. She gently slid her hands up and down his shaft until she slid her lips over the head, taking it deep into her mouth to suckle. Wanting to give the same incredible experience as he had just done, Gem's mouth opened, and he lifted up enough to watch her tongue slip into his slit, and it burrowed into him! Then, he felt her fangs pierce his tender flesh, and she drank.

Jaxx screamed out her name – not because of pain, but because of a pleasure he had never known as he felt her tongue inside of him, licking and suckling. Her teeth were buried on either side of his slit, and he thought he would go insane with abnormal lust! Feeling her hands close around his balls, she squeezed hard, and it threw him over the cliff! He had to bury himself inside of her – and now! But, Gem refused to release him!

"Gem!" he screamed.

Releasing him, she stared at him.

"Explode in my mouth!" she ordered.

"I want to explode into your womb, Gem! I have to do it!" he told her.

"Then, give me some of your semen to drink, first. Then, I'll mount you, and you can finish inside of me!"

Well, that sounded like a great plan! His balls tightened, and he felt his semen rise into his shaft.

"Then, you'd better get your mouth back on my cock – now!" he demanded.

She was happy to comply, and in less than a second, his balls tightened, and he exploded semen into her mouth. The moaning that came from her throat, as she swallowed his own, personal liquid, which only drove her to suckle him harder.

Gem tried to hold her need back, but she lost the battle, and while his semen was still shooting from him, she released his cock. It spurted out of him, and she quickly positioned herself over it, sinking down as he shoved his cock up inside her body – as deep as he could possibly go – right into her womb. He continued to shove his cock in and out of her. Breasts descended over his face, and he grabbed one tip, sinking his fangs into her breast.

Gem threw her head back as she wildly rode him up and down, while he slammed in and out of her, releasing semen in an incredible, never ending stream. She milked what seemed like gallons of semen into her mouth! And, she just didn't care! His hot liquid coated her womb.

With his last thrust, he flipped her over so that he was on top, and began to move slowly inside of her, working them toward another high. As his cock grew, he pulled out of her making her groan in protest.

"I'll be inside of you again, but first, I need you to do something," Jaxx whispered, panting with need and desire.

"What?" she answered with the same need.

He leaned over her, and kissed her nipples, then whispered.

"Get on your knees. I want to mount you from the back," he whispered to her.

She gasped, grinning wickedly as she rolled onto her stomach, and raised to her hands and knees. She turned her head toward him, and wiggled for him. Jaxx was behind her instantly, and his tongue licked her crack down to her wet opening. His tongue dove into her, and then licked her clit, finally suckling it hard. Gem jerked several more times as he did, until she felt a giant cock thrust upward into her body. His hands were positioned on her hips holding her still, so that he could drive into her.

Both of them cried out as he rammed her into oblivion. Her hips finally couldn't hold still, and she met him thrust for thrust, feeling his cock slam into her womb. She wanted whatever he had to give. She could do this forever!

With one, final, massive thrust that forced her onto her elbows. His balls burst, and spilled their contents! His desire for her to become pregnant was so strong, he let loose a special hormone that only his kind could make, and let it mix with his semen. It was designed to activate his seed to target a female's egg, and guide the seed into it. He tried, desperately, to hold it back, but he couldn't do it. His need for her to swell with his child was too great, even though he knew that there would be no child, he released it anyway.

Gem felt something different. An almost menthol warmth flowed into her womb, and attached itself to the sides of her womb. She knew what he was doing! He was trying to impregnate her! And, at that moment, she pushed back against him. She wanted this. Wanted to carry his child.

Jaxx filled her deeply. Once his body was empty, he slowly slid from her body.

"Gem, your ass is so beautiful!" he told her.

"Jaxx? Well, yours 'ain't' that bad, yourself! " she grinned, as she rolling and stretching like a well-satisfied cat.

Jaxx slid onto her body, and their mouths met. Her arms went around his neck.

"Ask me," she demanded.

"What?" he asked.

"Ask me if I want our child within me," she said.

"H-how did you know?" he stammered.

"I didn't," she told him, brushing his hair out of his eyes. "Not really. Just an instinct. So, ask me."

"It is an impossibility, my love, but the desire is there. So, Gem, will you let me try to impregnate you?" he asked her.

"Yes," she , then pulled his lips to hers. "And, it doesn't even matter, anyway, 'cause we can always work on it – a lot!"

Jaxx threw his head back, and laughed at his mate! She was adorable!

Then, they knew nothing else as deep sleep took them.

~ 12 ~
**"Why in the Hell do those 'in the Know', always
withhold vital information
from those 'out of the Know', and are surprised when
you say you "don't know", because you're not "in the
know"?
No takers? Yeah...me either!" ~ Taylor**

"Damnit!" Taylor yelled, when her head slammed against the far wall for the umpteenth time. Struggling to try and get to her feet, she couldn't, and slumped back down, and rubbed her head.

Rick struggled to get to Eloran, but the platinum bands that had his wrists tied were keeping his powers at bay. Platinum was the only thing that prevented the powers of both Onaerris and Anaerris from coming forward. And, that also included their mates for their powers transferred to them upon their mating. Rick had all the powers of Taylor, and therefore, could be bound just like Taylor. Eloran raised his hands, slamming Taylor into the wall, again, causing a huge dent. Rick charged and butted his head into Eloran, knocking him across the room. Taylor growled. Eloran was hurting her mate! But, because she, too, had the same platinum bands around her wrists, she couldn't help him, and that just made her all the more angry.

For the past hour and a half, Rick had watched his mate be tortured by Eloran, Delinear, and their gang of thugs. He was proud of her. She had not shown one sign of weakening. OK. So. He admitted – to himself, of course – that they truly had screwed up when all four of them had decided to return to their homes for some necessities that they really didn't need, but wanted. They had left their two children at Jaxx's home, which protected them, thank the Creator! At least they hadn't let all common sense disappear! They had promised to be good, and not break anything. And, any time their children promised something, they always kept their word. Honor was a very important thing in their family.

Two hours prior, Rick and Taylor had been dropped off by Stan and Stacy while they also drove home to get their clothes. Eloran, Imaerra, Delinear, and Mallorick had been waiting for them in Taylor's home.

"Well, well. The prodigals return! We knew it was a matter of time before you returned to your house, so we just waited. By the way, hope you don't mind. We also raided your kitchen," Mallorick sneered, licking his lips and fingers that appeared to have mustard on them. "Human food has its pluses!"

"Really, Mallorick! Why in the hell would you even bring that up?" Imaerra scolded.

"Uh..." he replied, licking his index finger. "I was hungry?"

Imaerra rolled her eyes at her mate. He was such a baby!

Delinear and Imaerra had surprised the two of them as they entered their house by grabbing their wrists, and tied them behind their bodies with platinum bands. Eloran had immediately slammed Taylor into the wall, floor, and ceiling several times.

Eloran sighed as if he was trying to be patient with a child.

"I will not ask again, Taylor. If you do not answer my questions, you will die," Eloran warned her.

Taylor struggled to sit up, balancing herself on one arm, and used her shoulder to wipe of part of the blood that ran from her mouth. Then, she turned to Eloran with disgust in her eyes.

"I will never tell you anything! Even if I did know something, which I don't, I would not tell you, you sleazy, son of a bitch!" Taylor told him without raising her voice.

Eloran screamed as he slammed her once again into the ceiling, then let her fall. This time, her leg broke. They all heard the snap. Even with tears in her eyes, running down her cheeks, Taylor defied him.

"That is *enough!*" came a voice from behind Eloran. At the same time, Eloran was immediately bound and wrapped with the same platinum bands that he had used on Taylor and Rick. "You have overstepped your bounds, and thus, by the order of the Council of Ages, you are hereby removed from the council forever!"

Rick and Taylor's bands fell from them with the wave of a hand, and Rick ran to Taylor's side putting his arms around her to help her stand.

"Kulana," Taylor breathed in relief, as she bit back sobs of pain.

"Hello, Taryln," Kulana said.

"How did you know they were here?" Rick asked, picking up Taylor in his arms, hearing her gasp of pain.

"I haven't trusted this bastard for a very long time, nor the rest of his cohorts. So, I have been watching them carefully."

Surprise was on everyone's faces seeing him in the room with them!

"Ha! Didn't expect me, did you?" he laughed.

Several others appeared in the room, obviously with Kulana, and had the other three in the same platinum bands, before they could even move. Eloran opened his mouth to speak, but Kulana beat him to it.

"*Do not speak!*" she ordered Eloran. "As for the rest of you? I also ban you from the council with the council's blessings. You will be immediately shipped to Tal'yae, where you will be incarcerated for not less than five thousand years. At that time, the Council in power will decide if your punishment continues, or you will released! But, since we don't change members, well, then...I guess you'll be there for eternity!" he snickered. "Get this scum out of my sight!"

While the other three were being marched out of the room, Eloran took one step forward toward Kulana, but was restrained by an enforcer from going further. He whipped his head around to the enforcer, then back at Kulana.

"Do not *DARE* to threaten me, Kulana! You will not get away with it! I told you! We will prevail, and Jaxxon will be destroyed with all his other minions!" Eloran said, looking pointedly at Taylor, whose juvenile self took over. She stuck out her tongue at him, earning an amused look from Kulana.

"I'll do whatever the hell I want! I am council leader, but in this case, it was unanimous for your banishment. You have lost." She turned to her guards, waving at them. "Take them out of here, and as fast as possible to Tal'yae."

The guards nodded, and disappeared in a whirl of black mist, along with all four insurgents.

"Well," Kulana let out a breath of relief. "That went well, don't you think? Now. I happen to have four vacancies on the Council!"

"I hope you'll be more *discretionary* with the next four," Taylor told her. Her face contorted in pain yet again.

"Well, I think the four I have in mind will be perfect," she smirked.

Before she could continue, they all heard a noise, and Stan and Stacy rushed into the main room, dropping their mouths at the destruction.

"Holy cow! What the fuck happened in here?" Stan asked in surprise.

"Oh, you know,"Taylor sarcastically answered him. Wincing between words, she just had to add, "Same ole', same ole'. Eloran, Delinear, and the others decided to come to dinner without an invitation..." Taylor quipped with gritted teeth. Then, added even more sarcastically, "...but they just didn't like what was on the menu! Who-da thunk?"

Another cry of pain escaped her lips, and Rick held her gently. Then, she pointed to Kulana.

"Ah! Sure. So. Kulana. Haven't seen you in ages. How are you?" Stan laughed at Taylor's sarcasm while in pain. She always managed to come up with something to make him laugh.

"I'm fine. I'm glad you two came. Saves me the trouble of saying this twice. It has been decreed that you four have been chosen to replace the criminals I just sent to Tal'yae."

Four faces just stared in disbelief at Kulana. None of them could comprehend what she had just said to them.

"Well?" Kulana asked.

Finally, Stan found his voice.

"Us? You picked the four of us?" Stan's voice broke.

"Of course. Why not?" she asked him.

"Well," Rick began, "if memory serves me correctly, you threw Stan off the council in, what? It was around the Middle Ages, wasn't it?" Nods were all around. "And, did you, or did you not, *replace* him with *Eloran*. So, why would you even want to appoint Stan, again?"

Stacy cocked her head sideways.

"Yeah. What he said," Stacy decided to put her 2 cents worth into the conversation. Stan picked it up.

"Yeah, what she said, he said," Stan repeated.

Kulana's eyebrows went up. "What kind of language are you speaking? And, what are you, Stan? Two?"

Stan shrugged.

"Look, Kulana. I was on the council for ages until…," and turning, he spoke to Stacy. He had never totally told her the entire truth. Glaring at Kulana to dare to contradict him, he explained, "Stacy this is what really happened. I wasn't thrown out like I told you, love. I left by my own design." He turned and glared again at Kulana who had opened his mouth. At least he had the decency to shut his it. "Look, love. I had no mate, nor did I have any desire to be a part of that dog and pony show! Words spoken; knives stabbed in the back; council members acting on their own volition – all of it was enough to make me puke – if I could."

He pulled Stacy into his arms, and continued.

"I hated the politics, and you know it! And, that has not changed! I STILL hate the politics! Luckily, within the week after I stepped down, I met my gorgeous, sexy mate, and I've never looked back," he said. "Thanks, but no thanks, Kulana. I won't be a party to the politics of the Onaerris and the Anaerris. I have better things to do with my time – like trying hard to impregnate my mate!"

Stacy's mouth dropped, and she slapped Stan on the back of the head. He turned to grin at her.

"Is there some reason you wanted to say that aloud, mate?" Stacy asked.

"Yep. I wanted everyone to know about our amazing sex life!" he teased, as her face reddened in embarrassment, which only caused everyone to laugh – even Kulana.

"Well, what about you, Taylor? The seat is ready for you."

Despite her broken leg, and her beaten body, she had an answer for Kulana.

"Uh-uh. No damn way! I have a mate, and two children. I'll be damned if I'll park this ass on one of those damned hot seats!" she complained. She yelped when Rick moved her just the wrong way.

Kulana looked at the four standing before her. He was relieved, and had been hoping they wouldn't say yes, but he needed to find out if they could be trusted. Now, he knew.

"OK, good. Now, that we have all that out of the way, and I have my answer," she began. Turning, he pointed to Rick to put Taylor on the sofa. Then, waving at everyone else to sit, he continued. "First things first. Rick, put Taryln down on the sofa, please, and I'll heal her leg."

Rick did as Kulana ordered. Kulana made a motion for Rick to move back. Once he was out of the way, Kulana went to work on Taylor's leg. While all watched, a bright light began to increase exponentially around both Kulana and Taylor, until the others couldn't move or see. When the light disappeared, Taylor was standing upright, completely healed! Everyone gaped, but Kulana didn't have time for their shock from his awe!

"OK. OK. She's healed. Now, down to business. So, just to let you know, I'm glad you all declined my offer. At least, I know who I can trust. I need you four to do some snooping for me."

"Snooping? And, just *who* are we snooping on?" Stan asked with narrowed eyes.

"Not who. What. I need you to find out if the TFM that held the peach ocean is intact. And, by that, I mean, you need you to find it as soon as possible!"

Stan and Taylor looked at each other. Neither of them had met their mates at time of the malfunction. Although they knew their mates could be trusted, could Kulana? Better to err on the side of caution.

"And, why?" Stacy asked him. "Excuse me, Kulana, but have you forgotten that the TFM had a *malfunction* ten-thousand years ago? And, you know that the peach ocean poured out of it, and mixed with the Earth's oceans? And, don't tell us that you didn't know it!" she narrowed her eyes. "I will know if you lie, and that was one. So, what's the real reason you want us to snoop, Kulana? Time to give it up."

Stan pulled her to him, and kissed her firmly on the mouth. A slight groan escaped her throat.

"Uh...hello? Over here, you two! Focus!" Taylor giggled at Stacy's red face as Stan raised his head to grin at her.

Kulana was trying to be cautious. Taylor was pretty good at reading others, while Stacy had become extremely adept at being able to spot a lie over the last thousand years, despite the fact that she was a human turned Onaerris. His mind quickly ran through all the scenarios without telling them all the truth – until he looked directly into Stacy's eyes. Her eyes stared at her as if to repeat what she had said earlier. *"Don't lie to us, because I'll know"*! Kulana took a deep breath, and decided to tell them the truth. He was really taking a chance.

"I need you four to remain calm at what I'm going to say," he stated. No answer came, just puzzled glares were all that met his eyes. "The TFM wasn't, um...actually designed for 'holding' the ocean, even though it worked out fine for our purposes in order to keep it out of the hands of the Onaerris," she said cautiously, not sure they could be trusted. "The ocean was placed into it for a totally different reason than we told everyone."

"Two things. First, what the hell does TFM really stand for, and second what *was* it designed for?" Rick asked, curious, yet just as cautious, about the answer.

"And, Kulana?" Stacy added. "Do not lie!"

Kulana nodded, licked his lips, then looked around him as if he expected someone to jump out at them at any second. Once satisfied, he answered in a very low voice.

"This doesn't go beyond this room. Deal?" Kulana asked.

All four nodded their heads in agreement.

"OK. It was designed for one reason, and one only," he answered.

"And, that would be...?" Stacy asked even more curious that the others.

"TFM? Well, it stands for 'Terra Form Machine'," Kulana answered in such a low tone, that if the others hadn't had superior hearing, they wouldn't have heard him. "Well, technically, the full name for it was AOTFM, or 'Anaerris Ocean Terra Forming Machine'.

Stacy, Taylor, and Stan gasped. Taylor tried to speak, but no words would form. Stacy and Stan just dropped their mouths in shock. They couldn't have uttered a word, even if they had wanted to do so! Rick's eyes narrowed in question. Rick was the only one who could find his voice.

"Uh, this is probably a really dumb quesiton, but what is Terraforming?" Rick asked, surprised when four pairs of eyes darted in his direction in expressions of disbelief. "What? I don't know what that is. Just saying!"

"Rick, terraforming is an immensely complex operation that is designed to allow non-natives of a planet to prepare an unsuitable world that is uninhabitable for their own species. Its sole purpose is to transform a planet into a habitable planet for them. The Anaerris commissioned it to be built when the technology was available." Kulana continued watching Rick's jaw drop even more with each word Kulana said.

"An invasion of other beings, not of the same world might not be able to survive in another planet's current state. In most cases, an invading species, trying to find a home, might come across planet that was perfect for them, but uninhabitable for their species. So, Terraforming allows the planet to be reformed into a habitable place for them."

"Holy Shit!" Rick said in shock.

"There is a slight drawback, of course," he told him.

"Do I dare ask?" Rick questioned.

"In all cases, the process destroys all living beings on the surface of that planet, allowing the invading force to take the planet for their own purpose. Many would never have a problem with destroying a whole planet and all living things – sentient or not – for themselves."

He didn't pay attention to Rick's widening eyes.

"Drawback? *Drawback*? You call wiping out an entire planet a *drawback*?"

"However, the danger of wiping out whole species everywhere just for the sake of one, was something that was forbidden by universal law from the Creator Himself. Anyone who dared to try it was, subsequently, punished with their own species being wiped out forever. An eye for an eye, as it were," he said in a matter-of-fact voice, but with a grin.

"What the hell are you laughing about, Kulana? Hell and damnation! Everyone knows it is

forbidden!" Stan yelled at him. "So, why the fuck would you even commission this TFM, knowing it was forbidden?"

"Yeah, and I'm still not completely clear on this terraf...whatchamacallit!" Rick asked again, knowing if he ever did understand what Kulana was saying, it would be bad. "I mean, I heard your words, and they didn't compute in my brain!"

Stacy answered Rick's question.

"Terraforming is used for one reason, Rick," she answered with a shaky voice.

"Throw me a bone," he said. "Please. Keep it simple for the stupid 'used to be human' in the room."

"First, remember. You are no longer human," then Kulana stopped. "Oh, right. I get it. So, for the 'used to be human', beings from another world go to another planet for whatever reason. Either they want to conquer another, or their own planet is dying. However, a planet is not always habitable for every species. If it is not habitable for them, they use a process called Terraforming by which they can make that planet habitable for themselves. However, in doing so, it kills anyone, or any animal, on the planet, because those cannot live in an environment from the invading beings," she explained, watching Rick's eyes widen with each world.

"Are you fucking with me?" Rick asked raising his voice.

"No, I have no intention of fucking with you," Kulana told him, solemnly. "I really don't think your mate would like it! But, hey...if you want me to, I'll be really happy to do...."

"*Hell no!*" Rick yelled.

Rick backed up, and flopped into his comfortable chair just staring at nothing in stunned silence, while processing what he had just heard.

"Yeah. It's a shocker." Kulana's voice dripped with sarcasm.

Stan continued to berate Kulana.

"Are you out of your mind? Were you actually planning on using it?" Stan asked her with a horrified expression on his face. "And, what planet were you going to use it on in the first place?"

"So, what were you planning to do?" Taylor, who had finally found her voice, butted into the conversation.

"The original plan was to re-Terraform Anaerris after the war. But...."

"Why is there *always* a 'but' in there somewhere?" Rick muttered, still in shock.

"Yes, there is, Rick," Stan agreed, turning back to Kulana. "*But,* what?" Stan demanded.

"*But*...we were ready to Terraform Earth," he held up her hand to stop gasps of outrage, then continued..."...*if* it was uninhabitable for our species. When we found out that...."

Stan flew off the handle, and interrupted, yelling at him.

"So, you're telling me, that if Earth wasn't habitable, you would have deliberately wiped out the human race just so we could live here? Kulana, that is *NOT* our way, and you know it!" Stan yelled.

At that point, Taylor had a revelation. Her eyes widened in horror as it came to her.

"Oh, Creator!"

"What?" Rick rushed to her side as he saw her knees buckle.

"The war! The war, Stan!" she cried. Then, she looked at Kulana. "This was never completely about Onaerris invading Anaerris, was it? It wasn't about the blood, either, was it? It was about that damn machine! Onaerris wanted the machine to Terraform what planet, Kulana? Anaerris? Or, Domaerra? Was that the real reason for the war?" Taylor demanded. When no answer was forthcoming from Kulana, Taylor yelled louder. "Well? Was it? Was that the reason for the war? Tell me, Kulana! All over that damn, fucking machine?"

Kulana closed his eyes, and slowly nodded his head.

"For the love of the Creator! What the *HELL* were you thinking?" Stan yelled.

"At the time, we were *thinking* that no matter what happened to us, we would be able to rebuild Anaerris! It never occurred to us that there would be so few of us would be left, nor that our moon was beyond repair! The machine was developed by an Anaerris as commissioned. Then, she made a deal with someone from Onaerris."

"Are you telling me," Taylor stated in a cold voice, "that we had a traitor in our midst, and you didn't know who it was?"

Kulana didn't answer. Taylor realized something.

"But, you did know, didn't you!" she screamed, trying to jerk out of Rick's arms, but he held onto her tightly.

"Taylor...please! We were trying to decide where we needed to go when we received a note from the Princess telling us to find our way to Earth, informing us that she had given the crystal to the one person that she would trust, but she did not tell us who that was," Kulana explained, continuing. "When we arrived on Earth, we were stunned to find that the planet was heavily populated. Our advanced scouts had not returned to us. We were not expecting so many humans to be here!"

"Wait! Hold it!" Rick interrupted. "That was ten-thousand years ago! Man has always believed that man was hunter gatherer at that point!"

"I know. It was a deliberate ruse to keep your species from knowing about the already, highly, advanced civilizations that were on the planet. Especially since we were directly responsible for helping the human species grow even more exponentially! After the great flood, we made sure that mankind would never remember any of them, nor did we leave any reference to them. Unfortunately, we couldn't erase it all. Things were found by very smart humans in archaeological digs. And, even more, humans have an uncanny capacity to pass stories, verbally, down through the ages, and we couldn't control all of them. So, the stories became legends, passing into mythology. While we were unable to keep them from knowing even a little bit, we did succeed, in a way."

"Go on," Stacy encouraged Kulana. "May as well tell us the rest, because we need to have all the variables."

Kulana nodded.

"When we originally arrived, as I said before, we found an island – a large one – in the middle of a newly formed, and vast ocean. It was here that we took up residence. "Azor took the name Poseidon. He was the first to fall in love with a human. He had loved all human females, and loved having sex with them. But, this one female was the love of his life, and he married her. Her name was...."

"Cleito," Stacy filled in the blank, earning surprised stares from everyone.

"How did you…?"

"Remember what Kulana just said? Humans passed their history down through repetition. When it became mythology, and writing was 'invented', the stories were written down."

Everyone stared at her.

"What? It was a passion of mine, before I met Stan. I liked hearing the stories, and trying to figure them out!"

"Yes. That's right. But, it was when they married that the most amazing thing happened. She had children. Not just one , but five sets of male twins! After that, he no longer wanted to be a "god", but stepped down, and Jaxx took over the mantra of Poseidon. Their birth was a miracle! As you know, neither Onaerris nor Anaerris can have children – either with the separate races, or together. We were the 'fallen' angels that everyone talks about. And, that's almost a correct term for us. Our powers on Earth were great. Without the radiation from our home sun, they grew exponentially. Even more so, because the humans believed in us as gods. You know we thrive on worship. But, once we realized that our powers were becoming stronger and stronger, and our race was able to mate with humans, and have children, we made the decision to stay here. And, the one who held the crystal, and we still never knew who, put it somewhere on Atlantis, and as if fated, it malfunctioned. Some say due to earthquakes prior to the inundation. And, quite frankly, that makes sense."

"I doubt that," Stacy said. "You're lying, Kulana."

Kulana's eyes narrowed at her.

"Sometimes, I wish that Stan had never found you! Your know the truth, and that's far too powerful for anyone!" Kulana told her. "In other words, Stacy? You're nosy!"

Stacy ignored him, and demanded, "Kulana? What is the truth?"

"Oh, hell! Seriously?"

"We're still waiting, Kulana," Taylor said impatiently, tapping her foot.

"Uh-huh. I'll admit it! I give up! What you do not know is that it did *not* malfunction," Kulana's voice was exasperating.

"It. Did. Not. Malfunction." Stan said in a dead tone, as if talking to himself.

"No. Somehow, Eloran found out where it was, but could not access it. So, he deliberately triggered earthquakes, hoping to activate it. He wanted to rule! With the mixing of our bloods, our own children would survive, and they were able to reproduce. So, he decided that it was time to wipe the rest of the humans off the face of the Earth. For no other reason than he felt himself superior to them. Most humans called our children 'Nephilim'. And, of course, he was successful to a point, but humans still survived. But, the crystal was lost, but where is the question. "

Stan started to pace. He couldn't believe what he was hearing! They'd all been lied to for the last nine thousand years! In fact....

"And, you let him *stay on the council*? What the hell, Kulana?" Stacy exclaimed.

"Well, Babe, I wouldn't say it that way," Stan said sarcastically. "It's more like Damn it all to Hell and the Council should all be assigned to Damnation, first!" Turning to Kulana after he took several deep breaths. "Is the machine missing, or stolen?"

"Like I said...we don't know what happened to it. It disappeared. We have speculated that it was lost in the deluge. Luckily, it didn't work the way he thought, because there was nothing inside it except the ocean. Someone gave him very bad intel. I've worked hard, and sent people to find it. But, we've had no luck."

"OK. So, what makes you think it would be around here?" Taylor huffed.

"The machine had an internal emitter. But, it never worked. Until recently. We have detected it on an extremely low frequency – too low for anyone but us to hear. We monitored it over the last several years, and have determined that it is somewhere within this area."

Kulana was tired, and moved to sit down on the long sofa. He dropped his head, and folded his hands. Correction. He clenched his hands together. After several minutes of quiet, he spoke.

"Where is Jaxx?" he asked.

The four looked at each other. Taylor shrugged, and Stan nodded.

"He's in the mating with Gem Elwood," she told Kulana.

At that, Kulana's head jerked up to look at them with wide eyes.

"Mating? Jaxx and...? Oh, fuck! How did *they* meet? That explains everything! And, why call her Elwood? Her last name is Sinclaerris!" Kulana shook her head.

Taylor and Stacy looked at each other, then at the men. Turning back to Kulana, Taylor answered her by pointing to one finger at a time.

"Sinclaerris? What the hell are you talking about? That's the name of our ruling family!"

"Yes? And?"

"How can she be a Sinclaerris?" Taylor was completely surprised. She did not see that one coming!

"Because she is." Kulana puzzled at why the obvious wasn't clear to them.

Taylor shook her head. She'd have to put that on the back burner right now.

"Well, first, they met at the library almost five years ago." Pointing to the next finger, she continued. "Next, she survived the massive storms that came through here over the last week and a half! They were weird. Of course, this is another something that we still don't understand. Wanna explain that to us as well?"

Silence erupted. Then, a horrible thought came to Taylor.

"Oh My God! The library! It was donated to Gem! The library belongs to the Sinclaerris family!"

Kulana nodded and rubbed his temples. He had a headache. A massive one! He knew that Gem would mate at some point or another, but he had never believed it would be with an Onaerris! And, certainly never Jaxx, of all Onaerris! His head jerked up when he realized what Taylor had told him.

"Wait! What storms?" Kulana said in surprise.

"The ones that seemed to follow her everywhere she went! The library was almost destroyed. Then, her truck was damaged, but Jaxx asked Stan to fix it, since it meant so much to her. Then, that same storm's lightning burned down her house. And, two nights ago, one followed her and Jaxx to the border of his property, only lightning struck the truck causing it to wreck and impaled Gem on a tree. She was dead!" Rick told him.

"Yeah," Taylor continued from Rick. "Then, her wounds healed miraculously leading Jaxx to believe that she was more than the jewel."

Kulana had to ask.

"The Jewel? What are you not telling me?" He paused, then jumped up, and his eyes became wild as if he was trying to find a way out of the house. He knew the answer, but still, "I demand you tell me!"

~ 13 ~
**"Have you heard the one about that fan that gets shit
thown at it?" ~ Gem**

"I asked you what are you not telling me? Don't try my patience any further!" he warned them, after a prolonged silence.

Taylor's head was spinning like a top. So, she decided to take each issue one at a time, starting with Kulana's declaration that Elwood was not Gem's name. And, until she had the entire story, there was no way in hell she was going to out Gem!

"Wait a minute, Kulana. There's too much going on, so no. We will not telly you anything without answers first! So, let's begin with why you said Gem's name was Sinclaerris?"

Kulana sighed. This was really going to be a mess!

"You may as well all sit down. It is going to take a while to explain."

"Oh, sure! Like nothing else took time, or was hard to explain!" Stacy muttered under her breath.

Everyone sat down except for Kulana, who paced back and forth, trying to figure out how to explain it to them.

"I'll have to start at the beginning, or it won't make any sense," she turned to them.

"What you are about to hear has been kept a secret since before we left Anaerris. It was not my secret to tell, but a very select few knew about it."

"Cut the crap, Kulana! Spill it!" Taylor demanded.

"Huh? Crap? Spill?" Kulana was really puzzled by the slang.

"Never mind. Forget it! Just begin."

267

"Once the Terraforming machine had been built, we were betrayed by one of our own,he notified the Onaerris that we had it," Kulana told them. "There were only about five of us who knew the entire truth, and we would never have told a soul. But, it was still enough for Princess Analyse to trust us – even after her transformation."

"Transformation?"   Stan   asked.   "What transformation?"

"Yes. You see, Analyse had fallen for another – an Onaerris, to be exact."

"Say what? You're saying our own Princess *fell for an Onaerris*? How is that even possible?" Taylor asked.

"I know! I know!" Kulana waved his hand at Taylor to drop her questions. "At this point, it doesn't matter. When we were told, we were sworn to secrecy about it. By 'we' I mean the King and Queen, myself and Faerron."

He began to pace, again.

"Yes. Secrecy," he said as if to himself. "What none of us foresaw was that our Princess would also be killed by an Onaerris."

"The one she was in love with?" Stacy asked stunned.

"No. By another. On the last day of the battle, she was perched atop a bluff at the edge of the peach sea – or at least where the peach sea had been. We had used the machine to drain the ocean just before the first attack, because we had received intel of the actual day and time. Anyway, her transformation was on that day by her Onaerris lover. Analyse had been on the bluff, when a rogue Onaerris drove a spear though her back, gutting her."

Both Stan and Taylor gasped in horror, while Stacy eyes bugged out, and slapped her hand over her mouth in horror.

"Yeah, well, the one who ran her 's was the Uncle of Jolinaer, Prince of Onaerris, and Analyse's mate. In

Jolinaer's anger at his own uncle, he cut his head off, then dropped to the ground to hold his love."

"She and the Prince? Jolinaer? Holy shit! How did that happen?" Stan asked, then wave his hand at her. "Go on. We'll talk after you finish."

"Yeah. We will," Taylor narrowed her eyes at Kulana.

Continuing, Kulana told them the rest of it, and what she told them shocked them even more than anything they had ever even imagined.

"Analyse was dying. There was no coming back from a spear of Onaerris, as you know, because our weapons are coated with a poison that can kill us. OK. I digress. You see, Jolinaer had offered to turn her into a Demon like him during their time together. Of course, she had refused every time – except this one. She either changed, or died, and her precious cargo would die as well."

"OK. I'm almost afraid to ask, but what cargo?" Rick asked.

"Something that was impossible. Totally and completely impossible! No one had ever foreseen it, because it had never happened before!" He paused for effect. It was obvious that he was ready to lower the boom on all four of them.

"Kulana! What?" Stan almost yelled.

And, the boom was lowered!

"The precious cargo? Oh. Right. The Cargo. Princess Analyse was pregnant with Jolinaer's child."

Four mouths dropped open. The silence was deafening. All of them were sitting in complete disbelief. No Anaerris nor Onaerris had ever been able to procreate!

"*WHAT? You said WHAT? No! Impossible!* Not possible! That is a lie! It has to be! Pregnancy can't happen with any of the 'fallen'! It's not possible, Kulana!" Taylor gasped in shock.

"I know. We said the same thing, but it was true. Analyse was pregnant, and the only lover she had was Jolinaer. When she realized that she was throwing up – morning sickness I think the humans call it – she was so excited that she told our King and Queen, her Father and Mother. Faerron and I were called in, and told about it. The shock and surprise was so great, we ran around for three days with smiles all over our faces. Of course, we were asked over and over what the hell was going on, but we never told a soul! Not that we didn't want to tell everyone, since it was so monumental! They had already realized that they would have to leave, but refused to give the destination to anyone. The battle began the fourth day after they told us. Well, to continue. Analyse was dying, of course, and it was then, and only then, that she agreed to the change. Jolinaer bit her, drained her, then gave her his blood, which, as you all know, is the only way another can be changed into"...

"A toothy monster?" Stacy finished for him, rolling her eyes.

Kulana huffed, then continued.

"We still do not know where they went, but they disappeared into history, never to be seen again."

"You mean you really don't know?" Taylor asked to which Kulana shook his head.

"Faerron believes that they fled to the Fae realm. Analyse was great friends with the Fae Queen. It was there that we believe she delivered a child – a little girl. These rumors ran wild. You know that time passes differently within the Fae realm than any other realm. I also believed that the child was brought to Earth by a Fae, and when grown, as the legend says, she would mate with an Onaerris, thereby allowing the royal lines of both worlds to continue. The combined blood lines would give her powers beyond anyone from both races. She would, then, become the most powerful being in history – all universal history. It was said that she would be called the "Anaerris Jewel", and would be charged with a book – codex – of Anaerris, which was written by Analyse and Jolinaer. When it was time, the Jewel would find it, and it would set off a chain of events that was designed to change our entire universe."

"Into what?" Rick muttered.

There was silence as Taylor, Rick, Stan, and Stacy contemplated Kulana's incredible revelation. Not only was Gem their friend, but this, combined with what they knew about Gem, confirmed that Gem was the Anaerris Jewel. Try as they might to wrap this around their heads, it was completely difficult despite the proof that Jaxx and Taylor had found her. Kulana saw Taylor's expression, and his eyes widened.

"You know, don't you? She found the book, didn't she, Taylor? Stan? You must tell me!" Kulana demanded. "She is in grave danger from Eloran!"

The two looked at each other, and back at Kulana. Both nodded their heads.

"She discovered the book, and is now..." Taylor hesitated.

"Now, what, Taryln?" Kulana asked.

"She has become a mate to an Onaerris," Taylor told her. Kulana gasped in shock.

"She what? Who? Where are they? I must have proof it has happened!" Kulana sounded as if he was in total panic.

The others looked at each other.

"Well, uh, you see..." Stan began. "Uh...it's like this, Kulana..."

"Yeah, well, it's like this...." Taylor began at the same time as Stan, then she turned to look at Rick. She was at a loss how to tell Kulana.

"I'm getting older just standing here! Spill it already!" Kulana said, using their slang and tapping her foot impatiently, knowing she was not going to like it.

"Well, you see...," Rick grunted.

"What?" Kulana asked, but maybe yell would be the better term for it.

"Well, uh...you see. Ah, hell! It's Jaxx!" Taylor continued. "He is her mate.

Kulana huffed. Why was she not even surprised about this?

"Why am I not surprised? Well, then. The time has arrived. A great war will be played out – on Earth – if we don't find that machine, before Eloran and Delinear do! If Eloran, and the others get their hands on it, well, Earth will go the way of Anaerris!"

"Wait! Was Delinear the one who betrayed us?" Stan asked. "Why?"

Kulana nodded once.

"Well, you see..." Kulana slurred his words. "You see, Delinear was the one who had been commissioned to build it."

"Oh, shit!" Taylor exclaimed.

"Exactly," Kulana agreed.

Gem stretched like a satisfied cat, even purring as she did so.

"Ouch!" she squealed, realizing that she was a bit sore. But, it was a *great sore!*

She reached out for Jaxx. He wasn't there, but she did hear some clanging, which echoed gently from the kitchen that was below this level. She swung her legs carefully off the bed, and sat still for moment, trying to regain her balance, since she'd been on her back for almost three days! She laughed a at that thought, and stretched again. She stood, crossed the floor to where Jaxx's blue, button down shirt laying across a chair in the corner. She grabbed it, and purposely buttoned one button in the center. As Gem strolled out the door, the shirt gently flew open revealing her curls – exactly what she wanted him to see. The "Dreaming" did nothing but make her horny. How could that be, she wondered? She stepped out onto the glass landing, and looked below her.

"Hey, Lola. You want some din-NER?" Jaxx asked her with a smile.

A little ball of fur streaked to him, and ran in circles around his legs jumping up and down, and panting! Gem saw him throw his head back and laugh. She grinned. Well, that was Lola! She always got excited – overly excited any time you mentioned food. Even if she was sound asleep, and someone went into the kitchen, she always jumped up to follow them, giving that little "I'm really starving, can I have some food, too"? Anyone who has a pug knows that look.

Jaxx set Lola's little dish with her food on the floor, then wondered how she had been fed while they were asleep? Shaking her head, that's when Gem realized he was still nude! She just hoped Lola wouldn't jump a bit too high, and nip his manhood! She laughed and made her way downstairs to the kitchen. When she reached the island bar, Jaxx turned to look at her, and he gave her a devilish grin. Moisture collected between her thighs at that grin. Just thinking of him inside of her made her all hot and bothered. Gem had to acknowledge what most girls her age always said. Once you've had it, you can easily become addicted. Well. that was so very true! She was addicted to his hard, kick ass body especially the appendage that hung between his legs! She licked her lips as she watched it go from limp to standing at attention, dripping with his own special brand of juice in a matter of seconds. Her eyes met his.

"Gem," he breathed softly.

Lola looked back and forth between the two of them. She was done with her eating, but she wasn't about to stay around, and watch these two engage in more games of sex! She toddled off quickly toward the arch that led to the ocean, and disappeared. Neither Jaxx nor Gem noticed.

"Jaxx," she breathed softly, and walked around the island straight into his arms.

He wrapped his arms around her, and his lips slammed down on hers kissing her fiercely as if he had never tasted them. His tongue darted into her open mouth as if he were a starving man. She tasted so good! When he drew back, he stared deeply into her eyes.

"Did you fix – uh – exactly what time is it anyway?" Gem asked.

"It's dinner time, and yes, I fixed us something to eat," Jaxx answered, flipping his cock at her with a grin.

"Mmmmmm! Just what I had in mind to eat!" she exclaimed, watching the glistening drops f.orm

"Good!"

He ripped his shirt off of her body, picked her up, and put her on the island. It was just the right height for him. He watched her spread her legs wide so he could see her slick wetness. He slammed his mouth onto hers as he rammed his cock up into her body.

Gem cried out as she felt his huge, thick cock pushed into her deeply, and begin to move fast and hard.

"I need it fast and hard!" he gasped, as he felt his balls continue to fill to the point of terrific pain.

"So do I!"

The two of them had been asleep for a while, and they were desperate for each other. Gem lifted her legs, and wrapped them around Jaxx who picked her up by her ass, and carried her just far enough to lay her on the dining table. He slipped out of her, then climbed upon the table watching her bend her knees, and spread them for him. He slid between them, and his cock found his home, again.

The sound of slapping skin, echoed throughout the cave as he pounded into her harder. Gem's hips met his hips with each thrust until they reached their climax quickly.

Jaxx was holding back to let Gem catch up, but he needn't have worried. He felt her tight channel clutch his cock hard, and begin to squeeze it as she screamed out with her release. In seconds, Jaxx felt his balls clamp down, tightened, and liquid of fire exploded deeply into Gem's womb.

When she had milked him dry, Jaxx dropped in exhaustion, but still held himself above her. Both of them were coated with glistening sweat.

"Oh, Jaxx!" Gem gasped with a tear rolling down her cheek. "That was so amazing!"

"It was!"

Jaxx's mouth found hers, and with one hand fondling her breast, he gave her a heart wrenching kiss.

"More!" she begged.

"Aren't you just a bit hungry?" he asked her.

"Well, of course I am – for you!" she trailed her fingers down until she gripped his soaking wet cock in her hands.

"You have to eat something, Gem. My cock will be there after you eat," he laughed.

Pretending to pout, she let him go. Jaxx helped her to sit up, and slide off the table.

"I need to clean the table," she said, looking back at the top of it.

"No. Look at it," he told her.

She saw a large puddle on it, then looked at him in question.

"I want our love to stay there. It is precious to me."

Gem just nodded, and followed him back to the kitchen. The smell of the food overwhelmed her desire for sex – at least for the moment. She really was hungry!

"What did you make?" she asked.

"Steak," he answered.

"Yum! I am hungry," she told him rubbing her stomach, an action that was not lost on Jaxx. "But, Jaxx?"

"Yes?"

"Watch your cock, will you? I don't want it to get burned with hot food!" she laughed.

"Only if you watch your tits, and make sure they don't get burned by hanging over the food!"

Both of them laughed out loud.

"Grab the wine and plates. I have the basket and four steaks ready to eat along with potatoes."

She frowned.

"Why?"

"We're having a picnic at the ocean."

"Great idea!"

While Gem laid out a large blanket, Jaxx opened the basket, and unpacked their meal. There were four steaks, two baked potatoes, grilled asparagus, and rolls. Next, he pulled out their dessert with a very wicked grin.

"Strawberries and whipped cream?" she wiggled her eyebrows. "Now, what do you plan on doing with those?"

He wiggled his eyebrows right back at her, making her laugh even harder.

"Ah, hell!" Lola thought when Lola saw them coming. She rolled her eyes, and trotted into another part

of the cave, so she could get some much needed sleep. She murmured to herself. "Well, after all, dogs sleep almost 24 hours a day! These 'gods' are just way to *obsessed* with sex!"

She curled on the sofa, and let the warmth of the fire soothed her to sleep.

While Gem and Jaxx indulged in a fantasy using strawberries and whipped cream, the others gathered what they needed quickly, and returned to Jaxx's home. The longer they were away from its protection, the more chances that Eloran's followers would appear.

As they sat around the library, something occurred to Stacy that she realized all of them had missed.

"Holy shit!" she exclaimed.

"What?" Stan asked her. Her eyes were glazed over, and she didn't answer. He shook her harder. Stacy turned around to everyone with wide eyes that resembled a catatonic state.

"Gem!"

"What about her?" Stan asked.

Stacy shook her head as if trying to get rid of cobwebs in her brain.

"It never occurred to me who Gem is!"

"And?" Taylor asked.

Stacy looked at Kulana whose eyes were quirking in a slight grin. When she saw the question in her eyes, Kulana nodded.

"Gem!" she looked around at the puzzled faces around her. "Don't you get it?"

Blank stares just looked at her.

"Gem is the Anaerris Jewel," Rick said.

"Yes, yes! I know that! But that's not what I mean!" Stacy said.

"And?" asked Taylor.

"Didn't you hear what Kulana said?" More blank stares. "Oh, for the love of …! Gem is the descendent of Analyse and Jolinaer."

"Again, and...?" Stan said.

"*PRINCESS* Analyse and *PRINCE* Jolinaer! Gem is the Princess of not just Anaerris, but of Onaerris! She is the heir to both!"

Kulana just smirked, then huffed at them.

"*Took them long enough!*" she thought.

"Crap!" Taylor said. "How did we miss that?"

"Exactly!" Kulana shook her head

Two hours later, after Stacy's outburst, they sat down to dinner. It was quiet, but at the same time, they engaged in small talk. After they finished, Taylor leaned back in her chair.

"OK. Look. This machine, Kulana. Does anyone have even an idea where it is?"

"No. We have no idea."

"We have to get to that machine before Eloran, or anyone else can get to it. We cannot allow them to Terraform Earth, if that is, indeed, their plan."

"Well, that's just swell and dandy! We have to find a machine that caused the Great Flood over ten thousand years ago...that went missing in that flood...and stop Eloran and Delinear from using it...and, I'll just wager, mind you, that they have no idea where it is, either...and, then, to top it all off, we have to find it before they do! Yeah! Right! It's just so simple!" Rick ran his sentences together.

"Well, like Rick muttered. That's just swell and dandy!" Stan huffed. "So, how do we find out?"

"Easy. The Fae know everything. We simply ask one," Kulana answered.

"I don't know any Fae," Rick said, turning to Taylor. "Do you?"

Taylor's eyes darted to Rick, then to everyone else.

"Well, you see...I do know one."

"*You* know a Fae!" Stan's voice was hoarse. "Why didn't you say something?"

"Because I made a promise."

"You. Made a promise? To one of those vile creatures?" Rick said loudly. "When did you lose your mind, Taylor?"

Taylor shrugged.

"The Fae revealed herself to me for a reason."

"OK. Then, where is she?"

"I hate to say this, but we need to bring Jaxx and Gem back – now," Taylor told them.

"What if they have not mated yet?" Stacy asked.

All four pairs of eyes turned to look at her in surprise.

"You have to be kidding, right? Jaxx not mate Gem?" Stan laughed.

"OK. Let me rephrase that. What if they have not exchanged blood yet?"

Kulana shook her head.

"It makes no difference. We can't wait. If they haven't, they will have to do it another time. We have a serious problem."

Taylor picked up her phone, and, feeling guilty, called Jaxx.

Gem kept inching forward as Jaxx slammed into her hard. She leaned down on her elbows to try and stop moving forward. The tilt gave him a better angle, and allowed him to descend into her much deeper. One hand on her hip, and the other fondling her breasts that were moving back and forth as he rammed into her, allowed him to move into her womb. Her internal walls tightened around him. He let the contents of his balls coat the inside of her womb.

Gem relished the incredible feeling it gave her – the feeling that she could do anything! She cried out until Jaxx gave one massive thrust, releasing the last of his seed. He stilled, leaning his head on her ass as he tried to stop shaking from their emotions. He could hear Gem breathing hard, and saw her lay her head on her hands. A euphoria came over both of them.

Jaxx finally found enough strength to remove himself from her body, and they both collapsed. He pulled her into his arms, and she lay her head on top of his chest, replete, and satisfied for the moment.

"Oh, Jaxx! That was...it was...oh, Jaxx!" she whispered in awe of the moment.

"It was," he agreed without description. "Are you Sleepy?" he asked.

"Mmmhmm," she murmured.

"Are you up for bonding one more time, before we sleep?" he asked her.

Her eyes flew open, and she tilted her head to look into his eyes. His left arm had been put behind his head helping him to lift it so he could look at her.

She kissed him gently.

"I do! I want to do it, again, Jaxx," she whispered against his lips. "And as often, and as much as you desire!"

He rolled her over on her back, and both of them let their fangs descend. Just as they were leaning toward each other, a sound yanked her out of her deep desire.

"Wait!" she said, holding his head still.

"What?" he told her.

"Listen. Isn't that the phone?"

Jaxx heard it, too. He growled as he raised his head.

"Damn it all to hell!" The anger in his voice was almost frightening. "Don't they know that you and I are in the mating?"

"Jaxx, be fair. Of course, they know that, but we are already mated. You and I both know it would take something truly bad for them to interrupt us. I think you know that."

"Yes, but what cosmic influences would choose *now* to interrupt us?"

Gem shrugged her shoulders. Jaxx got to his knees, and stood, reaching out his hand to Gem pulling to her feet as well. Together, they walked back to the cave where he grabbed his phone, and pushed the home button of his iPhone 7 plus.

"This had better be good, Taylor! You have interrupted our mating!" Jaxx growled.

"You haven't mated her? Yet?" she squealed. "What the hell have you two been doing? Playing a virgin reality...I mean virtual reality game? I'm really sorry for interupting, Jaxx..." she began with a bit of a snicker.

"What is so damn wrong, Taryln?" Jaxx almost yelled, reverting to her real name. "Well?"

"Well...oh, shit, Jaxx! Eloran and his hoard found us!" she told him.

"How!" he yelled into the phone, gripping his phone so tightly, Gem heard a slight cracking noise.

Gem wrapped her arms around him, when she heard him yell. She pulled his fingers from his phone to keep him from breaking it. Something was truly wrong.

"We, uh, well...we, uh...Went home to get some things?" she told him.

Jaxx turned his head to look at his mate as he crushed his phone to a pulp. Horrified eyes looked into his angry ones.

"Jaxx?" she asked.

"Get dressed, Gem. The jackasses went back to Taylor and Rick's house. Eloran and the others found them!"

"Oh, shit!" Gem exclaimed, as she quickly pulled on her clothing.

"Exactly," he agreed.

"Well? What did he say?" Rick asked Taylor, when she lowered her phone.

"Nothing. But, he sure did yell," she answered. "And? He called me Taryln!"

"Damn!"

"Exactly," Taylor agreed.

Eloran was angry. Too angry as they were led to their punishment. Each of them had been assigned two guards. Really? Did Kulana think these tiny, insignificant jailers would stop him? Stop them? His eyes met Delinear who imperceptibly dipped her head to him as she understood what he was asking. He also looked at Mallorick and Imaerra, who repeated Delinear's nod. In a move so fast the jailers did not see, the four whirled, attacked, and quickly killed all eight of them by breaking their necks. Their deaths came so fast, that the shock and surprise were frozen upon their faces. Mallorick pulled out his specialty, and threw fire at the bodies, and instantly, they were incinerated to ash as if they never were.

"Now, what?" Imaerra asked, already knowing the answer.

"Now, we eliminate Kulana, her mate, and the rest of the council."

"Yes, my lord," she grinned, and sarcastically curtsied to him.

He growled, and she laughed harder.

"Get into the air, find her, and bring her to me at the island," he ordered Imaerra. "We have the girl, and Jaxx will be at our mercy!"

"Get who? Kulana?" she asked him, rather puzzled.

"Do I have to spell everything out for you! Use your fucking head, Imaerra! Get the little girl you saw with Jaxxon! Bring her to me. It's obvious that she means a great deal to the others – and most especially to Jaxxon."

"You think she might be his mate?" Delinear breathed anger.

"She's human, you bitch!" he sneered. "What's the matter, Delinear? Mad because the cute little human got him when you couldn't?"

"No. She is nothing to me...nothing to any of us. She is purely human. He'll get tired of her soon enough!"

"Imaerra...*GO!*" Eloran commanded.

Imaerra nodded once, and in a heartbeat, her body began to shimmer and distort. Her face elongated as her mouth turned into a huge beak with a large head and coal black eyes on either side of her head. Her legs began to thin to the size of sticks, bending backward while erupting with long, sharp talons as her feet turned into claws. She hunched forward, and her body contracted as it grew, followed by feathers of glossy black, turning into wings, which began to protrude from the sides of her body. A feathered tail, that was split into three sections, grew from her butt as she changed into a bird of prey – a gigantic bird of prey with a wingspan of fourteen feet! She stopped when she heard Eloran speak, and turned her massive head to look at him.

"Make sure you do not return without her, Imaerra," Eloran threatened her. "You know the penalty for failure."

"Caw! Caw!" Imaerra whined as she lifted her wings, and with one swift push with her talons, she rose into the night sky. With no moon, it effectively would hide her from the humans.

"Now, Delinear...open the portal to the island," Eloran ordered.

Delinear grinned, and held her hands in front of her, palms facing away from her. Then, closing her eyes, she clapped them together. Her eyes opened, and a swirling, black Vorc'ara appeared out of nowhere, growing large enough for her to enter. She turned to Eloran with a wicked smile.

"Kind of dramatic, don't you think?" Eloran grinned.

She didn't say a word, but growled at him. Then, she turned, and stepped into the Vorc'ara."

"Your mate is a bitch, but you know that!" Mallorick grumbled in mock horror.

"Indeed," Eloran said, and both men cucked, then walked into the portal, where it closed behind them.

The two lovers walked out of the door of the little shed that hid the secret behind them, and into the night. Lola followed, when Gem had yelled for her to come. She had been a bit peeved at it, because she was all "snug as a pug in a rug", and sound asleep. The three quickly walked to the house. They were almost there, when a sound like rushing wind flew above them, and they stopped dead when they heard a huge screech reverberating in the night sky. All three looked up to see a massive bird diving toward them. It was horrible to behold.

"What the hell is that?" Gem exclaimed in terror.

"Oh, shit!" Jaxx screamed, as he scooped Lola up in his arms. "RUN, Gem! For fuck's sake, *RUN!*"

Jaxx got nowhere fast as the bird swept downward. He pushed Gem away from him, and planted his feet firmly between the bird and his mate. But, Imaerra dipped her left wing as she descended, knocking him sideways where his head hit a stone rendering him unconscious. Then, darting quickly back into the night sky, she rose high, only turning to dive bomb them, again. This time with the sole purpose to grab Gem.

Gem looked at Jaxx in horror as he lay on the ground not moving. Before Gem realized that the monster bird was coming after *her* this time, she ran to Jaxx, and tripped. She felt the bird graze her back, causing her to fall onto her stomach with the monster's first attempt to grab her! The bird missed, screamed loudly, and rose into the night sky, only to do what could only be considered a "U-turn in the air". It dive-bombed her, again. Imaerra missed once more, and her night cry of frustration was so loud, that Gem covered her ears, only to bring them down with blood on them. The sound made her ears bleed? Why was it after her? She turned her head upward to try and track the monster, only she couldn't see it against the moonless night. But, she sure could hear the flapping of giant wings!

"Lola!   Lola! Where are you?" she yelled desperately, as she realized that her pug was somewhere around.

She saw Lola under a bush shivering with fear, but, still thankful that she was hidden from the bird.

"Lola! Stay where you are, sweetie! Don't come out!" she cried.

What Gem didn't know was that it was not fear, but sheer anger that caused Lola to shake as she watched the giant bird dive for Gem! As the bird came closer, Gem saw the massive talons open reaching for her. She stumbled and fell. Gem turned to run, but stumbled, and fell, again. It took her a minute to realize that this time, she hadn't fallen. Surprise and terror gripped her when she realized that she was weightless as she was whisked into the sky. A tiny bark drew her eyes to Lola, who was grasped in another talon. She knew that Lola had been trying to rescue her. But, a second later, the bird tossed her down. Gem cried out as she watched, then saw that Lola was alright as she landed on all four feet. Lola looked up at her pet, and all she could do was berate herself for having failed to protect Gem!

Looking down as they gained altitude, Gem saw Jaxx sprawled on the ground with Lola standing over him, her head raised staring at Gem, barking. He was still unconscious, and he became smaller and smaller with every flap of the bird's wings. She had no idea what was happening, and her mind could not cope with it, so it just shut down. Just as she passed out, she heard a horrible screech that sounded as if the bird was shouting in triumph, and then, she knew nothing.

"Where the fuck is she?" Eloran asked Imaerra for the umpteenth time.

He'd asked Imaerra over and over for the last several hours, and all she would do was joke about it. He needed to ask the bitch questions about Jaxx. More than that, Eloran was positive that Jaxx knew where the book was. And, then, there was the unresolved issue about whether or not the Jewel of Anaerris was real. There was not really a doubt in Eloran's mind that there was a Jewel of Anaerris as the ancient rumors foretold, but as yet, no one had proved it. He was just as certain that the girl knew more about the whole thing, because she was Jaxx's mate. Well, at least that was what he thought. But, even if she wasn't, yet, she was a great bargaining chip! He had no doubt that Jaxx would begin looking for her, and Eloran had every intention of making it just too easy for Jaxxon to find her! Then, he'd be able to threaten her life, so it seemed a great place to start the "negotiations"! He would torture her slowly, over the course of hours, making Jaxx watch, if he did not tell the truth! Well, maybe not immediately! She *was* a beautiful woman. It wasn't as if Delinear hadn't cheated on him for years! He'd done same! Neither of them were exclusive. Perhaps he would enjoy tasting the bitch's cunt first? He thought about it, feeling his cock jump to attention, and his balls fill! He knew he wouldn't be able to stand the stench that surrounded her, and since Jaxx had fucked her already, well, she would always smell that way. That just about turned him off of doing so...but, well, maybe he'd hold his nose, and just fuck her in front of him He snorted, and turned his attention back to Imaerra whose legs were dangling in mid-air as he held her by the throat.

"I am sick of asking you, Imaerra! You will tell me! Where the hell did you put her?"

Delinear's evil grin appeared, and that scared Imaerra far more than Eloran. She hung her head, and gave an answer that made her laugh.

"What do you mean, where is she?" Imaerra asked. "Was this not the reason we took this island 'paradise'? Seriously? It was you who declared where all our 'guests' were to be placed – all of them! You did not specify anything different! I have always done your dirty work whenever you wanted to scoop someone up and bring them here. So, where would she be? You know where we keep our prisoners. We've always kept them there – well, until they burn, of course! Was that not your decree, oh great one?" she giggled nervously.

Eloran's head snapped up in realization of what she meant, and in seconds, he threw her against the steaming wall, then grabbed her by the throat once again.

"You fucking idiot! You put her below? *In the oubliettes?* I did not tell you to put her there! I told you to bring her to me! What part of that was unclear to you?" he asked, slamming her head twice into the wall.

Seemingly unfazed, Imaerra's eyebrows drew into a frown.

"I did bring her to you, oh mighty jackass! You weren't here, and I had better things to do than to wait for you to get back. Such as torturing the prisoners! It was certainly not to guard a stupid human until you returned!"

Eloran dropped her, then put his foot on her throat pressing hard. Their powers were almost useless on each other, so they had to resort to human tortures. They were a bit more effective, but in the long run, did nothing. It took the blade of an Anaerris, or Onaerris, to destroy each other.

"Bring her to me, now!" he ordered, then took his foot off of her throat. Holding his hand on the hilt of his Onaerris dagger that he kept at his side, he continued.

"If she has been turned to liquid, I'll kill you myself! Now, get the fuck down there, and get her out before she does fry!"

Slowly, Imaerra rose to her feet, and she heard the snickering of both her mate, Mallorick, and Delinear. Rubbing her neck, which really didn't hurt, she grudgingly obeyed as she turned to walk the long tunnels to fetch the human.

"Bastard!" she said to herself, albeit quietly. "I really hope that someday, Jaxxon kicks your ass, and makes sure you can never come back!"

~ 14 ~

**"Just where I always wanted to book a vacation...a
volcanic lava tube prison complete with lava!"**
~ Gem

Time became superfluous as Gem tossed and turned.
Her dream was miserable!

"This damn bed is too hard...and way too hot!" she
thought.

Volcanic ash, lava, and eruptions surrounded her! It
made the planet red, but part of it was black and gold as
well. She was sweltering in the heat. Her breathing was
labored, but Gem forced her eyes to open. She was
instantly hit with a heavy burning sensation. Gem shut her
eyes once again. She was also sweating heavily, and
completely drenched. Her hair was so wet, it was like
she'd stepped out of a shower, but it was plastered to her
head and neck and felt greasy. She might as well have just
been dumped by salt water! Hot salt water! Well, that
explained why her eyes were burning. Her body was stiff
as if she had been laying in the same position for hours, if
not days.

"This is just not right!" she muttered to herself.
"This dream is not real, so wake the hell up, Gem!"

Forcing her eyes to open for the second time, they
were also matted with a lot of gunk. It's the only
description of it at the moment. She rubbed her eyes
trying to remove it, before looking around her. Well, sure
she hadn't dreamed about the heat. Wherever she was, it
was horribly hot! Squinting, she realized that her focus
was off, but she managed to catch large features.
Overhead was rock. She tilted her head to the right to see
– rock. Then, she tilted it to her left knowing, but hoping,
it wouldn't be what she thought.

289

"Nope, that's rock, too," she muttered. That's when she remembered being kidnapped by a gigantic bird, and it took her into the air!

Rubbing her head, again, she asked the rocks, "Exactly, where in the heroine's handbook is it written that the captive has to be put in a jail of rock? Oh, right. The villain would find the best place where she could not be tracked. Well, this certainly qualifies!"

And, beneath her? Rock, what else? Confused, Gem knew it was far too hot, and any physical exertion just made her sweat even more. What she wouldn't give for a cold shower and a monster bottle of ice water right now! She licked her dry, cracked lips, remembering the giant bird that had swooped down out of nowhere! The wings had knocked out Jaxx as if he were a puff of wind, and then, grabbed her neck by its talons. That reminded her. The back of her neck was hurting, and she reached up behind her only to draw her hands away covered with sticky, drying blood. Her blood.

"Well, there's *not a surprise'!*" she muttered, again. Of course the talons would draw blood!

OK...no matter what, she had to at least force herself to sit, and take her bearings. Gem had to try and figure out where she was. Slowly, she maneuvered her sore body into an upright position. Wincing with each move, Gem glanced around, while frequently wiping off the salty sweat that was burning her eyes, so she could at least see. Doing so, though, just smeared blood all over her face, so she had to make a conscious effort to keep her hands away from her face. She looked around the room. It couldn't have been bigger than a small bathroom. Maneuvering was extremely difficult. But, she managed, and to her surprise, there were iron bars that "barred" her exit. She broke into loud gulps of scared laughter at her pun. Oh, hell! She was becoming hysterical as if she needed that in addition to everything else at the moment!

"Fucking get a hold of yourself, Gem!" she ordered to herself, and began hysterically giggling.

After her laughter died down, she was surprised at her, other senses. She smelled...sniffed a couple of times...smoke? Smoke? No. Not exactly smoke. More like steam with a horrible stench. It reminded her of chemistry class in school, because it was so nauseating. She tried to remember why, but her mind wasn't working. The heat made it difficult for her to concentrate. But of one thing she was certain. She was in a tiny cave. She looked closer at the rocks, and noticed it was catacombed with jagged holes, and in the dim light, the color looked dark rust except for the floor, which looked as if had been polished smooth. And, there was light!

"Where is the light coming from?" she asked herself as she looked around for a source.

Gem noticed that the reason she could see the rusty color of the cave was that there seemed to be something behind the rocks emitting a light! That made no sense whatsoever! Whatever that big bird was, how did it drop her into this God-forsaken place? She rubbed her back, and tried to stand, failing miserably, when her feet slipped out from behind her, landing her ass on the floor with a thud.

"Ouch! Well, that's just great! The rock is slippery!" she whined. She looked at the stone floor. A small pool of her blood was laying underneath where her head and back had been, and it was bubbling like a pot of water that had just begun to boil! That was enough for her to jump up quickly – a bit too quickly, and that caused her head to whirl.

Slowly, trying not to keep her head from falling off of her neck, she grabbed the wall to keep from falling down. Her hand drew back at the intense heat that met her palm. She held it out in front of her seeing the seared red palm, and fear gripped her. Feeling like an inchworm who could only move a quarter of an inch, Gem reached out to touch the rock wall, again, drawing her other hand back for a second time as she felt the heat coming from it.

"Bloody hell!" she yelled hoarsely, shaking her reddened and burned hand. "Where the fuck am I? It can't possibly get any worse than this!"

And, as always, the very minute you make *that* statement...well, we all know that is always when the shit hits the proverbial fan! And, of course, that is also the moment when she noticed some small flames coming from the back of the cave.

"And, there goes the shit hitting the fan! Of course, I shouldn't have said those fucking cursed words!"

She looked around, again, this time without touching the walls. She noticed a tiny hole in the wall at floor level was glowing a brilliant, almost a fluorescent orange. In seconds, she saw something that made her scream without a sound. The terror and shock that consumed her was so strong, she backed up against the nearest wall regardless of the heat! Was this the way her life was going to end? If so, just the thought of how she was going to die made her gag, and she begin to throw up.

Dry heaving after emptying her stomach's contents, she wiped her mouth, then her eyes fixed on the tiny, thickened, orange rivulet that was flowing toward her. OK. She just didn't have the time to fall apart right now! Gem's eyes widened in terror as she watched a thin ribbon of lava, but it was just a matter of time that the slow moving stream of orange would grow as it melted the rock around the tiny hole, and become a bigger stream. For a brief second, her mind wandered to her favorite author, H.G. Wells, and the book, "The Time Machine".

And, of course, she had seen the classic movie, too. The movie had used oatmeal dyed red to make the lava in it look real. Strangely enough, that's exactly what the little rivulet looked like! Shaking her head, she realized she was going into hysterics!

"OK. Now, I know that my mind is going! Why?" As if she couldn't leave things alone, Gem slowly breathed the one word you should never ask, because you usually never received an answer, let alone a satisfactory answer. Or, if you did, it was never what you thought it would be. Make that *should be*!

The rivulet of brilliant, glowing, orange liquid had tiny flames erupting now and then. Gem's brain worked overtime as realization crept into her brain.

"Holy fucking shit!" she whispered in shock. Louder, "Lava? It *IS* lava! I'm inside a damn volcano? I'm in a volcano, in a volcanic cave blocked by iron bars? In a lava tube? I'm in a volcanic prison? Seriously? Ah! Fuck! Fuck! Fuck!"

She felt stupid. No matter how many times she said it, she was expecting a different outcome! Yeah. Right. Like no one ever does it!

"And, the outcome will always be the same. I'm in a volcanic, prison cell inside a volcano. End of story!"

The cave reminded her of a dead, Jabba the Hut hollowed out fossil! The walls and floor had holes in it, making it look wrinkled enough. Why the hell was she even thinking about that right now? Really, Gem? That's all you have?

Reality grabbed hold of her as she continued to stare at the rivulet of orange. OK. So, she couldn't ignore it any longer! Terror gripped her as she saw the tiny rivulet growing as it melted the rocks around it! It had already doubled in size in the last few minutes, its path slowly heading for the iron bars! At the moment, she could keep out of its way, but she was certain that it wouldn't stay this way for long! Her life had just been cut short by lava! She was certain not many people would ever be able to say it! And, why? They were d.e.a.d.!

In minutes, she knew that the entire back side of the cave would be eaten through by the monstrously hot lava, and fill the cave! Looking beyond the bars, she realized that the cave that she was in wasn't actually a cave, but it must be part of even more tubes that had been carved by lava as it flowed through it in the past! Lava tubes were what they were! For the Creator's sake! Gem's heart pounded hard within her chest, and not only the roar of the lava behind her met her ears, but the roar of her blood vibrated within her body as well! Terrified of what would happen to her, she felt her "fight or flight" instinct arrive – only it would be flight! She sure couldn't fight lava! What should she do? Only one answer.

"Oh, God! I have to get out of here!" she cried, and asked no one.

Her eyes danced around the cave in an effort to find something! Anything? Nothing! Not a fucking, damned thing she could use! Breathing as deeply as she dared, she looked at the bars, and realized that the bars were really made of iron, and the lava stream was headed for the bars. They would melt if she could just find a way to keep it away from her long enough to burn through some of them, she might have a chance. OK, maybe it would be a gamble, but it was either that, or sit there and liquefy painfully. Nope. That wasn't going to happen! Not with Jaxx and Lola waiting for her! She noted that there were some stones, or pillow lava, sitting around. Some of them were very small. She quickly gathered some up, and started lining it end to end to divert the tiny stream toward the bars door. It might not work, but she would die if she didn't try something. She had to get out of there – now!

She watched for a bit, and noted that the lava was very thick, and very slow. The rocks might hold for a short time, but not forever. In the meantime, though, it was becoming hotter and hotter with every second. Now what can I use? Again, she looked around. The lock! If she could just find something to burn the lock away, she could get out of there much faster! There had to be something she could use! Long and narrow would work! Just as she was about to give up, she noted a group of stones that were piled up toward the back of the cave, and rushed to them. They weren't rocks, but bones! Bones of one who had obviously died in the heat, but if the lava had killed them, there would be no bones. So, probably the person had just died from the massive heat. And, that would be her fate, too, if she didn't get the hell out of Dodge!

"Well, bones, you'll be gone in minutes right along with me if I don't do something now!"

Gem sank to her knees with her head in her hands. She wasn't going to get out of here. It was a death trap!

"Oh, Jaxx! I'm going to die in here! We will never have a chance to finish our bond; never experience making love, again; never will I have a chance to carry our child inside of me! Oh, Creator! What can I do? I have to get out of here! Please? Please give me a way out!" she cried out in her misery.

Thirsty...so thirsty! Her mouth was more parched than if she were in a desert! Just moments later, a calm descended over her, and she lifted her head. Well, if this was how she was going to die, then she sure as hell not going to embarrass herself, her mate, or her friends! She flopped down by the bones, and leaned her head back.

"Well, buddy. Soon, your bones, and mine will be turned to melting fluid, and you and I will become a part of this cave forever. Or, we'll be pushed down the tubes, and maybe out to the fresh air, and become part of the outside world," she told them, and looked down.

Eyebrows frowning, she noticed a shiny object that was in the skeleton's hand. She leaned over, and pried it out of the bone's hands, breaking several of them.

"Holy shit!" she exclaimed. It looked like a small piece of iron, but what was it?

Opening her hand, she looked at it. It was a key? A key? How in the hell did a key get into his hand? Her eyes darted to the lock, and back at the key. She jumped and fled toward the door just ahead of the lava, putting the key into the lock. Nothing happened. She kept trying, looking backward now and then to see how close the growing lava stream was to her. Damn! It was flowing faster! She had to do something! That's when an idea hit. As crazy as it sounded, she knew she was dead anyway, so she had nothing to lose. Turning to the lava, she looked at the cooling, crusted lava on the side of the stream. Hesitatingly, she slowly put the tip of the key into the top, and jerked it back out fast. The tip glowed, and began to melt. Gem ran to the door, and put the key into it. Bouncing up and down, she waited to see if the tip could burn the lock, keeping an eye on the fast approaching stream. In moments, the lock caught fire, and burned through it!

"Thank the Creator!" she murmured.

She pushed the door open, and darted out into the tubes. Gem refused to stop, even with the strange crackling and roar that raced behind her. She never even had a chance to wonder why she was running so fast that she could outrun the volcanic flow that raced behind her...and...it was approaching...fast! Coming to another intersection, Gem had only an instant to decide to go straight, right, or left. On impulse, she turned left, and ran for her life! The heat surrounding her was causing it hard to breathe, but she also remembered that she didn't need to breathe. She still didn't know why, but she deliberately stopped breathing. When she did so, Gem felt power flow into her legs allowing her to run even faster without air. She funneled as much of that power as she could into her body.

On and on she ran. Faster, faster, and still faster. Gem continually hit intersections, and her instinct had her go left one more time followed by straight the next. She let her instincts rule.

When her body felt a coolness ahead, she let her breath take over for a second. She smelled air! Fresh air! Behind her, the lava was still flowing. Although she couldn't see it behind her, she could smell the sulfur in that second she took to breathe. Gem ran toward the fresh air.

If Gem had looked to the right when she had turned left at the "T" junction, she might have glimpsed Imaerra just appearing. Imaerra had only missed Gem by seconds. She walked leisurely down to the cave where she had placed the girl. She stopped at the odd crackling sound that she had never before heard. Suddenly, a massive wave of heat hit Imaerra, and all she had was a split second to see a massive, ceiling to floor lava rushing toward her.

"What the hell?" she barely had time to say, only to be hit by said wall of lava, splashing and dividing into all three directions at the "T". Her body was incinerated, before the lava ever reached her. She never even had time to be afraid, nor did she have time to scream! Any other left in th lava tubes had no chance in Hell of surviving.

Bursting into the open air, Gem chanced a deep breath while moving quickly out of the way of another tube she passed. Finally, coming to a stop, she began to pant. She'd made it! Nothing was going to stop her! She tilted her head up as she heard the gushing sound of the lava and the roar of flame and fire. Not stopping, it flowed toward a cliff, and in seconds was rushing over it. Gem sniffed. The fresh air was eliminated as quickly as it came. Now, it was almost impossible to breathe anything other than the sickening stench of sulfur, but a fresh, fragrant scent reached her nose. A fragrance of water and salt. Ocean?

Gem took a moment to look around her. There wasn't just one flow, but many! Other lava flows were scattered here and there. Much of the ground on which she stood was blackened by ancient lava flows, reminding her of the photos she had seen from Hawaii and Iceland – most recent, the scene in Thor: The Dark World. Other parts had tiny sprouts of greenery peeking through the lava. Apparently, it had been a while since the last flow. Gem didn't stop to look at the scenery, but headed toward the smell of the ocean.

Dimly, she heard shouts and screams from everywhere around her. Turning her head, she saw that not only was she trying to avoid the lava, but now, there were guards running after her! And, they were far too close for her comfort! She quickly came to a dead stop. Where was she going to go? She was blocked by several, smaller lava streams on one side, and another about a mile away. She could see that other stream as well as the one that was just a few yards away from her. Luckily, it wasn't large, so she didn't feel the entire heat. But, she just didn't have time to wonder how her eyes could be that good. As far as her speed, well, that would just have to wait, too. She could freak out later. Right now, she had to get away from the lava, and at the same time, away from her captors!

In seconds, she had to make her decision. Down, or up? Which way? Either way, she could smell the richness of water. Up. That's it! She'd go up the side of the mountain, and follow the smell of the ocean – the cool ocean! She was looking forward to getting wet! Turning she embraced her speed faster than before, and ran. Again, somewhere in the midst of everything, she wondered why she wasn't tired?

"Don't think, Gem. Just run!" a voice told her.

Gem didn't stop to analyze the voice. She ran. Another mountain in front of her, just looked as if it reached into the sky forever! Just when she thought she'd gotten to the top, another run over the rise only served to be a "false" top.

"Are you kidding me?" she muttered. "Damn it! Just where the hell was it written that there has to be a false top past the false top? Oh! Of course! In every freaking book ever written no matter what form it took!",

Just how high was this damn thing anyway? Finally, she topped the last rise. She had a short time to survey her situation hearing shouts and yells that followed somewhere behind her. Crap! They were on her damn tail! Taking off again, Gem ran using her survival instincts. She had to get away, and just had to get back to her mate! She had allowed herself to dream about their life together. Growing close, having children, growing old. But, right now, if she didn't get away from the crazy loons behind her, those things would never be hers! What was it that her Father had told her when she was asking him what "freedom" really meant? She called up her memory from that day.

"Gem, not everything is set in stone. Life surprises us with both good and bad. But, sometimes, one has to fight for what they believe in, for what they want to keep,

or even to just preserve it. And, it might very well be our lives. For our freedom is inborn inside of us even before we enter this world. Without that inborn desire for freedom, we are at the mercy of those who would put us in cages for their own twisted desires. And, many would pretend to promise those with weak minds that they, too, would gain great wealth and power with them, as long as the elite tell them what to do. Essentially, they turn them into slaves, before they even realize it!"

"I don't understand, Daddy," she had asked him. "If it's 'free', then why must we fight to keep it? That doesn't make any sense. My teacher says that it's a flawed concept – Freedom. She said that man was never meant to be free. A few, but only a few, were meant to keep us 'safe', and to do so, we must work for them in exchange. It sounds reasonable, doesn't it? I mean…it does to the rest of the kids."

Her Father had snorted.

"Your teacher is wrong! Feedom is the most basic instinct that is in all of us, whether human or animal. Freedom, my little firefly, is never free. It never has been, and it will never be. Many have fought, been maimed, and even died for their families and our country to preserve the very freedoms that we take for granted and others abuse. Our "Constitution of the United States of America" gives us the precious freedom of speech to praise this country, while at the same time also gives those who disdain this country, that same right."

Seeing her frown in confusion, her Father had continued.

"You see, some seek to destroy our freedom from some warped idea that they know better than anyone else. These are people desire to enslave and rule over the rest in the guise of mercy, because they think you and I have no mind of our own. And, even more, that we too ignorant *to not know what is best for our own lives. But, it is that mindset that is flawed, Firefly. But, there's more. They not only want to make decisions for us, but they seek to take our minds to a level of stupidity by taking away knowledge. With the removal of knowledge, we would just blindly follow them. Follow me."*

She had followed her Father into the living room where a huge mirror hung over the sofa. He pointed at it. She climbed onto the sofa so she could see in it.

"What do you see?" he had asked.

She had turned to him, then looked into the mirror.

"You and me, Daddy!"

"What else?"

"I don't understand," she had told him.

"Look again."

She shrugged, and looked again.

"I just see you and me," she had repeated.

"Do you know what I see?"

She shook her head.

"I see a man with a beautiful daughter who can do, or be, anything she wants to be. I see myself as a man who can do, or be, whatever I want to be. There is no cage around us, and no one to tell us what we can, or cannot, do. We are free to be whatever we wish to be, do whatever we wish to do, go wherever we wish to go, and no one can stop us. Now, look again, and see a cage around us."

"But, I don't get it. There is no cage?"

When he answered, the most amazingly, brilliant words came from his mouth – ones that she had never forgotten, which gave her the knowledge she needed. And, they were the words that she used in her report that had earned her a tongue-lashing from her teacher, calling her a "stupid girl", as well as an "F" on her paper.

"Ah, my little firefly! A physical cage is not always needed. In fact, in many countries, especially in the past, the people lived in cages where none exist."

"How can that be, Daddy? Why would they not fight for their freedom?"

"Fear, Gem. Fear and physical force. This is what is instilled into them, and the poverty in which they are forced to live. Always, and forever, one small group of elite people want all to be slaves under them. That fear is enough to keep them in a cage without bars, and subservient to others. Yes, there are cages with bars, but in the long run, there are far more cages without bars. And, that is why we have to fight off and on through the eons to keep our freedoms. It's so simple, I am still amazed at how so many willingly follow them these cages the same way as the children who followed the Pied Piper. These are people who fight to be in a cage through the promises of the elite. They mislead the masses by promising that they will be part of the ones who rule the others. Unfortunately, it is not until those freedoms are taken away, that they realize what they have done. By that time, it is almost an impossibility to get those freedoms back. Therefore, they will remain in captivity for years – even thousands of years – before, and if they are lucky, they rebel. Do you understand, now?" he had asked.

She had just thought she had understood her Dad. However, for the first time in her life, now Gem *truly understood* what her Father had meant. She had been in a physical cage below with bars, but now, if she didn't find a way to get away, she would be in a cage without bars. And, then, fear would keep her where she was. Nope! Not happening to her! That spurred her legs faster. Finally, she reached the top of the mountain coming to a surprising, and sudden stop, flailing her arms to keep her from falling over the edge of a great abyss!

Screams were heard by Eloran, and suddenly, their human guards were running down the hallway. Looking at each other, Quazer, mate to Imaerra, along with Eloran and Delinear suddenly felt a massive pain in their heads. As if a voice was suddenly silenced. It took them a few moments to determine that the screaming, which met their ears, was from one of their own.

"What the fuck?" Quazer gasped, holding his head, before he collapsed to his knees, and whispered, "Imaerra! *NO!!!!*"

"What has happened?" Delinear cried, almost falling to her knees in pain.

"S-she's gone!" he cried.

"Gone?" Eloran asked. "As in...?"

"Dead! She's fucking dead!"

"Impossible! We cannot die!"

"That's a bunch of bullshit! You know that's a lie! We can be killed! When we came to this world, we discovered that the internal fluid of it could destroy us! It's not like on Onaerris! I feel nothing from my mate! *NOTHING*! Do you understand that you bastard? Do you understand what that means?"

Eloran stormed out the door, and grabbed the first person that ran past him.

"The girl! Where is she?" he demanded.

"Let me go! We'll all die if we stay here!" the pathetic, slave of a human said, struggling to get out of Eloran's hold.

"The girl! I will not ask again!"

The human looked up at him in terror, but he wasn't afraid of Eloran. His head turned to look behind him. Lava began to flow toward them.

"Let me go! We're going to die! Will you fucking let me go?" he screamed.

Eloran's eyes narrowed.

"Oh, have no fear. I'll be glad to let you go," Eloran promised.

"Thank you, my lord!" he cried.

Eloran immediately broke his neck, and dropped him, as his own eyes widened at the lava flow gaining on them. He stuck his head in the door.

"The fucking volcano is erupting! We have to get out of here!"

Eloran ran followed by Delinear, who was dragging Quazer behind her.

"Will you come on? We have to get out of here!"

She pulled harder on Quazer's arm.

Quazer jerked his arm out of her grasp.

"*NO!* She is gone! I will not go with you! I cannot live without her, and you know it!"

He pushed Delinear forward. Delinear stopped for just a moment as their eyes met. Then, she shrugged, turned, and ran, following Eloran. Seconds later, the two heard the screams of Quazer, echoing as he was turned to liquid in the lava.

Delinear caught up with Eloran, and they darted out the door to the building where their headquarters had been for a while. Suddenly, a huge earthquake rocked the land beneath their feet, throwing them off balance, and they fell.

Gem came to a dead halt, and flailed her arms trying to keep herself from falling. Finally, she fell back, and landed on her butt, breathing hard.

"Man! Was that close!"

After catching her breath, she got on her hands and knees to crawl slowly toward the edge, and peeked over. She wasn't on a mountain! She was on an extremely high cliff – more like an escarpment than a cliff! It was a sheer drop below. Her mouth dropped open. Several places on Earth vied for the highest cliff. The main one was the Romanche Fracture Zone, where if the water was gone, it was about four miles deep, and yet, water would still be at the bottom!

"Ah, hell!" She shook her head. It was always her lot to come up with some completely random fact in a moment of real terror.

She remembered something on another channel about a 4500 feet vertical drop, but she was absolutely sure that wherever she was, this vertical drop was at least twice, or even three times that high! It was almost unimaginable, even though, it stared her in the face! It was hard to gauge the height at this point. A moot point, because there was one thing she was sure about, and that was she was definitely not on Earth! And, that boggled her mind more than anything. It sounded like a good scene for one of her books, but this was real, and she had only two ways to go. She looked out to the black ocean below (and what caused it to be black, she really didn't want to know), and saw nothing but water far below her. She heard yells behind her, and she turned to look at others jumping, darting back and forth, all the while trying to dodge the lava.

She turned her head to the right then the left. There was nowhere for her to go, but the vertical drop. She was trapped! There was no where else to go, but back, or to jump. Now that her shock had disappeared, fear appeared! The sight was so incredible that she couldn't take her eyes off of it – until she felt the ground under her begin to rock. Pulling away from the edge, she turned around, and saw the massively high volcano, reaching far into the sky, explode! She knew about pyroclastic flows, and now, there was one coming straight at her! Shit! She looked at the cliff, then back at the flow. Great! Her choice of death was either to be incinerated, or death by jumping off an escarpment that was so high, she would probably be dead, before she fell halfway down it! Voices were yelling at her. Gem turned to see Eloran running with Delinear only seconds behind her.

"Going somewhere, Miss Elwood?" Eloran yelled at her. He stopped, and glared at her with an evil grin.

"Hell!" Gem answered him, quietly.

"But, my dear. You have nowhere else to go!" Delinear grinned. At that moment, she looked like the Wicked Bitch of the West!

Gem's eyes widened with fear, but it did not deter from her decision. It was far better than the alternative! At least she would die in freedom! Turning back to Eloran, Gem straightened up with her shoulders back. A slight sneer adorned her face as she looked back at Delinear.

"That's what you think, you bitch!" Gem smirked.

In seconds, Eloran realized what she intended to do, and made a bee-line to stop her.

"You will *not* keep me in a cage! I am free, and I choose to die in freedom rather than let you keep me in one until you are done with me. He will come after you, and you will know every kind of torture ever known!" she yelled back, then turned. Hearing Eloran storming toward her, death was very preferable than life – or lack thereof – that Eloran had in store for her – and she knew it!

Before Gem could think, which just might cause her to chicken out it, she sped to the cliff's edge, closed her eyes, and whispered, "Jaxx, I love you!".

Gem turned back to Eloran, grinned an evil grin at him, reached out her arms, and closed her eyes. Then, she jumped.

Flying off the edge of the cliff with her eyes closed, Gem just knew she was going to die. She knew that her heart couldn't take it as she fell. No one's could. OK. So she had survived being impaled on a tree branch, but this had to be a whole lot different, right? At least eight-thousand feet stood between her and death! What a great choice she had made, but in her gut, she knew that these two were truly evil, especially after hearing them talking in the library. Something odd was happening inside of her. She suddenly felt protective not only of Jaxx, but her friends, and the planet Earth. Whatever it was they wanted with her, she couldn't let them succeed. And, she just knew it had to do with Jaxx.

"I'm sorry my darling," she whispered, tears rolling down her cheeks, while she was waiting to feel the fall. "If only I could have carried our child."

She had jumped off at a great speed, but didn't fall immediately. She waited to fall. Then, she frowned. All thoughts flew out of the window – or in this case...flew off the cliff...when she didn't fall. Her eyes jerked open in surprise.

"What the hell?" she said aloud to no one, as she looked around her.

How could she have missed the edge? She knew she had jumped! But, where she should be falling like a lead weight, Gem stood on solid, unshaking ground – at Jaxx's home! Her home! She was home? How? Then, one of her rare anxiety attacks grabbed her. It always happened when she was confronted with a massive crisis of some sort, but usually did not appear until after-the-fact. Her heart beat so fast, it felt as if it would burst right out of her chest! She couldn't focus or breathe, and her head and stomach hurt. Her only option was to lie down, and fast. She needed something to drink with sugar in it, but sometimes, if she could lay down fast enough, she could control it almost immediately. She dropped like a rock, and laid on the ground for a couple of minutes. She was in time. After her heart stopped beating like a shuttle being launched from Earth, she became dizzy and nauseous the way she always was after her attacks. When she was sure it was over, she slowly climbed to her feet, and began to walk, albeit unsteadily, toward the house. All she wanted was a hot shower, and a warm bed preferably with her mate in bed with her – naked. They needed to complete their bond. Her head swirled. Wait! They had already done that, right?

Tired. So...tired. Stumbling, Gem walked toward the mansion. Walked to freedom. Walked toward the only thing that kept her legs moving one step at a time. Jaxx.

Eloran and Delinear were following their slaves, and their eagle eyes saw the girl almost fall off the cliff, then fall on her ass.

"We have her!" Delinear shouted, as she ran just behind Eloran.

Despite the lava flows all around them, and the ground shaking beneath, she grinned. The two of them slowed to a walk, knowing that the edge of the cliff was a sheer 8500 foot drop! She would never kill herself! She was human! Humans were always weak, and weaker in mind.

"Yes, she is! She is trapped. It's either us, or she jumps," Eloran agreed.

"She's human. She won't jump," Delinear told him confidently. "Humans are weak – terrified of their own shadows! They'd rather live in slavery than to die!" she laughed at him, as he raced ahead of her.

Without answering, Eloran used his super speed. They couldn't let her get away, because their plans would be ruined. He stopped.

"Going somewhere, Miss Elwood?" Eloran yelled at her. He stopped, and glared at her with an evil grin.

"Hell!" Gem answered him, quietly.

"But, my dear. You have nowhere else to go!" Delinear grinned.

"That's what you think, you bitch!" Gem smirked as she turned, and jumped.

Eloran and Delinear dropped their mouths at her words. Then, stunned, they could not believe what appeared in front of Gem! It wasn't possible! She was human! When Gem jumped, their slaves also came to a dead halt right behind them!

"*NO!!!!!!!!!!!!*" Eloran tried to scream, but his voice froze in motion.

"*FUCK!!!!!!!!*" Delinear yelled, her voice hoarse and raspy. "How the he...!"

"No way! Not possible! It can't happen!" Eloran echoed, barely making a sound. "How in the fucking hell was she able to open a Vorc'ara?"

All Delinear could do was shake her head. She was in total shock after what she had seen.

"What is she?" she gasped at the very moment the volcano blew its top.

The entire island shook harder, and they knew that it was coming apart! The pyroclastic flow, while appearing in slow motion thanks to Delinear opening a Vorc'ara, was still coming far too fast. While their slaves were screaming for help, Eloran and Delinear just stood in shock at the idea that somehow – someway – Gem had opened a Vorc'ara! There was only one race who could do this! But, she was human! How could this be?

"I do not know, but we will find out, Delinear. Good thing opening a Vorc'ara slows down time a bit. Let's get the hell out of here!"

While all around them, men and women were falling into the abyss of the planet that was opening beneath their feet, or being gobbled up by the lava flows, these two remained unharmed as they floated several feet above the surface. Without a word, they looked at each other, while Delinear quickly opened the Vorc'ara. They both walked through the vortex, leaving their minions behind to die. Just before Delinear walked into the Vorc'ara, she turned back to look at Eloran.

"Promise me that we will find the bitch, and kill her!"

A short, quick nod from Eloran made Delinear smile as she stepped through the Vorc'ara, first, followed immediately by Eloran. But, not before he answered her.

"Yes. Then, my love. I'll kill you, too! No one will rule by my side! No one!" he said to her, only she could not hear him.

Eloran stepped through the Vorc'ara, and as it closed, the island began to sink behind it.

~ 15 ~
"You never, ever want to discover a Fae is around!" ~ Jaxx

"I am beyond sorry, Jaxx," Kulana appeared to him in his unconscious mind. "Eloran, and the others have escaped from my guards! You must protect Gem at all costs! Now...for the Creator's sake, Jaxx! *WAKE THE HELL UP!* You must find her, before they realize who they have! We had Eloran and Delinear, but they got away!"

Jaxx was completely out, but his first though"t was how did Kulana get into his mind, since that should only belong to his mate. Second, Jaxx had never panicked in his entire life, but right now, even he was beyond that part of his nature! Panic and anger didn't even begin to touch how he felt! He struggled to wake up, but whatever Imaerra had done to him, he just couldn't move. His mind, though, was intact. Even as he continued to try and wake up, he also thought that it was bad enough that Gem had been yanked right out from under his own nose! Now, Kulana is telling him that her own guards allowed Eloran and his "gang" to get away from them? Just as he asked the question, he knew the answer. He slapped his forehead. Well, of course! No one had betrayed either race for thousands and thousands of years. In consequence, Kulana had been loathe to mete out real punishment when it was needed for fear of offending the two races. Because of that lax in judgment over the years, the guards were probably not really protecting their prisoners with the caution that they should have given to them. The PC crap in the human world was bad enough, but they had ignored, or at least pretended, that they were above the humans in the politically correct universe.

However, they were no better than the humans...less even, because they had recognized it, and ignored it! Because of this, they had underestimated Eloran's power and following. Jaxx, knew, and had fought like hell to have him thrown off of the council, but he had been met with too much opposition.

So, now, here they were! Backed into a corner! Jaxx was angry and stunned beyond belief when he had seen Imaerra swoop down in her bird form! He had thought that she was after him, since they didn't know about Gem, and who she was. But, no. She was after Gem, and he knew it was because of him, and more than likely, they thought they would use her as a bargaining chip to get Jaxx to talk! Whatever had been in Imaerra's razor sharp wings, it was something of which Jaxx had no knowledge. All he knew was that whatever it was could not exist on Earth. So, if that was true, then where the hell had she taken Gem? She couldn't have used a Vorc'ara, for only Anaerris royalty could open the vortex. His eye began to droop, and he passed out again.

Grrrr! Slurp! Slurp! Grrrr! Jaxx heard the sound, but also noted that his face was wet. *Was it raining?* Struggling to wake up, he opened his eyes a fraction. Lola was licking his face!

"Ewwww! Seriously, Lola?" he griped, wiping his face with the back of his hand. He pushed Lola off of him. "Was all that drooling really necessary?" She just cocked her head to look at him.

OK. Truth be known, it *was* her licks that had brought him back to consciousness. He looked around frantically for Gem.

"Where could that monster have taken her, Lola?" he asked to no one. He turned to see not Lola, but a tiny figure. "Who...?"

"Don't even bother, Jaxx! I will explain later," she replied in her high, squeaky voice. Tears running down her cheeks, Lola added, "I did not protect her, and for that, I will be forever shamed!"

After an admission from Lola that she had been assigned to Gem's family eons ago, until the time came where the Jewel of Anaerris would arise, he had been even more surprised! Lola had helped Jaxx to the library, and sat him down. Simple though it was, his wounds broke open even worse, and blood ran down his face, arm, and side where Imaerra's wings had sliced his flesh.

"It was not your fault, Lola. I am her mate. It is I who am responsible for her! Your protection ended when she became my mate."

Lola narrowed her eyes at him.

"That has to be the single, most fucking stupid thing you ever said!" she admonished him. "Never mind. I'll get Taylor. In the meantime, I can use my magic to help somewhat. If I knew what that bird had put on her wings, I could probably counteract it, but right now, I have no idea. I'll just have to try different things."

"Whatever. Just do what you can do. Then, I am going after Gem!" he promised, removing his shirt.

"Call me for what, Lola?" Taylor asked as she walked into the library. Her eyes widened at the slices in Jaxx's torso. "Oh, my Creator! What the hell happened, Jaxx!"

"Why?" Jaxx ignored Taylor, and addressed Lola grinding out between his teeth in anger.

Lola knew he wasn't angry at her, but still, it unnerved her to see an Onaerris up close who was losing it! She hadn't seen any of them lose it in eons, but revealing herself to him was important. They were both on the same side – to find Gem. Using her magic over one of the facial wounds, she answered him.

"I would like to say that I was sorry for the deception, oh great one, but I am not. I was assigned to watch Gem by my Queen. The reason was, of course, to protect the Jewel of Anaerris. I have completed this task, and it's time for me to..."

"So, you're running out on her? Sounds like a damn Fae!" Jaxx growled.

"What is it with you Onaerris and even the Anaerris?" she said, frowning at Taylor, too. "You interrupt what I am saying, before you let me finish what I need to say!"

She whacked him in the back of his head.

"What the hell, Lola? What the fuck did you do that for?" he demanded, rubbing his head.

"How about just shutting your mouth long enough to understand what I'm saying!" She looked him in the eye to see if he would keep quiet. After a few moments, she nodded, satisfied. "When the mated Anaerris and Onaerris left the world of Anaerris, they came to the Fae world."

Jaxx opened his mouth, but thought better of it when Lola glared at him. After she was satisfied – again – that he would keep quiet, she continued.

"Who knew that all of you would not only lose your damned heads when you are mated, but you also lost your common sense as well!" she growled. Then, she continued, before Jaxx could question her. "An ancient Fae prophecy arrived at our door – literally. It was said by the most ancient of Fae, long before I was even born, and as long as we have existed, that a child would be born who would change the entire universe, and that she would be a being unlike any other. Earth, as you know, was a good, neutral area. No Anaerris or Onaerris would have thought to ever bother with it, so it just verified who Gem was when Analyse told us where their child should be raised."

Lola sneezed, and then puttered around dusting off a couple of tables, before she finally climbed up on the arm of the chair opposite of Jaxx. She quickly checked to make sure his wounds were healing, then she put her elbows on her knees, and leaned forward with her gleaming, dark, rose-colored eyes. Well, she gave a new meaning to "rose-colored glasses"!

"We were stunned when we were told about this. It's not often that we meet a true prophecy in person! In addition to all of this, Analyse also told us that she would be writing a book that could only be read, or even opened, specifically by the Jewel of Anaerris in the future. We truly believed this to be a very bad idea, when Jolinaer, her mate, told us that the book and the Jewel would not be brought together until the time came for them to be joined. After hearing their plan, we felt that it would be a while before the Jewel would appear, and so, we agreed to it. We knew that the time would come when all would be at risk. If the Onaerris who started the war made it to Earth, then there would be hell to pay."

"And, yet, they came anyway!" he sneered.

"Yeah, yeah! I know, I know! That's a given! We just hoped it wouldn't happen. So, sue us!" Lola told him in a sarcastic tone. She took a breath, and then said, "The idea to Terraform Anaerris was front and center by the Anaerris, and they knew that they could not let Delinear be in charge of Terraforming, even if she did invent the crystal. They were already suspicious of her. So, they made sure the peach ocean was drained thoroughly, before the war began. They knew it was the only way to preserve their race, since the ocean contains all the DNA of all Anaerris."

Jaxx interrupted her, again.

"Oh, yes! And, we all saw how great *THAT* worked!" He frowned. "Exactly whose idea was it, Lola? Whose idea was it to hide Gem? The Fae's?"

Lola truly felt remorse at this, and nodded. Jaxx shot up, and stomped toward the fireplace. He was shaking with anger, and for the first time, Lola was actually scared of him. The admission had sent him over the line, and she knew it. All she could do was continue.

"Bloody hell!" Jaxx was beyond angry, now, and even her saying she was sorry didn't help.

"For that, I am truly sorry. Our queen was a good friend of Analyse, so she agreed to help both her and Jolinaer. Although, some of my brothers and sisters wanted to preserve the Anaerris, they wanted to destroy the Onaerris," she said hanging her head in shame. Finally, meeting the blood red eyes of Jaxx, she gulped, and continued. She could see he was having a problem talking at this point.

"When we realized that the Anaerris and Onaerris had been all but wiped out – something that we did not foresee – the idea was no longer feasible to Terraform Anaerris back into the world it was. The planet was too badly damaged, and all that was left was a black ball of rock. Nothing survived. Terraforming must have some form of life, no matter how small, in order for it to work. So, and as you know, the Anaerris and the Onaerris who had fought beside each other decided to form a Council. This council would decide matters of both races," she sighed. "I know that a few of you decided to "transplant" to Earth. The council was just being formed and, those who were chosen later were heartily against it. We thought it to be a bad idea on your part, not accepting the appointment, but, well..."

Jaxx just watched as she hesitated, and said nothing.

"...the choices were made, and you refused to be on it."

Waving her hand at him to keep quiet, she continued.

"In reality, only a few of both your races survived. It was a bloodbath, and almost an extinction event. Analyse and Jolinaer came to us after Analyse had been changed. As a friend to our queen, there was no doubt that she would help. When I met them after they had come to our realm, I was known as the keeper of the histories of all races."

Jaxx gasped when she said that she was the "Keeper". The "Keeper" was thought to be the most sacred of beings, and quite frankly, he thought she was a myth! And, here she was in person! He had no idea that he was in the presence of one of the most honored Fae to ever walk the face of the – well realms! He began to kneel.

"Stop that, Jaxx!" she told him as she slapped the back of his head, again. His eyes darted up in astonishment. "I've been in this world so long, I think of it as my home, now. So, get over it! Anyway, Gem is my family, and now, of course, you. The one thing that the Fae wanted to preserve – at all costs – was the Anaerris Jewel. After our "healer", Minoth, had determined that the Jewel would have only Anaerris and human DNA, it actually surprised both Analyse and Jolinaer. They asked how their daughter could not have his DNA, and our Queen sought out our "seer", who foresaw that Gem would be mate to an Onaerris. It would be necessary in order to activate the book at some point. If she had Jolinaer's DNA, well, she could, inadvertently, trigger the book before it was time. We were all puzzled, but she refused to elaborate, saying that if we knew, we might accidentally interfere with what had to happen."

"What the hell does that mean?" Jaxx asked.

Again, Lola shrugged, then sighed.

"Analyse was a very smart woman as was Jolinaer a smart man. They would not accept that answer from Minoth, so, Minoth acquiesced, and explained only a small portion of what was to come. She further told them that when the time came that the Onaerris joined with the Jewel, something evil would raise its head. What that was, Minoth refused to tell them. So, in order to make sure the Fae agreed without any possibility of backing out of it, the two of them exacted a blood oath with our Queen, Laquana. She agreed, and her word was law."

Waving at him, again, she added more. "I was assigned to keep watch until the Jewel was born, as I have already said. I jumped at the chance, because I was always writing down histories, but I never got to live them! I have appeared in different forms, since the day I was volunteered for the honored position," she said. Then, for a moment, her eyes became fixed as she said, "You know? I actually prefer being on Earth than in the Fae realm. I love these humans. They are unpredictable, and just downright fun to watch!" She shook her head, then continued. "But, I digress. After a kind Earth couple was found for her, I took the form of a pug, because it was what Gem wanted. So, I just sort of showed up on their doorstep, and without hesitation, her Father tried to find my 'owner'. Of course, he couldn't, so he "adopted" me. And, I have remained at her side ever since. I will protect her at all costs, Jaxx." She stared him in the eye. "Remember that! At. All. Costs! However, at this moment, I wouldn't worry too much about them killing her. They only believe that you have finally found the book, and it is that they want more than her. They do not know that she is the Jewel of Anaerris, and we need to keep it that way as long as possible. But, Jaxx? You must complete the blood bond. Until you do, she will be vulnerable, and more than that, she will not receive her full powers until you do."

"Relax, Lola. The blood bond has already been done. Now, what powers?" he asked.

"Each of your races has specific powers. Even though they are different, your powers are not stronger than the other race. This is a fact. The Creator did not want each race toto be able destroy each other."

"But...?" he began.

"I know. Destruction still happened. That's because several Anaerris, one in particular who was greedy for rule, decided to betray not only their people, but your people, and told the Onaerris about the "Terraforming jewel". If Analyse and Jolinaer had not taken it away from Anaerris, it is highly possible that evil would have reigned – much earlier. Then, trying to correct that evil might have meant destroying the Universe much faster."

Jaxx thought about that for minute. It was true. His kind had always tried to find a way to take Anaerris. If they had gotten their hand on the jewel, who knows what kind of damage they could have done!

"OK. I admit that you're right about that. My kind are far too explosive," he paused. "So, where is she, Lola? I'm going crazy not knowing!"

"I know not. The giant bird? Do you know where it came from? I'm worried sick about my little pet! But, the truth is I don't really know where she is, and that is making me even more nervous!"

That worried Jaxx even more. If Lola – a Fae – was nervous, then by damn, this was about as serious as it could be!

"She was taken by Imaerra, Jaxx."

"What? And, just how is that possible? I thought the Fae knew everything at all times?"

"Well, that's normally true. But, something is affecting my senses, and I don't know what it could be. At the moment, though, we can only hope she'll surv...." Lola started to tell him, but froze when a scent reached her nose.

Both felt a disturbance in the air. Jaxx sniffed, too.

"Gem!" he yelled, and shot out the door at super speed, almost knocking Stan, who had just opened the door.

Rick reached out to steady Stan as he whirled in a circle, then turned to hear his mate voice their concerns.

"What the hell, Lola? Where is he going?" Taylor asked.

Lola just shrugged her shoulders.

"You heard Jaxx. She's home."

"Home? What do you mean home?" Taylor asked. "Whose home?"

"Gem's back from her 'vacation'", Lola answered in a sarcastic tone, leaving the others with expressions of "what the hell?"

Jaxx had never run so fast in his entire life! He followed the same path that Gem and he had taken, before his love had been snatched by that bitch from hell! It hadn't been even twenty-four hours, since he had held her tightly in his arms after making love to her! And, that was just way too long! He slid to a halt as he saw a form stagger towards him. In seconds, he took in her appearance and smell. Her own scent had been muted, and she was surrounded by the stench of sulfur! That was the only clue that he had where she might have been. Gem stumbled, and before she could fall. He knew there was no way in hell that she could stand, let alone walk a straight line.

The moon was high, so he could easily see Gem's face. His first up close look at her made him wince in horror. She was filthy. Absolutely filthy and covered with what looked like dirty snow. Her bright red hair was no longer red, but pinkish gray. Her clothing was covered in blood, and her face had bloody smears all over it.

"Jaxx?" she whispered, barely getting his name out of her mouth. She was so tired. So blankety-blank tired. Too tired to even think of a cuss word!

The decaying odor coming from her almost knocked him off his feet! She smelled as if she had been rolling in rotten feces somewhere! He stopped his breath, so he wouldn't have to breathe the stench. His piercing canines appeared, and his eyes turned blood red. But above all, he never wanted her to know how she smelled. Well, truth be known, she had to know. Wherever she had been, the horror on her face was enough to keep him silent about it, for now. Did she know it was one of his kind that had kidnapped her?

Picking Gem up in his arms, she kept muttering, "Hot! So damned, fucking hot! I am so very sorry. So, high! No. Cannot let Eloran and Delinear imprison me, again! Jumping is the only way. I just know I'll be dead, before I'll ever reach the ocean!"

Hot? Why would she be hot? Frowning, he turned, and sprinted back to the cave. If a human had seen him, they would see nothing at all, or they might see just a slight blur. Quickly, Jaxx placed her in his shower – their shower. Then, he removed her clothing, and threw everything in the fireplace to burn. Nothing would ever remove the smell from the fabric. He returned only to find her sitting on the floor under the hot spray of the water, and his heart broke when he saw her. Her knees were drawn up, and her hands covered her face as she leaned back against the tiled wall. Tiny shudders racked her body over and over from silent tears that poured down her face. Blood washed and swirled in a red river towards the drain. She looked so forlorn; so sad! He quickly undressed.

"Gem?" he asked softly, as he stepped into the shower.

Gem looked up at him, only partly believing she was home, and safe. And, her mate – her naked mate – was standing before her. She tried to stand, but Jaxx gently pushed her shoulders back down as he knelt to the floor to keep her still.

"Don't try to stand, Gem. You're too weak."

Despite the fact that Gem shook her head, he asked no questions. And, for that, Gem was grateful. But, she needed to get it off her chest. If she didn't, she couldn't go on with her life.

Before Gem could speak, Jaxx took shampoo in hand, and cleansed her hair thoroughly until her hair was bright red, again. Then, using soap, he started to bathe her back, where he moved his hands in slow, circular motions. He found the broken skin under her hair, and made sure he was very gentle.

His touch was almost like a caress and a massage at the same time. Gem moaned in relief as he cleaned the stench of the sulfur from her body, as well as the dirt and blood. Then, Jaxx moved around to her front, and she leaned back against the tile, relishing in the slightly warmer water that fell from the ceiling like rain. She let her face, eyes closed, turn upward to feel it's healing power. Then, she felt Jaxx begin to rub her face and neck gently. He worked his way down her body with the gentlest of hands. When he reached her breasts, he was very tender as he cleansed them. Even with her eyes closed, she could feel the tips turning hard with desire. How was that even possible after everything she had been through? Warmth pooled between her legs as she felt his hands bathe her body down her stomach to the apex of her thighs. Without a thought, she parted her legs. Still with her eyes closed, she felt his gentle hands drop between her legs. He worked his magic slowly over her clitoris and the opening to her sex. He took the hand held shower, and gently sprayed the area clean of the soap.

He had already scented her arousal before he cleaned her, but now, looked up into her open – and red – eyes! Gem glanced downward to his lengthening cock, as it became hard with every second her eyes stared at him. He desired her more than life itself, now, and lust began pouring out of his every pore! Gem felt it! He saw her nod once, and he lay down between her legs, while she watched Jaxx's mouth water staring at her soaked pussy. She needed this! Needed him! Needed to remind herself that she was still alive, no matter how tired she was. She needed to believe that she was finally safe. When his tongue swirled over her clit, she cried out in desperate need. Hard; fast. That's what she needed to erase her brush with death, and imprisonment. When his tongue began to dart in and out of her opening, she felt her climax explode into his mouth, and she pressed her sex into his mouth, so that he could drink of her special nectar.

"Oh, Jaxx!" she breathed. "Please? I need you! I need you inside of me!"

Without a word, he slithered up between her legs to suckle one nipple, while he squeezed and caressed the other one. Then, hearing her moans, he switched nipples, and paid the same, loving attention to her other one.

Gem couldn't think! Not with the incredible pleasure he was giving to her. It was exactly what she needed. She could tell him about her ordeal later, but right now, she needed his huge, ripe cock inside her. She needed his hot seed to explode into her womb!

In a move so bold and strong, she yanked his mouth to her lips giving him a kiss unlike he had ever had! Jaxx let himself go, and kissed her passionately, possessively, as if he had been through hell waiting to do so. He lifted her face to his. Like her, he needed her desperately. Needed to bury his cock deep into her body; to release the contents of his balls that were heavy with seed. Jaxx knew that he needed to feel her hands closer to his erection, so he took her hand, and moved it down to the tattoo just above his cock. When she began to move lower, she traced his tattoo, and he sighed in desire.

"Touch me, Gem," he whispered into her ear. "Please, touch my cock. I need to feel your hands on it!"

Gem was mesmerized. She couldn't stop touching him. Her eyes dropped to his hard-on that was pointing directly at her, and moaned. When he ordered her to touch him, she couldn't resist. That hardness was something she needed to feel beneath her hands – then, inside of her, pounding her into oblivion! Her hand gently cupped around his cock. Feeling its size in her hand caused her eyes to close in total desire. She wanted it – now. Wanted it inside of her – now.

Jaxx bowed his head toward her, and in a split second, his lips met hers, even while her hand continued to gently stroke him. He reached behind her, grabbing her naked ass and pulling her tightly into his body. Slipping his fingers between the folds of her sex, he felt how wet she was for him! Wonderfully, gloriously wet! So wet, it even coated his hands! She was ready for his invasion, and released her hand from his erection, so that he could grind it against her, then brought her arms up as he used one hand to hold them above her head. He wanted to dominate her! To take her body, and invade it! His head dipped, and crushed his lips against hers, again! His mouth ravaged hers as if he were a pirate bent on taking his woman!

She threw her arms around his neck feeling and needing his possession of her. One of his hands slipped down behind her, tracing her crack with his fingers, then allowed his hand to dip further underneath! His cock jerked hard at the anticipation of taking her. Slowly, he stroked her sex, earning moan after moan from her, that only served to harden his cock. He yanked his mouth from hers. Breathlessly, their chests heaved with desire. Still stroking her silky wet core, he plunged one finger into it, causing her to cry out in pleasure. His finger moved inside of her fast, even as he thrust a second, and third finger into her wet heat! She was hot inside. His balls filled even more with his seed, as he felt her slick entrance and walls close tighter around his fingers. He groaned out loud.

"Creator, Gem! You're so damn, fucking wet for me!" he growled. He needed to feel her around him to make him really believe she was with him. "I love you, Gem. Even while I was out cold, I was so scared I would never see you, again!"

Gem arched I thought I would die, never to see you, again in this life!" She gasped. "What do you want to do to me, Jaxx?" Say it! Please!"

His head buried into her neck, he could smell her blood just underneath the skin; feel her speeding heartbeat. He raised his eyes to hers. The desire to sink his teeth into her neck became overwhelming.

"I want to fuck you senseless!" he whispered to her.

"You mean...with this hard part of your body? Your, uh, now, what is it called?" she giggled.

"Say it, Gem! I want to hear you say it!"

She stared up at him, then answered.

"Your cock of steel feels like velvet to me," she panted, stroking him. "I want your penis inside of me – now!"

He laughed.

"Demanding little bitch, aren't you?" he said jokingly.

She pulled his lips to hers.

"As you are my little bastard!" she added. "Now, are you going to fuck me, or not?"

"That is a direct question, and it deserves a direct answer," he said.

He lifted her with one hand, thrusting into her wet sheathe.

Gem cried out as he filled her body! After everything she had experienced, and she almost lost her life in a volcano, she needed to reaffirm her life by creating a life with the man she loved more than any other. Her eyes began to darken to a red that was almost black.

Jaxx pulled back from her lips while moving his hips back and forth, burying himself inside of her to the hilt. They stared into each others' eyes, and she pulled her lips back over her teeth, revealing her elongated canines. Jaxx sucked in his breath at her eyes and teeth! His own widened as his lips sprang back from his own canines.

"Are you ready to bond with me, again, Gem?"

"I thought we had already done that?" she whispered.

"We have. But, bonded mates re-bond a great deal. But, this one is different. Just before our first climax is reached, we will bite each other, and drink. Then, we mate from behind," he explained with his eyebrows wiggling at her.

"Behind?" she asked with a slight grin.

He leaned down to her ear to whisper.

"You will be up on your knees, and I will plunged deep into your cavity. And, then, Gem, my beautiful mate, I will try to impregnate you with my seed.."

Gem jerked in pure desire. Pure lust.

"Do you think you can give me our child?" she asked him, panting hard.

"If I cannot, then you and I will certainly try again and again!" he smiled as he opened his mouth, and sank his canines into her neck.

Gem jerked at the momentary prick, then cried out in ecstasy as she felt his cock become impossibly harder and larger as it pounded into her body, while his mouth sucked on her blood! In seconds, she opened her mouth, and sank her teeth into his neck, and began to suckle his blood into her! They both began their climax almost immediately, and she felt his hot seed spurt and she met each thrust with the same fervor. Her walls clenched down tightly on his cock as if it was in a vise! She milked every single drop of his seed from him, and still, her channel clamped down on him wanting more! Quickly, he pulled from her, and flipped her onto her knees. He used his hand to rub the tip of his still-hard cock gently up and down her crack, while watching his seed spill from her body onto the tile floor only to be rinsed away by the falling water.

"Damnit, Jaxx! Fuck me!" she begged. "Please!"

"My pleasure!" he told her, and plunged back into her body. Deeper and deeper he thrust into her from behind, his fingers digging into her luscious, smooth ass, until he entered her womb. The moment he did, their release came. Both lovers screamed out at their violent climax!

Gem collapsed onto the tile floor. It was not only cool, but felt like a mattress to her after that damn cavern! She felt Jaxx collapse next to her as well. For several minutes, all that could be heard was the raining down of the warm water onto them, and their frantic pants as they waited for their pounding hearts to slow.

When Gem began to return to the world, silent tears reigned down her face. Without a word, Jaxx pulled her into his arms, and held his mate tightly, letting her cry.

Gem let the tears fall for what seemed like hours, completely ashamed of herself after what she had shared with Jaxx. She never meant for him to feel bad or sad, but she just couldn't stop the tears! When he pulled her even tighter, her crying included huge, gulping sobs, because he was so tender, and didn't ask her a thing. She knew she didn't need to do so.

Jaxx knew everything that Gem was thinking, now. The blood bond was firmly, and permanently, in place between the two of them. As his mate cried, he was able to catch glimpses of what had happened to her when she was taken from him. But, when he saw lava coming toward her, while she was locked in a tiny underground, volcanic cave, he had to restrain himself from shaking with anger! When Gem's crying began to lessen, he finally began to see the entire picture through her eyes, and what he saw, had him shaking with more anger than he had felt in the last ten thousand years, and his warrior nature erupted from him as he let her show him what had happened to her!

~ 16 ~

"Some days, you just find out things you'd rather not know – especially if it concerns you!" ~ Gem

Since, Jaxx had been knocked cold by whatever poison was on Imaerra's wings, he had not seen what had happened. Jaxx watched through Gem's eyes – watched her grabbed by Imaerra's razor-sharp talons biting into her shoulders. Gem watched in horror seeing Imaerra's poison laced wings swipe against him, rendering him unconscious. Moments later, Gem passed out from sheer terror from the attack on both of them. The next thing he saw, was when she woke up in a volcanic cave. He was immediately blasted with a horrible heat. How in the hell had Gem not burned? No human, or Anaerris could have possibly withstood that type of heat! Only he and other Onaerris could withstood that type of heat, since their planet was volcanic. Lola had told him that she had no Onaerris within her, so, how could she stand the heat without turning to ash?

He pushed that thought aside as he realized that Gem was deliberately showing him the next scene. He saw the small hole and tiny rivulet of magma that flowed from it, which became larger by the minute. He puffed up with pride as he watched her solve the real dilemma of how to get out of that cell! She had done it brilliantly!

Gem smiled in his arms, when she felt the overwhelming pride that Jaxx felt for her. It had taken a while to realize how the two of them could communicate with each other by the unification of their minds.

Next, Jaxx saw her running for dear life as the lava broke through, and began to pour into the lava tubes. Screams of terror rocked the inside of the tubes. It took Jaxx a minute to realize that it was because there were other prisoners within the tubes that were left behind to melt. He felt her cringe as she discovered that she would hear those screams for the rest of her life. That's when he saw the lava rush toward her, and sent Gem into an unbelievable run, when she looked back just as she burst out of the tubes, and darted quickly to the left to avoid being hit by the blast. When that was over, he saw her run wherever she could – faster than she should possibly be able to run. Squinting his eyes, he tried to place where she was? It was an alien landscape with steam rising from the crust. Very little green was visible. When she looked up to see the volcano that rose above her, he gasped. One thing he did know. It was higher than anything that could ever be found on earth. It reached and stretched into the heavens, far into the clouds of the volcanic, orange sky. Where in the hell had Imaerra taken her? He squinted, trying to find something familiar, but could find nothing. Gem jarred his mind again, and he found himself standing on an escarpment. Looking down there was a massive, black ocean stretching in front of her, but the drop was unbelievable – even by human or Onaerris standards! Looking behind her at someone calling to her, he saw Eloran and Delinear! Those assholes! Gem's next memory drug him from his anger. Gem made a decision. She either jumped, or succumbed to Eloran and Delinear, letting them take her away forever. But, he also felt her hesitate.

"Eloran? It was Eloran and Delinear?" he asked, which just confirmed for him that Kulana was right.

"Y-yes."

Suddenly, it dawned on him. How did she know about them?

"How do you know who they are, Gem?"

"I know, because I was listening at the door when you guys were in the library," she said sheepishly.

"You didn't stay in our room?" he yelled.

"NO! I did not! Just because you tell me to do something, what makes you think I'll do it? I'm a free agent, Jaxx, even if we are tied at the hip by a blood bond!"

She refused to let anyone tell her what to do! She wondered why Jaxx had not figured that out yet? Oh. Right. He was a man. Er, an alien man. Apparently, men could easily be dicks all over the universe! And, they always thought with them, too! She fed him the next scene that had him growling even more in anger at her. He grabbed her shoulders, and shook her.

"What the hell, Gem? You were going to kill yourself by jumping off the escarpment? What the fuck were you thinking? You're mine! How dare you even think of it!" he raged, angry that she had made the decision to jump from the escarpment. "I would have found you! Why would you do that?"

Her mouth turned up in a smile, as she fed him the next picture. His mouth dropped as he watched her actually step off into nothing – but didn't fall?

Gem shrugged as she leaned back to look into his eyes.

"I don't know what happened, Jaxx! I mean...I took a step forward waiting for the fall, but nothing happened. When I opened my eyes, well, I was back home! For the life of me, though, I don't know how I ended back out in your yard!"

"Our yard," he absentmindedly corrected her.

Jaxx knew, but he could hardly believe it! She was Anaerris, after all, but it never occurred to him that opening one could be involuntary. Every Vorc'ara he had ever heard of had been deliberately opened! But, obviously Gem had no idea what it was, let alone how to open one. Somehow, Gem had opened a Vorc'ara without knowing about it! It was the only explanation! HE wondered whether it was inborn in all Anaerris to open one even unconsciously, or was it only Gem who could do so? That was a bit of information that the Onaerris never knew! Hell! For once, he was glad they did not know about this!

"I opened what?" she yelled, when Jaxx uttered the weirdest word she had ever heard through their bond. "What the hell are you talking about, and what the fucking hell is a Vor-ca-whachamacallit? What do you mean I didn't open it consciously, because it is inborn in all Anaerris? What do you mean the Onaerris didn't know about it?" she demanded, as she sprang out of bed in one movement.

Ah, crap! He'd forgotten to shut his own thoughts off from her while he watched hers. He looked at her wondering how he could explain what one was. Well, he really couldn't. She needed another Anaerris to explain it, and teach her.

Gem was so hot when she was angry,and he licked his lips in sudden lust. Jaxx lunged at her in a speed so fast, Gem hadn't even seen him move! Jaxx picked her up, and threw her back onto the bed, jumping in, and laying down on top of her with his hard and erect organ cradled between her wet thighs. He started fondling her breasts, and suckling her nipples, when she pushed his head up to look him in the eye.

"Uh-uh, lover boy! No more down here until you start explaining," she demanded pointing at her apex, but with a small sexy smile on her lips.

Oh, man! That sexy smile was almost more than he could handle as he felt his cock rising quickly. He sighed. She wasn't going to leave this alone, until he explained.

"You are damn well right about that, lover boy!" Her grin took the sting out of her words.

"OK. We still believe that you are the Jewel of Anaerris. You are not just human, but are also the product of an Anaerris and Onaerris.

Gem's mouth dropped.

"W-what d-did you say?" she squeaked. "A-re you saying that..."

"You are not fully human? Yes."

"I-I don't understand, Jaxx!"

"OK. You are both like me and like Taylor, but only one-third of each race. That's why you healed from the wound. Surely, you suspected you weren't totally human?"

Gem narrowed her eyes at him, and deliberately crossed her arms underneath her breasts pushing them upward – on purpose. OK. So, yes. She had suspected it. Now it was confirmed, what was she going to do? She saw Jaxx's eyes were fixed on her perky little nipples, and licked his lips, again.

"Jaxx?" she pressed his head upward to change the direction of his heated gaze. She pointed toward her face. His face was fixated on her breasts. "My eyes are up here!"

"What? He jerked his eyes back to hers, then grinned wickedly earning a roll of her eyes. "Oh, right. Yeah. Well. Like the Onaerris, the Anaerris have certain powers, too, Gem," he began.

Gem's eyes popped out at that, and she dropped her hands as she sprang up into a sitting position.

"Powers? What the hell? Where did that come into it?"

"Well, several powers, actually," he continued as if she hadn't spoken. "And, now, being mated to me as well as bonded by blood, you will be developing many more."

Was he joking? Playing with her?

"But, wha..."

"Hold on. Let me finish. The Anaerris have this one, very important, and particular power that no other in the universe has. And well...." he trailed off trying to figure out how to break this new information to her without her getting upset. She hadn't responded well a few minutes ago. He shook his head. Nope, Jaxx. There is no other way! Jaxx just had to tell her up front.

"Well....what?" Gem flipped him sideways, and pushed him back onto the fluffy pillows behind him.

"Now, don't get panicky about this," he said seeing her breathing pick up speed, causing her breasts to bounce gently with each breath. "Well, you see? The Anaerris have the ability to open a Vorc'ara."

Seeing her eyebrows draw into a frown, he explained further.

"Yeah, yeah. Cut the crap! What IS that?" she demanded.

"I guess the best way to describe it is that it's, essentially, a stable wormhole."

Gem's mouth dropped, and she sat back on her knees in shock just staring at him. A wormhole? Did he just say a wormhole?

"A wormhole...you mean like in Stargate SG-1?" she squeaked. It had always been one of her favorite science fiction shows.

"Basically, yes."

"But, how is that even possible?"

He shrugged.

"Well, I really don't know. It's a heavily guarded secret by the Anaerris, and I know of no one outside the royal families who even know about it, let alone accomplish it."

"And, of course, there are no other royals around, right? Then, how am I supposed to learn how it works...?"

"Well, one, you already opened it. How do you think you got back home, and escaped from Eloran?"

"But, *how* did I do it?" Her eyebrows went up in surprise. She really opened a Vorc'ara? Then, as if to reinforce this idea, Jaxx just grinned.

"I wish I knew. Wanna tell me?" he laughed. She punched his arm with a smirk.

"Yeah. Sure. I'll tell you all about that deep, dark secret that even I don't know!" After a couple of minutes of silence, she thought of an answer.

"What about Taylor? Was she a part of the royal family? Taylor would know, wouldn't she?"

"She would," he answered.

This was getting far too involved, far too fast for Gem's liking. First, when he had said the word "home", it made her feel all ooey and gooey inside. He was right. She was right here, in the home and bed of her mate and lover. Second, she was surrounded by all the incredible people she loved most in this world. Third, when Jaxx was inside of her, she knew she would always be "home" no matter where they were in the world. Gem narrowed her eyes, and like always, she rattled off her nervousness by speaking fast, listing everything that was bugging her. And, she did so rapidly, without a breath.

"Whatever," waving her hand at him. Taking a deep breath, "OK. So. Let me get all this straight. I am being pursued by some crazy group of people from an alien council where almost half of them want to kill me only they don't know I'm me, but they are really after you, because they think you know where the book is, and I've been chased by monster storms created by these nutcases, almost killing my pug, burning down my house, impaling me on a tree, but I healed, because I'm some sort of half-alien and, now, I am thought to be some kind of super being, or something else, and found a book that everyone and his aunt wants to get their hands on, but I'm some sort of "Jewel" who is the protector of said book. I've found my 'mate' who happens to be one of my own Professors who, I never knew was so hot, he sizzles my skin and womb, until I see him waiting for me after dark, and almost have sex with him on the side of the road in my truck! Then, I almost had sex with you – again – and discovered a son-of-a-bitch – and a bitch – who have no compulsion in killing you, who wants to kill me, too. Then, I find a very secret, massive cave that is your home only to find out that you are filtering an alien peach sea that accidentally was let loose into the Earth's oceans through some crystal, when you guys pretended to be the ancient gods of mythology, and the sea was supposed to be used for Terraforming Anaerris, but couldn't, because it was burned out, so instead, it was given to you for safekeeping, and brought to Earth, and now wants to be stolen by the evil bastards to Terraform Earth. And, if that's not enough, I'm kidnapped, taken Creator knows where – but certainly it wasn't Earth – and almost killed by boiling hot magma, while the same kidnappers just happened to be the same evil crew that stood in your library threatening you, only to step off an escarpment intending to die, only now, I've discovered that because I'm part Anaerris, I can open a Vortex..."

She stopped when she saw Jaxx rocking with laughter, listening to Gem as she condensed everything that had happened without stopping for one single breath!

"V-vorc'ara," Jaxx interrupted her with a correction in between gulps of laughter from her diatribe.

"*Careful, mate,*" she warned him through their bond. It just made him laugh even harder.

"Oh, come on, G-Gem! You have to admit that was amazingly hilarious!"

"Jackass," she muttered under her breath. More laughter came from Jaxx. *"Shut it! OK...Vorc'ara...which is nothing more than a wormhole, for the Creator's sake! And, now, I've had the most amazing, earth-shattering sex with said hottie, not to mention blood bonded with my mate so that I can receive even MORE damn powers, and while this is all happening, I'm still trying to figure out just why I am some damn protector of some damn book! Just what the hell is in that book anyway?"*

She was magnificent! Jaxx was mesmerized by her lips, even while laughing at her! With every single word, his cock had hardened, and he desired to implant it into her delicious body! He felt wet on his stomach, and looked down to see his tip was leaking his own droplets. His sexy eyes darted back up to her, drinking in her breasts that were heaving with her long-winded speech! He couldn't help himself! He had to have this strong woman, and needed to bury himself deep into her body, again. She would be with him forever, and he knew he would never get enough of her.

What he didn't realize was that Gem was more than ready to mounthis hard cock that lay on his stomach, jumping and flexing! Without a second thought, she rose, and positioned his cock at her entrance. She sat down on him – hard – taking him into her body with a speed worthy of an Anaerris female! And, she didn't even realize it! All she did know was that from the moment she had taken his blood into her body, she had become a wild, nymphomaniac, and she was loving it! Even though she was distracted by everything, she needed him to erase everything she had been through. She needed to know that she really was home. And, it appeared from Jaxx's eyes, and the grip of his hands on her hips holding her as he pounded his way up into her, that he needed to know it as well. One hand left her hip, and stroked her breast gently as she rode him.

"Harder, Jaxx! My tits need to feel your hand harder on me!" she cried, throwing back her head, and jutting them out at him.

"Harder, my little nympho?" he laughed wickedly.

She glared at him. He had to ask her?

"Yes!" she demanded.

He became rough as his other hand joined its mate, and there was no other description for what he did to her next. He man-handled each breast with his hands. With each grasp, squeeze, and rubbing of her nipples, she screamed out his name only serving to drive him harder into her, and fondling her even harder!

Then, suddenly, she stopped. His cock hard inside of her was throbbing while her walls were clamping down on it. Jaxx frowned. He was ready to spill his seed! His balls were clenching ready to release their contents.

She leaned over him as she laid down on him bracing her arms on either side of his head. Gem gently slid her nipples over his face, his eyes, his nose, his lips, tempting him while his cock jerked inside of her, and she moaned.

"Open your mouth, and bite me, Jaxx!" she whispered to him.

"Bite you?" he said in surprise.

"Yes!" she purred.

"Then, woman, put your luscious tit in my mouth!" he demanded, and she pushed one nipple into his mouth to suckle.

Jaxx sat up to suckled his mate's nipples, drawing them into his mouth hard and deep. His fangs descended, and he positioned them on either side of her nipple. Then, he bit down, and began to suck her blood! At the same time, he really wanted to shove his huge cock into her mouth, and release his seed into it! There was something extremely sexy knowing that he wanted to remove his cock covered with her juices and his semen, and jab it into her mouth! He wanted to feel her mouth as she sucked him until he came! He wanted to spill his seed into her mouth, then wanted to share it with her. When his fangs retracted, he started to heal her wounds with his tongue, but stopped when Gem said something that made him go still.

"No, Jaxx! Let them stay, and heal normally. I want to be able to look at my breast, and see your mark on me!" she whispered into his ear, dragging her hard-tipped breasts against his chest.

OK. He'd never thought about those "marking" her as his, but it was OK with him! He just licked off the small amount of blood, then leaned backward staring at his marks. She wouldn't be the only one to see them when he looked at her! That just made his cock jerk with need.

As if Gem knew exactly what he had been thinking, she slid her silky, wet sheath off of his cock, and stared at it longingly. She needed to suck him! Needed to let his seed spill inside her mouth! She wanted to share it with him...to drink deeply of his milk!

They stared at each other panting hard. Then, Jaxx had to ask.

"Gem. Suck me? Suck my cock! Let me spill my seed into your mouth?" he asked in a sultry tone.

Gem's lips swept up into a huge, evil grin as she slid off the bed, and onto her knees. Silently, she leaned her neck upward, and opened her mouth for him. Jaxx's excitement reached a fevered pitch as he watched her nude body slide to the floor. It became even stronger when she leaned her head backward with her mouth open. He slid to the edge of the bed, and stood. With his hand, he guided his juice-coated cock into her mouth. Her lips closed over it, and she began to suckle his wet, velvety steel.

She had never tasted anything as good as he slid his wet cock inside her mouth! She gently gripped it, running her hand slowly up and down his massive shaft, while Gem increased the pressure of her mouth against the tip. She circled her tongue gently around the tip that was oozing with so much of his liquid, while she felt her insides go weak as water at the incredible taste of him! Again, her lips encompassed his tip, and she slowly slid them up and down his massive cock, listening to him groan in desire and excitement. She suckled harder and harder wanting his semen inside her mouth. She let go for a moment, her sexy eyes staring at him.

"You're so wet, Jaxx! We taste so good on you! Come for me!" she ordered, as she squeezed his engorged balls gently with her hand.

Jaxx took his cock, and began to pump it inside of her mouth faster and harder. He felt it hit the back of her throat, but all Gem did was moan in need. He increased his speed feeling his balls contract under her delicious fingers, and seconds later...he screamed her name loudly as his semen jetted into her mouth.

Gem couldn't believe how much creamy, white liquid shot into her mouth. So much, she had to swallow some of it, so that she could hold some of it in her mouth for her to share with him. She moaned with every single pulse of it! After a few minutes, he finally had ejected every single drop inside her as she had sucked him hard with each thrust.

He yanked her up to him, crushing her tender breast with his marks against him, pushing his still hardened cock against her stomach.

"Feed me, Gem!" he commanded, as he pushed her mouth against his, and opened it.

His own seed spilled from her mouth into his, and they shared it back and forth, twirling their tongues in the creaminess, before they swallowed. His cock was already hard, again, and as their lips parted, Jaxx fell with her onto the floor, flipped her onto her knees, and mounted her. She screamed as he thrust into her! She pushed back against him with each thrust, meeting him as the wet sounds of their bodies squished and slapped together, until he shot his seed into her once more. He saw Gem try to stop them from reaching the rug, and he brought her hand up to his lips, kissing it gently, reverently.

"But...Jaxx, we can't let it get on..."

He put a finger to her lips.

"Forget it! Let it flow, Gem. Just let it flow."

At some point, he had picked her up, and placed her onto their bed as she slept. Jaxx, technically, did not "sleep" as humans knew it, but he had never meditated as deeply as he did that night. Time had no meaning at the moment. He heard Gem moan, and he felt her hips push against his hard erection, which was constant, now. It just never softened around Gem! It was always throbbing, and pulsing with desire for her. Without turning, he lifted her top leg, and draped it backward over his. Then, he slowly rubbed himself against her crack, feeling their juices coat him. His eyes closed feeling each stroke of his hardness.

Gem awoke. Her dream had been incredible, but this was no dream! Her mate was stroking her crack, and all she could do was to remember every single moment while she had been awake. She moaned gently feeling Jaxx's hard-on that was gently rubbing her crack up and down! She pushed her hips against him, and felt his hand gently lift her leg over his while he slowly – very slowly – pushed into her soaking wet channel. She was surprised to find semen still flowing from her, but it just made it easier for him to enter her body. This making love was slower. She relished his movements in and out of her tight sheath, and pushed back against him as he began to increase his thrusts into her.

Jaxx wanted to stay inside his mate forever! He never wanted to leave her body! It was his home. He never felt as content as when he was inside of her. Never felt desire this intense. And, he loved it! Hearing her moan made him thrust harder, until his seed spilled from him once again.

"Oh, Jaxx!" Gem moaned softly as she felt him thrust one last time into her. "That was so...beautiful!"

Silently, Jaxx pulled from her, and turned her over, so he could see her soft, satisfied eyes staring up into his.

"It was. I never want to leave your body, or your side, for eternity."

Smiling, but tired, she pulled him back to her lips, kissing him softly once again.

"Jaxx, nothing will ever keep me from your side. No matter what happens; no matter where we are – apart or together – I will never leave you," she murmured just before her eyes closed, and she fell deeply asleep next to him. Jaxx followed in meditation. As happy and sated as he was at the moment, he couldn't help but wonder if Eloran and Delinear had seen her open the Vorc'ara, then how long would it be before they realized just who his mate really was! Grating on his brain, he finally had to admit that it would not be long. He pulled Gem into his arms a bit tighter.

"And, where are we going this time?" Delinear demanded of Eloran, as the emerged from her Vorc'ara for the fourth time. They had tried several other planets, but none satisfied Eloran, and she was getting pissed!

When Eloran refused to speak, she repeated it, but much louder.

"Eloran! Are you even listening to me? Where the hell are we going? We can't go back to the island on that world of ocean! It was the only damn bit of land on the whole planet!"

Eloran was deep in thought, still wondering how that little bitch of a *human* girl could open a Vorc'ara! But, the fact that the colors of red and white for a Vorc'ara did not exist, according to Delinear! For the life of him, he couldn't understand! He'd wracked his brain since the moment they had seen her step through it! Still thinking, he walked into a cloud bank followed by Delinear, although he ignored that she was there. In fact, truth be told, Eloran had forgotten Delinear altogether in his desperate attempt to make sense of the entire thing. Shaking his head, he was in complete confusion. He was never confused. There was always an answer to every question, but this one had him totally stumped. There was no way a human could open a Vorc'ara. That was reserved, specifically for the Anaerris royals. It was just another thing that angered him towards the Creator – for the billionth time, and he silently cursed the Creator for granting them that power. The Anaerris were weak fools! They had proved that by burning their planet to a cinder! But, then, he had talked Delinear into betraying them. Everyone had assumed it was a jewel, since they all used them for storing information. But, what if it wasn't a jewel? He came to sudden stop. He had never factored in that the Anaerris would drain the precious ocean he craved, resulting in the moon burning permanently. Nothing could ever grow on it again. Eloran needed all three of them – the crystal, which started the war in the first place, the book, and the Jewel. He wanted his hands on it! He wanted to rule the entire universe! His plan was to Terraform certain planets into a volcanic oasis for the Onaerris, while the Anaerris, and other beings, would be planted on the others, forcing them to become slaves. To think that he would have an unlimited amount of slaves for his own nefarious purposes was enough to drive his obsession to possess the jewel as well as the crystal. Without the three, it wouldn't be happening! Huffing, he began to pace once again.

Back to the girl. She was human, and couldn't open a Vorc'ara, but he had also never known it to be opened by any other but an Anaerris. Then, another thought occurred to him that brought him to a halt, once again. He was almost hesitant to ask. Delinear plowed into his back, causing her to bounce off him, and fall flat on her ass.

"Damnit!" Delinear growled, as she stood and brushed the sand from her butt. "Will you wake the fuck up, Eloran! We have to have some kind of a plan!"

Back on the last planet that was lush and green, Delinear had been trying to get through to Eloran any way she could – including stripping naked, and practically raping him. Eloran hadn't even shown any interest! He'd flicked her off of him as if she was a fly. She was horny to a fault, but Eloran hadn't put out for her! Neither of them had ever gone that long without sex, and she was in dire need of it – now! She had been angry at the little bitch all week, and she needed sex. so she could at least get through her hate and anger. Especially hate, which always caused her to have heightened desire, making her wet constantly. Eloran had never failed to take care of her ass – until now!

"Well?" she repeated, yet again.

"Mmmmmm?" he replied.

Delinear slapped his face, and he looked down at her in anger – enough to want to kill her!

"How dare you...." he began.

"Shut the fuck up, Eloran! We have to have a plan!" she demanded.

With unfocused eyes, Eloran asked a question – one that he had asked many times.

"Delinear? Can a Vorc'ara be opened from the other side at a different time and place by someone else?" he asked.

Delinear's face showed shock.

"Huh?" she asked.

"Damnit, woman! Pay attention! Can someone else open a Vorc'ara from the other side for someone else to cross?" he repeated impatiently.

Delinear blinked.

"No, of course not! I've told you that hundreds of times that it can't be done! When are you going to get it through your damn, thick skull that it must be activated by an Anaerris from the same side."

"It can't be opened long distance?" he asked. "You're absolutely sure?"

"Yes! Without a doubt!"

"Then, who opened it for girl, Delinear? The *Human Girl*! So, did you open it?" he accused her. He never took Delinear for granted. He knew that she would betray him if she found a way she could do so. "The only possible explanation was that *you* opened it for her! I just want to know why?"

"Are you on crack, Eloran?"she asked, using the vernacular of the young people on Earth. She really liked their verbiage and slang.

"Crack?" he repeated. He looked around, puzzled. "What crack? Your crack?"

Delinear shook her head. Eloran never could keep up with the times.

"Never mind! And, no, I did not open it! Why in the hell would you ask me that same question, knowing I have told you over and over that I didn't?"

"You're sure?" he asked her again.

"That is enough! Look, Eloran, and listen this time! Each Vorc'ara is as individual as a finger print. As individual as an eye. It cannot be copied by another. It's all based upon the color of the Vorc'ara," she sighed, explaining for the umpteenth time over eons. Why he couldn't understand, or remember it, she didn't know.

"Explain," he ordered.

Delinear walked a little further, stopped, and turned around.

"One last time, Eloran! I will never answer this question, again!" she commanded. "Each Anaerris royal blood has a color based upon their own powers. Mine, of course, is black. You've seen it."

Eloran nodded, and waited.

"Taryln's color is a lime green. Therefore, her Vorc'aras are lime green," she told him in a placating tone, as if speaking to a two-year old.

"Who has the color of read and white, then?"

"Huh?" Delinear frowned. She'd never thought about it before. Therefore, it hadn't occurred to her to even wonder about it. That's when her eyes widened.

"No Anaerris has that color! You know our planet had every color except for gray and black in the Creators universe."

"Yes, yes. Go on!" he waved at her to continue.

"I have, honestly, never seen the color red and white from any Anaerris, Eloran. E.V.E.R!" Delinear told him.

"Well, then...why was that Vorc'ara red and white?"

"You are right! Why didn't I notice it?"

"Maybe because you were seeing hatred through your eyes?"

"Fuck you, Eloran!" she whispered quietly. And, then, she realized what he was saying. Gasping as she suddenly realized the answer. She sank to her knees in shock, and said, "There's only one explanation, Eloran."

"And...that would be?" Eloran said.

"The girl!" She stood up slowly to face him.

He frowned.

"The girl?" he repeated.

She nodded.

"It's the only possible thing!"

His eyebrows jerked up in shock.

"Wait. You mean...?"

She nodded to him in complete shock.

"It had to be the girl, Eloran! She has to be..." Delinear almost couldn't say it aloud.

"What does she have to be? Delinear?" he ordered, even though he knew the answer already.

Quietly, her eyes met his in stunned disbelief.

"Anaerris. The girl! She has to be Anaerris! The only people who can open a Vorc'ara is royalty!" Delinear's eyes widened, as a horrible idea came to her. "She has to be what we have been looking for over the thousands of years!"

Shaking his head, stunned, he couldn't believe what she had just told him.

"Wait, that would have to mean..." he yelled. "Have you been taking nephera, Delinear? You're insane!"

"You're a total dick, Eloran! It is the only answer! She's the one! The Jewel! We had her in our grasp, and didn't even know it!" Then, "Oh, shit! She has the book! If so, does she also have my crystal?"

"S-she is Anaerris? Anaerris royalty" his voice stuttered, as he asked the question, and kept repeating it as if trying to believe what she was telling him. Finally, Eloran let reality hit him. "She's the Jewel? *She's the Jewel*? You mean, the Jewel really is real?"

"Shit & damn! We had the Jewel of Anaerris – right here – and she opened the Vorc'ara herself!" Delinear stopped for minute, then said quietly as if to herself, "Did she know what she was doing?" She turned to Eloran with wide eyes as realization struck. "She doesn't know!"

"Or didn't!" he said. "Fuck!"

They both reached the same conclusion, and stared at each other.

"Exactly," Delinear replied.

~ 17 ~
"Someone, please! Just tell me the truth!" ~ Gem

"Lola," Taylor asked, just after Jaxx had almost mowed down Stan in his hurry to get out of the house. "What the hell just happened?"

Lola looked at her, then turned, and trotted into the library on her tiny little legs. For a tiny little dog, she was fast!

"Well, I'm going to assume that Lola wants us to follow her?" Stan asked to no one in particular.

The four immortal beings followed the immortal pug, and each took a seat. They all knew that Lola wouldn't talk until she was satisfied that she had everyone's full attention. She really hated to repeat herself. After several minutes, Lola transformed into her Fae appearance, and she began to speak.

"Gem's back," she said.

Taylor's mouth dropped.

"Back? What do you mean, back? Where is she back from?" Taylor asked.

"Gem was kidnapped by Imaerra, but she's back, now."

Everyone shutup to stare at Lola. Taylor was aghast; Rick became rigid; Stan put his head in his hands; and Stacy just blinked at Lola. The silence melded into minutes, and still, no one could say a thing.

"Well, that went really well," Lola muttered under her breath, and morphed back into her pug form.

For the next hour, there was silence.

"Now, what?" Rick asked Taylor, breaking the silence and startling everyone.

"I don't have a clue," she told him.

Lola shook her head. Truth be known, she was really beginning to like being a pug instead of her normal Fae presence. People treated her as if she was the sweetest thing in the world! She liked it! Sighing, she knew nothing was going to happen soon, so she flopped down onto the sofa, yawned, and fell asleep. And, there was silence once again.

Gem stretched slowly as she turned over in the bed, feeling for Jaxx. For a moment, she panicked when she didn't feel him next to her, then realized that he probably was somewhere else in his "man-cave". She grinned at the description all men use for their "special place" – and felt extra special that she was allowed in it!

"Ouch!" Gem said, feeling the soreness in her body.

Her body was extremely sore from their repeated sex-a-thon, but it was a *good sore*! Gem stretched, smiling that secret smile all women smile, when they have the special "secret". She stretched once more, stood, and slipped into his massive shower, washing her hair, and body. After she had dried herself with a huge, thick, forest-green towel, Gem stepped into the bedroom, wrapping it around her. Looking around, she didn't see her clothes from yesterday. Well, they *were* torn to pieces. And, that just brought back the memory of her ordeal. She almost wanted to throw up at the thought of putting them back on her body. Yuck! The stench that had been covering her must have been horrible! How Jaxx could have stood to be around her, she would never know! Gem stepped over to the dresser, and opened the top drawer. It was filled with his underwear and socks, so she proceeded to the next drawer. Inside were some black t-shirts, so she pulled one out, and pulled it over her head. Well, she couldn't really put on his briefs, so she decided not to wear anything. That gave her naughty thoughts! She giggled, and looked into the mirror, grinning wickedly at the sexy images that danced through her mind at the though of having nothing on underneath. Even more that Jaxx would like it!

Suddenly, a loud buzz descended on her ears and she grasped both sides of her head in terrible pain. She shook her head, but that didn't work. The buzz just got louder.

"Oh, Creator!" she yelled, and sank to her knees.

The sound of her scream sent Jaxx running into his bedroom only to see his mate in horrendous pain. He quickly reached down, and pulled her to him.

"Gem! Gem?" he asked, but she couldn't hear him. The pain in her head was far too great.

"It hurts!" she cried.

"What is it?" he asked.

Gem heard a garbled sound coming from Jaxx's lips, but that was all she could hear. She tried to concentrate on his lips, and finally realized he wanted to know what was happening.

"My head! It hurts, Jaxx! It's as if a billion bees were buzzing inside of it!" she cried in terror.

Jaxx thought about it a minute.

"When did it start?"

Reading his lips, she answered.

"Right after I got into the shower!" she yelled, not realizing that he couldn't hear her words.

"Look at me, Gem!" he ordered. When she didn't immediately obey him, he yelled, "LOOK AT ME!"

That did get her attention. His mind joined with hers, and felt the excruciating pain that was in her head.

"Concentrate on my thoughts."

"I-I c-can't!" she cried.

He gave her a sharp shake, which made her look up at him.

"Yes, you can, Gem! Do it!" he commanded.

Gem looked into his eyes, and didn't look away.

Jaxx's heart almost turned over in fear as he saw the haunted look on her face. But, she didn't back down, and that was a good sign.

"Listen only to my voice," he told her. "Now, breathe deeply. Don't think of anything else but my voice."

She nodded, and concentrated on his beautiful voice as he spoke to her gently. In seconds, the buzzing pain began to cease until it was completely gone. She leaned her head against his chest, before he turned her to the mirror in front of them. Jaxx held her so lovingly it brought tears to her eyes.

"That's it, my love." He looked into the mirror, and into her eyes. "Feeling better?"

"Y-yes," she said, "I-I think so."

"Good. Now, can you tell me what you were hearing?"

She nodded. She really didn't want to admit it, but she believed she knew what was happening.

"It was a buzzing – like bees," she told him. "But..."

"But what?" he asked.

"Well...I really can't explain it, but I wasn't the one in pain. Something else was calling to me. It was in pain!" A sheepish grin on her lips, she added, "Silly, huh?"

"No. It's not. A buzzing sound like bees," he whispered to himself, staring into space forgetting she was there.

Gem waited...and waited...and waited...and...waited....

"Well?" she asked, after at least ten minutes had passed.

"What?" he shook himself out of his reverie. Gem cocked her head, and raised her eyebrows. "Oh. Right. Nope. I got nothing!"

He grinned at her, and she swatted his arm in playful frustration, turning her to face the mirror, again. Then, she realized that by relaxing, she knew what the buzz was. She met his eyes in the mirror.

"I know what it was, Jaxx," she said in surprise.

"What?"

"It was the book! It's in danger!"

"Huh?"

"It's in danger...or, at least, is going to be in danger."

"How do you know that?" he asked surprised.

"I-I guess, well, maybe I really don't know, but I just know it!" She looked at him, seeing confusion on his face. "I have to get to it – now!"

He nodded at her.

"Are you sure?" he asked.

She gave him one nod.

"Right now?"

Gem thoaght a moment, then shook her head. "I don't think it's in danger at this very moment, but it seems to know that danger is imminent."

"Hmmm. If you think it's safe for the moment..." he began, watching her nod once again, "...and, I trust that wherever you put it, it is safe."

"Yeah. I think it's OK right now, but it obviously feels that danger is near. Jaxx, as much as I'd rather stay here, and have raunchy sex with you, I think we need to go get it. It needs our protection."

"Ours?" he asked surprised.

Gem's eyes grew larger as she realized that it was true. It needed both of them!

"Yes. Ours. I don't understand it, right now, but it needs both of us." Gem closed her eyes as she felt the book speak to her, but she wasn't going to admit that to Jaxx. It would make her sound like a raving lunatic!

"No, my love. You aren't a raving lunatic! But, it must be why it called to you. You really are its protector!" Jaxx said in amazement, as if he hadn't believed that she was the Jewel before this very second in time!

"Oh, crap! I forgot you were in my brain!" Gem complained, who gave him a lazy grin.

"Apparently," Jaxx said, sudden lust slamming into his groin.

"Huh?"

"Yes?" He had become distracted by her wearing his t-shirt. Her nipples were pointed and hard against the material.

"My eyes are up here, you know," she laughed, as she pointed to her face.

"What? Oh. Right. Damn!"

Jaxx's eyes were red – again – indicating he was thinking about sex. He bent his head, and nibbled on her shoulder. Then she looked into the mirror to see hers were also red. That's when she had a thought.

"Jaxx? My eyes are red!"

"Mmmmm hmmmmm," he murmured. Creator! She was delicious, as he licked her gorgeous neck.

"No. Heeeelllllloooo!" she tried to get his attention to look into her eyes. "My. Eyes. Are. Red!" she repeated.

His head came up, his eyes staring into her red ones. "So?"

"Didn't you say that the only ones who had red eyes were Onaerris?"

"Well, uh, yeah?" he answered completely puzzled by her question. That is until....

"But, doesn't that mean that I am not completely Anaerris or human?" she asked him in shock.

Jaxx's eyes darted up to look her directly in her eyes.

"I think we have established that point, but that you have no Onaerris DNA within you, so I don't get what you are asking."

"Jaxx! How can I not have Onaerris DNA? I have red eyes just like you – at least when I'm horny as hell!" she exclaimed. Another thought came to her. "What does the legend actually say about the Jewel of Anaerris?"

Jaxx had to think about it. It had been a very long time since he had not only heard it, and he wasn't sure he could remember it completely. Maybe verbalizing it would help?

"Let's see. The legend basically says..."

"No. Not basically. Think. What does it *actually* say?"

"Well, I'm not totally sure, Gem. It's been so long since I really heard it in complete detail, I don't know if I really remember all of it," he told her.

"Well?" she asked, tapping her foot.

Gem cocked her head at him without saying a word. He rolled his eyes. There was only one way for him to remember all of it, and he shied away from what that was. It was dangerous, and could get them both killed!

"Take your time, but hurry it up, will you?" She wanted to know – now.

"Seriously? Take my time, but hurry up?" he asked her in surprise. She nodded. "Well, OK. But, I'll have to step away from you, because you are just so damn hot right now, and there is no way I can concentrate!" he grinned at her.

Seeing him step away, she simply rolled her eyes at him.

"Oh, alright. If you just have to!" she giggled, her eyes straying downward toward something pretty darned hard and pointing at her.

Smiling devilishly, Jaxx pulled on his briefs, much to Gem's dissatisfaction, then sat down in one of the two, black leather wingback chairs in the room, and closed his eyes. Remembering wasn't going to be easy. So, he decided to put himself in an ancient state of catalepsy – a state wherein he becomes rigid and pulls himself out of reality. But, there was a danger. He would be unable to connect with the reality around him, and he wouldn't be able to protect Gem. He had already failed at that, and it was just not an option this time. He looked at Gem. Her eyebrows were drawn downward in worry. OK. He could do this as long as....

"Gem. Promise me that if I do not awaken within one hour, you will say anything – do anything and everything – you can to wake me?"

"Uh...why?" she drawled out the word, as she sat down opposite him, pulling a soft blanket around herself.

"The only way to remember the entire legend is to put myself into a near catatonic state."

Surprised, her eyebrows went up, and her eyes popped out of her head.

"You can do that?" she said.

"Yes. But, there is a real danger here, and I want you to know about it before I begin."

His words weren't reassuring, and it was causing her stomach to draw into a tight knot. This did not sound good. Not at all.

"Maybe...maybe...," she sputtered grabbing his arm. "Maybe this isn't such a good idea, Jaxx? Let's just forget it, OK?"

"Maybe it's not a great idea, but baby, it's the only way. It's just been a long time since I tried this. That's why I need you to wake me up," he looked at her with a slightly worried expression that he quickly hid.

"Are you really sure about this?" she asked. "No. That doesn't sound good at all, Jaxx! Forget about it!"

"Yes. We are going to do this. You are right. We do need to know as much as possible," he said, pacing back and forth. Then, he stopped, turned, and looked at Gem. "You know, it's very possible that the legend has been diluted throughout the eons, and my people probably don't remember it correctly. In fact, I doubt anyone remembers the *original* version."

Gem just shook her head no. He stood, and pulled her into his arms, kissing her gently on the forehead.

"I'll be OK. Just remember to wake me if I don't wake up in an hour."

"What happens if I can't awaken you?" she asked, scared of the answer.

"If I don't wake up, I'll – uh – change," he explained, not meeting her eyes.

"Change? Change how?" she questioned.

"Well, it's hard to explain, but...well...I will change into my true form." Jaxx looked into a pair of stunned eyes.

"Do I dare ask what that is?" she frowned.

"It's better that you don't ask. But, more importantly, it's better that it not happen," he explained, again, without explaining.

"Jaxx! Please! What are you talking about?" Gem demanded. "What form? What do you mean by form?"

Jaxx didn't really want to explain all this right now. He knew it would freak her out if he did tell her, so hoping to distract her from asking a question he did not want to answer, he decided to give her a sort-of truth. Better she not know about his true form and powers.

"Let me put it this way, mate. I'm not exactly human, OK?"

Watching Gem cross her arms with an eyebrow raised, he knew he'd have to give her something.

"And?" Her left eyebrow went up, and she crossed her arms.

"OK! OK! My true form is difficult to explain, but suffice it to say that it looks more like energy than solid form."

Dropping her hands, Gem gaped. He wasn't solid? But, how...?

"Not solid? What do you mean you are not solid!" she indicated, waving her hands up and down his body.

"Well, it's true. The Onaerris are a bit different than the Anaerris. But, the same form that we take as our true selves, made us always think that we could not procreate – or at least that's what we believed."

Shit! Why the hell did he let that one slip? He waited for it to permeate her mind, and then...

"*Believed*? What do you mean *believed*?" Gem's voice raised several octaves into a squeak that really hurt Jaxx's ears. To make his point, he stuck his fingers into his ears to which she made a smart-ass remark.

"Very funny. Ha ha. Give it up, smoke and mirrors man!"

Jaxx yanked her to him, and placed a mind-blowing kiss onto her lips. When he pulled back, her eyes were dazed – and red! He turned her to the mirror, again.

"Look at your eyes."

She opened them, and dropped her head in defeat.

"If you are who we believe you are, then yes, Gem. We do need to know. You are right. But, baby, it doesn't matter if you are, or are not, the Jewel of Anaerris. The Anaerris Code believes that you are, and it speaks only to you. That's all we really need to know. But, we need to find out, because if you do have Onaerris blood inside of you...? No matter how diluted...we need to know." He let his voice fade away.

Finally, he saw her eyes get it.

"Does that mean I might not be the jewel?" That had never even occurred to her.

"Honestly? At this point, I just don't know any more. Lola says you have no Onaerris within you, and she believes you to be the jewel. But, I wonder, now, if it was something that got pushed to the back somewhere in your genes, which slowly disappeared over time."

"Well, OK, if you're sure? I love you," she said, kissing him lightly on the lips.

"Uh-uh. None of that!" he smirked, swatting her on her ass, before sitting back down.

"What you are saying is that if you take whatever form, then, if I have Onaerris, I may be able to do the same?"

"Yes and no. I have no idea, really. But, I suspect that if you are of human, Anaerris, *and* Onaerris blood, you will be the only one ever to have descended from all three, and if that's true? Then, Gem, we don't know what you *could do*! We already know that you can open a Vorc'ara – unintentionally, that's true."

"Well, shit!" she said as she realized what he was saying. Tapping her chin, she wondered, "Hmmm. Can't we call it a "vortex" instead? It's less of a mouthful."

Ignoring her, Jaxx continued.

"And, it could also be that your mixed DNA keeps you from being able to take the form of an Angel or Demon. In other words, you might not be able to do so – or – it might mean that your true form may be something entirely different than anyone has ever been. Whatever it is, it may also need some sort of catalyst to release it," he stared at her. "I mean...obviously, your capture released your ability to open that Vorc'ara."

"Vortex," Gem absentmindedly corrected him, earning an annoyed look from Jaxx.

Still wondering how she had done it, she decided to push this entire conversation to the background for the moment, and let Jaxx get down to business.

Nodding, Gem quickly opened the timer on her phone.

"How long?" she asked, pausing her finger above it.

"Oh...no longer than fifty minutes, I should think. That should be enough time for me to remember, and time enough to wake me up," Jaxx told her, while adding to himself that it should be a safe enough interval, before his body would transform into his red-hot volcanic and fiery persona. He didn't want Gem to ever see that side of him. He could easily hurt her. "Remember, Gem. This is truly important. No longer."

She nodded, and watched while he put himself into a trance-like state. She nibbled on her thumbnail, waiting for him to remember. What if she couldn't watch over him? What if she couldn't wake him? What if...oh, hell! It never does any good with "what-ifs"!

Jaxx realized he was really taking a chance, but he slowed his breathing, and concentrated on the legend itself. He pulled himself out of time and space, pushing his consciousness further into the past than he had ever gone. Very far into the past to the day he had first heard of the legend. He was on Anaerris just before his brother and his mate left forever. Oh, he knew they were both still alive somewhere, but "where" was the question.

He really hated doing this. It was something none of them wanted to do – ever. It could release a monster that would decimate everything around him. And, he could hurt Gem. And, as far as he knew? He was the only one to ever go this far into the past, and he had no idea of the consequences.

Concentrating, it felt as if he was swimming through a thick, grayish mucous – without air – before he surfaced, and then, he was in the past. His unconscious memories began to surface, and he remembered that his brother had ordered him to the secret place, where he had discovered that Jolinear and Analyse always met. He remembered his anger at having been summoned as if he were a little boy. Also, he had a war to win against his own people, and his brother demanded he take "time-off" to meet him? And, worse? How he had to reach this secret place! With each step, Jaxx's anger grew as he trekked across a dead, burned-out moon to the location of the only mountains on Anaerris. Following his brother's directions on how to find some sort of a doorway into the tallest mountain, it seemed as if it took forever, before he found it. But, when he did, he walked through a long tunnel, which opened into a large cavern. What he hadn't realized was that he actually had walked through a Vorc'ara opened by Analyse. But, the tunnel had been so dark, he hadn't seen it form. A light appeared just in front of him, and he stepped onto a landing complete with crystalline stairs going up on the left, and crystalline stairs down to another level to the right. A single set of carved, stone stairs wound down to the floor below. It was light, but there was little to see. There were a couple of wood chairs, a wooden table, and an empty, hole in the center of the floor. His brother stood at one of the doorways into another part of the cavern, waving up at him. Jaxx walked down the stairs to the main floor. It was the first time that he had seen what would, eventually, become his own, personal hideaway. Nor did he realize that it was not even on Anaerris, but was somewhere else. And, it was where he would bring his own mate eons later.

"Impressive, isn't it?" Jolinaer had asked, meeting his brother's eyes.

"Yes, it is," Jaxx had answered. "Enough small talk. Do you know I didn't have time for this shit? What's going on, Jolin?"

Sneaking a look behind Jolin's shoulder, Jaxx had noticed something – or more correctly - someone who was moving behind Jolinaer in the darkness beyond.

When Jolinaer spoke, his eyes jerked back to Jolin.

"I need you to...," Jolin began.

"Who is that?" Jaxx had asked.

Jolin turned. "Who? There's no one there, Jaxx. We're alone," he said innocently..

"Try again," Jaxx had demanded. Even so long ago, Jaxx struck fear into the hearts of anyone. His brother, however, was actually a kind soul, and hated the terrible war as much as did he. But, in his wildest dreams, the next thing out of his brother's mouth floored him, until the proof of his words walked out of the shadows of the depths of the cavern. It was the red-haired beauty he had seen earlier.

Jaxx felt as if a huge door had been raised that had been shut for eons, and everything that he had forgotten flowed back into his brain as he began to remember everything.

~ 18 ~
"After having lived so long, you kind of forget some very major details over the eons!" ~ Jaxx

Gem was still gnawing on her nail almost as soon as he blacked out to discover the truth.. It's what she always did when she was excessively nervous. And, nervous was putting it mildly at the moment! She didn't want to take her eyes off him, but she had to check the clock. She realized that it had been just barely ten minutes.

Ten minutes? It seemed like hours to her! That's when she heard a gasp that came from Jaxx's lips. Gem shifted her eyes to his open, but almost dead, black eyes. Whatever he was doing, he didn't need his eyes closed for the entire time. But, his eyes were just way to creepy. Waiting was giving her a headache, so she tried to take her mind off of it. Even though it was a bit silly, she tilted her head, wondering how he would look with a mustache. He already had the scruffy look down to a fine art. Why had she not noticed his drop-dead gorgeous looks, before any of this other crap happened? She almost stood to wake him, when she realized his eyes were moving from side to side as if he was looking at someone.

"No! Not looking at someone. He's in REM sleep, maybe?" she whispered to herself.

And then came a "voice" out of Jaxx's mouth. Gem shuddered in shock as she realized she was listening to a conversation Jaxx was conducting with someone else! She mouthed "holy shit", then began to listen to a language she did not know – at least for all of two seconds. She reached up and grabbed the amulet around her neck that she had put back on right after she had returned. She had taken it off in Jaxx's cave, and left it on the night stand, before she was abducted. Suddenly, she was able to understand what he was saying! And, truth be told? She almost wished she could not understand the words! But, with no other choice, she did.

"Jolin? What the hell are you doing here? Who is she?" Jaxx looked around, then, "And, just where the hell is here?"

"It is good to see you, too, Jaxx," Jolinaer said, reaching out to take Jaxx's forearm in the traditional greeting of the day.

Although Jaxx took Jolinaer's forearm, he asked, again, before dropping it.

"Where in the hell are we, Jolinaer?" Jaxx meant business, because he used his older brother's formal name! It usually meant Jaxxon wasn't going to tolerate any funny business.

Without saying anything, Jolinaer walked to one of the wooden chairs at the table, and sat, leaving Jaxx no choice, but to do the same. Crossing his arms across his massive chest, Jaxx waited.

After several minutes of quiet, Jolinaer finally spoke.

"I know this is very strange to you, Jaxx. It was to me, too...at first."

Jaxx narrowed his eyes, and waited without speaking.

Clearing his throat, Jolin continued.

"I have fallen in love, Jaxx," he told him.

"What?" Jaxx yelped, jumping to his feet. "That's not possible! Love cannot enter into any Onaerris!"

Jolinaer nodded in agreement.

"That's what we all have believed for our entire existence. But, it was not true, because I have fallen in love," he added, watching the numerous displays of emotions raging on his brother's face. After several minutes, Jaxxon was speaking.

"And, just who is it?" he sneered. He was really skeptical of the answer, but what Jolin told him next was never, in his wildest dreams, what he had been expecting.

"Analyse, brother. Analyse," he answered.

Jaxx's mouth dropped in stunned silence.

"D-did you just say…" he stuttered, dropping right back into his chair, his legs giving out underneath him as if they were spaghetti.

"…Analyse? Yes."

Analyse? He was in love with the daughter of the ruler of Anaerris?

"*Analyse*? You're in love with the enemy? What the hell are you thinking, Jolin?" Jaxx muttered aloud.

"She is *not* the enemy, Jaxxon! You should know that better than anyone else! You are the leader of this rebellion, per se!" Jolinaer growled.

"Then, what do you want me to say, Jolin?" Jaxx had finally been able to grind out through his gritted teeth.

"I'm not expecting *you* to say anything," he said, while Jaxx was just waiting for the next shoe to drop…and, sure enough, here it came! For the first time in his entire life, Jaxx was rendered speechless! "There's more, Jaxx. I need you to be open to this, because what I'm about to tell you will not be easily accepted."

Jaxx frowned. What more could there be, than the fact that his own brother was in love with an Anaerris? But, if the statement that Jolin was in love with Analyse wasn't enough, the next statement out of his mouth completely shocked him to his core!

Jolinaer stood up, and walked back toward the opening in the cavern. He reached out to take first a hand, then an arm, and then, an entire body with brilliant red hair – a female who had just a hint of a tiny, protruding stomach – walked straight into Jolin's arms. He led the woman toward Jaxx, and that's when Jaxx stood up so fast, his chair fell backward, skittering backward in shock. It was a woman with the red hair he had thought that he had seen from afar earlier when he spoke to Jolin! And, there was more. He hadn't even wanted to believe Jolin was in love with Analyse! But, this woman wasn't Anaerris...was she? Red eyes? She had red eyes? And, then, Jaxx received the shock of his entire life! It looked as if...it looked like...no, it couldn't be...it was...was she...was she...? He gasped, then moved so fast, no one saw him coming – even Jolin – as he grabbed the throat of his brother, and lifted him well off of the floor!

"What the bloody hell have you done?" he yelled.

Looking down at his brother, Jolin grinned. However, his grin quickly turned to anger.

"Yes. I turned her, Jaxx. I had to do it. She was dying thanks to an immortal lance that was thrust into her chest by one of our own! Our own *uncle*!" Jolin told him without remorse. Seeing Jaxx's shocked face, he continued. "Yes! I killed him! Then, I changed her into one of us, because I would be damned – even more than we are now – if I had not saved her life! After that, a miracle occurred!" Jaxx watched him gently place his hand over hers that cradled her stomach. With a tear in his eye, he turned back to Jaxx. "She is with child – my child. Jaxx?"

Jaxx was too stunned, shocked, speechless, motionless, and any other word one could say, to hear Jolinaer! He looked at the woman standing before him in utter silence. The ruler of Anaerris was no longer Anaerris, but she was Onaerris! Her red eyes gave proof to that fact. But, the gentle swelling of her belly also attested to the fact that she was, indeed, swollen with child! His head moved from side to side in denial, even while his eyes could not deny what he beheld as truth.

Then, he made the mistake of saying aloud what he was thinking.

"Well? Are you going to say anything?" Jolin asked him, once more.

"This is not possible! How could that be? It cannot possibly be your child! But, how she could have gotten pregna..." the words flowed from his mouth in disgust. Then, before he realized what he had done, Analyse's eyes and fangs descended as she lunged for him. With no pause, her teeth barreled into the flesh at the base of his neck. She began to suck blood from him quickly, and would have ended his life, if Jolin had not grabbed her, and begged her to stop.

Jaxx felt his life declining with each suck, along with his own strength. He had been taken by surprise, so he had not been prepared for a fight let alone an attack! He had been wrong, and he knew it in that instant. Jolin begged and pleaded with her, trying to reach her through the bloodlust and anger that had consumed her from being insulted.

Finally, Jolin managed to coax her into letting go, then pulled her back into his chest, quietly speaking to her, while her anger subsided. When she was able to exhibit coherency, she looked at Jaxx in horror. Her hand covered her bloody mouth as her eyes returned to green. Jolin said something to her, and she nodded. He had sunk to his knees during the attack, and was breathing in stutters. She had taken a lot of his blood, and he felt extremely weak. Jolin had picked him up, and laid him on a pallet that was on the floor near a massive opening in the wall. A fireplace, he assumed, or at least it could be.

"I'm so damn sorry, brother!" He looked back at Analyse. "She was so concerned with hurting others that she brought us here to keep her out of their way, until her bloodlust was contained."

"Oh, Jaxx!" Analyse cried softly. "I am so, so sorry!"

Jaxx pushed himself up onto his elbows. He took a deep breath, even though he didn't need one.

"I understand. Analyse, it's OK," he repeated when he saw her shake her head. I was wrong, and I am sorry. It just took me by surprised. Who would have thought this could happen? No one has ever been able to become pregnant. As for the bloodlust? It's part of who the Onaerris are. And, a new one is far stronger. Your need for blood would be magnified a thousand fold. But...are you OK?" he asked her.

"Y-yes. I guess so." To Jolinaer, she asked, "Will he be alright? I drank an awful lot of blood from him."

"Yes. He will."

"That was more intense than ever before," Analyse muttered. "Why?"

"Ah! That's the question," Jolin teased, while at the same time, realizing why. "Hormones, my beauty!"

She looked up to see Jaxx grinning, and she grinned back at him.

"Hormones. Right. Let's use that one!" she giggled.

Jolinaer laughed aloud, then turned to his brother, ripping into his wrist. He fed his own blood to Jaxx, who sucked greedily, but knowing he would only take just enough to become strong, again. Once he finished feeding, Jaxx was able to stand once again, and Jolinaer and Analyse explained everything to him.

Sitting at the table, all three drank a glass of wine together. One thing he was happy about was the fact that his kind loved the food from Anaerris. It was one of the many reasons why they attacked her world. A few pieces of meat and wine were always the perfect compliment to blood.

"So, other than the obvious, I get the feeling that there is another big secret?" Jaxx asked.

Putting her wine down, Analyse answered him.

"I can't be with my people, again, nor can I go around others with our child within me – especially with my blood lust uncontainable. They might want to dissect me to find out how this could happen."

Jolin nodded. "She's right."

"But," Jaxx asked, watching Analyse rub her belly gently, "how did it happen? I don't get it."

Jolin and Analyse looked at each other and shrugged. Then...

"We don't know, Jaxx! We do not have an explanation," Analyse told him. "Both of you should know better than all others, that He can do whatever He wishes! But, I'm not going to question Him any longer. I am going to accept that this may very well be the beginning of a whole new life for us!"

Jaxx looked at Jolin, who just shook his head as well.

"We just do not know, Jaxx."

"There is only one explanation, Jolinaer," Analyse said to him.

"NO! I refuse to believe it!" Jolinaer said angrily.

Analyse reached over, and took his face into both of her hands.

"We must realize that there is no other reasoning for it!"

"OK. Just for the record, Analyse," Jaxx said, "what?"

She turned to him, and told him her suspicions.

"The Creator, of course," she said, her voice sounded reasonable.

"But, why?" Jolinaer asked her the same question he had asked her several times. "Why would the Creator do this?"

The three of them looked at each other. There wasn't another explanation, and they knew it. But, the question of why still remained. And, Analyse had the only answer possible.

"It's not always for us to understand His reasoning Jolin. But, there must be something that is going to happen, and He needed this child for whatever reason. We all realize that we were in the wrong when we went against Him. The reason that we united into a small army, now, was because we needed to stop the evil that attacked Anaerris. Were we all not trying to redeem ourselves in some way? Sometimes, it's just easier to accept what is."

Again, the three looked at each other. Deciding that whatever the reason, they were going to have to leave this question unanswered. Perhaps, the Creator would explain at another point in time.

"Tthe two of you have to get out of here!" Jaxx said in a panic. "Holy shit! If anyone of either race found out about the two of you, the ramifications would be...," he trailed his words, and stopped speaking.

"Well, we need to get off of Anaerris, so this cave is my 'getaway' off world. Right now, this is the safest place I could think of, because no one knows of it. I found it long ago, and used to come whenever I was upset, or just needed quiet and peace. Later, I brought my mate here, and well, you get the idea," shyness taking over her eyes.

Jaxx rolled his eyes. "Shyness, Analyse? Really?" Then, he and Jolin laughed.

After properly slapping Jolin's arm, she turned back to Jaxx.

"You came through a Vorc'ara, Jaxx. One that I created."

His mouth dropped. "I did? B-but...I didn't see it?"

Seeing her smile, he understood, in that second, why his brother had fallen in love with her. He knew she would have been a fabulous ruler, but now...things were never going to be the same, again – for any of them. They were no longer rulers, but to all intents and purposes, they were now, just average fallen angels. Well, technically, "outlaw" fallen angels.

"So, what now?" he asked, and Jolin answered.

"We are leaving, Jaxx."

"He's right," Analyse added as she saw Jaxx frown. "A friend of mine in the Fae world has been kind enough to invite us to stay there until our child is born, and that should give us some time to figure out what we are going to do. But..."

Oh, shit! Another shoe was about to fall!

"Before we go, though, we have one more thing to tell you. What I'm about to trust you with goes no further than the three of us," Analyse finished.

Jaxx's eyes narrowed, but he didn't speak. He watched her stand, and go to the table pulling something from underneath. She came back to the two of them, and stretched out her hand. Jaxx opened his, and Analyse dropped something into it – large piece of crystal the color of peach.

"A crystal?" He looked up at her as he held it. "I don't get it? These are everywhere on both worlds."

"Look at it again, Jaxx. It's not just any crystal," Jolin told him. "It's a machine. A Terraforming machine."

The silence was deafening, while Jaxx turned the crystal around in his hand. He looked from one of them to the other, and back to the crystal. It had been altered. They had all been warned by the Creator, as they were cast out of His realm, to never try to alter the crystals that were found on the two moons. If anyone did so, His wrath would be immediate, and they would be destroyed. He wanted to give those who followed the evil one, a chance to redeem themselves, although none of them knew this.

"Terraforming was strictly forbidden by the Creator for both races!" he muttered, unnecessarily. "Where did this come from?"

"Delinear," Jolin answered.

"What?" Jaxx was surprised. He had been having a relationship with her for years, now.

"Jaxx, she's evil incarnate. She is involved with Eloran, and they conspired to Terraform Anaerris after they burned it."

"Look, Jaxx. We know how you feel about her, but the simple fact is that she is a traitor to her own kind. The two of them want to rule both races! And, they do not want to stop there! They want to rule everything!"

Jaxx thought about that for a bit, then something occurred to him.

"How did you get this if Dilinear had it?" he asked.

Analyse looked at Jolinaer, who nodded.

"I stole it from her by using my true form while she was, uh, engaged in some, uh, activities in the bedroom," Analyse explained. Then, waving away Jaxx's objections, before he voiced them. "Don't worry. I saw nothing. Look, I know it is forbidden, Jaxx. She and Eloran have been colluding behind our backs – behind yours. I stole it so that they could not utilize it. When we realized that this world was beyond Terraforming, we heard rumors that they would be Terraforming another world. One that was inhabited. And, that was something that we could not allow!"

"Agreed. But, which world?" Jaxx was curious.

"It is called Earth, and is in the Terran system," Analyse explained. "It's very far away from us."

Jaxx wrinkled his brow, and shook his head. He'd never heard of it.

"Never heard of it," he said.

"Nor had we. It was the Fae who told me about it. And, we want you to go there, covertly, and hide the crystal. We both doubt that Eloran and Delinear will go there, now. Without the crystal, they can't do any harm. Make sure that it is not used, and make sure that you protect that planet! But, I'm almost sure they will show up there at some time in the future." He turned to Analyse. "At least, that is what Analyse has foreseen."

The Anaerris had been given powers for them to use, but they were limited in their scope. Opening a Vorc'ara was one of them. And, only a small handful of Onaerris even knew about this. The ruling family were given the power of sight as well. They could see what would happen in the future, but again, it was limited in scope. They saw the future, but they did not always see details. In contrast, the Onaerris had the ability to influence others by becoming invisible as well as the power of illusion.

The Anaerris, like the Onaerris, could revert to their true form at will. Where Onaerris became red with volcanic power, the Anaerris became a glowing white being of great light. Both had once had wings, but they were clipped when they were banished by their Creator to the two worlds. Being left with these small remnants of their original glory had always been a source of irritation, but at least they still had them. However, long ago, both the rulers of both worlds had decided to make sure that neither could use their powers on each other, and had, thus, forbidden any to use their powers at all.

But, never had there ever been a traitor on either side. Delinear, Jolin had told him, and Eloran were traitors – not only to their own kind, but to the Creator! And, they had every intention of destroying not only Onaerris and Anaerris, but also other planets and beings. Jaxx looked down. He held, in his hand, the means by which they would have accomplished those goals. He closed his hands tightly over the crystal feeling it cut into his palms. He would protect it with his very life!

"OK. I will make sure this never falls into their hands," he vowed.

Giving a visible breath of relief, Analyse leaned over, and kissed his cheek. Her belly had also touched him, and he felt a soft flutter that made him look down in surprise. In there was his – whatever it might be called. There was no word in their language for the life growing within her. It wasn't until he reached Earth that he heard the terms of nephew and niece. After they had disappeared via another Vorc'ara, he never heard another word from either of them, and he didn't know if his little nephew or niece was alive and well. He had been astonished at how much he cared about that tiny little being!

Thanks to the Vorc'ara created by Analyse, after they had left the cave. Jaxx rememberd even more. The accident with the crystal happened a couple of thousand years later. Surprises came almost immediately with those who had made it to Earth as well. Analyse and Jolinaer had made sure that everyone in the rebellion had knowledge of where to go. The first shock was that their kind discovered they could have children with humans! And, that brought a huge increase in children being born to the "gods", which they were now being called. Even more so, the shock of even the female "gods" being able to bear children, ripped their entire belief system away! Azor, aka Poseidon, really got out of hand when his female, Cleito, not only presented him with one set of twins, but the two of them were like rabbits, and had procreated four more sets of twins! Until then, the Onaerris and humans produced children who were giants. But, now, something else happened, and while their children were obviously gorgeous, they were also larger than normal humans, but not so large to be thought strange. They also had great strength as well. Once they realized they could have normal children, the other "gods" went on a whirlwind speed of knocking up more human females, producing more of them. One of the most famous of these was Heracles – or Hercules, as he became known.

After his last set of twins was born, Azor decided that he didn't want to be a "god" any longer. He had actually fallen in love with Cleito, and wanted to stay with her as her life dwindled away. So, he stepped aside, and Jaxx took up the mantra of Poseidon. Of course, the twins were attributed to him, which bugged him to no end! As time went on, though, he just accepted it, and gave up trying to convince people that they were not his children.

Next, he wondered what to do with the crystal he had carried around for thousands of years. He was really tired of carrying it, so Jaxx solved the problem by having the people build a gigantic statue of himself, complete with horses, and chariots, and before it was to be moved to its permanent place, he entered the construction zone at a time no one was working, and carefully put the crystal inside the left, back chariot wheel. And, that was where it stayed for thousands of years. However, the planet he was on had other ideas. It was alive.

A massive earthquake rocked Atlantis, and the statue fell, causing the crystal to crack. The leak from it poured the peach ocean of Anaerris into the mighty ocean of Earth. When Atlantis began to sink due to the rising of the oceans, which actually made it only look as if it were sinking. In reality, the ocean levels rose suddenly and virtually overnight. While Jaxx had managed to rescue the crystal, before the island was covered by the waters, but it was already too late. The damage had been done. Once it flooded the entire Earth, it destroyed the wickedness of man that had engulfed the Earth for eons. As time progressed, humans repopulated the Earth, so the last thing the surviving inhabitants had time for was preserving their histories. They were far too busy trying to survive everyday life to pay attention to anything else. Finally, time pressed forward, and humans had more time after the work of their day to listen to the tales told around campfires. It became a form of entertainment, when they began to cluster into communities and villages. Bards were born who had an uncanny talent for remembering the stories of the past. There was no written language at that time, so recitation became the form of preserving their history. And, the tales spread. Bards wandered from town to town, regaling the populace with amazing stories of ancient "gods". The people even named their own children after the legendary "gods", as well as their children, and there children's children. Eventually, those lapsed into legends, and finally, dissolved into the mists of history in the form of mythology. And, the ancient "gods" were left behind, causing them to reinvent themselves through the eons many times. Today, they were captains of industry, politicians, and wealthy beyond most people's understanding. No matter what, though, they had always needed to help the humans to higher and higher forms of civilizations.

As time went on, the anger of Delinear's deception was buried within him, and he began to let that anger go. He had to expel her betrayal from his mind and his body. And, with only one way to do that, he allowed his volcanic energy to build, until he became a molten entity that could kill with a touch – the very thing he had been afraid to allow.

The alarm on her phone rang, and quickly, Gem tried to wake Jaxx. Even after ten minutes, he would not wake! She tried everything she could! She shook him; she pushed him; finally, she hit him in the face with her fists! Nothing happened! It was within the time period he had told her to use! So, what the hell was wrong? She sat back on her knees with tears rolling down her face wondering what to do, when she saw Jaxx's form begin to change.

"Oh, shit! Creator!" she squealed, as she watch the fiery form that was Jaxx began to flash toward her. Gem's eyes widened in terror as she felt the heat! She turned – and started to run as if hell was on her heels! And, truth be known? That's exactly what Jaxx had become! Hell on legs! She was sure that he would kill her!

Only she got nowhere fast as Jaxx reached out and caught her. Gem was frozen, waiting for her body to burn! His entire being blazed like fire, but when he touched her, all she felt was ecstasy! He didn't burn her at all! Her eyes widened in shock, looking down at his fiery hands. She felt nothing but cool next to her skin!

"Jaxx?" she asked him in a shaky voice.

Without a word from his fiery form, he drew her into his arms, thanking the Creator that he had not killed the love of his long life. She gasped, as his fiery lips dipped to her creamy white neck, and without a word, he picked her up, and carting her back to his bed for the most amazing and erotic "ride" of her life!

~ 19 ~
"Time to leave, but remember this...never feed a Fae Pancakes!" ~ Rick

Everyone decided that they would sleep late the next morning. After awakening, and after checking on their still sleeping children, Taylor strolled into the kitchen, where Rick was actually beginning a huge breakfast for all of them. Taylor leaned against the cabinet, watching her mate cook, and finally began to speak.

"So, where are they?" she asked, her eyes twinkling.

"Where do you think, Tay? It's right where I want you!" Rick said, waggling his eyebrows at her, only earning a slap on the forearm. "Ouch! Why did you hit me?"

"Because you can be such a dick sometimes!" she laughed.

"Uh-uh! Language! We have two rug-rats in the house!" Rick grinned.

"Like I said. You are such a dick!" she repeated with a grin. "Well, I dunno. Perhaps we should go look for them," she suggested with another grin.

"Oh, yeah! That'll go over great with them!" Rick flipped the sausage that was in the pan watching it sizzle slowly. Then, Rick tossed Taylor a towel. "OK, woman! Get to work, and make the pancakes. Our two lovers will probably be starving when they get back."

Taylor pulled out the pancake mix, and stirred the ingredients together, then put it aside to wait while the burner heated up the griddle. Her brows turned into a frown earning a raised eyebrow from Rick.

"What's the matter, Tay?" he asked.

"I'm worried, Rick."

"So am I, but what should we do?" he asked.

"After what happened to Gem, I'm just really worried, Rick. I mean...since Eloran was able to breech this house, our house, and the grounds of Jaxx's estateeven after Jaxx had banished Delinear, safety is the utmost priority."

Wiping his hands on the towel after grabbing it from his shoulder, he turned toward Taylor, and reached across to grab the mixing bowl of batter.

"I am not going to argue that point, Tay."

"Of course, it's not safe. And, neither is Earth, now," she told him.

"*We* are not safe on this planet any longer, Tay," he stopped to wrap his arms around her, holding her to his chest. Light tears appeared in his eyes. "There is no one as saddened by this as I am, Taylor. This is *my* home. This is *my* planet. Our children were born here! We have to leave, and *you* must open a Vorc'ara to let us do so."

Her eyes met his in shock. She couldn't imagine living anywhere else!

"B-but..." she stammered.

He placed his fingers on her lips, shaking his head.

"No, Taylor. We must leave. Your kind – and I don't mean any disrespect, my love – have literally caused all of this. The humans around us will be in danger if this escalates."

Nodding, she knew Rick was right, but it didn't make it any easier.

"So, what now? Where do we go?"

"First things first. We are getting the kids out of here. I don't know where we could send them, but let's ask Lola. She is Fae. Maybe she has an idea. Second, the minute Jaxx and Gem return, we have to get the hell 'out of Dodge'!"

"Well, we certainly cannot go into the Fae realm. That's a given. No one can go into it without an explicit invitation, and they have always been very paranoid about other realms," Taylor said. A thought occurred to her. "You know, I was thin...." only to be cut off in mid-sentence.

"Third. Eloran is bent on becoming ruler – not only of us, but the human world as well. We cannot allow this to happen!"

"Thanks for that beautiful piece of deduction, Sherlock. I know all that! You're right, though. We are going to have to find somewhere else to go," she agreed. "How can we save Earth if we are not here?"

Rick's eyes bulged. Neither of them wanted to even voice the third step that needed to be done.

This world was their home. She loved it, and didn't want to leave it. Unfortunately, unless Jaxx came up with another idea, there might be no other choice.

"Jumping to conclusions is not the best course."

Taylor nodded slowly, and sighed.

"I know. And, maybe Jaxx just might have an alternative solution."

The pancakes were burning, but Rick didn't care. He put his arms around Taylor, and held her tightly.

"Oh, my love! Let's wait and see what he has to say when he and Gem get back. He is a warrior just like you are. Gem will not want to leave, either. So, let's wait, and not jump to conclusions," he said. "OK?"

Quietly, she lifted her head to quickly kiss her mate.

"You're right, Rick."

"That's my girl!"

"Yep, I am, but honey? The pancakes are burning," she grinned, even though it really wasn't necessary to point it out to him, because he was already scooping the burned pancakes off the griddle and into the trash, then added more batter to it.

"By the way...where do you think Lola will suggest for the kids?"

Before she could respond to Rick's question, a tiny voice came from behind them.

"Are those pancakes?" she squealed, hopping up on one of the chairs using her Fae magic to pull the small, but full, platter toward her. One of the great things about this realm was the food! And, her most favorite food of all was pancakes! Lola scooped up three pancakes, slathered them in butter, and poured the thick syrup over them. She cut her first large piece, and shoved it in her mouth.

"Mmmmmm! You can cook, Rick!" she said, after she had swallowed it. "These are amazing!"

After a few more bites with Rick and Taylor staring at her in shocked silence, she answered their question.

"Oh. Well, that's an easy question. The Queen has agreed to take your kids for protection," Lola said as if it were the most logical answer in the world.

"How do you know?" Taylor asked cautiously. "But, how are they going to feel about having two hybrid children there?"

Lola was already busy slathering more butter and syrup on the next three pancakes, and her mouth was full as she answered.

"Alrdy tlk ta er bot ti, duh! I gng to scort the du a dm into the Fre Rlm," Lola said, not really caring if any one understood her. When she finally swallowed her food, she finished what she was saying. "And, they will be under the specific protection of our Queen, so you will not need to worry about it. She has offered her personal protection to them." Lola shoved more pancakes into her mouth. "I wll sway wit er in er plas."

"What?" Taylor asked with a laugh, watching Lola just shake her head, and stuff more pancakes into her mouth.

Rick looked down at Taylor in complete confusion and shrugged. Taylor only grinned at him. Whatever she had told them, they trusted Lola to be on top of things! Even with a mouthful of pancakes!

An hour later, Gem sauntered into the house arm in arm with Jaxx, and looking at each other with googly eyes. At least that was what Marcus and Shirley were calling it. In seconds, Lola had taken off to the kitchen to change back into a pug. No one really wanted Gem to know that she was Fae, yet.

"Ewww!" Shirley snarled her nose.

"Yeah! Ick!" Marcus said with the same facial expression as his sister.

The adults around them laughed heartily, including Jaxx and Gem.

Gem couldn't resist them as they ran to her practically throwing themselves into her arms. Then, they followed by doing the same to Jaxx. Both laughed, and grabbed the urchins as they hugged them.

"Well, give yourself a few years," Gem giggled. "You'll change your minds!"

Vigorous shaking of two heads followed.

"No way, Aunt Gem! Ewww! I won't ever want to look at a boy that way! Ewww!" she repeated in emphasis.

"Yeah! Me, neither! Ick!" Marcus echoed – with different words, of course, and adding, "But, geez, Aunt Gem! You stink!"

What? She still smelled like a sewer? Gem had thought she had been able to rid herself of that gross smell. Guess not. Everyone's head turned toward her. Jaxx, who just dipped his head, looked suspiciously sheepish. Neither said anything.

After the greetings and sticky kisses the children gave them from eating pancakes, Marcus and Shirley were hustled up the stairs by Lola when Taylor told them to go get baths. Gem frowned as she watched Lola herd the kids – as if she understood what Taylor had said, and was determined to see that her orders were carried out to the letter. Gem looked at everyone, but they stood around, looking really innocent. That clued Gem to finally not only admit to herself, but also to realize that there was something wrong with Lola. She had no idea what it was, but after experiencing Jaxx's real, volcanic form, she was beginning to realize that nothing around her was human. After he had awakened, his entire body erupted in a yellow-orange fire. He had cornered her in the kitchen. She had no where to run. The fiery form reached for her hand, and she had screamed. Moments later, though, she realized that his fiery hands were cool. He had yanked her to him only to wrap his very cool arms around her. Now, Gem humphed, wondering if it could also include Lola?

Taylor frowned looking at Gem realizing that something was different.

"What the hell happened to your hair, Gem? Half of it is missing!" Taylor was stunned by the fact it looked as if it had been burned! "The tips of your hair are black!"

Gem's eyes darted to Jaxx, then back to Taylor who caught the look. The next thing Jaxx and Gem knew, Taylor was up in his face.

"You DIDN'T!" she accused him point blank.

"Didn't what, hon? What did he not do?" Rick asked.

Without answering, Taylor's hand came up to slap Jaxx, only to be stopped by Rick's grasp.

"What the hell, Taylor?" Rick asked, restraining her attack on Jaxx.

Jaxx shook his head.

"Rick.   Let Tay go. She is absolutely right to admonish me – even with a slap to my face!" Turning to Taylor as she was released, "I know, Tay. I shouldn't have, but I had no choice."

"No choice? Don't give me that crap, Jaxx! You have a choice! What is wrong with you? Don't you know that you could have killed Gem?   What were you thinking?" she yelled.

Gem stepped in between Taylor and Jaxx, holding up a hand to stop Taylor's advancement toward Jaxx.

"Stop, Tay! Please! I understand why you're so mad. But, don't be mad at Jaxx. It was my doing. I asked him to do it for me," Gem said.

"Doesn't matter! His form could have killed you!" Taylor cried.

"But, it didn't!"

"Just for the record," Rick yelled loudly to be heard over them. He continued. "and for those of us who have no idea what you are talking about, exactly *what* did Jaxx do?"

Gem, Jaxx, and Taylor looked at each other, then turned to Rick. Before anyone could say anything, a noise behind them caused them to turn. Stan and Stacy walked through one of the three doors into the kitchen.

"What's the beef?" Stan asked casually, taking into account everyone's anger.

Stacy jabbed him in the gut.

"That's 'where's the beef' you idiot!"

Stan cocked his head at the others, then answered his mate.

"Nope. I'm right! '*What's* the beef?'" he asked, again.

Jaxx was breathing hard. Stan had been his best friend since they had come to terms over the five sets of twins eons ago. It was something Stacy knew nothing about. It would hurt her too much if she ever found out about it, because she had been trying to become pregnant for years.

"Well...," Jaxx stammered.

"...you see," Gem continued.

"Ah, hell, Stan! I turned to my fire form, and I could have killed Gem!"

"But, it's OK, Stan. Really. He only burned some of my hair," Gem told him in a matter-of-fact tone.

Stan's head jerked toward Jaxx in shock. There was only one way that could have happened.

"What the fuck did you two do?" he demanded.

Well, at least he was blaming both of them, Gem thought.

Silence ensued, and Rick took that time to make some more pancakes, and put a full platter on the table. Everyone automatically dipped into them, and spread butter and syrup on them, before anyone said anything.

"It was my fault, Stan," Gem murmured.

"What?" Stan yelped.

Suddenly, Gem and Jaxx started to talk...and, they stumbled over each other trying to explain.

"I asked him about the myth of the Jewel of Anaerris, and if he remembered the truth..."

"..Yeah. Then, I told her that I didn't remember everything, because it had been so long. You know that's the truth. None of us remember the entire thing..."

"And, I told Jaxx we needed to know, and he said that the only way was to put himself in something called catalepsy, and it was dangerous if I didn't wake him up when he said I should..."

"...and, I did it, and was able to remember everything..."

"...but, I couldn't wake him up, and I tried everything I could think of...but, then he began to glow hot and red, and I realized that was what he had been talking about, and why he was dangerous if he couldn't wake up, and I turned and ran, but not fast enough, and fire burst around him, and I just barely made it out of his reach, and my hair caught fire, so I stuck my head into the waterfall to douse the fire, and I was really upset, but then, he touched me, and he shocked me with the cool touch of his fiery hand, and..."

"...then, I changed back, and believe me, Stan, I was horrified by what I had done, so I ran to her, and saw her hair was burned, then I grabbed her and apologized..."

"...yeah, and then I told him there was nothing to apologize for, and he said that Taylor and Stan would be so pissed at him. And, he believed you guys would probably try to kill him, and I told him, no, they wouldn't do that, and he said that you would, and..."

"...we came back..."

"...and I told him that you two would not bug him about this, because it was an accident, and that it could happen to anyone, but I was really happy I saw him in his true form, because after being in the volcanic prison, and almost melted alive, I wasn't as scared as I had been, and after all, I had escaped that prison, too, so why would I not escape Jaxx's burst of *firepower*?"

Gem and Jaxx exchanged a look, knowing that they had no intention of telling them the whole truth.

After the two of them finished their diatribe, both of them were breathing hard, because she said all of that without hardly taking a breath. Both she and Jaxx stood looking at the four people in front of them hoping they'd understand. Then, Stan threw back his head, and began to laugh so hard, his knees actually sank from underneath him, and fell to the floor in apparent hysteria! In seconds,

Stacy and Rick were laughing right along with Stan, leaving Taylor glaring at the three of them in frustration. She whipped her head around when she heard laughing from Gem and Jaxx.

Two little urchins were staring at the grownups, watching them laugh like hyenas! They wondered if all other grownups reacted this silly?

And, as we all know, laughter is catching. And, Taylor wasn't immune to it. So, while she was still extremely angry with Jaxx, she couldn't help the burst of laughter that came from her...and it continued. OK. So, she guessed it was a bit funny, but still, her best friend could have been killed. And, Taylor just began laughing right along with everyone else.

After what seemed like hours, but was really only minutes of stomach-hurting laughter, everyone finally began to calm down, but interspersed with sporadic laughter that could not be contained.

Finally, Stacy wiped her eyes of the tears that had been running down her face, and grabbed Gem's hand.

"C-come o-on, G-Gem," she managed to say.

"W-where?" Gem laughed.

"Let's go take care of the mess Jaxx's 'firepower' made on your hair!"

That just sent everyone into wails of more laughter all over again.

"F-firepower!" gasped Stan. "N-never, e-ever, h-heard it called t-that b-before!"

Stunned, Gem said, "*Firepower?* That is what you all are laughing about? Because I said he had *firepower*?"

"S-sure?" he stammered between gulps of laughter.

Stacy snickered behind her own hands, desperately trying to get control over her own laughter. She pulled at Gem's hand, and the two of them made their way up the stairs into Jaxx's bathroom.

Giggling, Stacy parked Gem on the stool at the vanity that Jaxx had added to his bathroom just for Gem, and said, "W-wait r-right here, Gem! I'm going to get my hair trimming kit, and I'll be right back."

Gem turned to her with a huge grin, "Well, OK. After all, where am I going to go – this time?"

Stacy roared with laughter as she left the room only to return a few minutes later. By that time, the girls had calmed down, and Stacy looked at Gem in the mirror. She pulled the damaged hair up, and shook her hair, then grinned.

"I know you've had that same hair style all your life, Gem, but there is too much damage. I'm going to have to cut your hair shorter to get rid of it."

Gem had always had the same style. Granted, the tips of it were burned away, now, but she really didn't want to change anything. She really hated change. She cocked her head as she looked at Stacy who was waiting for the go ahead. For someone who hated change so much, her entire life over the last few weeks was filled with nothing but change! Why not the way she looked, too? She had no idea what Stacy could do with her messy locks, but she nodded.

"OK."

"I promise. Your hair will look amazing when I'm done!" Stacy told her. After all, this was what she did for a living. She was a Master Hair Stylist, so she set to work on the worst hair she had ever seen in her life – but she would never say that to Gem! "OK," she told Gem as she took the first hair strands, and snapped her scissors quickly together just so she could watch Gem cringe at the sound, then grinned. "Here we go!"

"How long have they been up there?" Rick asked not really caring.

Taylor shrugged, then went back to reading a book on her iPad that she had downloaded the other day. She was fascinated by a new three book series, called the White Wolf Prophecy Trilogy.

"I don't know, but they've been up there a long time!" griped Jaxx, who was busy tapping his fingers on the fireplace mantel, before he stopped. He raised an eyebrow when he realized he had been doing that an awful lot lately!

Stan grinned as he looked up from working on a carburetor that he had brought into the library to work on, while they waited.

"Oh, get a grip, Jaxx! Stacy's a pro at these things, and you know it!"

"Yeah, but it wouldn't have been necessary if it hadn't been for me!" Jaxx whined.

"It was an accident, for Creator's sake! Get a grip, and will you, please, quit whining, Jaxx!" Rick admonished him, hearing Taylor snicker without looking up from her iPad.

"I. Do. Not. Whine." Jaxx growled at him, enunciating Each. Word. Separately.

"Uh...Yes. You. Are." Stan said pointedly, earning an outright laugh from Taylor, who still didn't look up from reading.

"No. I'm. Not." Jaxx said with a slight smirk.

"Yes. You. Are." Rick added grinning like an idiot.

Taylor looked up, and rolled her eyes with laughter in them.

"You guys really sound as if you are in the first grade!" she giggled, then bent her head to read, again.

"*No. We. Don't!*" all three men whined together, and laughter erupted from the three of them, which stopped when Stacy blew into the room with a flourish.

"Ladies and gentlemen! May I present the new – and much improved without burned hair – Gem Elwood!"

Stacy bowed, and stepped aside to allow Gem to enter slowly. Blinks and gasps were heard all around the room making Stacy stand up taller in pride!

"Holy shit!" Rick said with his mouth open.

"I don't believe it!" Taylor said in shock.

"That's my girl!" Stan added as he rushed to her side, seeing her look appropriately proud, but embarrassed at the same time. "You look gorgeous, Gem!"

Gem felt a bit shy as she looked at Jaxx whose eyes were about to pop out of their sockets! That was good, she thought, right?

She was a vision of beauty, Jaxx thought to himself. Just like...just like...his mouth dropped in complete shock as he realized, for the first time, who she resembled! He was dumbfounded as he realized it. How had he not noticed before this?

Gem turned slowly around, so everyone could see her new look. Stacy had been a miracle worker, and Gem had never been as pleased as she was, right now, with the way she looked. Stacy was, indeed, a miracle worker. She loved her new shorter style!

At first, she thought that Stacy had just kept hacking away at her hair. Gem didn't think she'd have any left from the sound of the shears attacking her hair over and over. Stacy had even huffed when she saw a couple of tears run down Gem's cheeks! No doubt at all that Gem was truly afraid to change her looks. After her hair was done, Stacy carefully applied makeup to her face. Gem wasn't a big lover of it, but she deferred to Stacy in this. Partly because she was curious, but mostly because she didn't want to hurt Stacy's feelings. However, when Gem saw the finished result in the mirror, she had been totally speechless!

"I-i...is that really me?" she had asked Stacy, who watched Gem's mouth turn up as she began to smile so wide, you could even see her gums!

"Yep! Now, we need to get you dressed!"

Next, they had run to Stacy's room to get an outfit for Gem to wear.

There were all kinds of colors in Stacy's closet. So many, Gem was stunned! She must have brought everything from her home!

"Were you expecting to live here forever?" Gem had teased jokingly.

Stacy just stared at her as if she had grown two heads, causing Gem to laugh.

"Well, you just never know what a girl will need!" she answered, as if that explained everything.

That made a strange logical sense – to Stacy. Stacy was the diva of all three women!

After debating for a long time, they both chose the same outfit at the same time as their hands met on the hanger! They grinned at each other, and in moments, Gem was dressed. The girls giggled, and almost jumped up and down with delight. Gem's feet were also the same size, so Stacy had her don a pair of silvery sandals that wound upward just over her ankles. The result was breathtaking!

Seeing the gleam in all the mens' eyes just confirmed the fact that she was as amazing looking as she hoped. Before them stood an absolute beauty. Stacy had cut Gem's hair just above shoulder length in a cropped and blunt style. She no longer had curls, but her hair was wavy, and softly bounced around her face. Her makeup had been enhanced to make her green eyes stand out boldly with long, black mascara framing them. A highlighter had been placed just under her eyebrows that had been tweezed and waxed, which allowed her eyes to be even brighter with lavender eyeshadow on her eyelids, and the dark green liner below and just above her eyelash line. She wore a bright green dress that had a gentle sheen, which left her shoulders bare. A high waist emphasized her cleavage while disguising her large breasts. A large, silver medallion was clipped just under her breasts, and the skirt fell softly around her body, stopping just above her knees.

Unabashedly, Jaxx's eyes were full of lust and desire as his eyes traveled up and down her body. She looked exactly – almost to a T – like Analyse! The resemblance was uncanny! Of course, she was a younger version, but the look was the same. Without doubt, he now believed that she was the descendant of Jolinaer and Analyse. She really had been pregnant that day in the cave, and it was obvious that the child had lived, or Gem wouldn't be here right now – looking like the most delectable dish served on a platter to a starving man! He couldn't wait to get her alone, and unwrap the present that stood before him!

"Oh, man!" Rick said in admiration.

"You said it!" Stan agreed.

"You are the sexiest thing I have ever seen in my life," Jaxx said to her softly. Her blush was perfect with her look!

"Well, she's all dressed up, but nowhere go go," Taylor said with a snarky grin.

"What are you talking abo...Oh! I get it! You're being a little bitch!" Stacy smirked.

Taylor darted a look at her, and glared darkly for a few moments. Stacy just grinned at her.

"You know?" Taylor mused. "I haven't used my ability for a Vorc'ara in ages. How about we go to someplace where we can get a great meal?"

"With Eloran out there?" Rick asked.

"I doubt Delinear wouldn't be able to use the Vorc'ara for at least two weeks. so...."

Taylor and Stacy were already running upstairs to dress with Stan and Rick nipping at their heels, leaving Gem and Jaxx happily alone.

"Creator! Gem! I want to rip that dress off of you, and plunge myself inside of you!" Jaxx admitted.

Grinning, Gem pressed her mouth to his in an Earth-shattering kiss that left them both gasping.

"After we go out to eat, Jaxx," she told him to which he growled deeply in disappointment.

"But, after?" he asked, eagerly making Gem laugh out loud.

"After?" she asked in a sultry tone, her eyes raking over his body stopping at the huge bulge that pushed against his pants. Her desire ridden eyes raised back to his. Quietly, she put her lips to his ear, and whispered so only he could hear her. "Well, when we do return, if that large cock of yours isn't in me fast, I'll make sure I will take you!" she grinned, and received another fabulous kiss. She pulled back, and finished. "And, I don't care if you take me out into a back alley to do me!"

Then, she skittered up the stairs as the other men came down with an excuse that they girls needed her help. Just at that moment, Stan bounced into the room, but had not heard all the conversation.

"So, who's doing who?" he quipped.

An hour later, all three girls entered the library where the men waited for them. Lola was lying on a comfortable chair, and no one had better move her. She could, quite literally, destroy all of them without moving. She glared at them, but they paid no attention to her when the men saw the three women walk into the room, and a slow, appreciative, whistle came from Rick and Stan.

If there were three other women in the world who were more attractive and desirable as these three, not one of the men could name one. They were the epitome of all mens' wet dreams. Not really realizing until now, all three women represented all three types of women – a redhead, a blonde, and a brunette.

Lola wrinkled her nose. Yuck! It stunk from all the testosterone and estrogen in the room. What was it with them? Was it really necessary to think of sex on a constant basis? Her own kind were not immune to it, either, but they were an ancient race, and had learned to control their libidos! She huffed, dragged the soft, fluffy throw from the back of the chair, and buried her nose into it to escape the scent.

Gem, dressed in green with her green eyes and red hair was absolutely breathtaking alone, but Taylor and Stacy added to the beauty in spades.

Taylor was the tallest, and had donned a shimmering, golden Roman style dress that dropped to her ankles. It had deep slits slicing both sides of the skirt, showing off her golden sandals, which laced upward to just below her knee. With one shoulder bared, and her arm sporting a slave bracelet on her upper bare arm in gold, her eyes glittered with excitement, while her dark, brown locks of hair had been pulled up on one side, and clasped in a golden barrette, glittering with yellow diamonds. And, at her neck, glimmered a simple golden chain. She was dressed as a goddess, Rick thought – and she was his!

In total contrast, Stacy twirled in a circle, allowing her brilliant, red dress to flare softly from her smaller frame. It was a soft, v-neck dress that dipped low revealing a lot of cleavage as well as dipping low in the back. Sleeveless, both sides draped to her upper waist that was held by a silver, filigree broach. The skirt flowed directly from it, and moved softly with any movement Stacy made. She wore brilliant, tall stiletto heels that were so high, it raised her shorter height by at least three inches. Stan gulped as he beheld her beautiful blonde, straight hair falling softly around her shoulders with a gorgeous head ornament that was placed on top of her head coming to a point on her forehead and shined with brilliant red jewels. A small ruby drop hung from the center, which rested on her forehead, between her eyes.

The men were similarly dressed in their own version of dress-up, but each as individual as the girls' dress.

Stan wore a simple pair of khaki pants, a black turtleneck, and a tan blazer with elbow patches. A brown belt and slip on shoes completed his outfit. Since he was bald, he didn't need any grooming there, but in place of his normal scruffy chin, he was clean-shaven. Stacy hadn't seen him shave in years, and she felt her heart skip a beat, reminding her of when they first met.

Rick, on the other hand, was dressed in a semi-shiny charcoal gray suit complete with a snow-white dress shirt, and a tie that was printed with different shades of gray. A black belt, and black dress tie shoes had been added. His dark brown hair was slicked back, which only emphasized his darker brown eyes.

Finally, after having torn himself away from Gem, Jaxx showed up in almost typical Jaxx attire, but with a couple of differences. Instead of a black t-shirt and jeans, tonight, he sported a cream colored turtleneck sweater over which he wore a black leather duster, and black jeans. With his messy black hair, and a scruffy beard on his face, he was heartstoppingly gorgeous to Gem. A black studded belt, and black riding boots completed his own look.

Taylor was just about to open the Vorc'ara, when Rick grasped her arm.

Lola blew out an exasperated breath as she saw everyone ready to open one of those damned wormholes again. Seriously? When would these so-called immortals ever learn, she wondered. As if opening one wasn't going to draw every single enemy to them! Right! Nah! They'd never learn. They hadn't learned in eons, so why would they start now? Her eyes met Gem's, and Gem was convinced, in that moment, that Lola was definitely no more human than the others!

"Are we sure about this? I thought that when one opened, other Anaerris could sense it?" Rick asked.

Taylor looked up at him, and nodded.

"Essentially, yes. That is true, but..." she began.

"Hold it! Wait! Are you saying that every time one of the, uh, wormhole thingies open, the evil guys know it?" Gem asked, surprised that five sets of eyes whipped around to stare at her. "What? I'm just saying!"

Taylor shook her head, and turned back to her mate, ignoring Gem.

"As I was saying...yes. That is true – in most cases...."

"I feel a 'but' coming," Stacy muttered under her breath, receiving another glare from Taylor.

"*BUT*," Taylor said with emphasis, earning an eyeroll from Stacy. "We're talking about an inter-dimensional Vorc'ara as opposed to a planet Vorc'ara."

Shock registered on Jaxx's face. The Anaerris kept all kinds of their powers secret, but this was new to him!

"What?" he said – very loud!

"Oh, put a sock in it, Jaxx," she rolled her eyes, while turning back to everyone else. "Opening a Vorc'ara to another dimension or across space alert others, and is what exhausts the Anaerris who opens it, lasting for up to two weeks, before they can open another. However, when the Vorc'ara is open on a planet, only, it takes little to no power, so we can quite literally open as many as we want with little to no detection."

Taylor stared at Gem.

"But, there is a catch. If, say, Delinear opens an off-world Vorc, we might, or might not, be able to detect it? However, it is quite apparent that Gem can also open them, so even if one of us gets tired, the other one can open another one!"

Gem was fascinated, now. She had opened an inter-dimensional, and had no idea how she had done it. But what was Taylor saying? That she had the power to open one on Earth, and not be tracked? Hell, she had no idea how she had opened one in the first place! She needed to talk to Taylor to find out how to actually open one.

"But, Taylor," she began, "I don't know how to...."

Taylor waved her silent.

"Tut-tut, Gem. I know you don't understand how you opened one, but that's OK. I am going to teach you. One thing I can say," she turned to all again, "we have several advantages over Eloran and Delinear, among which we have the Jewel of Anaerris – whose name actually lives up to the legend – and she not only has the power to open Vorc'aras, but she can read the Code."

Rick pulled Taylor to him, and kissed her forehead.

"So? What are we waiting for? Let's go to dinner before the guys decide to take you all back to our rooms for ravishing?"

Taylor rolled her eyes right along with Gem and Stacy, while the men laughed.

"Lola? You got this? Stay with the kids and protect them?"

Lola snorted her answer, and laid her head back down. These people were really idiots! As if she wouldn't stay with the little tadpoles!

"Good. Thanks," she said to Lola, hearing Lola snort a second time. "OK, Gem. Come here. I'm going to show you the secret even though you stumbled onto it by accident."

Gem walked to stand beside Taylor, who bent to whisper into her ear. Gem's eyebrows rose markedly in surprise.

"That's it?" she asked.

"That's it!" Taylor told her with a grin.

"No shit!" Gem said in amazement.

"Nope. No shit," Taylor answered. "You want to try?"

"Sure. Why not?" Gem said.

Gem positioned herself, and simply did what she did before. She closed her eyes, raised her arms, and called up an exit! Feeling a rush of wind and cold, Gem's eyes opened in surprise, and she stared at the Vorc'ara whirling in front of them.

"Oh, wow!" she murmured.

"Wow, indeed," Jaxx said wrapping his arm around her. "Ready?"

She nodded, and the group stepped through the Vorc'ara to the destination Gem had imagined.

~ 20 ~

**"Time for a little R & R! It's always good for the soul;
bad for the old bank account!" ~ Stacy**

"This is perfect, Gem! Why did you choose here?" Taylor asked curiously, looking around at all the pigeons fluttering in the massive square.

Gem shrugged. She really didn't know why she had picked this particular city, but still, it was perfect!

"I don't know. It popped into my mind, and I opened the 'Vorc'," she explained to Taylor.

Everyone's heads shot to Gem.

"What?" Stan asked. "What the hell is a 'Vork'?"

All four agreed with him, as they frowned.

"Huh?" Gem said in surprise, then giggled as it dawned on her that they would be confused by her nickname for it. She giggled a bit, before she told them what she meant. "Oh! Well, you see? I think Vorc'ara is a bit of a mouthful, and kinda old-fashioned. And, hell, it's way too much of a mouthful. And, quite frankly, it is a vortex, after all, so I decided it was time for a change in wording. So, Vorc is what I decree it should be!"

"You *decree*?" Jaxx repeated, but she knew he was teasing her, because his words were accompanied by his normal, sexy smirk.

"Are you serious?" Stan muttered.

Taylor nodded, then broke into a delighted laugh.

"Well, it's really not a bad idea!" Then, she had another thought. "You know...it could come in handy later on if we need to open one in front of our enemies! It's close enough to Vorc'ara, but the shortened version just might give us a slight edge, because they wouldn't understand what we are talking about, immediately!"

With that Earth shaking decision made, they wandered to a local sidewalk café surrounding the square in the city where Gem had taken them. OK. She had always wanted to visit this city! Venezia, Italia! Then she sighed in happiness.

After they had given their order, they sat back, relaxed, and discussed all kinds of subjects that were about anything without mentioning the current circumstances. They did not notice how difficult it was for those passing by not to stare at the three gorgeous couples sitting at the café. Most people had never seen that many gorgeous people in one place at the same time, so naturally, anyone passing by would have no other option but to look. They wouldn't be able to help themselves. The problem was that the group didn't really care about what others were thinking about them, because they were too busy talking to each other. Finally, Stan broke the taboo subject.

"So, what are we going to do? We need a place to hole up until we can figure out what to do," Stan leaned back in his chair.

"Thanks so much for that buzzkill, mate!" Stacy grouched.

Everyone ignored her, and sipped their drinks, while considering options.

"Is there even a place that Eloran and Delinear won't find us?" Stacy asked the billion dollar question. The sixty-four thousand dollar question was long gone due to inflation, of course.

"Well, at least we don't have to worry about the kids!" Rick mentioned, getting a kick from under the table by Taylor. "OW! What the hell was that for?"

"You idiot!" she hissed, shooting her thumb at a stunned Gem. And, that was enough.

"OK. I've let you all get away without telling me some things, but this one you need to answer. Where are the kids going?"

No one answered. A waiter approached, asking if they wanted another round of drinks. Stacy answered for all of them.

"Yes. I think so. Thank you," she told him.

He left to get their drinks, and Gem slammed her fist lightly on the table, making the dishes clink a bit.

"Come on! Is there anywhere that they cannot find us?" she demanded.

Jaxx looked at Taylor who looked at Rick who looked at Stan who looked at Stacy who looked back to Jaxx.

"Will you *please* stop doing that!" Gem voice was frustrated. "Why can't you just tell me the truth?"

Taylor looked at Jaxx who looked at Stacy who looked at Stan who looked at Rick who looked back at Taylor.

"Gaaahhhhh!" squealed Gem, and standing, she marched in the opposite direction of the others. She threw up her hands in exasperation. "That's it! If you won't respect me enough to tell me what's going on, I'll, by damn, go back home, and find out myself!"

Gem headed for the closest road off the square to open her Vorc. Jaxx jumped up, and intercepted her before she made it. Grabbing her arm, she stopped, but refused to look at him.

"Gem, please?" he coaxed her, trying to get her to calm down.

She said absolutely nothing to him, light tears running down her cheeks. She was sick and tired of being left out of the loop! All of this shit was happening to *her*. If she didn't know what the hell was going on – all of it –

then, how the hell could she protect herself or others if she didn't know the whole truth and nothing but the truth?

"Gem?" Jaxx begged. "Please?"

Gem realized that jumping up, and storming off was simply overreacting. But, she wasn't going to give them the satisfaction of acknowledging it, no matter how embarrassed she was! She knew these people hadn't told her everything, because they thought that she just wasn't ready. Telling her might have made them believe that they would push her over the edge. But, she had been alone since she was seventeen years old, and had done just fine taking care of herself right along with Lola. That thought had her pull up short, and she froze where she was.

Lola? Lola wasn't what she appeared to be! Gem knew this without being told. Perhaps she had always known it. If the rest of her friends who had surrounded her all her life were from a supernatural world, and she was from a supernatural world, even if she had just found out about it, then would it also follow that Lola may be from some other world as well? Keeping her voice low, but knowing that Jaxx could hear her.

"Lola isn't a pug, is she?" she almost hesitated, but glad she didn't. Waiting for the boom to be lowered was never a good idea.

Pulling her tightly into his body, Jaxx whispered into her ear.

"No, my love. She isn't."

Gem darted her eyes to his in surprise. Why she should have been surprised, she didn't really know. But, it was one thing, thinking that in the first place; another thing asking the question; yet, hearing it answered in the affirmative was a shock.

"W-what is she?" Gem stuttered.

"Well, she's a...," Jaxx stopped, then shook his head. "No. Let's go back home. I think it's better if you heard it from her."

"Is she not like you?" Gem said with her eyes wide. "I-I mean us?"

A shake of his head told her everything.

"But, she's still supernatural?"

A nod followed without speaking.

"Look, Gem. We've all finished dinner, so let's go home so she can tell you, OK?" he placated her.

Gem nodded, and the two headed back to their companions.

"Ready to leave?" Jaxx said, then was stunned to see both Stacy and Taylor leap to their feet.

"Leave?" Stacy squeaked.

"Leave?" Taylor followed with her own squeal.

"Uh...yeah?" Jaxx said tentatively.

"Oh, hell, no!" Taylor answered him.

"Why not?" Gem just had to ask.

"Yeah. What she said," Rick pointed at Gem.

"You don't *seriously* believe that we would come all this way – to Venice, no less – and *not* go shopping?" Stacy answered him as if he was a total moron.

"Shopping." Jaxx couldn't believe this! "Shopping? With all that's surrounding us, and you want to go *shopping*?"

Taylor, Stacy, and Gem looked at each other, then turned, hands on hips, as one to face the guys.

"Yes!" all three said together with mischievous grins.

"We have enough time to go check out the leather shops for shoes and bags!" Taylor said, as she walked away with the other two girls, leaving the three men staring at their backsides in stunned silence.

Rick cocked his head to the right.

"Did they, or did they not, just walk away from us?" he asked the other two.

Jaxx nodded along with Stan.

"Yep. That's exactly what they did!" Stan said with amusement in his voice, then coughed when he saw Stacy turn to glare at him. "Uh...I mean...why, uh, no! Of course they didn't!"

Jaxx and Rick glared at him, and he cleared his throat. Time for this to be in safer territory!

"So...anyone ready for another round of drinks?"

Looking at each other, the three men sat back down at the table, and ordered another round of booze.

"Well, we may as well get comfortable! When women go on their shopping rants, it's best if we just curl up, and drink ourselves silly!" Rick said, seeing the other two men nod.

Four shopping hours later, and by that definition meaning six hours later, the three girls returned with several bags in hand to find three men as drunk as they could be! And, worse? Music was playing, and Stan was dancing – on one of the tables to the applause and cheers of the other two along with everyone else in the restaurant!

Both Gem and Taylor whipped out their cells, and began to record the whole shebang!

"Oh, shit!" Stacy said, while a wave of red ran up her neck to her face in embarrassment.

Taylor and Gem just laughed at her, continuing to film them. Gem put her arm around her friend's shoulder.

"Hey! Don't worry!" she told Stacy

"Oh, crap! I'll never live down this embarrassment!" Stacy moaned shaking her head with her hands over her face, and head bowed.

"Gem is right, Stacy. You'll never see these people, again, so no worries! So, we definitely have to grab blackmail pics whenever we can!"

"Ahhhh," Stacy said, finally getting the point.

And, then, Gem and Taylor started laughing so hard, that Stacy had no defense against the laughter, so she joined in with the festivities by whipping her own phone out, and with the other girls, videoed the guys – and the excitement went well into the night.

Jaxx awoke to the smell of coffee, and stretched. Yum, that smelled so good! Then, wafts of bacon, sausage, and eggs made it to his nostrils. Yes! So good! He sat up quickly, and his head began to pound while his stomach began to roil. He barely made it to the bathroom, before everything he had eaten the day before came up in great quantities.

He stood up from the toilet when he was able to get his legs back onto dry ground, but everything still continued to spin. He staggered over to the sink wiping his mouth as he went, then put his hands on the cabinet, and looked into the mirror.

YUCK! He looked horrible! He couldn't imagine any woman, let alone his own mate, wanting to be around him at the moment. His mouth tasted like the sewer, his eyes were black and blue with broken veins, and his skin looked drawn and old. OK. So, not as old as he really was, but at the moment? He sure as hell felt like he was that old. He barely made it into the shower, before he threw up, once again. The smell only served to gag him more. It felt like hours before his body was finally finished, but in truth, it was only about fifteen minutes. There wasn't anything left in his stomach, anyway.

He showered – slowly – then, brushed his teeth at least three times, and finally, meandered into the bedroom to grab a pair of clean, black briefs, a black t-shirt, and a pair of black jeans. When he was done, he sat down in the wingback in front of the fireplace, and hung his head. His stomach had settled, at least, but he was too embarrassed to go downstairs and let everyone see his condition. He put his chin on his hand, and reflected on the absolute stupidity of what the three of them had done the night before after the girls took off to shop. Well, honestly? He didn't really remember much of it, but he did remember some of it. After he and Rick had laughed at Stan dancing on the table, everything became blurry. He had no idea how in the hell the girls got them back, but right now, that wasn't a priority. He had to apologize to Gem for his momentary lapse of college party mentality.

As if the very thought of her entered his mind, she appeared in the doorway of their room. Jaxx was too ashamed to even bother glancing at her, but he did hear her as her light footsteps advanced toward him. Gem sat down in the other wingback across from his. She said nothing at all, but finally, Jaxx sighed, and looked at her. Surprise floored him when he saw her grinning like a cat who ate the canary!

"Hello, lover boy!" she grinned.

"What?" he asked in surprise.

Shocked, he watched as she moved her hand to her left breast, and fluttered her eyelids with her mouth partially open.

"Y-you m-mean...y-you don't remember, last night?" she whined. Then, "Oh, Jaxxon! I'm so hurt that you don't remember the amazing kiss at the restaurant! I mean..." she fluttered at him again. "...it was the most amazing kiss in history! And, it wasn't even me!"

His eyes widened in surprise and humiliation, until he saw her mouth turn up into a huge grin, and she began to laugh. The horror on his face was completely hilarious!

"O-oh, Jaxx! Your face...it's s-so...p-priceless!" Gem knew she was pushing him, but then, he had made this way too easy!

Jaxx scooped her in his arms, his stomach forgotten, and threw her on the bed. He splayed his body on top of hers, and then...well...you know what they say about payback being a bitch! But, Gem was ready for him, and he proceeded to "punish" her thoroughly!

An hour later, the two lovers, having showered – twice – finally made it down to the kitchen. Everyone was there, including the kids.

"There you are!" Rick smirked, earning a slap on the arm by Stacy.

"Mind your own business!"

Smiling at the slap her mate just received from Stacy, Taylor told them, "I have breakfast, ready...I mean...brunch!" she chuckled.

Gem rolled her eyes, while Jaxx gave Taylor a pointed look that said she'd better not say one more word. Taylor just giggled, and spooned some food onto plates for the two of them. Both Gem and Jaxx shoveled the food in their mouths as if they hadn't eaten a large dinner the night before!

While Gem helped Stacy clean the kitchen, the others met in the library. The two girls joined them after they were finished, and the kids were up in their rooms playing.

"So. What now?" Stan asked slapping his hands on his thighs, sitting down on the sofa next to Stacy.

"Well, one thing is for sure," Taylor said, "We are not safe here any more. None of us."

"Will you guys *please* stop saying that?" Stan demanded. "We already know it isn't safe, so why does everyone keep repeating it?"

"Repeating what?" Ric said with a straight face, launching everyone else into laughter.

Gem looked from face to face. This was really all about her. She was the one keeping everyone in danger. Even her own mate! If she left, maybe she could keep them all safe. Jaxx knew what she was thinking.

"Fuck that, Gem! I can't believe you were even thinking about leaving!" Jaxx said.

She turned to him. Oh, crap! She really needed to learn to protect her thoughts!

"But..." she began.

"No 'buts'! We are your, uh, bodyguards whether or not you want us!" he growled at her.

"Jaxx is right, Gem. You are our responsibility. Where you go, we go," Stan agreed.

Gem sighed, and leaned back against the chair.

"OK. So. What are we going to do?" she asked the group.

"I have no idea, Gem," Stan answered. "Everything is so different, now. I don't know what to think. I only know that we can't stay here."

Taylor nodded in agreement.

"Doesn't *someone* have an idea what to do? I can't let the kids remain here, so it's a given that Lola will escort them to the next realm, and..."

Gem interrupted her.

"Hey, wait!" She turned to Jaxx. "You told me that you would tell me what is going on with Lola. So?"

Silence ensued, until a tiny voice answered Gem.

"You're right, Gem. It is time that I told you who and what I am," a tiny voice spoke behind her. "I am Fae."

Gem jumped at the voice, and whipped around to see Lola. Her eyes widened as she beheld a tiny little being who stood next to the chair, looking up at her – way up at her! Gem's hand reached to her throat. The tiny being had silver eyes. Her Fae form was exquisite! Her skin was milk white with not a blemish in sight. She was very tiny, and had platinum blonde hair that reached down to her tiny butt. Wings of translucent gold fluttered behind her. Her clothing reminded Gem of Tinkerbell, because they were spring green in color, trimmed in gold, and sandals of gold were on her feet. Above her silver eyes, impossibly long lashes fluttered as she blinked. Looking into her eyes, not only did she know it was Lola, but she looked into the eyes of someone who was very ancient.

Gem slowly sat back down, and bent her head to Lola's figure as close as possible. The two companions stared at each other for a very long time, before either spoke.

"Lola?" There was no way that Gem was not hurt. And, it hurt Lola to know that this confrontation had arrived.

"I'm sorry, Gem," she murmured with tiny little tears flowing down her cheeks.

"Why?" Gem asked.

"I know this is a surprise to you, but I couldn't tell you about me. I've been under orders for almost ten thousand years," Lola said. She extended her tiny wings, and fluttered up to the arm of the chair where Gem was sitting once again, and promptly sat down on it.

"OK, Lola. Give. You know more than you are telling, don't you?" Jaxx said.

Lola nodded.

"Well?" Gem was getting impatient.

"OK." Lola stood and paced up and down the arm of the chair. "The war between the Onaerris and Anaerris wasn't exactly a secret from our realm, but it was among the beings everywhere else as well as other realms."

Gem eyes widened. "There are other *realms*? And, just for the *record*, exactly how *many realms* are there?"

Lola glared at her. Gem knew that glare. It was the same one Lola always gave when she was frustrated with Gem. Gem backed down – as she always did.

"Sorry."

Lola tilted her head in that cute little pug way, yet even though she was in Fae form, she was still just so doggone cute! She nodded when she was satisfied that Gem would listen.

"The war brought some Anaerris and Onaerris together, as you, now, know. And, that included your parents," Lola said.

Eyes flew wide. All except for Gem, who was too busy trying to sort things out as Lola spoke.

"You don't mean her parents, Lola," Taylor said. "You mean Gem's ancestors."

Lola turned toward Taylor, and slowly shook her head as if for emphasis, while her expression said, "Are all of you really *that* dumb?" Yep. They are!

"No. I mean *her parents*."

It took Gem a couple of minutes, before she realized what Lola was saying.

"Just a minute! That's not possible!" Stan exclaimed, before anyone else could get a word out their mouths.

"No way!" Taylor yelled, jumping to her feet.

"What in the bloody, freakin' hell are you talking about, Lola? What do you mean '*her parents*'! That's feasibly impossible! It's been over ten thousand years!" Jaxx interrupted.

Laughing nervously, Gem said, "Yea. What Jaxx said. I mean...there is no way I can be that old! None whatsoever! That would just really...really...really...! No! I don't believe it!"

The others nodded in agreement with Gem. There was no possible way that Gem was the daughter of Analyse and Jolinaer. It just wasn't possible!

"Yeah? Well, shows me you all are either the dumbest beings I have ever met, or totally clueless!" Lola barked. "You are thinking in terms of *linear time.* In other realms, even you should know that time doesn't exist in the same manner, or have you forgotten that?"

Jaxx, Taylor, and Stan's eyes widened as they realized that her statement was true.

"So, what? You're saying my mate really is the daughter of my brother?" Jaxx's voice came out n a strangled sound.

"Brother?" Lola said. "You don't have a brother, imbecile! You were created individually. No angel has a brother or sister – Fallen or otherwise!"

Jaxx's eyes narrowed when he "lost it", and jumped at Lola, catching her between his hands.

"You fucking little bitch!" Jaxx was beyond angry! He was so mad, he did not feel Gem and Taylor tugging at his arms, trying to stop him!

"Stop, Jaxx!" Taylor roared, trying to get through to him.

Lola morphed into her pug form, bit his hand, and he dropped her with a loud "Damnit"! Then, she re-assumed her Fae form, brushing off her tiny dress.

"Rein in your damn mate, Gem! I will not continue if I am attacked, again!" Lola vowed with narrowed eyes.

"Please, Jaxx! I need her to tell us everything," Gem begged, still holding onto his arm. Taylor had let go, but stood silently by Jaxx just in case he flew off the handle, again.

"OK. If you are finished with your juvenile temper tantrum, Onaerris, I'll continue." She turned back to Gem. "Your Mom and the Fae world had formed a bond long before you were born. Because of your Mother's favored status with my Queen. They had become great friends over the ages, and she accepted both your Mother and Father into the Fae realm – despite the fact that Analyse had been turned. She was not foolish to know that Analyse would have died had he not changed her. And, Analyse was unstable in her current form. However, by being in the Fae realm, she would become stable, and be able to give birth to you. Once you were born, Gem, your parents fled the Fae realm to make sure that you stayed safe with us. The threat was truly never contained, but it was diverted from you. You see, the longevity of all Anaerris and Onaerris do not appear before the age of five, and therefore, susceptible to all dangers."

Gasps were heard around the room at that revelation. Neither Anaerris nor Onaerris knew this. So naturally, they were shocked. Jaxx opened his mouth, and Lola shot him a "don't mess with me" look. His mouth snapped shut.

"Yes. Well, as I said. Your Mother considered my Queen a great friend. And, she, in turn, offered to help Analyse if ever need be. So, when the unbelievable occurred, she petitioned to come to the Fae realm to protect their precious child, who was to become the greatest, and most powerful being ever to exist. It was obvious to us that the Creator had some great future plan," Lola told them. "We accepted this."

Gem was overwhelmed, and was having a lot of difficulty trying to process it all. But, what did Lola mean by "being"?   Her mind came to a halt when Lola continued.

"We also knew about the Terraforming crystal given to Jaxxon by his brother – who is *not his brother*, of course," she repeated for emphasis. "And, the only way we knew this was because we were told when the two of them crossed the ancient veil into our realm. We really didn't know what was happening outside our realm, so we took care of Jolinaer, Analyse, and you, after you were born. But, Analyse knew that to remain with you was a serious danger, so she and Jolinaer made the conscious decision – and it hurt like hell – to leave you in our care, and then both of them vanished to another place to keep you safe, and to divert all attention away from you."

Taylor and Stan dropped their mouths, then their accusing gazes shot to Jaxx, who just shrugged.

"What the...." Gem began, only to be cut off by Lola.

"In our realm, time moves differently. Thousands of years may pass in this realm, but only days in mine. It's all in one's perception. We do not see time as you do," Lola explained.

"Oh," Gem muttered, not really understanding anything.

"So, what you're saying, Lola, is that Gem..." Stan started.

"...was in our realm in our time," Lola finished Stan's sentence. You see, I was assigned, specifically, to be Gem's protector. At first, I was extremely angry at my Queen assigning me – a scribe – to babysit a child! And, a non-Fae one at that!" She looked at Gem's disappointed face, and her eyes softened. "When I saw your face, it broke into a smile to end all smiles, and was the sweetest that I had ever seen! In that instant, I knew my destiny was to watch over you. So, my Queen told me that she had made a decision that, when it was time, I would take you to the human realm, and find a kind couple to adopt you. I transformed myself into a pug, and with a little Fae magic, I convinced your Earth parents to adopt both of us. The Elwood's were the nicest couple, and I fell in love with them. They loved you so much, as if you were their own. How could I not feel the same? And, strangely enough, they actually loved me, too! So, I watched out for not just you, but them as well. After all, they were raising the Jewel of Anaerris."

Silence fell over the room as light tears ran down Gem's cheeks.

"Now that you know the truth, I will take Shirley and Marcus into the realm of the Fae. My Queen is waiting for them. And, there they will stay, no matter how much time passes here, until this is over. I have already told them."

"How did you contact them?" Stacy asked.

"That is a secret of my people. I have been in contact with my Queen for all these years. Anyway, Rick and Taylor, she has promised me to keep them safe. and to teach them what they will need to know. Nothing will happen to them there."

"OK," Taylor murmured, tears in her eyes at having to leave her children in the care of another realm. "Rick, will you get them?"

"On my way." He stopped, and looked back at Taylor, grinning like the Cheshire Cat. "And, you, my dear, get to tell them what's going on!"

Taylor just groaned.

Rick continued up the stairs, before Taylor could answer. It seemed only minutes before the two children stood next to Lola who was, again, in pug form.

Taylor knelt, and began to explain things to her children.

"OK, you two. You will be going with Lola, right?" Two tiny little heads nodded in silence, tears in their eyes. Rick, too, knelt down, and took Taylor's, hand while she continued. "Lola is going to take you to a safe place."

"Why?" they both asked.

"It's a really long story, kiddoes," Rick answered, "so, you will just have to trust us."

"Some friends in another realm will be taking care of you, and keeping you safe." Taylor waved her hand demanding silence as Marcus opened his mouth to ask another question. "I know. Questions. But, this time, you'll have to trust us. Your welfare is at stake, and there are some, here, who would use you. Where you are going is called the 'Fae' realm." Both children perked up at her words. They had been told about it, but they always thought it was something their Mom and Dad had made up out of thin air. "Yep. It's a real place. You both behave, OK? Lola will watch after you, and you both will see some amazing things that no one has ever seen – and will never see. You'll meet the Queen of the Fae, and you will see Lola in her true form. You are going to love it there, because it's beautiful!" Taylor said hugging both of them. "And, very, very few have ever been lucky to see it! You, my two little darlings, will be among those very few, now."

"And, we will come for you just as soon as possible...as soon as it's safe to bring you back," Rick added.

"OK, Mom," Marcus said.

"OK, Daddy," Shirley echoed.

After one last huge hug by all the adults in the room, Lola snorted, then trotted ahead of the children leading them to the realm of the Fae. Marcus and Shirley turned for one last glimpse of the people they loved, then all three disappeared in a brilliant, blinding white light. They were gone.

All six adults just stared at the place where the children left.

"Wow! That was...," Stacy breathed.

"Yeah. What you said," Stan agreed, because he had never seen the opening to the Fae world before, and he was awestruck.

Jaxx then asked, "Now what?"

All of them looked at each other in silence. They really didn't know what they needed to do. Finally, Gem spoke.

"I know what I need to do," she stated. Their eyes bore into hers waiting for her to finish. "I am the Jewel of Anaerris, right? I am protector of the Anaerris book, right?"

"Yes," Jaxx said pulling her tightly to him. "So?"

"I have to retrieve it, Jaxx! I don't know why, but I need to retrieve it, now. It's almost too late!"

"Too late? What do you mean 'too late'," Taylor asked.

Gem shook her head.

"I don't know. But, I feel it, Tay. I can feel it; I can hear it calling to me. It's scared!" Her eyes shot to Jaxx, and she grabbed his t-shirt in a tight grip. "Please, Jaxx! Help me get the book!"

Jaxx stared into her eyes, but against his better judgment, he nodded once, then turned to the others.

"We retrieve the book tonight," he said.

"Do you really think that is wise?" Stacy asked, nibbling on her nail.

Sighing, Jaxx said, "Probably not. But, if the book is in danger as Gem says, then we need to bring it to where we can watch over it. Gem, where did you put it?"

Gem looked at him. The Anaerris book had been hiding inside the library for who knew how many thousands of years! And, who was she to declare that it was no longer safe there? It had been safe for a very long time! But, nevertheless, the calling of the book was getting louder, and she knew, without a doubt, that no matter what she did, she had to save that book. Somehow, she knew that the three were bound together, even though she didn't know why or how.

She let her lip curl up at her mate, and her eyes turned a brilliant green in mischief as she answered him.

"Where else do you keep a book? In the library, of course!" she giggled, trying to lighten the mood. Everyone already knew where it was, and she knew that was not what Jaxx was asking her.

Everyone glared at her, and she laughed out loud.

"Ha, ha. Trying to be a comedian are we, Gem?" Jaxx asked. Sarcastically. She just grinned at him. The shit was about to hit the fan, and she thought everyone needed to lighten up a bit. Jaxx continued, "OK. Let's get a plan together. I think that the safest place for it, and us at the moment. will be in the cave," Jaxx said, rolling his eyes at his mate's shocked face.

"The cave? But, we can't go there! It's impossible," Stan protested.

"Well......technically, yeah," Jaxx told him. "But, while the Vorc'ara was invented and designed by Analyse, and made it only for me to go through, and eventually, my mate, we do have someone else who can override her invention."

He turned to Gem who looked at him puzzled, and wary.

"You are Analyse's daughter. You have the same signature in your DNA as does she. You can override your Mother's Vorc'ara, Gem!" he told her.

Her eyes widened, and she shook her head slowly.

"No. Listen. You can. It might just be once, but I believe that she deliberately designed it that way for a reason!" He grabbed her shoulders, staring directly into the eyes of the woman he loved so much. "Listen to me, Gem. You have her DNA; you have my brother's DNA. You are the product of both Anaerris and Onaerris! The only one of your kind. You have the power of the Vorc'ara within you. You released it when you were held prisoner without conscious thought. You opened it for us to go to Venice. Unlike everyone else, you have no training whatsoever for it! It's instinctive!"

Taylor's face lit up as she realized what Jaxx was telling her best friend! Gem's power was greater than anyone. She just hadn't used it yet! Stan nodded in agreement. He had come to the same conclusion as Taylor did a moment ago.

"He's right, Gem. Those of us who have the power of the Vorc'ara must be trained from birth how to use it correctly. I cannot use the Vorc'ara to enter the cave. I know. I've tried before at Jaxx's request. I couldn't pierce it. But, you! There has to be a reason for your parentage and your DNA! It has to be part of the Creator's design!"

Even while shaking her head no, Stan finished.

"That's it." He was matter of fact.

"What's it?" Taylor asked turning her head to stare at him.

"That's why her conception was so amazing!" He turned to Gem, his eyes wide with amazement. "The book hasn't been seen, or heard of since Analyse and Jolinaer disappeared! But, still, Gem found it easily! The only way anyone can change everything is the one who has the power of the gods within her! You are more than just Anaerris and Onaerris, Gem!"

"What are you talking about, Stan?" Jaxx asked, not really sure where Stan was going with this.

"The island where she was being held! Correct me if I'm wrong, Taylor, but aren't your Vorc'aras specific?" Stan asked.

"What do you mean?" Taylor asked, puzzled. Her brows drew together.

"Specific...as in protected?" he asked.

"Oh. Yes, but you know that," she answered still frowning. "Care to explain?"

Stan huffed and puffed just like the Big Bad Wolf in the fairy tales.

"*Come on, Taylor!*" he growled. "I mean as in P.R.O.T.E.C.T.E.D!"

Everyone looked at each other, then shook their heads.

"How many Anaerris have the ability to open another's protected Vorc'ara?" he explained.

Dawn showing on Taylor's face, she gasped out loud.

"Holy shit!" she murmured almost to herself.

"Well?"

"None! No Anaerris can override another. In other words...an Anaerris can call up a Vorc'ara. But, we can only call it up on whatever side that the Anaerris is on, but not on the original location. They are specific to the one who opens it. Each has it's own design and color, and until that one decides to leave, no one else can do so," her voice with a whisper. She looked at Gem.

"Well, when Gem was on that island, then just how did she get back? Gem wouldn't have been able to get back, in theory, since Delinear's Vorc'ara was in play, right? What does it all mea...?" he demanded.

Sudden understanding came over all of them at once.

"Oh, man!" Jaxx exclaimed, and looked at his mate in awe.

All five of them stared deeply at Gem, who became uncomfortable as the stares continued.

"What?" she asked, still not getting it. "Look. You guys seem to think I should know all this supernatural crap! I don't, or have you forgotten?"

Ignoring Gem's outburst, Taylor explained, albeit in shock.

"Gem! Don't you get it? You opened a *protected* Vorc'ara that Delinear had in place! It's basically automatic any time one of us opens one! Another Anaerris cannot open one while another Anaerris has, well, basically, jurisdiction! Just like your Mother has one in front of Jaxx's cave! It's in our DNA, girl! Look, you overrode Delinear's DNA.! You opened a Vorc'ara on Delinear's turf!" Taylor almost shouted in shock. "It's impossible! You shouldn't have been able to do it! Yet, you did!" Taylor shook her head as realization came over her. "Gem! You have an ability unlike any other Anaerris! The fact that you can breach a Vorc'ara...*any of them*...is, well, is....Oh, hell! I don't even know what word I would use!"

Gem's eyes widened at the implication! Seriously?

"Wait! Are you saying that I can..."

"Go through any protected Vorc'ara? Yes! That's exactly what I'm saying! Remember that the Anaerris who have that power are the only ones who can open and close their own!" she repeated. "But, you? Somehow...*someway*...you must be able to open and close – *anyone's from any origin or destination*!"

Stacy began to laugh until she was bent over trying to take big gulps of air. It released the tension that everyone was feeling, and they turned to look at her as if she had lost her marbles.

"What?" she snickered. "Think about it! Delinear must have been beside herself, when she saw that you had penetrated her own Vorc'ara!" Stacy laughed. "I'd have loved to have been a fly! I would have paid money just to see her face! It must have been priceless!"

There was sudden silence except for Stacy laughing. Then, the very thought of the shock Delinear must have felt, caused everyone in the room to roar with laughter.

"Yeah, and imagine what Eloran must have felt when he saw it!" Rick's booming laughter felt as if it shook the house.

"P-price-less," Taylor tried to get out, but failed miserably as she gasped for breaths between laughing. "T-that's j-just hil-hil-larious!"

"In other words, Gem," Stan said to clarify it to her. "You can go *anywhere*, at any *time*, through *anyone's* Vorc'ara! In other words, Gem...you are not bound by any of the rules!"

Gem just stared at him. Now, she understood what she had deliberately been trying not to do!

A sudden thought hit Stacy, and her laughter slowed.

"But, can anyone go through hers?" she asked, stunning everyone.

After several minutes of silence, Jaxx answered her.

"I don't know, but perhaps we can find out!" Jaxx declared. "How about it, Gem...Taylor. Wanna give it a try?"

Taylor thought about it.

"It's an unknown. Honestly, I don't know if it would be dangerous," she answered glaring at him.

"Can we not test it some way?" Rick asked.

"Well, we enter it, you close it, and then see if Gem opens it."

"OK. I'll pick something like the kitchen. That way if something goes wrong, she can just walk back in here."

"Well, at least it's a plan!" Jaxx muttered.

Taylor opened a Vorc'ara, and Gem stepped through. In seconds, Gem opened another, and stepped back into the room.

"Holy shit! It is true! You can override other Anaerris – and that's something that I know Analyse could never do!" Taylor gasped.

"Well, right. We know it works for Gem, but has anyone thought that if Gem opens one, no other can breach it? We may as well try it to make sure."

Gem nodded, and opened the Vorc'ara to the kitchen, and Taylor stepped through it. Taylor tried to open her Vorc'ara from the kitchen, Stacy tossed a rat into it from the library. Instead, a loud shock wave hit both rooms, while at the same time, put both Taylor in the kitchen, and the others in the library on their butts as they were flung backward.

"Hells Bells!" Stacy said sitting up, and rubbing her head. "That was some 'test'!"

"Ahhhhh!" Gem whined, sitting up.

"Yeah," Jaxx said who had been thrown into the fireplace, and landed on his ass. He stood slowly, looking at his mate in awe. "Well, I guess that answers the question!"

After everyone had stood, and rubbed whatever had been hurt, there was one other question that Rick asked. Well, several, Rick decided. Just to make sure, Gem re-opened her Vorc'ara, and stepped through it. Then, she opened it, again, and both Gem and Taylor appeared back in the library.

"Seriously, Stacy? And, where the hell did you get that rat?" Jaxx snickered.

In a juvenile display, Taylor grinned and stuck out her tongue.

"OK. Everyone OK?" she asked.

Several heads nodded.

"Wow!" Rick exclaimed.

"What?" Jaxx asked.

"Can she invoke the powers of the Onaerris, too? You know...bypass even their powers?" Rick asked.

All mouths dropped open, and eyes darted to Gem whose eyes had become the size of saucers. Finally, Stacy broke the silence.

"Interesting thought!" she answered. Then, with a grin, "So...does anyone know where we can find another rat?"

"Too bad Lola's gone!" Jaxx gritted his teeth, turning to the liquor cabinet in search of some rum.

"No rum?" Stan grouched, and paraphrased a favorite line in Pirate's of the Caribbean. "Why is the rum never in the cabinet?"

~ 21 ~
"A little bloodletting is good. Getting rid of an annoying mate is even better!" ~ Eloran

Seeing the ridiculous expressions on the faces of her companions, Stacy threw out two arms with palms up in a "what" gesture. She smirked.

"Oh, come on! You know you were all thinking it!"

They were all looking at her as if she had large ears, a tiny nose, and long, skinny tail, resembling Gus from "Cinderella"?

"No takers? Really?" She huffed, and muttered, "I thought that was pretty damn good!"

"That's OK, Baby. You did just fine," he petted her shoulder as if she were a little child.

The others ignored both of them, and proceeded to come up with some type of plan. And, with that temporary plan, they decided to test Rick's idea about Gem's ability as an Onaerris even if she did not have the DNA of one. After multiple tries with both Jaxx and Stan guiding her, she couldn't do a damn thing! One of the powers of the Onaerris was the ability of invisibility. They could "cloak" not only themselves, but everyone and everything around them.

"Crap!" Gem echoed everyone else's thoughts.

"Crap indeed," Jaxx growled.

"Maybe she needs to develop it?" Taylor guessed.

Shrugging, no one else had any explanation, so they decided to proceed on the idea that Gem might have the powers, but they had not yet matured. Since they knew, now, that Gem could bypass any other Anaerris' Vorc'ara, it gave them a slight advantage. But, now, they knew that Delinear knew it as well, since she had seen it in action. It was possible that Delinear had no idea, but none of them would take a bet on it. That was only one of the many kinks in their plans. However, they put their plan into operation anyway. That book had to be rescued from the library – and fast, according to Gem.

Their first plan included letting Taylor just open her Vorc'ara, and Gem would go through into the library, and bring the book back. Unfortunately, Taylor nixed it. Wherever she opened a Vorc'ara, the destination was deflected to another place.

"Damn it!" Taylor exclaimed after the fifth try. "Something is impeding me!"

"Look, guys, I know I'm new to all this shit, but what if the library is actually warded, and won't let just anyone open a Vorc'ara into it?" Gem asked. "I mean, is it possible that someone warded it against certain people?"

"Well, that kinda makes sense. So, now what? Do we just drop it?" Stan asked. Then, grinned as a thought occurred to him from one of his really favorite movies, "Field of Dreams". He snapped his fingers. "I know! 'If you open it, they will come'!"

"Seriously? You just are a real buzz-kill, you know that?" Gem rolled her eyes, receiving a huge grin from Stan.

After another discussion that lasted way too long, no one could be absolutely sure that Gem's own Vorc' would not also draw the others. And, that ended the whole discussion!

"We can't get into it that way. Not without Delinear being drawn to it," Jaxx reasoned.

"Wait!" Gem said suddenly. All eyes turned to her. By now, each couple had spread out around the room lounging in chairs, on the floor, or on the sofa. "Correct me if I am asking a stupid question, but do you know if Delinear or Eloran have ever been inside the library?"

Taylor perked up, and scooted to the edge of Rick's lap where she had just sat down in defeat.

"No. Not that I can recall," she answered.

"Why?" Gem asked the simple question. "Anyone?"

"Because of a spell, perhaps? A ward?" ventured Stacy.

After another round of silence, Gem asked another question.

"Is it possible, Jaxx, like the cave, could someone ward the library against unwanted intruders?" Jaxx frowned. "No. I'm serious. What is the difference between them? You basically 'invited' the bitch into your home with your lack of vision from ages ago. But, once you uninvited her, she had no choice but to leave. That was painfully obvious!"

"And?" he asked warily. He was already irritated at himself at his idiocy in afterthought, but he knew that Gem was trying to tell him something.

"The cave, though, was warded by not only Analyse for you and, eventually your mate – me, of course," she grinned, as she leaned forward to give him a quick kiss, which he turned into a very hot show of affection in front of everyone. And that just caused a round of cat calls from their audience.

"Get a room already," Stan groaned, but with a huge smile on his face.

Ignoring him, Jaxx pulled back reluctantly, so that Gem could continue to say what she wanted to say, but seeing the promise of more later from her dazed eyes.

"Huh? What?" Clearly she was throw for a loop. "Oh. Right. The cave. If the spell worked for the cave, then why not the library? Taylor and I have a theory that it came from an anonymous benefactor, you know. And, it isn't that hard to figure out that whoever it was warded it."

Taylor's eyes widened, when she realized what Gem was implying.

"Are you saying what I think you are saying, Gem?" she asked in shock.

That's when Jaxx caught onto what Gem meant.

"You're saying that the library, which held the book all this time, was warded?"

"Through a Vorc'ara itself?" Taylor added.

Gem nodded.

"Why not? If no one could find the Anaerris Code, until I discovered it, then the obvious conclusion would be that neither Delinear nor Eloran were able to enter the library, and I doubt they even could have detected it at least until it was found! And, if that is fact, then it had to not only be warded, but..."

"Cloaked?" Stan gasped.

"You mean they didn't even know the library was here?" Stacy asked.

"No! I mean that the *book* was *cloaked*! Every attack on me came from *outside* of the library!" Gem reminded them.

"But, wouldn't they be suspicious when they couldn't get into it?" Rick asked them.

"Maybe not. Maybe, just maybe, they never had a reason to suspect the library at all! Why would they have reason to go into it in the first place, when they were following me?" Gem went into stunned silence as something else occurred to her. "Only...only, I don't think that they were following *me*, Jaxx! I think that they have been following *Lola*!"

"B-but, we can't detect Fae," Stan shook his head. "No. No..that wouldn't be possible."

"Are you sure of that?" Gem asked.

"We were surprised, when she revealed herself to us!" Taylor said. "I didn't detect her! So, that can't be right!"

Gem cocked her head at her best friend.

"But, you hadn't been trying to find Lola."

"Are you telling me that we didn't detect her, because we're stupid?" Stan growled at her. Then, hearing Jaxx growl at him, he backed down. "Sorry. No disrespect intended to your mate, Jaxx, but how could it be that we did not detect what Lola was?"

"Of course you guys aren't stupid, Stan! How can you even think that? My point is that you have all been living among humans a long time," Gem said, then turned to Jaxx. "How long have has it been since you used your full powers? Is it like humans who, if we don't exercise our abilities on a daily basis, might diminish over time? Humans say, 'Use it or Lose it'. Can that also apply to other species? Delinear and Eloran haven't lived among us, and they have obviously not lost *their* powers. Wouldn't it make sense that they might know a Fae was around. And, even if you couldn't have detected her, what does that mean? Unless something tipped them off? I mean, how else could they have known, unless there was a traitor among the Fae, and would that even be possible?"

"Hmmm," Taylor mused. Looking at the others who had never even thought about it, she continued. "Well, Gem might have a point. We haven't been able to protect Gem or Lola. And, it's not as if we haven't tried, but maybe...maybe Gem's right. Maybe our powers are not as strong as they should be. After all, we don't use them unless necessary, and there just hasn't been anything pressing until recently. Tipped off, huh? That never occurred to me," she continued in a muted whisper. "But, who could it have been?"

Somehow, that made sense to Jaxx. He hadn't used his powers in ages, and that included their ability to scent others. He had cast his wards many, many years ago. But, honestly, he couldn't remember having used them for anything else since. And, he knew, for a fact, that neither Taylor or Stan had, either. And, his own protection over Gem had not worked when she was taken. He had wondered, albeit briefly, why he was unable to protect Gem. Another thought had occurred to him. Everything revolved around scent. Gem smelled like Lola; Lola smelled like her. His brain couldn't rap around this fact, so he felt he had to come up with a better explanation.

"But, Lola wasn't always with you," Jaxx put forth. He was trying to find an excuse, although deep inside himself, he knew Gem was right. They hadn't "used it", so had they, truly, "lost it"?

Gem thought about that for – like – two seconds! The answer was obvious to her.

"True. But, remember. Animal owners bear their scent all the time! Lola's scent is *always* on me!"

Her words were like being hit over the head with an iron rod. Jaxx had just been thinking that, but rapidly disregarded it, because he just couldn't believe that they were that ineffective. Who they are was what they were! And, yet…?

"Holy crap!" Stacy said. "She's right! Oh! Shit! If they did see her open the Vorc, it won't take them long to figure out exactly who Gem is, and that she was the one that Lola has been guarding!"

Everyone looked at each other as they realized the truth.

"OK. We have to admit it. We fell down on the job! Eloran and Delinear may have seen her open a Vorc'ara, but maybe they still didn't know that they were looking for Gem when she escaped the Volcano tunnels. But, they almost have to know who she is, now," Taylor added. "So, until we know all of Gem's powers, we need to get that book, then figure out where we are going to 'hide' until we can figure out what to do in the long term,"

Rick, Stan, and Jaxx all snorted at the word "hide", but knew that she was right.

Rick thought maybe Taylor's Vorc might work right at the site of the library, instead of from the house. And, if hers didn't, Gem's would. But, the sad thing was that, now, they had no other choice.

"Well, I guess that's all water under the bridge, now, so no use crying over that spilled milk," Gem told them. "And, I know...you guys don't like 'hiding'. Quite frankly, neither do I, but what choice to we have?"

"Absolutely none, whatsoever," Taylor answered. "We can get the book, but we are going to need a diversion. All we can hope for is that we can throw them off the trail. They have to at least suspect that Gem has the book, now, so they won't stop trying to get it, and her. At least, we know we can walk into the library to get it. Oh! And, don't forget the crystal! That's the most dangerous thing of all! So, does anyone know where that crystal is?"

Silence met Taylor's question.

"No one knows?" she asked, again.

"I don't see how we could know. Maybe it did 'drown' in the Atlantic!" Stan answered. "Let's hope so!"

Gem shot a quick look at Jaxx, who barely shook his head at her. She almost huffed, while everyone shrugged. If their experiment worked for real, then they would still be on borrowed time. Once they got into the library, Gem would procure the book, then leave. Hopefully, before Delinear would show herself, and find they had left.

The plan in place, it was time to leave. After changing into clothing that would not be seen in the middle of the night, they all piled into two of the SUV's, and using the temporary invisibility of both Jaxx and Stan, they climbed into the vehicle, and drove away from the house. Care was taken not to exhaust their powers, but they could only hold it for a short time, due to the many years of non-use.

"How long can you two hold it?" Taylor asked.

"Maybe, what, Stan?"

"Between the two of us? Oh, say...a half hour at most? Maybe shorter? Not really able to tell," Stan told her.

"OK. Let's plan on half an hour, and just hope that it works. That leaves us twenty minutes to drive there, and another ten minutes to get in, get the book, and get out," Rick muttered.

Stan turned to Jaxx.

"Fifteen minutes? A piece?" Jaxx nodded. "Well, hell! There was a time when we, each, could hold a cloak for several hours, at least!" Stan looked to Gem. "You know? You have a damn smart mate!"

Jaxx grinned, as he turned to look at her, too.

"Oh, yeah!"

"That'll work," Gem had not heard them. "It has to! All I need is few seconds to grab the book! But, where are we headed after that?" To herself, she muttered, "*So glad Lola isn't here!*"

Stacy spoke up with an idea, and didn't know why she hadn't thought of it before?

"Great idea, Stacy. It's secluded and off the radar!" Taylor exclaimed. To Jaxx and Stan, she asked. "And, if you can't hold the cloak?"

"We're fucked?" Rick interjected.

"Exactly," Taylor answered. Man, they so needed to get a new end line!

Eloran and Delinear were trying to figure out their next move, but neither of them had a clue how to proceed. Eloran paced back and forth on the sand. Delinear was still having trouble believing that a little slip of a girl was able to penetrate her Vorc'ara. She just couldn't believe it! And, it rankled. How in the hell was she able to do it?

"I don't get it! How?" she mumbled to herself, as Eloran passed in front of her. He stopped.

"What?" he inquired.

She looked up, and shook her head.

"I just don't get it? No other Anaerris can breech another's Vorc'ara!" she muttered for the umpteenth time, since they had traveled to an odd looking world where the grass was pink, the sand was crimson, the ocean was purple, and the sky was green.

"Will you stop worrying about that?" Eloran almost yelled at her. While he didn't exactly yell, it was as if his voice just bounced off a wall that dampened sound. Their voices didn't carry further than their words, and in order for them to hear each other, they had to shout.

Delinear had had enough! It was time she called Eloran by his *real* name – that being his first name was "*Jack*", his middle being "*Ass*", and last name "*Hole*"!

"Look Jack, you overindulged son-of-a-bitch! I need to know how she did it, because it can mean the difference between succeeding and not! Seriously? All you care about is shoving that stick up Jaxx's butt!"

"Bitch!" Eloran growled, yanking her body to his. He ground his hard erection into her stomach as his mouth crashed down onto hers. Delinear groaned loudly feeling his hardness, and pushed her pelvis hard against him. He lifted his mouth off of hers.

"I want to fuck," he demanded.

Delinear felt the wetness between her legs at the words, and slowly backed away from him. With a thought, their clothing disappeared. A thick quilt appeared underneath their feet, and she laid down, knees up, and spread apart for Eloran to see. Eloran dropped between her legs, and Delinear watched his head disappear between them as he assaulted her wet sex with his tongue. Delinear cried out in pleasure as she felt his tongue circling her clit, diving in and out of her entrance. She grabbed his head, and pushed it even closer to her.

Eloran had never found total satisfaction with Delinear, nor she with him, and both had no qualms about fucking other women and men. However, Delinear was as close as possible to being sated as he could get in between. He had a penchant mostly for human females, but his evil was massive, and many human females did not survive his lust. He would fuck them so hard, they would die, bleeding to death. Their bodies were frail and could not hold up to his desires. Then, he would discard their bodies as if they were trash. Those few who did manage to survive were never the same, again. He destroyed their ability to have sex, as well as their ability to have children. And, that just gave him pleasure! And, most, eventually, committed suicide, because they couldn't live with themselves, and their damaged bodies.

But, with Delinear, he could be as rough as he wanted, and she could do the same to him. Their coupling was hard, fast, and their claws drew blood. Afterward, Delinear sighed in semi-contentment – blood oozing over her large breasts from the gashes that he cut into her body, while Eloran panted in his short-term satisfaction. In seconds, he rolled off of her, and their bodies immediately healed showing no cuts whatsoever.

"Good thing our bodies heal, considering the fact that human bodies cannot," Delinear gasped, her hands spreading their blood all over her body seductively. She, too, took human males many times, leaving with the same devastation as did Eloran. She, too, destroyed the mens' ability to father a child. She turned, and slid over Eloran's own blood covered body, rubbing against his still hard erection.

"More?" she grinned, as she placed her opening on his tip.

"Yes! We'll figure everything out afterward. *Fuck me!*" he yelled, and slammed up inside of her, letting his debasement loose on her body. As he pounded his cock into her, his thoughts went to the Jewel of Anaerris, and all the powers that would be at his command if he owned her! Even with his eyes never having beheld her, he desired her more than any woman he had ever met. It literally fueled his lust higher than ever before, and Delinear screamed in pleasure. Rage gripped him as he realized that he would just have to be satisfied with Delinear, until he had the Jewel underneath him! He deserved that power! Certainly not that tiny slip of a girl! As his balls squeezed, both he and Delinear screamed out their release. His erection burst forth with his seed, and he knew that nothing, not even his own mate, nor the Jewel and her mate, could stop him from obtaining it! *He would have her body* and *her power*!

Twenty minutes later, the two SUV's drove up to the library.

"Why don't Taylor and I just use the keys to get into the library? Remember? We can just walk inside the building? And...I mean...if necessary, we can use a Vorc to escape. After all. We do work here, and we have them," she grinned, swinging the keys from her index finger. "If we don't open a Vorc, maybe it will take longer for Delinear to find us? If so, then we can buy time just by using the key."

Everyone gaped at her.

"Well," Jaxx smirked, "I feel sheepish!"

"Really? That's what you have, Jaxx? A line out of 'Aladdin'?" Gem laughed along with everyone else.

Something so simple had never occurred to most of them! Taylor and Gem quickly walked up the stairs, unlocked the doors, and went into the building, followed on their heels by both Stan and Jaxx. That left Stacy and Rick driving each of the SUV's, or as Gem said, they were driving the "getaway cars"!

Jaxx and Stan stood guard outside the building while, Gem and Taylor entered the library. When Gem started to flip on the main lights, Taylor grabbed her hand and shook her head.

"Let's not give anyone a cause to suspect something is wrong here, Gem. Here's my flashlight. Do you think you can find it just using it?" she asked Gem quietly.

Gem merely nodded, and took the flashlight, since she had forgotten. Sweeping it side to side to aid her walking, she turned back to Taylor who was standing guard at the door. Gem found the CCR room, unlocked it, and entered the room. Quickly, Gem dropped to her knees, and fumbled a moment as she pulled out the books that hid the precious book. In seconds, she had the Anaerris Code, and left the room, making sure the door closed without a sound behind her. Once she reached Taylor, they left the building, and the four quickly ran down the steps, springing into the waiting vehicles. Then, driving like bats out of hell, both SUV's headed straight for the border of the town. Once they reached it, they kept on driving. The plan was to head for the remote location, where Stacy's family had a cabin, deep in the wilds of Colorado.

"Anyone hungry?" Rick asked. Nodding their heads in his direction, he called the other SUV, and while they also agreed, they decided to drive as far as possible, before stopping to grab something to eat. When they arrived, they would pick up some food. Even though it was remote, there was a small, general store close to it.

Little did they know that they had just missed Delinear and Eloran arriving at the library.

"Well? Where are they?" Eloran demanded.

"Hell if I know!" she answered.

"I thought you said you heard its call?"

"Yeah, I did."

"So, Bitch! Why isn't it here?" he growled, and grabbed her arm.

Jerking her arm out of his grasp, she added.

"It's not an exact science, you nimrod! I only feel a draw to it, and it's usually a delayed response! I've told you this before, so don't pretend you don't know what I'm saying," she growled, seeing his scowl grow in irritation.

"And, now?"

"I don't feel it at all. It's as if it never was!" Delinear shook her head in bewilderment. It wasn't often that she felt this way.

"But, why? Why can't you feel it? Seriously? I thought you had this all worked out, you fucking whore!"

If look could kill at that moment, Eloran would have dropped dead right there with Delinear's eyes staring daggers at him.

"Do not *ever* call me a 'whore', again, you bastard!" she warned him. Then, continued. "How in the hell should I know?" She stomped toward the door to the library. "Maybe it was hidden?"

Ignoring Eloran, she started to cross the threshold – and ran right into a "wall"! She was thrown backwards, down the steps, landing on her back. Sitting up, she rubbed her neck.

"What the fuck?" she asked.

"What the hell was that?" Eloran demanded, not bothering to help her to her feet.

She shook her head.

"I don't know, but there is one thing I do know!" She pointed toward the library. "That building is not what it appears to be! The book was in this area. I'm sure of it! But, now it isn't, and I can't get a read on it at all!"

"That is unacceptable, Delinear. I suggest you get off your ass, and figure out what is going on! I need that book, and I need the Jewel. I need them to take over this world!"

"And, I need the crystal! The only way to take it over is to kill every single inhabitant on it by Terraforming!" Delinear added, seeing Eloran nod once. A thought occurred to her.

"Could the invisibility of the Onaerris cloak it, so I couldn't read it?"

"Shit!" Eloran gritted his teeth. "Yes, it's possible!"

"Well, that's just perfect, isn't it! Let's get the hell out of here! I need time to concentrate, and I won't be able to do it here!" Delinear told him, and opened a Vorc'ara.

Both went through it, and back to the world they had just left. Once there, he pulled her into the purple ocean. His anger was so great that he pushed his cock deep into her body with one, hard thrust, and she gladly accepted it.

As they began to climax, he let her know that he would be doing this to the Jewel.

"Rape her, will you?" Delinear gasped, feeling his thick, long cock deep inside her body.

"Yes!" he cried, as he felt his seed spill into her.

"And, I will rape Jaxx!" she cried out, feeling his hot semen flood her womb.

Walking from the water, they collapsed onto the sand. Eloran suckled her nipples, before he answered her. His head came up, and stared into her eyes with great lust.

"You can't rape the willing, Delinear! He will be willing. But, she will not – at first. But, she will! I have something she has never seen before, or felt! Then, we will fuck them together as we lay side by side with each other!" Eloran whispered against her breasts.

The vision excited them even more as the tension built between them once again, and she straddled his cock. She stroked her wetness against his hard length, feeling his hands and claws dig into her breasts, while hers dug into his massive chest. She impaled herself onto his hard cock.

"Yes!" she cried, feeling the blood run down their bodies as their orgasms climaxed.

The rest of the night was spent driving in silence, before they reached Stacy's remote cabin. It was so far off the beaten track with all the turns and twists on the back roads, the only person who wasn't lost was Stacy. She and Stan were in the first SUV leading the way, while the other four were in the second one. They had agreed that Gem needed as many around her as possible for protection. During the drive, more than once, Gem had felt the book sigh in contentment at being in her hands. She didn't understand how, but it told her that she belonged to it. She constantly stroked it gently. It was so obvious that it felt safe and secure – until it completed its mission, which was to transfer it's power to her. Including the fact, she was even more surprised that it was self-aware.

Driving up to the cabin, both vehicles stopped, and everyone jumped out of them to walk up hill to the cabin that sat just above a large lake.

"Wonder if Delinear felt the book at all?" Taylor murmured.

Stan stopped short of the front door, and turned.

"Good question...unless?"

"Unless...what?" Jaxx asked.

"Unless she doesn't know where it is," Stacy said in a matter-of-fact tone.

"What do you mean, Stacy? The book calls out to all Anaerris," Taylor's eyes widened, and turned to Gem in surprise.

"Unlessssss...?" Gem hissed the question, when they all turned to face her.

"Unless...unless *you* are masking it somehow?" Taylor finished.

Complete silence ensued..

"What? I'm not doing anything!" she denied. How could she be? "You did make it invisible, right, Jaxx?"

"No, I didn't, Gem."

"I-I don't understand. Stan?"

"Then, h-how…?"

"Maybe you are doing it," Jaxx said, standing next to her. "...maybe...I mean...is it possible that *you* have, somehow, cloaked the book yourself?"

"What? What are you talking about?" Gem asked, again.

"Gem...if somehow, you have made the book untraceable, well, it's no wonder they haven't found us yet!" Jaxx's voice was quiet with awe as he stared at his mate.

Gem's face morphed into surprise, if not complete shock. She looked down at the book in her hand, then she realized something. The book was actually talking to her!

Mouth dropped open, she began to gently caress it, as it told her....

"*I cloaked myself!*" the now, familiar voice said to her.

"It cloaked itself!" she whispered aloud, as she stood in shock.

"What?" Jaxx raised his voice.

Gem turned to him.

"It told me that it cloaked itself! How is that possible?"

"*Through the blood of the one,*" it said to her.

"The 'blood of the one'?" Gems stammered. "What does that even mean?"

Jaxx just gaped, until Taylor broke the silence. They had arrived at the cabin.

"Look. Let's just go into the cabin, then we can talk. I feel completely vulnerable out here in the open."

Everyone nodded, got out of the SUV's, and entered the cabin. Jaxx was the last one in and shut the door. They bustled about turning on the electricity, which let them check the cabin's condition. Other than a bit of dust, and sheets covering the furniture, it was virtually clean. Stacy checked the water faucet, and it worked just fine. She was happy as a clam that she had the foresight to put in electricity and water. While they tested everything and cleaned it up a bit, everyone ignored Gem in their effort to make the cabin liveable for a short time.

"What do we have in the way of food?" Stan asked.

"Trust you to talk about food," Stacy laughed.

"Well, what do we have?" he badgered.

Both he and Stacy rustled around in the kitchen area after finding several cans of soup in the cabinet. A tiny refrigerator occupied a corner in the kitchen. Stan opened it, and shut it fast.

"OK. Trust me! We do *not* want to eat or drink anything from this!"

"What's the problem, Stan," Jaxx asked, grabbing the handle while Stan stood back, and plastered a smirk on his face. Jaxx opened it, and slammed it just as Stan had done. "OK. Ewww!"

That was enough for all of them. No one was going to ask what was in it, but it was clear that whatever it was had actually grown legs, and was trying to get out of it!

"OK. There's a small general store down the road. Taylor and I'll run down, and pick up some drinks, bread, and things," Rick said. As Taylor walked out the door, Rick turned, and laughed. "We'll just let you guys clean up the refrigerator while we gone. We don't mind!"

Stan stuck out his tongue in a juvenile way, while Rick's laughter followed him out the door. Stacy looked around, and while she found some old cleaning bottles that appeared to still be in good condition, even though it had been almost five years, since she and Stan had come here. She pulled out the cleaner, and turned to Stan.

"OK. I'm going to open the door, and you can catch it as it runs out!" Stacy snickered.

Standing in front of the refrigerator, Stan was ready with a trash bag in hand. He nodded, and Stacy opened the door. A gigantic spider leaped into the air, and Stan caught it in the bag. He twisted it quickly, then stomped on the movement in the bag. Both he and Stacy sighed in relief, and while Stan threw the bag at Jaxx to take outside, he tackled the refrigerator with gusto, emptying it out quickly, so Stacy could clean it.

~ **22** ~

**"What happens when you let an ancient book filled
with instructions talk to you?
You get more instructions!" ~ Jaxx**

Gem sat in a rocking chair that she had commandeered, caressing the book constantly. She didn't want to let it out of her sight! While the others talked, no one noticed that Gem's eyebrows had gone up, as she realized the book was speaking to her, again. Something she had to ask it three times to repeat, because she couldn't believe what it was saying! It wanted her to open it, and read it – wanted her touch! And even more than that, it said that it wanted to….

"Oh, crap!" she squealed, looking up at Jaxx in surprise. "Jaxx...it-it...I-I mean...the b-book wants to...."

Jaxx grabbed her hands, and pulled her out of the chair, and to his chest, kissing her gently on the lips sandwiching the book between them.

"What does it want, Gem?" he asked, aware that there was an audience around them. He turned, and jerked his head toward the back door of the cabin. Stacy and Stan stepped outside.

Gem looked up at him.

"It wants to – uh – it wants to..." she began, her cheeks flaming red.

"What?" Jaxx urged.

"It wants to fuck me!" she said so softly, Jaxx almost didn't hear what she said.

He held her away from him, shocked at her words.

"The book wants to *what* you?" he asked loudly.

"What, Jaxx? What, Gem? What?" Taylor demanded. She had just entered the door with Rick, when she heard Jaxx's shocked voice. She gave the groceries

442

she had in her hand to Rick, then went to stand by Gem. "What?"

"You can't be serious, Gem!" Jaxx said, shaking her shoulder lightly, ignoring Taylor.

"I can, and I am, Jaxx! It just told me!"

"Exactly how in the hell could it even accomplish that? That's the most insane thing I've ever heard in my whole life! Even more insane than when we attacked Anaerris!"

"I-I don't know, but that's what it is demanding!" Gem said, tears rolling down her face that had turned pale as death itself.

She was certain that Jaxx thought she was crying, because she was scared, but that was far from the truth! Gem *wanted* to give it what it wanted! She *wanted* to feel it move inside of her! But, she felt guilty even mentioning it to Jaxx. He was the love of her life, so why in the hell did she want to lay with the book? To let it place whatever was inside of it, inside of her? But, she couldn't help it! It's as if she needed to do it! Laying the book down on the nearest table, she turned back to Jaxx. A sudden awareness from her low whisper gripped Jaxx as he turned to everyone else.

"OUT!" he yelled.

"But...," Taylor began.

"I said OUT! NOW! All of you!" Jaxx demanded, his eyes wild. "Run far from this cabin!"

None of them said another word as they poured out the door as fast as they could go, leaving Jaxx and Gem all alone. He yanked Gem to his body.

"No," he growled.

Gem looked up at him. His eyes were murderous! Then, she realized what was actually wrong, and her mouth dropped, before she shot him a sexy, slow grin.

"You're jealous of a book, Jaxx? Isn't that a bit ridiculous?" she asked.

"I'm not jealous of a book." He pointed to it laying on the table. "No one – or thing – is going to fuck you but me!"

That's when Gem knew what had to happen. He was right. A book couldn't have sex with her, but her mate could! It was Jaxx who was to be the vessel of the book – not her! They had it all backwards. Yes, she could read it and protect it, but it also had to join with the Jewel of Anaerris! It had always been him! It was the only way that Gem could complete whatever transformation she needed to undergo. While she didn't really know why, it was absolute. And, it made sense. He was Onaerris. She was Anaerris and human! He could transfer to her what was needed easily, if it *became* a part of his body! But, how the hell did she get the book into him?

"Yes, yes. I know. I know. No one is going to enter my body in anyway, but Jaxx. But, how?" she asked the book, looking at it to answer her. Her expression was clearly surprised by its answer.

"Is it talking to you, now?" Jaxx demanded of her in surprise.

Nodding her head, she placed her hand upon the book. In a split second, it imparted its need to her, and began to tell her how it planned to accomplish the task. After the merge was completed, it would give the knowledge to her through her mate by joining with her physically. Next, she listened carefully as the book proceeded to tell her exactly why Jaxx had to take it within him, and how he had to do it. Images flew at her mind in seconds, and then, it stopped. She slowly turned to Jaxx, who stepped backward in shock when he saw her eyes. He gasped! They were the strangest color he had ever seen on anyone! Orange! They were a glittering, florescent orange!

"Shit!" he said. Then, "W-what are you?" he asked.

Jaxx was dumbstruck! He began to speak, but Gem held up her hand for silence.

"Be at peace, Jaxxon, Prince of Onaerris, fallen angel of the Creator. I am the spirit of the Anaerris Code, written by my maker, Princess Analyse, and spelled by Prince Jolinaer – your brother and friend. Within my cover is all that was Anaerris, and all that will be Anaerris, again, only much stronger with the addition of new seed. Gem was fated to be my protector, but for her to do so, I must merge with her – physically. I must transfer all knowledge through the one thing I do have – uh...DNA, I believe the humans call it. Only through this DNA will I be able to fill her with the knowledge that is inside my cover. This is to belong to both of you – you, Jaxx, because you are her mate, and you are charged with her protection. It must go to Gem, because she is human and Anaerris. Even though you have exchanged DNA by blood from within, it does not bond to her DNA. She must become what she was always meant to become – the Anaerris Code in bodily form. And, the only way to do this is through the act of physical bonding. It's a bit disgusting to me, but it has to be done. She must accept the Onaerris gene that is bonded within the skin of my cover as well as the pages. The DNA of the Onaerris was infused into my pages, and it must bond to her DNA. She *must contain* all three DNA codes within her to be able to understand the book completely. I must combine your powers. However, when I impart the DNA to Gem, it will also change yours as well. The three of us must become fully as one. Until this is completed, I will be in danger from anyone who wishes to use my powers. I can feel the evil that is coming. Gem is not yet physically capable of using all her powers, and to add Onaerris to her body is the only way she will receive all powers that are her birthright. Therefore, I must merge with you, for only you can protect me – and her – until her powers are developed fully."

The book stopped to listen to Jaxx."

"And, the powers that she will have?"

"Unimaginable!"

"But, her red eyes? They are the eyes of an Onaerris! How can she not have Onaerris blood somewhere inside of her?"

"Her red eyes came about, because it was the only thing that was given to her in the womb. Analyse was turned *after* Jolinaer impregnated Gem. When her Mother was changed, Gem's eyes were given the ability to turn red with her emotions. And, they will always continue to turn red when her emotions were very strong. You must also accept her DNA as well."

"What? I'll also have human and Anaerris DNA?" he asked in shock. "And, what do you mean that we have to become one? We have already done this!"

"I know this," she told him, and shook her head. "You must merge my pages within, and then, you and I must impart her with our knowledge by giving her your DNA, and my knowledge through your seed."

"M-my seed?" he stuttered.

"Remember, she has no Onaerris blood inside of her. While she was in the Fae Realm, Analyse specifically requested that human DNA become part of her makeup to protect both Gem and me from evil, and the Fae were the only ones who could actually accomplish this, while Gemma was within her womb. The Fae have always chosen certain humans to become their companions. It has always been thus. The Queen, Analyse, and Jolinaer chose a young, human girl, of only two years-old. Finally, Gem's DNA was merged with her human DNA. Her human parents were honored that their daughter had been chosen. She was not hurt in any way, and her family was forever lifted to high status in the Fae realm. But, it is a monstrous undertaking that rivals all other procedures, and only the Queen has the knowledge of how to do so. It was imperative to keep her Anaerris DNA and her Onaerris blood separate until the appropriate time. But, another needed to be added to make sure that, once exchanged, no one will be able to gather the knowledge. This was Analyse's orders. We were kept apart until it was time, which has now arrived."

Jaxx frowned at Gem.

"So, she is not truly Jolinaer's child?" Jaxx was really trying to understand, but it was all still a bit above even his knowledge.

"Oh, that she is. But, she is missing his DNA, as I have told you."

"I'm confused. That is not what our stories say. It is said that the Protector has all three races within her already. In any case, how could he have not given her his DNA? I mean...that makes no sense!"Another thought came to him, and he thought he would be sick! "Unless...! Oh, Creator! I've been sleeping with my own niece? My mate is my niece!"

Gemma laughed.

"Of course not, Jaxxon of Onaerra. She is is his real, biological daughter, and you are not his brother by blood, but by friendship, only. Surely you know this!"

Of course, she wasn't his niece! What the hell was wrong with him? He and Jolinaer had been brothers in arms, and as close, or closer, than any two brothers could be. From what the book was saying, they had been all wrong? All of them? That's when he realized what the book was trying to tell him.

"You," he pointed at Gem. "I know what you are! You're in need of a – a host! You're like a parasite, aren't you?"

A short nod from Gemma acknowledged it.

"As close to an explanation that you can understand, I guess. However, it is not so much a host that I need as much as a delivery system. Your brother's DNA is within my cover. That is why she needed an Onaerris mate, and why you were chosen by Jolinaer to protect his daughter. He and Analyse chose you to give her the DNA of Onaerris. She needed a conduit to deliver his DNA, and you are that person."

"But, I can't touch you!" he complained. "Isn't it dangerous, or are the stories about that false as well?" It was something he had never wanted Gem to know. To touch the book would be his doom. Of course, she knew this, but the truth was, she didn't know how dangerous this really could be. The stories, however, never said anything about joining with a book! Only about the bonding!

"No. In that case, your stories are highly accurate. This is very dangerous."

"And, what? Exactly how *dangerous* is this plan?" Jaxx answered with a sneer.

"You will suffer great pain upon the knowledge that will pour within your mind and body, Jaxxon of Onaerris. Much will enter your mind and body. So much, even your immortal body is at extreme risk of injury, or...."

"Or?" he asked.

Gemma shrugged.

"You die," she stated in a matter-of-fact tone. "However, I must tell you truthfully, that I do not know what will happen. But, I do know that pain will come, because while the protection was Jolinaer's, the written words are by Analyse. What you do not know is that I was written with Analyse's blood upon these silver pages, *before* she was changed. Because of her change, she was no longer able to touch the book. Jolinaer solved the problem by carving the skin off the body of a burned Onaerris. Then, they fashioned the cover, and attached it to my silver pages without touching me, and thus, placed his wards upon my cover. In other words," Gemma said as she saw confusion on Jaxx's face, "her DNA is on each of the silver pages, whereas, Jolinaer's DNA is in the cover. The knowledge that she wrote down, also had another purpose. She not only wrote down all of Anaerris and Onaerris history, but..."

"But...what?" he asked warily.

"The final touch? The last pages are made of crystal. Analyse transferred everything, except the ocean, into those pages. It is made from the same crystal as the terraforming crystal that Jolinaer gave to you, and instructions on how to terraform another planet."

Reaching into his pants pocket, Jaxx pulled out the crystal, before they had left for the cabin. He certainly couldn't leave it. And, he had already checked out that the peach ocean had been fully separated, and was still inside his cave. Other than Gem, no one else even knew where it was. Right now, he was glad that the crystal was useless. He rolled it around in his hand, looking at it. Grasping it tightly, Jaxx's knees buckled underneath him, causing him to sink to the floor stunned. His face turned toward the book. He realized, in seconds, what that meant! Not only would he be filled with the knowledge of the Anaerris and Onaerris, but the crystal – the Terraforming crystal pages – as well after it joined with him! And, even so, the cover could be touched by an Onaerris, but the pages could not be! The opposite was true as well –

except, of course, for Gemma, who was able to touch all of it. Gem had been able to read it, but she had never had the time to actually do so.

Unwilling to believe any of this, Jaxx had another revelation.

"But, the Crystal! After the accident, it broke, and out flowed the peach ocean! It mixed with the Earth's oceans, and I've been separating it for thousands of years! I've been protecting it, thinking that it was entirely intact, except for the ocean!" he exclaimed.

"Analyse took the crystal from Delinear. When the war came, she took away its ability to be fully used in Terraforming, and thus, rendered it useless. From there, she created two crystal pages," Gemma told him.

"Just how did she do that?" he asked.

"How is not necessary for you to know."

"What do you mean? Of course I need to know!"

"Get used to disappointment, Jaxx," Gem smirked.

He narrowed his eyes at her. She had no intention of telling him. He tried another tactic.

"But, the peach ocean flowed from the accidental crack! How did the…?" he began to ask.

"…ocean get into it? It was quite easy. The crystal may be small, but inside, Delinear designed it with another subspace dimension."

"Another dimension? Wait! My brother *lied to me?"* he grasped his chest as his breathing, that he really didn't need, took off at super speed. Never would he have believed that Jolinaer would have deliberately lied to him!

"Did he? Did he lie to you? What did he tell you – exactly, Jaxx?" she asked him.

Jaxx, still sprawled on the floor, looked up at her. Then, he closed his eyes. What did his brother say?

"The crystal is the way we will rebuild Anaerris," Jolinaer had told him. *"It contains the peach ocean, and is the key to Terraforming a new Anaerris."*

No. Wait. He didn't say that it was the key to terraforming. What he actually had said was *"...and is only* part *of the way to terraforming a new Anaerris."*

Then, he remembered the rest of the conversation.

"What!?" Jaxx had gasped in shock, almost dropping the crystal in his hand.

"Terraforming, Jaxx. There is a machine that can Terraform any planet. It will kill the indigenous population if it is ever found, and if unleashed, will destroy any inhabited planet."

Had Jolinaer told him the crystal had actually contained the Terraforming engrams? No! He didn't! He only told him that there was a Terraforming *machine*, and that the peach ocean was contained within the crystal! So subtle, and yet it never occurred to him that it would have two different meanings. To protect it, and not let it fall into the wrong hands! Realization struck him at the same time. His eyes flew open. He looked up at Gemma as he slowly rose to his feet. Then, he looked into her silver eyes, and saw his reflected within hers. She nodded, and continued.

"First, Analyse used the device to harbor the peach ocean. Second, she removed the part of the device that would be able to contain everything else. Once that was done, it left the crystal holding only the ocean, Jaxxon, mate to Gemma Elwood. It contained nothing else."

"Then, where is it?" Jaxx asked completely puzzled.

"It is where one least expects it to be, and where one would expect it to be," Gemma told him.

"Well, thanks for being so cryptic! You have to give me more than that!"

"Then, it is time for you to use your mind and heart. You know where it is, Jaxx,"Gemma said.

At first, he had no idea what she was talking about, and suddenly, his eyes widened as the realization of where it was came to him.

"In the book!" he exclaimed, suddenly. "But, where? Gem has already opened it, and she mentioned nothing about crystal pages being inside!"

"That is very simple. The pages are there, but have been hidden by eyes other than the one who will see them!"

"What are you talking...," Jaxx stopped mid-sentence, feeling sudden fear inside for the first time in his life. "Then, just what do I need to do?"

"What do you think you must do?" she countered, before one short nod from Gemma confirmed his growing fear. He leaned on the wall behind him. No! He couldn't, even though he knew it was not her, his love for her overwhelmed him to the point that he would agree to anything if it kept her safe.

His original training returned to him with such a vengeance, it surprised him. It had come from his own brother, Jolinaer, as they trained.

"Remember, Jaxxon, one must accept fear, to know fear; in order to conquer fear, is to accept fear. Only then, can you fight!"

"I understand," Jaxx told her.

"Good. The first crystalline page details the instructions on how to use the machine; the second page *is* the machine! It was for this reason that you were deliberately made by the Creator to become Gemma's mate. He always has a purpose in whatever He does, and in this, it was for Analyse's daughter to mate with an Onaerris – you. My cover cannot be unlocked without the merging of the knowledge within my cover, and the key to unlocking it is with Gemma, and the blood of both of you. Once unlocked, Gem must also spill her blood on the top silver page, and then you will both need to place your hands upon the top page of silver."

"But, Gemma has read it!" he said.

"True, but she has not read the entire book. The pages are deliberately concealed until you both unlock it. You will be filled with all the knowledge that Analyse imparted into my silver pages as well as the crystalline pages. These pages will dissolve forever within your DNA. This action belongs only to you. Both of you must slice one palm for one crystalline page, and again, the other palm for the second one. Once this is done, you will be filled with all knowledge of the machine, and everything within it. The book will crumble into ashes. It is then that you will be called upon to impart the knowledge to Gem through the act of copulation, and she will become the Anaerris Code – the savior of all races."

"But, will any other be able to sense you within us?"

Shaking her head, Gem, or the voice of the book through Gem, told him the truth.

"The truth is I do not know. We must err on the idea that it is no, and hope it is correct. Once my task is completed, I am hoping that they can no longer sense me through your cloaking spell, but honestly, I do not know if that can be. However, if it does work, then it will be possible to finish what was started so long ago."

"How long do I have to choose?" he asked, knowing he would choose yes, but he wanted to understand.

"Now," Gem answered. "There is no time that was built within me. It must be now, or others will be able to take me from you. All hope will be abandoned if that occurs."

Jaxx paced back and forth for several minutes, before she spoke again.

"Your decision, please, Jaxxon of Onaerris, Prince and Heir to the Planet of Onaerra."

He whipped around. Prince and Heir? No! That was his brother! He had caught the book in a lie!

"What? I'm not the heir to the throne. Jolinaer is Prince and Heir!" he disputed.

Sadly, Gemma shook her head.

"In order to put the powerful ward into my cover, and to atone for his great sin for the desecration of another by skinning them for the book cover," she held her hand up to continue, "and to atone for the attack on Anaerris, his punishment was banishment, forever, from Onaerris. Therefore, he can no longer be the heir. The title falls to you."

Shock overwhelmed Jaxx. His brother could never go home? Oh, he always knew that they wouldn't go back there, but he always had held out a small bit of hope that they could. He stared at Gemma's silver eyes, knowing it was her, but not. He would never go home, either. This was his mate, and wherever she wanted to go, he would stand by her forever. And, for him – and her, now – that was an eternity. As if the Code knew what he was thinking, it answered him

"Oh, no, Prince. You will both go home as one, *if* you succeed in your tasks. And, know this. If you do, the world you will create will be the most unbelievably beautiful world in all the Universe, and entire galaxies will flock to you in friendship. Your world will be the true Jewel of Anaerris."

She stared at his mouth, and Jaxx quickly shut it, wiping the drool that had formed in the corners. Oh...he just had to do that now! Gem turned him on so much, he was always ready for her – even when it wasn't her. Or, was it? Confusion was so not his forte!

"But, beware. There is another thing that must be used to read and to open the book, and only that is possessed by Gem," she told him, silencing him when she had something else to add. "Gem has something in her possession that is the key to the book. She will know when it is time. Now, Jaxxon, Prince and Heir of Onaerris, mate to Gemma, Jewel of Anaerris, Princess and Heir of Anaerris. Are you ready to truly mate with me? With us?"

"Princess? Oh, right! Of course." A thought crossed his mind. "Wait. Can you answer one more question?"

"I have been given the ability to answer all your questions, Prince," she nodded once.

"Did you say 'daughter' of Analyse? Did you not mean that Analyse is her ancestor? That Gem is her offspring after thousands of years?"

He needed confirmation of what Lola had told them earlier – that Gem was her daughter. It still seemed almost impossible to him that Gem was the age she had told them. That she was kept in the Fae realm until she was placed upon Earth.

Gemma threw her head back, and laughed heartily.

"Oh, no, dear Prince. She is the *daughter* of Analyse, Queen of Anaerris, and Jolinaer, former Prince of Onaerris. How many times must you be told this? Jaxxon, Jaxxon! You have had this explained on numerous occasions, now. Or, perhaps, I need to finish it. She was not born on Anaerris, but within the Fae realm," she began, and then saw in his eyes when he realized Lola had told them the truth.

"She stayed as a baby in the realm until the time came for her to come to Earth," he stated flatly. "I know."

"Yes. Time passes a great deal slower there than in the human realm. And, then, a couple was chosen – a human couple – to care for her until she became of age. Like you, Gemma is the true Princess and Heir to the world, and people, of Anaerris – no matter where that world will be. A princess and prince you both are; a Queen and King you will be as our Creator has planned. Now, are you ready?" she asked with a smile.

"How long will it take?"

"That, my Prince, is up to your body, and I cannot answer that question."

"Will you remain within Gem, now?"

"I am only using a conduit by which I am able to connect with Gemma, so that you both would know what is to happen. Once this begins, I will return Gemma's consciousness to her, and return to the book to be absorbed by you."

"What of the others with us?"

Gemma's eyes began to glow as she shook her head.

"Your friends must not be here. They must stay away for the power that is about to enter this building, will destroy it in the end. And, it can also destroy both you and Gemma as well, if you are not strong enough to endure."

"May I go tell them?"

"Of course," she said, and gave him a quick nod. "But, do not tell them what is to happen."

"Well, that's no problem, because I don't know what that is!"

"Very true, but you cannot tell anyone afterward, either. It will be secret between you, Gemma, her Mother, and your brother, for all time to come. Not even your own offspring may know what occurs here this day."

Considering her words carefully, Jaxx finally answered.

"So be it. I agree."

She bowed her head to him, then Gem collapsed. Jaxx caught her before she fell, and placed her gently on the sofa, before he stepped outside to call the others who came to him quickly.

"Gemma, I mean, uh, Gem, and I will be undergoing something that I cannot explain, because neither of us understands it ourselves. Only that this is the Creator's will. Listen to me carefully. No matter what you see; no matter what you may hear, do not – I repeat *do not* – enter this cabin until we come for you," he looked around at their friends. "Get as far away as possible. If you do not, you *will* die."

Startled, Taylor said with hands on her hips as if to impress it upon him.

"NO! I don't understand it! I won't stand by and let my best friend go through whatever this is alone!"

She started toward the cabin, when Rick caught Jaxx's eyes. The look was so terrifying, he reached out, and pulled Taylor back.

"Let me go, you big lug!" she demanded as she wiggled, trying to get away. Jaxx stepped up.

"Listen to me, Taylor! Listen! She will not be alone. I will be with her. It is not just her that it affects, but me. A change is coming, and quite frankly, I don't know what's going to happen."

He turned to Stacy, gently taking her hands in his.

"I am sorry, Stacy, but by the time whatever is happening is over, your cabin will very possibly no stand. I know how important it is to you, but this is much more important than either you, your family, or your cabin. I hope you understand."

Stacy smiled sadly at him.

"It meant something long ago to me, Jaxx – when they were alive. The cabin have been rebuilt hundreds of times throughout the years! Building another is nothing."

"Thank you," Jaxx stated. He turned to Rick, and took his forearm in the ancient form of greeting, saying good-bye. "I have enjoyed knowing you, my friend, even if it may have been for only a little while as our time allows."

"As I do, Jaxx. Tell Gem not to worry about Taylor. I did not meet her until two thousand years after the Great Flood, give or take a decade. She will be safe with me. Always."

Jaxx took Stan's forearm next.

"My friend...it has been an honor to know you, to have fought beside you, and to fight once again for freedom!"

"As is mine, brother."

Jaxx dropped his hand, then stood back. He nodded his head in respect, then looked at everyone.

"Stacy is there another place you guys can hole up until this is done?"

Stacy frowned as if she was remembering something.

"Yes. It's on the other side of the lake. There is an old cabin that belonged to an old man who had no heirs. It's been there for a long time, but it should be more than adequate for our needs."

"Good."

"Jaxx?" Gem's shaky and confused voice came from the doorway.

"I am done. It is time," he told her walking to stand by her side.

Their friends watched in sadness and anger as they raised their hands in farewell. Once they disappeared from sight, Gem and Jaxx turned to walk into the cabin, and quietly shut the door behind them.

~ 23 ~
"Never trust a magical book. You will not like the outcome!" ~ Gem

Flipping over to her stomach, Delinear luxuriated in the massive shower at the small, exclusive island hotel bungalow that they had rented for the time being. The ocean was just a few feet from their door, and she loved being nude constantly – every bit as did Eloran. They had sex every second that they could, and neither were ever satisfied.   That would never happen until she was underneath Jaxxon, while he pounded into her with his massive cock! Closing her eyes, she dreamed about those days when she was satisfied! Then, she frowned as her anger grew knowing that instead of her, that bitch was under him, on her knees with him, letting him inside of her over and over again!

"It should be me!" she muttered as she stood, her shower ruined.

"What should be you, little whore?" Eloran asked, as he walked into the shower, his hard cock standing at attention.

Seeing him ready for her again, she channeled her anger into stroking her breasts with one hand, while stroking her sex with her other. Eloran licked his lips as he grabbed himself, and began stroking his cock without restraint. He stepped to her.

"Kneel in front of me!" he ordered, and Delinear complied immediately.

She groaned as she felt him stroke the tip of his hard cock in a circular motion over her hard nipples, wetting them down with the creamy liquid that poured from his slit. In seconds, he pumped his cock hard, and huge spurts of red-hot semen shot from his cock covering her breasts completely. He was extremely proud of how much semen he could always make.

Delinear always loved a man's hot, wet semen shooting all over her tits! It was something that turned her on so much, she'd give him anything he wanted! And, Eloran knew it! He knew how to push her buttons, and she gave in just as she always did. Standing up, she raked her silky, semen-infused breasts against his chest. Hearing him groan, she needed his hardness within her!

"Take me, Eloran!" she begged.

He grasped her hair, yanking her head back hard.

"How?" he asked her.

"How do you think?" she smiled wantonly.

"Then, get on your knees, and put you ass in my face!" he ordered. She was on her knees in a second, and he positioned his tip at her entrance. "Say it! I want to hear you ask for it!"

"Fuck me!" she yelled.

Delinear was barely on her hands, before Eloran rammed his hard cock up into her!

"One thing I can say, Delinear," he gasped as he rocked his hips forward and back in massive thrusts.

"What?" she asked breathlessly, enjoying each thrust inside of her.

"Your pussy is always so damn wet, and it grasps my cock, milking it hard!" he answered.

"My pussy is always wet, because we are both never satisfied, and you know it!" she gasped.

"True! We are never satisfied, and we won't be unless we get what, and who, we want!"

"I can't wait!"

Moments later, both flopped onto the shower floor panting hard. Then, Delinear jumped up, whirled her hair at him, and grinned.

"Beat you to the ocean!" she cried, already on her way.

Eloran grinned, and followed her quickly to the edge of the ocean, where the two of them swam for hours. Oh, there were a few beasties in the purplish ocean, but they were nothing to the two of them, and they quickly made food out of them. Dragging their last kill upon the crimson sands underneath their feet, they fed each other the remains of the large creature beneath the ocean. Little remained of what it had looked like before they had dug their claws and teeth into them.

Delinear sighed as she licked her fingers clean of the last bit of green blood that came from the creature. She lay back on the crimson sand, followed by Eloran. Above them, the sky began to darken, and the ocean grew black. Five moons threw their light onto the small planet where they were.

Stretching her arms upward to the dark sky, Delinear laughed.

"The fools! Little do they know that we have amassed an army from all over the universe!"

"True. But, still, we have a problem," Eloran said to her. His hand was lazily stroking his cock while he spoke.

Delinear turned her head to meet his eyes, but at the same time, couldn't help but drop down to his hand. He laughed at her gaze.

"Love your dick much?" she guffawed, shooting her eyes back to his.

"Well, you have to admit it is damned amazing!" he answered.

"It is indeed!" she absentmindedly said. Then, she asked, "What problem?"

"Getting them onto Earth."

She rolled her eyes, and sat up crossing her arms on her knees with her chin on them. They had worked for thousands of years, amassing a massive army, but like the Anaerris, only a few Onaerris were left. They had been set to training the others that they had gathered. Yet, still they did not know how to get them to Earth. Her own Vorc'ara was nowhere near strong enough, nor could she keep it open long enough for thousands of troops to emerge. So, Eloran was right. It was a problem. Oh, sure! Delinear had not had a problem betraying her own. After all, she had done it numerous times. That bitch, Analyse, had caused all kinds of problems, which had led to Delinear's ousting from the Anaerris Council, where she had sat since the beginning – or the casting out to be sent to prison, which was a more accurate description! And, all because Delinear invented the Terraforming machine against all rules and laws. Then, she had easily seduced and killed a young guard, who she had enlisted to help her. She did so by opening a Vorc'ara to a world of pure ice where he would freeze to death in seconds. When it had disappeared, she had every intention of finding out where it was, and stealing it back, but the War of the Exiled had begun and. When she did find out where it was, she was angered, because it had been burned to the ground. But, not by the Onaerris! But by the Anaerris to keep anyone from getting their hands on it! Frustrated, she had immediately joined Eloran, and furiously helped the Onaerris destroy the Anaerris. She took great happiness in killing her own kind! Her desire and sexual lust drove her to want to rule, and enslaving both of their kind was her strongest wish! Just the thought of having slaves to do her every whim fueled her sex.

"DAMN!" she shouted to no one.

Restless, Delinear stood and stretched uncaring that she was nude, or that Eloran was lusting with his eyes even as his hand pumped his own hardened cock. The two of them adored watching each other give themselves orgasms. And, then she'd give him what he wanted! But, it was fun to flaunt her nudity in front of him. After the stretch, she put her hands on her hips staring out at the ocean before her, and slipped deeper into thought. Frowning again, neither she nor Eloran ever believed that Analyse and Jolinaer would escape to another world, dimension, plain of existence, realm, or another place!

Rumors and legends of a "Jewel" began running rampant to the point where Eloran began to believe it was not an object, but a person, that was in the stories. Once they realized this, they had spent the last several thousand years trying to figure out where the Jewel was. This person had the power and knowledge of the Anaerris from before the fall not to mention the knowledge of everything else! With that knowledge, they could finally challenge the one who had confined them to this universe, and get rid of him! But, they believed that they couldn't get rid of the Creator without the Crystal, and of course, the Code of Anaerris that had been hidden long ago. They had failed at every turn. But, it had only been just a few weeks ago that rumors abounded from Imaerra. She was convinced that she had discovered a Fae was living in Colorado, in the guise of a tiny little dog with a human slave. So, Eloran had sent both Imaerra and Quazer to spy on the Fae to make sure of it.

Delinear grinned on a side note that sprang into her mind. There was one thing that was great about the inferior humans, and that was their colorful words and phrases. The entire council, and all others, used them quite frequently. The word "Fuck" was her favorite of all! It turned her on so much, that any time Eloran, or her many other lovers, said the word, she would spread her legs, and let them do it! She turned to look at Eloran who was licking his lips, then her gaze drifted to his huge hard-on. She needed to ride him now! As she walked toward him, she continued her thoughts.

They had realized that the Fae bitch was dancing around a young, human woman. No one could enslave, or confine a Fae, while they were in a different form, either. They were far too powerful. But, they could make her so damn miserable that she just might tell them what they wanted to know! So, together, both Delinear and Eloran had ordered Imaerra to follow the tiny Fae with storms that grew wilder and wilder with each manifestation, hoping that it would force her to turn into her true form. Then, she could be coerced into telling them who the Jewel was. Delinear frowned as she gazed into the darkness while she approached Eloran. But, it didn't work, so then, she had tried to kill its human pet by capturing her. Until that moment, not one of them had ever entertained the idea that a human could use any powers at all! When, oh hell! What was her name? Gina? Gong? Gem? Yes! That was what Imaerra had told them! Gem! When she saw her open a Vorc'ara, Delinear's mouth had dropped open in surprise. Delinear stopped in shock! That's when it came to her that Gem was not just a human! She had to one of her own! She had to be Anaerris! The one they had been looking for over thousands of years, who most believed was myth! And, she was protected by a Fae! They had to do something! She stopped and stared down at Eloran, who was still stroking himself, and felt wetness flow from her sex. Well, maybe after she rode him! They had time! After all? Where could she go even with her protectors? This Gem didn't even realize that she was from another world and universe...and, they had obviously not told her!

"Fuck," Eloran smirked flipping his massive cock at her, his balls distended to almost a full ten inches.

She grinned at the word. He knew her so well! She walked to stand over him, so he could see her wetness as it dripped onto his cock, then sank slowly over it. As she sat down on him, taking him inside of her, he reached for her very large bouncing breasts.

"Fuck," she agreed, and screamed when she felt him slam his huge cock into her body.

"Now, what?" Gem asked Jaxx.

Jaxx pulled his mate to him, slamming her body against his. Gem relished the feeling as she felt his hardness press up against her.

"Excited to see me?" she quipped with a smug grin.

"I'm always excited in your presence. I know I'll be spending our entire existence together hard. I will always be hard for you, when I'm both with you, or apart from you. Just thinking about you makes me hard!" he grinned against her mouth as he punished her mouth with his.

Several minutes later, he broke off the kiss, and she stroked his cheek with her left palm, while her right hand was gripped in his.

"You know what we have to do, right?" he asked her.

She nodded her head, then added, "I never felt such incredible power from anything as I did when the book spoke through me, Jaxx. Whatever is to happen isn't going to be easy, nor is it going to be gentle."

"We are going to experience a lot of pain, Gem. Are you certain you wish to do this?" he asked, frowning at her.

She smiled sadly at him, and pulled his head down so she could lean her forehead against his.

"Oh, my love. It is what our Creator wants, so how could either of us deny it?"

"Because, He gave us free will – all of us, Gem. It is, and has always been, our choice," he told her. "Each of us have one life, but infinite choices. We must choose wisely, my beautiful mate."

"But, how do we use wisely in the face of everything?"

"Wisdom is not chosen by chance, but by what is right. If we choose right, then the choice is wise."

She grinned up into his gorgeous eyes, and stroked his cheek gently.

"You are wise, Jaxx, but choosing what is right is always the hard thing to do."

"But, the end result will end in something beautiful. Regardless what it may do to us, the end will not justify the means, but we will be worthy of the final outcome."

Gem thought of that for a moment, then, looked at him. He was right. But, the truth be known, she was terrified. Who was she that she was chosen? She had no idea, but he was her mate. He was right, and therefore, any pain created by this process would be worth it if it kept the book's knowledge out of the hands of Eloran and Delinear.

"Then, we do this – now," she told him, and he nodded once, leading her to the book that lay on the table.

"First, according to the book, there are apparently three things needed – my blood upon the cover, yours upon the pages, and something you possess that must be used to help open it along with my blood. I will go first since the cover must be opened by my blood, and while you can touch it, you cannot open the hidden crystal pages that are the real Terraforming machine."

He turned to look at her.

"Are you ready?" he asked her.

"Of course not! I'm not going to lie, and tell you I'm not scared stiff, Jaxx. I don't really have a choice in this, but you? I am so sorry that you are involved in all of this," she told him. "And, exactly what do I possess that we need?"

"I don't know, but Gemma said that you do. Think, Gem! What could it be?"

Gem shook her head. "I really don't know, Jaxx. I can't think of any...." Gem stopped as she realized something. She grabbed the amulet in her hand, and pulled it out showing it to Jaxx. "This! This is it! It's an amulet that my Dad had hidden. I found it right after the fire!"

Jaxx took the amulet, and stared at it. It was like nothing he had ever seen, but what shocked him most were that the symbols upon it matched all three moons!

"You know what it is?" Gem asked him.

"I do." He looked up at her. "This amulet contains all three symbols of Anaerra, Onaerra, and Domaerra. There has to be something on the book, or in it, that will activate it!"

Gem thought a moment.

"What if...Jaxx! What if this is what is keeping the crystalline pages hidden?"

"I never would have thought about that! It makes a lot of sense. We will proceed with that knowledge. Gem, I am just as afraid as you, because I never even thought of anything like this. We should be, because the power of the Creator is great, and should be respected at all costs."

Pulling her toward the table, he pulled out an ancient dagger that she had never seen before.

"How did I not see that?" she asked, shaking her head.

"Oh, probably, because you had your eye on, uh, something a bit bigger?" he laughed, and she joined him in his own nervous laughter.

"Indeed. And, to tell the truth? I love the thing that's a 'bit bigger' better anyway!"

Jaxx jerked her to him for one final kiss, before they touched the book.

The two of them stood in front of it, looked at each other, not knowing if neither would survive, and proceeded as they had been instructed by the codex.

Letting her hand go, Jaxx, first, took his dagger and sliced his palm, letting his own blood drain on the cover of the Codex. Nothing happened. They looked at each other in puzzlement. Suddenly, they heard a loud twanging sound, that made each of them turn back to look at the book. The cover was slowly becoming blood red. As it took shape, they saw the symbol that also matched Gem's amulet in shape, design, and size. It began to glow silver with the first symbol of the river, which they both realized was the peach ocean of Anaerra. Then, immediately followed by the smoking mountain,which was obviously representing Onaerra. And, a snow-capped mountain, which represented Domaerra, glowed silver, swirling just like any Vorc'ara. Finally, there was a starburst at the top, and could only be one thing. Destruction of everything they knew. Gem looked at Jaxx, and at his nod, she placed the amulet down where it settled easily into its special place.

A sonic boom followed by a brilliant light, burst from the code so brightly, both Jaxx and Gem were blinded by it. Gem screamed. Then, nothing.

Taylor wasn't happy about any of this, and turned to run back to the cabin, when Rick caught up with her, and wrapped his arms around her to hold her back. She glared at him when he shook his head in warning. Narrowing her eyes, she turned back to look at the cabin that was across the lake. She huffed, turned, and stomped up the steps, walking into the cabin behind her, and slamming the door in his face. She plopped down onto the tattered sofa that was covered with dust and dirt over years of neglect, and sneezed as it flew everywhere. Then, she broke into tears.

Rick knew how upset Taylor was, because he was just as frustrated at Jaxx as Gem. It was a huge mistake for something to happen in their world that no one knew about, and even worse, when they couldn't help the one person they both loved like a sister. Rick sighed, climbed the same steps, and opened the door. He walked into it, and saw the love of his life in tears. His heart broke. It had been more years than he could remember since she had last cried. Slowly he approached his mate, and silently sat down beside her, pulling her into his arms. She buried her face into his chest, and he sat holding her tightly as she unleashed a tide of tears.

Outside, Stacy and Stan were talking about what they had planned to do in case something went horribly wrong.

"I don't know, Stan. What do we do, now? It has already gone south, but could it get any worse?" Stacy asked him.

Stan shook his head at the obvious answer to her question.

"Of course, it could get worse! Why did you even say that? You know what happens whenever someone says that! Look at who and what we are, Stacy." Stacy just frowned at him, then turned to look toward her cabin where they had left Gem and Jaxx. "OK. I mean look at all of us. I'm not human, Stacy, and despite the fact by mating me, I gave you your longevity, and even given your almost invulnerable and immortal status, you are still human."

Stan paced back and forth, trying to find the words he needed to say. He stopped and looked at her as if he had come to a decision.

"Look," he said pulling her to him. Oh, she was mad, and he knew it, but he needed to make her understand. "I know I told you about our war, but I never told you all of it."

Stacy's head jerked toward him in surprise.

"Huh?" she asked.

"Yeah."

"But, why?" Stacy was very puzzled.

"Because, the carnage and the blood that flooded Anaerris was even sickening to those of us who did not believe in attacking the people of Anaerris."

"Blood?" she said, then her eyebrows went up, and her eyes opened in total shock. "Oh, shit! It was a thousand times worse than anything you told me, right?"

"No. Try a million times worse," he told her sadly.

Stacy looked up at him. She wanted to know.

"I don't care. Show me," she demanded.

Stan shook his head, but Stacy wouldn't accept it.

"I demand it, Stan! I'm your mate for the Creator's sake! I am due all that I am entitled to as your mate. That is what you said."

"Well...," he started.

"No. No 'well'; no 'I'm not sure'; no 'I don't think that's a good idea'; no nothing! Show me!"

Hanging his head, he nodded, then raised his hands to her head holding them on either side of her forehead. He slowly lowered his own to hers until his forehead touched hers.

Stacy gasped as images flooded her mind. In seconds, tears, in an unending stream, flowed down her cheeks as she realized why Stan had never showed her all of it. And, right at that moment, she wished she had kept her damn mouth shut! The violent scenes of mutilation and blood were already making her stomach churn. But, what was worse was the wide River of Blood that wound its way toward the brilliant red moon of Onaerris, looking for all the world as if it was actually flowing straight into it. He showed her why the river was filled with blood by centering his thoughts at the beginning of it. Stacy started to gag, and in seconds, she was bent over throwing up anything that was in her stomach. Stan had been right! She would forever remember the dismembering of the Anaerris people as knives and swords sliced their bodies open allowing their blood flooding into the river. And, it wasn't just a few! There had to be thousands more Onaerris waiting their turn for the bloodletting! The faces that she saw as Stan continued to bring them up were covered in the blood of the Anaerris as they drank the blood of their enemies, even before draining the rest into the River of Blood. But, when she saw her own beloved's face covered in that blood, she threw up all over again, while Stan held her hair back, and cut off the images that he had poured into her mind. He regretted showing her his own face during the purge, even though he was not a part of it.

"I'm so, so sorry, my love," he said softly, as he held her in his arms when she collapsed.

Stacy could only shake her head. Her lover's face was still prominent in her mind, but she had no one to blame but her own stupidity.

"Don't," she begged, pushing against his chest. She lifted her eyes to his. "It's not your fault. It is mine. It was I who wanted to know. I understand why you didn't want me to see it."

"I did so against my better judgment, Stacy. I'm sorry you saw what I looked like."

"But, I know it wasn't the reason your face was covered in blood," she told him.

Shock crossed his face. How could she possibly know that?

Pulling his head down, she placed a gentle kiss on his lips.

"How did you know?" he asked still surprised after she raised her lips from his.

"Because, it's you," she stated simply.

Stan closed his eyes, and sniffed his mate's scent. How did he ever earn this beauty? He didn't deserve her.

"Of course, you don't deserve me!" she giggled. "Here's what you do deserve."

Pulling him down to the ground, she proceeded to show him his just desserts.

Moments later, a large, sonic boom covered the area, followed by a brilliant light. Rick and Taylor almost tripped over each other as they ran outside to join Stan and Stacy who were frozen in place, looking across to the cabin across the lake – a cabin that once stood there.

The four used their super speed to go around the lake.

"Where are they?" Taylor cried frantically.

There was nothing. It was all gone – including the cabin and some of the trees around it! But, there was also no sign of either Gem or Jaxx. Silently, the girls sank to their knees in tears, while their mates just stood looking at where Gem and Jaxx should have been.

"Where are they?" Taylor cried, again.

Stan and Rick looked at each other, and shrugged.

"Shit!" Stan said.

"Exactly," Rick replied.

EPILOGUE
"Oh, damn! I am so screwed!" ~ Gem and Jaxx

Gem opened her eyes, blinking at the night sky above her. It was so beautiful, and loaded with brilliant twinkling stars of every single color in the world. A beautiful planet of many colors, reminding her, in a way, of Joseph's coat of many colors from the Bible.

"Whoever made that place truly wanted it to be more beautiful than any other!" she thought

Peeping out from the left of the globe was a smaller globe, shining down on her with its glittering countenance! Geez! That is strange. For a few minutes, it didn't dawn on her she wasn't on Earth. Then, she frowned…

"Where in the 'sam hill' am I!?" she exclaimed. "And, why is it so damned hot! What is this, hell?"

Why was she hot? Oh, come on! Not again! She was way too hot! In fact, she felt as if she were back on that volcanic island! It was the very same feeling. Sweat poured from her, and she wiped it away with her hand, only to have it reappear immediately. Salt began to sting her eyes when it dripped into them, and she was heavy. Really heavy – as if the gravity had increased greatly.

Suddenly, a loud pop, and swooshing sound was audible. Looking behind her, she gasped.

"Oh, fuck!" she said, looking at a steam vent just behind her, steam exploding from it.

She didn't want to look, so she shut her eyes quickly! No! She wasn't going to open them! No way! Surely this couldn't happen – again? Slowly she raised her head, and even more slowly, opened her eyes!

Looking around, she finally scratched out, "Jaxx?"

She waited for an answer, but none came. She tried, again.

"JAXXON!" But, her voice was even less, and no answer.

Gem was barely able to rise to a standing position so she could see around her better.

"Oh, my GOD!" she tried to say, her voice dying in her throat from the sulfuric acid wafting into her nose. It wrapped around what little air she did have to breathe, and stifled every breath! Just like the stench in the volcanic cave, it burned her nose and throat, and the stink was so bad, it was causing her to gag! She would throw up if her stomach wasn't dry. Unlike the cave, though, where the outside had greenery, water, and even a black ocean, here, no matter how far she could see in any direction through the steam, her eyes brought her stinging vision nothing but white steam, blackened earth below her feet, steam everywhere, and even orange and yellow lava flows all surrounded her!

She saw a movement from her peripheral vision on the left, and turned her head. Several figures, maybe about three, were moving toward her. She couldn't see them due to the heavy steam that surrounded them. She began to slowly back away as they continued to advance. Swords and staffs emerged, before their faces, and she stumbled, and fell on her ass. Her eyes grew larger as she saw the figures begin to take shape.

She brushed her sweaty, soaking wet hair out of her eyes, and with the emergence of the figures, her heart pounded in her chest with fear for the sharp, gleaming white teeth appeared first, before their faces. Where was Jaxx?

"I am So. Damned. Fucked!" she squeaked, then screamed when she saw what appeared to be arms reaching for her. Gem passed out, falling in the ashes below her.

Jaxx awoke slowly. Cold! So, fucking cold! Why was he so damned cold? He tried to sit up, then grasped his head as a red-hot pain shot through it.

"Ahhhhhhhh!" he yelled, and laid back down. Such pain! He had never felt this kind of pain in his entire existence!

After a few minutes, the pain subsided, and he tried opening his eyes once more. This time, the pain was, at least, bearable! He looked around the room, then his eyes shot back to a figure sitting beside his bed. He couldn't focus, though. Who??? He tried to speak, but couldn't. He tried, again. Nothing. When he tried a third time, the figure spoke.

"Relax, Jaxxon," a soft voice said. "You're alright. Your eyes will adjust soon enough."

He frowned at the figure. He knew that voice, but he couldn't place it.

"Your voice will return as well. It will just take a bit of time."

He shook his head just a bit, and that caused the pain to shoot through his head, once again. So horrible, he knew he was slipping back into unconsciousness, but a soft hand brushed against his forehead, which eased his pain.

"Rest, Jaxxon. You are safe," the voice repeated.

"But, what about Gem?" he tried to say, shivering uncontrollably, before he slipped away. *"Where is she? Where is my heart? And, since when do I feel c-cold?"*

"How is he?" a male voice asked, sounding as if he had lost his best friend.

"He is cold, but I am worried as to why he is cold. He shouldn't be cold!" she said with tears in her eyes. She hitched up her black leather coat around her, even though she really didn't need it. But somehow, it helped her ease the pain of loss and worry, and to keep it at bay. But, the truth was, it wasn't working at all. "What happened to Gem? Why is she not here with him? Why did they not come together?"

"I do not know," he said, looking down at Jaxx with worried eyes, watching Jaxxon shake. The man turned to her, taking her hand in his, which gave her a little bit of comfort. "But, we *will* find her, my love. On this, I give you my vow!"

He kissed the white hand, which had a huge emerald adorning it, and then, turning to scoop up Jaxxon into his arms, he secretly hoped that he would be able to keep that vow to his mate!

~~∨~~

I want to thank my Creator for giving me such a vivid imaginataion! I am truly blessed by Him. I also want to thank Patti Champion and Tonya Rose, for contributing to this book, and taking the time for doing so. I want to thank my husband and daughter who, without their incredible support, I would never be able to do this. I also want to thank all my great Twitter and Facebook followers and friends for having so much faith in me. I am truly lucky to have such wonderful support throughout the last 3 years! You humble me, and I thank you!

LK Kelley

I invite you to my webpage, and hope you'll enjoy it!

Twitter @lkkelley1

https://www.facebook.com/lk.kelley.5

http://firebird4554.wixsite.com/white-wolf-prophecy/the-anaerris-code